The Further Adventures
of
Langdon St. Ives

The Further Adventures
of
Langdon St. Ives

James P. Blaylock

Illustrated by J. K. Potter

Subterranean Press 2016

First Edition

ISBN
978-1-59606-782-0

Subterranean Press
PO Box 190106
Burton, MI 48519

subterraneanpress.com

Table of Contents

Introduction to
The Further Adventures of Langdon St. Ives

MY LIFE (IN PART) AS A READER AND WRITER

A WRITER WHO STARTS writing early in life and keeps at it discovers that things change, particularly the writer. P. G. Wodehouse was apparently the same writer at ninety years old that he had been at thirty-five, as if he had been dislodged from time. But he was a rarity, perhaps an enviable rarity. When I wrote my first steampunk story, "The Ape-box Affair," back in my mid-twenties, I was still occasionally asked to haul out identification when I ordered a drink in a restaurant. A couple of months ago the same thing happened, except that there was no drink involved: I was hoping to get the senior discount at the local movie theater. It occurred only once, and the phenomenon was instantly amusing. But it came into my mind, as it had forty years earlier, that youth isn't the only thing that is fleeting; everything is fleeting, and that there's an absolute family resemblance between a mirror and the clock on the wall, both of which are reminders of our own mortality. I'm writing this as an introduction, but one can't introduce something until one knows what it is, and so every introduction is an afterword after all.

One of the distinctions between the new writer and the old writer is that the world of books and stories is the new writer's oyster. He or she might become any sort of writer at all, or so he or she supposes, perhaps a literary genius, and Shakespeare might as well start shifting chairs in order to make room in the panoply of literary greats. The writer who has been at it most of his life looks back and very clearly sees what he (in my case) has become. He's perhaps closer to Shakespeare than he was when he started, but there'll be no rush to shift any chairs. That being said, if he's generally happy with what he sees when his books and stories are lined up in temporal order, he's very fortunate indeed, and is even more fortunate if he still sits down at the desk in the morning and adds a few hundred or a few thousand words to the living thing that his writing has become to him.

Not long ago, when I was in a looking-back mood, I realized that the books I read when I was a child and teenager had an outsized part in shaping who and what I would become as a writer. The course of my literary life was being mapped before I knew that I would have such a life. I learned to read, literally, in the last three months of the second grade, after my teacher, Mrs. Rice, who had a haircut like Moe from the Three Stooges, sent a fortuitous note home to my mother saying that I was reading so far beneath grade level that I was in danger of failing. My mother got hold of a book titled *Why Johnny Can't Read*, popular among mothers in those days, which she tortured me with for those three months insufferable months. Instead of getting into trouble with my friends after school, I sat at the kitchen table and sounded out words, read paragraphs aloud, and took spelling tests. It turned out that the book worked. I was meant to be a reader all along, but simply didn't know it, and when I went into the third grade, I was a sort of reading whizbang.

Christmas of that year my aunt and uncle gave me a copy of *The Complete Short Stories of Mark Twain*. (Or perhaps it was the following Christmas. In "A Child's Christmas in Wales," Dylan Thomas wrote, "I can never remember whether it snowed for six days and six nights when I was twelve or for twelve days and twelve nights when I was six.") It was years later that I figured out the gift must have been suggested by my mother as part of her grand scheme to turn me into a reader; my aunt and uncle weren't readers of any sort and were far more likely to give me a bow and arrow. *Why Johnny Can't Read* had disappeared into the drawer by then, thank God, and I was free to run around in orange groves again and spend long afternoons wandering along the railroad tracks searching out ant lions.

And yet, due to my mother's insidious scheme, I was inclined to spend more and more time reading, which is to say occupying other worlds.

I opened my Christmas gift (I have a clear memory of it) and started out with Twain's "The Notorious Jumping Frog," happy to discover that Calaveras County, which apparently had a surplus of prodigious frogs and comical people, was in California, within driving distance. I tackled "Cannibalism in the Cars," and was disappointed that there was no cannibalism to be found in it, and then "An Invalid's Story," in which a man's deterioration and death is brought about by a disguised Limburger cheese. I had no idea what Limburger cheese was and had to ask my mother, who told me that it stank very badly but that Europeans were fond of it. Much of what I found in books was deeply mysterious, but I can still recall the strange change that came over me when my world was no longer limited to the comparatively small town of Anaheim of the 1950s.

Twain's language was like no language I'd ever heard, and I wished it was my own. My mother brought home an illustrated edition of Tom Sawyer, which in time I read literally to pieces. I took to saying "what in tarnation...?" a lot, and memorized the spunk water chant that cured warts, and badly wanted a "sure-enough" Barlow knife, as Tom Sawyer put it. My father cheerfully gave me a Barlow when I asked him about them, he having collected knives over the years, and it being okay in those days for a kid to carry one around, a notion that strikes terror into people today. I carried mine around religiously, just in case I had the urge to whittle on a stick. I wanted a corncob pipe, too, since Huckleberry Finn smoked one, but I was informed by my mother that I wasn't of pipe-smoking age.

(Here's a sad business: all these years later I believed I still owned that Barlow knife, so I searched around in my study today and found what I thought was it. I discovered after blowing off the dust, however, that it had a suspiciously plastic-looking handle rather than a bone handle. The name "Barlow" was etched into the stainless steel bolster at the top just as it should be, but on the base of the blade were etched the words "Made in China." That "sure-enough" Barlow that my father gave me had vanished some time in the past fifty-five years. Maybe goblins had stolen it and left the cut-rate Barlow.)

It turned out that by learning to read I hadn't lost my taste for railroad tracks and orange groves at all. To the contrary, they meant more to me than they had before. The world glowed more brightly now that Tom

Sawyer and Huckleberry Finn were living in it and always would be living in it (unlike a Barlow knife, which can disappear out of it). I was curious by now about other writers' books, and I went searching through the volumes in my mother's library (a built-in room divider of four shelves with a copper planter in the top filled with philodendron). I found a set of books by Steinbeck and pulled out something called *The Long Valley*. I didn't understand half of what I was reading, although even then I was particularly fond of "Breakfast" and still am (both the story and actual breakfast). I undertook to write opening scenes in the manner of Steinbeck: the sun coming up over the hills above Salinas or Monterey, a man ambling along a country road, the smell of a river and the sound of the wind. After a couple of paragraphs of literary mimicry I would inevitably run out of steam, and of course I had no idea that I was practicing what would one day come to be my craft. I found a copy of *The Return of Sherlock Holmes* around this same time and was infected with the image of gaslamps glowing along foggy London streets and the rattle of hansom cabs. That particular book impressed upon me the notion that the best books very often had a black cloth cover with red or gold embossed print, a black-and-white frontispiece illustration, and the wonderful smell of dusty old paper. In short, I began to develop a love of books as objects, which is often looked upon as a variety of insanity and should be kept secret.

My mother, seeing that I had begun to browse avidly through her books, began to take my sister and me to the Stanton Free Library on Tuesday afternoons. On one of those trips, very early on, my mother handed me copies of *20,000 Leagues Under the Sea* and *A Journey to the Center of the Earth* (or was it *The Mysterious Island* or Wells's *The First Men in the Moon*? Did I check out two books on the third Tuesday or three books on the second Tuesday?) I remember absolutely that both of the books passed the binding and frontispiece test. The language was slightly archaic, which was another requirement. They had the right effect. My brain (perhaps literally) began to take on the finny, fishy submarine shape of Captain Nemo's Nautilus, and I began to think a lot about the possibility of worlds in the center of the Earth.

My sister Lynn and I started swapping books, and I borrowed her Black Stallion books and the Howard Pease merchant marine mysteries (copies of which books are now in my own library.) Around then she discovered a book called *High Times* beneath the philodendrons in the room divider—a story about three retired women who cut comical capers while out seeing the world. There was a picture of a martini glass on the dust jacket, and so we read the book secretly, thinking that it was fairly scandalous stuff. I remember lots of solitary reading and secret reading in those days: under the covers with a flashlight at night, of course, and up in an orange tree in the middle of a ten-acre grove on a spring afternoon, one eye on the lookout for the unpleasant owner of the grove, who carried a shotgun loaded with rock-salt. These crimes would lead to further wickedness, a *Mad* magazine hidden inside a Pee Chee folder at school, for example. Reading had become a vice.

I look back and see my life in those days as a succession of books, alternate universes without end. Alexander Smith, the English essayist, wrote that "The world is everywhere whispering essays," and it seemed to me then (and still does) that the world was everywhere whispering stories. I wasn't competent to whisper any stories myself yet, but that had clearly become my destiny.

I finally wrote my first story in the 5th grade, which means I was eleven years old at the time. I had a book-loving teacher named Mr. Borden, who read out loud to us every day. I remember that he asked us to choose between *Tom Sawyer* and *The Yearling*, and how disappointed I was when the class chose *The Yearling*, even though I had already read *Tom Sawyer* two or three times by then. Mr. Borden asked us to write a story of our own as homework, due in a week. It happened that a couple of days later my friend Johnny Hatley and I were walking along the railroad tracks killing time—throwing rocks, stealing oranges out of adjacent groves, and searching for horned toads (writerly research, it would turn out) when he told me about a terrifying film he'd just seen, a film titled *Macabre*. He was having nightmares about it. Not having the foggiest idea that the word "macabre" existed, I immediately (and I'll insist sensibly) thought of a corncob pipe. I went home and wrote a story about a walking skeleton named McCob, who smoked a pipe and terrorized a family in a farmhouse. I remember thinking that it was particularly brilliant, so it's a good thing that the story doesn't survive: I can go on thinking that way. I also remember that I didn't care much about motivation. The skeleton had no particular grudge against the family in the farmhouse. Peering into windows was evidently the sort of thing that walking skeletons were put into the world to do. And I'll admit that several months earlier I'd been immensely impressed by *The Seventh Voyage of Sinbad*, which had primed me for a lifelong passion for animate skeletons. A couple of years later I would watch *Jason and the Argonauts*, which featured an entire regiment of skeletons. I was certain that nothing more glorious had ever been seen on Earth, and (although I can't swear that this is true) I was no doubt happy that my story "McCob" had tied into the Universal. I'll cheerfully give that to literary critics who in some dim future will want to write learned articles about the walking skeleton theme in Blaylock's work, although I suppose it's even-money that none will step forward—critics, that is to say, not skeletons.

I've written a great deal elsewhere about how I came to write early Steampunk stories along with K.W. Jeter and Tim Powers back in the 1970s and 80s. I wrote it on and off for 15 years and then not at all for a period of time. And then by a happy chance my brother-in-law gave me a copy of James Norman Hall's collection of historical seafaring stories titled *Doctor Dogbody's Leg* (which you should read) and it came to me that I missed the cast of characters who figured into my steampunk stories and novels. The result is the collection of novellas in this book. It's a cliché to say that characters "take on a life of their own," but sometimes they do, at least in the writer's mind. And the more we write about them, the more likely that is to happen. Mine seem to have taken up permanent residence. In *The Art of Fiction*, John Gardner wrote that the world of the novel can become more real to the writer than the actual world, and that's also true, and is another thing that sounds like lunacy. Writing is a dangerous profession.

Reality comes highly recommended, but it's not a bad thing to take leave of it now and then, especially into the pages of a book. And with that I believe that I've said what I wanted to say. It's my great good fortune once again to be able to sit down at my desk in morning in order to find my way into another story—an afternoon's stroll down a railroad track heading for nowhere in particular, but ideally a place worth discovering. Thanks for reading this introduction (which is an afterword nonetheless) and the book that goes along with it.

—Jim Blaylock
Orange, California
January, 2016

The Ebb Tide

CHAPTER 1

Merton's Rarities

W E WERE AT the Half Toad one evening early in the month of a windy May—Langdon St. Ives; Tubby Frobisher, and myself, Jack Owlesby—taking our ease at our customary table. Professor St. Ives, as you're perhaps already aware, is one of England's most brilliant scientists, and her most intrepid explorer. The Half Toad is an inn that lies in Lambert Court, off Fingal Street in London, frequented by men of science down on their luck: three rooms to let, William and Henrietta Billson proprietors. The inn is difficult to find if you don't know the turning or if you fail to see the upper body of what is commonly called a Surinam toad leaning out of the high window over the door.

The carving of the toad was carried out of Guiana in the mid-century by Billson himself, aboard the old *William Rodgers*. The nether half of the creature blew to flinders when the powder magazine exploded in the dead of night, sinking the ship and half the crew in a fog off Santo Domingo. Billson found himself afloat and alone with half the toad, and he clung to the remains for close onto a day and a half before fishermen hauled him out nearly drowned. He went straight back to London on a mail packet, only to discover that his old father had died two months earlier and left him something over five hundred a year, and so he counted his many blessings, married his sweetheart, and set up shop in Lambert Court, where he put the heroic toad in the window.

In his seagoing days, Billson had been an amateur naturalist, and had sailed as a young man with Sir Gilbert Blane, popularly known as Lemon

Juice Blane, the great anti-scorbutic doctor. Billson's collection of fish and amphibiana was housed in the back of the inn (and still is). It was the man's deep interest in Japanese carp that led to his correspondence with St. Ives in the days following the incident of the break-in at the Bayswater Street Oceanarium in the time of the Homunculus.

St. Ives had recently resolved to keep a room the year round at the Half Toad, despite—or rather because of—its obscure location, so that he had secure digs when he came in from Chingford-by-the-Tower to London proper, which happened often enough. Billson wasn't a man to be trifled with, nor a man to ask questions, both of which attributes suited St. Ives down to the ground. Henrietta Billson, a ruddy-faced, smiling woman, once beat a customer half silly with a potato masher who had put his hands on the girl who makes up the rooms. Her fruit tarts and meat pies would make you weep.

Enough people frequent the Inn to keep Billson busy in front of his fireplace spit long into the evening, and on the night in question he had a joint of beef rotating, done very nearly to a turn, and he was looking at it with a practiced eye, his carving knife ready at hand. Beneath, to catch the drippings, hung a kettle of those small potatoes called Irish apricots by the Welsh, and there wasn't a man among us who didn't have the look of a greedy dog.

This particular May evening at the Half Toad, I'll point out in passing, took place during that lamented period when St. Ives had been forbidden entrance to the Explorer's Club because of a minor kitchen mishap involving refined brandy and the head and tentacles of a giant squid. The great man's temporary banishment and subsequent reinstatement will have to be the subject of another account, but in those dark days St. Ives came to appreciate the homely luxury of the Half Toad, and in the years following his reinstatement he visited the Explorers Club but rarely. I should say "we," since I was (and am) St. Ives's frequent companion when the great man comes into London.

But as I was saying, I remember that May evening in '82 well enough, for the Phoenix Park murders were being shouted high and low by newsboys out on Fingal Street. That unforgettable joint of beef was turning on the spit, there were kidney pies baking in the oven and puddings boiling in the copper, and, of course, there were those potatoes. The Billsons' halfwit kitchen help, a Swede of indeterminate age named Lars Hopeful, was drawing ale from the tap, and all of us, you can be sure, were looking forward to making a long night of it.

I hadn't so much as put the glass to my lips when the door swung open, the street noise momentarily heightened, and we looked up to see who it was coming in with the wind. Surprisingly, it was St. Ives's man Hasbro, who should have been in Chingford tending the home fires, so to speak, and collecting the post. Alice—Mrs. St. Ives—was in Scarborough with the St. Ives children, little Eddie and his sister Cleo. My own wife, Dorothy, had gone along, the lot of them staying with Alice's ancient grandmother, which explains how St. Ives and I had come to be temporarily bachelorized. Hasbro had the air of a man in a hurry (not his usual demeanor) and you can imagine that we were suddenly anxious to hear him out.

Without a word, however, he produced from his coat a recent copy of Merton's *Catalogue of Rarities* and opened it to a folded page, which he passed across to St. Ives, who read the piece aloud. There was offered for sale a hand-drawn map of a small area of the Morecambe Sands, the location not identified. The map, according to the catalogue copy, was stained with waterweeds, tobacco, and salt rime, was torn, soiled, and ill-drawn as if by a child, was signed with the letter K and the crude, figure-eight drawing of a cuttlefish, and was offered for sale for two pounds six. "Of questionable value," Merton had added, "but perhaps interesting to the right party."

Merton had found the right party, and had doubtless *expected* to find it, because he had sent the catalogue out to St. Ives Manor by messenger, not suspecting, of course, that the Professor was already in London. St. Ives stood up abruptly from his chair and uttered the words, "Kraken's map, or I'm a fried whiting." He slid the catalogue into his coat and along with the waiting Hasbro strode toward the door, shouting a hasty goodbye to Billson, who gestured his farewell with the carving knife. Never a potato did I eat, I'm sad to say, and the same for Tubby Frobisher, who was fast on my heels, although the man could have had no idea what any of this meant.

Night was falling, and the temperature with it, as if the world had tilted and spring had slid back into winter. Lambert court was deserted aside from a workman in dungarees, who was inordinately tall and sneery, lounging on a pile of excavated dirt and rock with the air of a man having avoided a day's work. Twenty minutes earlier there had been two of them, the other squat and with dangling, heavy arms, and the comical contrast between the two had stayed in my mind. Now the tall one was smoking a pipe over the remains of the day—Balkan Sobranie, my own tobacco of choice, and perhaps a little elevated for a workman's pocketbook, something I remarked to Frobisher when the wind blew the reek past us in a cloud. The man gathered himself together and left just as we came out through the door. He disappeared back through the Court with a certain celerity, as if he had an appointment to keep.

Fingal Street, never particularly active, was possessed of an evening quiet. St. Ives hailed a Hansom cab that happened to be passing, and he and Hasbro climbed aboard and whirled away. "To Merton's!" St. Ives shouted back at us, and Tubby and I were left to follow as best we could. We set out on foot, making our way down toward the Embankment at a fair pace.

"Look here, Jackie," Frobisher said, puffing along beside me. "What on Earth is this business of the map? That was my kidney pie just coming out of the oven, and now I'm left to starve."

"I can't be certain," I said. "I can only speculate."

"Then speculate me this: a map to *what*? Gold and jewels, eh? Something of that sort? The problem with all this," he told me, "is that anything lost in the Morecambe Sands will stay lost. I've heard stories of coaches and four sinking into the quicksands of Morecambe Bay with all hands on board, never to be seen again. A man might as well have a map of the Bottomless Pit."

"Merton surely knows that," I said. "His 'of doubtful value' makes just that point. Do you remember poor old Bill Kraken?"

"Absolutely. Not a bad sort, although half the time off his chump, as I recall."

"Not so far off as it sometimes seemed, I can assure you," I said. "The antics of a lunatic are a natural ruse."

We hailed a passing cab now, which reined up, Tubby cramming himself in through the door like a stoat into a hole. "Merton's Rarities," I said to the driver. "Hurry!" He hi-hoed at the horses and off they went, throwing us both sideways, Tubby pinning me heavily against the wall. "The point is," I said, "if Bill drew such a map, and it's come to light, then we've got to take up the scent, or we'll lose it again."

"The scent of *what*, Jack? *That's* the salient point, you see."

"A lost object. It was what you might call…a device," I told him.

"Ah! A *device*. Just so. For spinning straw into gold, perhaps?"

One didn't keep secrets from one's allies, especially from a man like Tubby Frobisher, who did as he would be done by, so to speak. "You recall the so-called Yorkshire Dales Meteor?" I asked.

"Plowed up a meadow owned by a country parson, didn't it? Burnt a hedgerow. There was some element of it that made it worth the attention of the press for a day or two. I seem to recall a ring of floating cattle round-about a manure dump, although it might have been floating swine."

"It was the murder of Parson Grimstead that attracted the press. They were more or less indifferent to the flaming object—not a meteor, I can assure you. The Parson found a strange device, you see, in his cattle enclo-sure, and he hid it in his barn. He suspected, probably correctly, that it wasn't…of earthly origin."

Tubby gave me a look, but he knew enough about St. Ives's adven-tures over the years so that the look wasn't utterly dubious. "The Parson sent word to St. Ives," I said, "whom he had known man and boy, and St. Ives flogged up to Yorkshire to arrive the following morning, only to find the Parson dead on the ground inside the barn door. He was carry-ing a fowling piece, although he hadn't apparently meant to go hunting, at least not for birds. There was no sign of the device. A local farmer had seen a wagon coming out of the Parson's yew alley before dawn, driving away westward. It turned out that the device had been spirited away to the Carnforth Ironworks. According to a worker, a container of wood and iron had been built to house it, the interior of the container sealed with India rubber. As for the floating cattle, St. Ives found the report vitally interesting, but to my mind it simply encouraged the press to make light of a good man's murder."

"*Spirited away*?" Tubby said. "*Built to house it*? By whom?"

"You know by whom, or can guess."

"Ignacio *Narbondo*? What does he call himself now? Frosticos, isn't it?" He was silent for a moment. "We should have fed him to that herd of feral pigs when we had the chance. We'll add that oversight to our list of regrets."

Fleet Street was annoyingly crowded with evening strollers, and we crawled along now, the cabbie shouting imprecations, our pace quickening again as we rounded onto Upper Thames Street toward the Embankment. "The map, then?" Tubby asked. "You must have found this device and then—what?—lost it again?"

"Just so. What happened," I told him, "was that we three took the device out of the Ironworks under the cover of night, St. Ives, old Bill, and myself. We were waylaid near Silverdale at low tide, and Bill set out across the sands alone with the wagon despite St. Ives's reservations. He had the idea of fleeing into Cumbria, going to ground, and waiting for us to catch up. If the wagon became mired in the sands, he would draw a map of its exact location, although the odds of our recovering it were small. The virtue was that the device would be out of the hands of Frosticos, who would surely misuse it, whatever it was."

"It had a use, then?"

"Apparently, or so St. Ives suspected. The long and the short of it is that Bill disappeared. We fear that he went down into the sands somewhere in the vicinity of Humphrey Head. Did he draw his map? We didn't know. All these years we've assumed that the map, if there was one, sank along with the wagon and poor Bill."

"And so ends the tale," Tubby said. "Your device is lost, and two dead men to show for it."

"One last, salient bit. Merton, you see, frequents the Bay, where he has family, and years ago St. Ives asked him to be on the lookout for anything remotely relevant to the case. Lost things turn up, you see, sometimes, along the shore, sometimes in dredgers' nets. This is our first glimmer of hope."

"Well," Tubby said gloomily, "give me a kidney pie and a pint of plain over a glimmer of anything, especially if it's buried in quicksand." But Tubby was always a slave to his stomach, and there he was sitting beside me in the cab as we reined up in front of Merton's, game as ever.

Merton's Rarities, very near London Bridge, is part rare book shop, part curiosity shop, and a sort of museum of old maps and arcane paper goods, scientific debris, and collections of all sorts—insects, assembled skeletons, stuffed creatures from far and wide. Where Merton finds his wares I don't know, although he does a brisk trade with sailors returning from distant lands. In his youth he worked in the stockroom at the British Museum, where he established a number of exotic contacts.

The shop was well lit despite the hour. Tubby and I hesitated only a moment in the entryway, spotting St. Ives and Hasbro bent over the body of poor Merton, who lay sprawled on the floor like a dead man. Roundabout the front counter there were maps and papers and books strewn about, drawers emptied. Someone had torn the place up, and brazenly, too. Merton's forehead was bloody from a gash at the hairline, smeared by the now blood-stained sleeve of his lab coat. Hasbro was waving a vial of smelling salts beneath Merton's nose, but apparently to no consequence, as St. Ives attempted to staunch the flow of blood.

"*Back room. Wary now,*" St. Ives told us without looking up, and Frobisher, no longer mindful of his kidney pie, plucked a shillelagh out of a hollow elephant leg nearby. He had the look of a man who was finally happy to do some useful work. I took out a leaded cane and followed him toward the rear of the shop, where we came to an arched door, beyond which there was a vestibule opening onto three large rooms: a book room, a storage room full of wooden casks and crates, and a workshop. The book room was apparently empty, although the storage room afforded a dozen hiding places. "Come on out!" I shouted, brandishing the cane at the shadow-filled room, but I was met with silence.

Then Tubby called out, "He's bolted!" which didn't altogether disappoint me. I found Tubby in the workshop, where a door stood open beyond a row of heavy wooden benches littered with half assembled skeletons. We looked out through the door, discovering a pleasant, walled garden with a paved central square surrounded by shrubbery. An iron, scrollwork table lay on the pavement, its feet pushed into the shrubbery along the wall, which the attacker had no doubt scaled, kicking the table backward when he boosted himself onto the copings.

We set the table up, which was very shaky, I might add, with a treacherously loose leg, and while Tubby held it steady, I climbed atop it and looked up and down the empty by-street, which dead-ended some distance up against a shuttered building. It lead away downwards towards the river, winding around in the direction, roughly speaking, of Billingsgate Market.

"Gone," I said out loud. "No sight of him." And I was just leaning on Tubby's shoulder to climb back down when I saw a boy come out of an alley down across the way. He stood staring at me, as if trying to classify what species of creature I might turn out to be. To my utter surprise, he headed straight toward me, waving a hand in the air. ⟶

CHAPTER 2

What Happened to the Map

W HAT'S *THIS* NOW?" I said, and Tubby, still holding steady, said, "Enlighten me," with a good deal of irony, as if he was miffed that his only useful business was to anchor the table while I took in the view.

"Begging your pardon, sir," the boy said, breathing heavily. "There was a man came over this wall. I seen him."

"How long back?" I asked.

"Not ten minutes, sir. I followed him down toward the market, but lost sight of him. I thought at first he'd taken an oars downriver, but then I saw him duck into a gin shop, what they call the Goat and Cabbage."

"Send the boy around to the *front*," Frobisher said a little pettishly. "I'm not a damned *pi*laster."

"Right," I said, and was about to convey the suggestion when the lad took a mad run at the wall, sprang up, latched onto the copings, and heaved himself over, landing on his feet like a cat.

Tubby shouted and trod back in astonishment, letting go of the table, which toppled sideways, pitching me into the rock roses, thank heaven, and not onto the paving stones. It was the boy who helped me to my feet, dusting off my coat and asking was I injured, which I said I was not, although I gave Tubby a hard look for shirking his duty with the table. The boy might have been twelve or thirteen, and was in need of a haircut and a new pair of trousers a good three inches longer than the pair he wore.

"Finn Conrad, at your gentlemen's service," he said, holding out his hand, which I shook heartily enough. I immediately liked the look of the boy, who reminded me a little of myself at that age, but with considerably more gumption.

"Jack Owlesby," I told him. "And this is Mr. Frobisher. They called him Pilaster Frobisher out in India, where he spent a great deal of time in the sun. If you'd just lead the way inside, Mr. Frobisher."

"It's a pleasure to meet you, young comet," Tubby said to the boy, bowing in his portly way and shaking the offered hand before heading in through the open door "I'm speaking to an acrobat, I don't doubt?"

"Duffy's Circus, sir, born and bred. But I ran away two years back, after my old mother died, and I've been living hereabouts since, making my living in what way I can. Are these your whacking sticks?" he asked, gesturing, and we said that they were. He collected the leaded cane and shillelagh where they lay atop the workbench, surveyed the bones and skeletons as if they were pretty much what he expected to find under the circumstances, and went on into Merton's like an old hand.

Merton wasn't dead, thank God, but was sitting in a chair now, in that comfortable little browsing parlor he's got at the front of the shop. He held a glass of brandy and wore a bandage round his forehead. St. Ives and Hasbro sat opposite, and Tubby and I took the two remaining chairs. Through the window I could see London Bridge. Upriver lay the Pool, the masts of the shipping just visible, and faint on the air you could hear bells and whistles and other sorts of nautical noise. "I saw his face clearly," Merton was saying to St. Ives. "It was a broad face, nose like a fig and small eyes. Not a dwarf, mind you, but a small man. Apelike is the word for him. Quite horrible in appearance."

"In a brown coat," young Finn said, "begging your pardon, sir, and a watch cap. That's the very man I was telling these gentlemen about."

"What have we here?" St. Ives asked.

"Finn Conway, sir, at your service. I seen him come over the wall out back. 'What's this now?' I asked myself. Why would a man come over a wall when there's a door out front unless he's up to no good?"

"Quite right," Tubby said.

"He didn't see me," Finn said, "because I didn't want him to. He headed straightaway toward the river with me following after him, and went into a gin shop in what they call Peach Alley."

"The Goat and Cabbage," I said helpfully,

"That's the one. I took a look inside, nonchalant like, but I didn't see him. Maybe he's gone on through, I thought. There's a lot of what you might call *passages* down along there by the river. I waited for a bit, thinking he might come out from where he'd gone, but then a man came in and told me to clear out."

"Can you take us there in the morning?" St. Ives asked, and Finn said that he could, and then assured us that he could find very nearly anyplace a second time if he put his mind to it, just as easy as the first time. He had lived hereabouts long enough to know the riverside, he said, although he was presently without an address and was looking forward to summer and to less of this wind.

St. Ives asked him if he could find us a bite of supper, and sent him off with a handful of coins, considerably more money than was necessary, enough to tempt him if he were a rascally young hypocrite and not who he seemed to be, and in any event to get him out of the way while we reconnoitered.

"He'll be back right enough," Tubby said. "He's a game one. You should have seen him scale the garden wall, speaking of apes."

I could see that Merton was in a state, glancing fearfully about him as if at any moment his assailant might return to finish him off, but he calmed himself with an effort, and for the next quarter of an hour he laid out the facts as he knew them, and we pitched in with comments when we were able. Merton, it turns out, had been given the map by his uncle Fred, a sand pilot on Morecambe Bay who lives in the area of Grange-over-Sands. Fred takes excursions across the sands at low tide, Merton told us, out into the cockle beds off Poulton-le-Sands, or back and forth from Silverdale to Humphrey Head if the moon is right. Uncle Fred—a legend thereabouts—had been mired in quicksand, caught up by the incoming tide, run afoul of smugglers, and suffered all manner of perils and had lived to tell the tale. He wasn't one of the Queen's Guides, mind you, but that's what made him useful to certain people, especially that class of dredger who fished the quicksand by night.

Fred had found the map—it was as simple as that—near the top of the Bay. It was corked up in a bottle that had suffered some leakage. It looked curious to him, and he kept the map as a souvenir, putting it into a drawer and after a time forgetting about it. Then one day two weeks past he sorted out the drawer and found it again, and when Merton and he ran into each other at their Aunt Sue's house in Manchester, he gave it to Merton as a curiosity. Merton put it straight into the catalogue without a second thought, although he'd been cagey with the description, in case there was more to the business than met the eye. Then he sent up to Chingford-by-the-Tower to alert St. Ives.

"More *what* than met the eye?" Tubby asked, in his usual impatient way.

"The thing is," Merton said, "Uncle Fred talked the map around, you see, after he found it again in the drawer."

"Talked it around to *whom?*" asked St. Ives, looking at him narrowly.

"To the lads in a pub there in Poulton-le-Sands, over a pint, you know. Natural sort of thing, if you see what I mean, passing the time. Except there turned out to be two men sitting nearby, listening hard. One of them asked to see it, but Uncle Fred made up an excuse for not having it with him, although he did, right there in the pocket of his coat. He didn't like the look of either of them, and didn't know them, although he could describe them right enough. The one was a tall, scowly sort of fellow, swarthy, Fred told me. Unpleasant. A murderer's face, Fred called it. The other had dead white hair, and a face that looked as if it had been carved out of ice. There was something wrong with this second man that you couldn't quite name—Dr. Fell comes to mind. It was the tall man who did the talking."

St. Ives gave us a glance at this juncture. The detail of the white hair and the unnamable malevolence suggested that our man was indeed Ignacio Narbondo, now known as Dr. Frosticos, or sometimes Frost, St. Ives's longtime nemesis and the last man on earth I wanted anything to do with. He had gone out of our lives some time back—out of the world, I had hoped. His interest in the map would be as avid as that of St. Ives, although he would be considerably more ruthless in its pursuit.

"I take it that you saw these same men again?" Hasbro asked.

"Just the tall one," Merton said. "The first time was there in Manchester. Fred saw him on the street and pointed him out to me. He was loitering in a doorway and smoking a pipe. That could have been a coincidence, of course, or perhaps another tall man with similar features. We were on the other side of the street, you see, and it was evening. But then I saw him again, shortly after I was back in London, and no mistake this time. He followed me to the shop, and he wasn't clever at it either. Bold is the word for it."

"You're certain he followed you?" St. Ives asked.

"Yes," Merton said. "The second sighting there in Manchester might have been coincidence, but the third time always smells of a plot."

"And the white haired man?" I asked him.

"No. Only the tall one. The catalogue hadn't been distributed yet, but he asked straightaway to buy the map, said that he'd heard it had fallen into my hands. No preamble, no beating about the bush. 'I want the Morecambe Sands map,' he said."

"And you told him to bugger off," Tubby said.

"Not in so many words," Merton said, pouring himself another glass of brandy. He swirled it in the light, looking shrewdly at us. "I played the fool, you see. Denied knowing anything about it. He accused me of lying, and I told him to get out. Then two days later there he was again, but with a copy of the new catalogue, Lord knows where he'd gotten his hands on it, which he laid on the counter along with the required sum, accurate to the penny. I told him I'd already sold it. He called me a liar, which of course was accurate, and walked out without being asked. I hoped that was the end of it."

"But he sent his simian cohort back in tonight and bloody well took it," Tubby said.

"Ah! Ha ha! He *believes* he took it!" Merton said, brightening up, but then shut his eyes and held his forehead with the pain of laughing, and it took him a moment to get going again. St. Ives had a keen look on his face.

"Now, here's the long and the short of it," Merton continued, looking around again, his voice dropping. He tipped us a wink. "I *hoped* I'd seen the end of the gentleman, you see, and yet I'm a careful man. I set to work and devised a false map on a piece of the same sort of paper—but quite a different part of the Bay and with the landmarks changed. Correct in all other ways. I doctored the ink so that it ran, as if the paper had been soaked in seawater, but not so much that the map couldn't be made out. Then I colored it up with dyes made of algae and tobacco and garden soil, and I slipped it into the box under the counter, where I keep small money to make change for the customers. Our man searched for it, as you can see, throwing things around the floor. Then he spotted the box, helped himself to the money, and found the map. Of course I played my part. 'Take the money,' I said to him, 'but for God's sake leave the other! It's of no value to you.'" Merton sat back in his chair now, smiling like a schoolboy, very satisfied with himself, but then his face fell.

"His response was to hit me with a length of lead pipe. Quick as a snake. Perfectly unnecessary. I hadn't so much as twitched."

"The stinking pig," Tubby said, and of course we all voiced our agreement, but what I wanted to know was, what about the map, the real map? Merton had it safe as a baby, it turned out—rolled up, tied neatly with a bit of string, and thrust into the open mouth of a stuffed armadillo in the window. No thief, he informed us, would think to look for valuables inside an armadillo.

Merton leered at us for a moment, making us wait, and then said, "Fancy having a squint at it?" He was enjoying himself immensely now. He was resilient, I'll say that for him, but perhaps too enamored of his own cleverness, which the ancients warn us against. Still, he had done what he could to help St. Ives, and had nearly had his skull crushed into the bargain. He was a good man, and no doubt about it, and his *ruse de la guerre* seemed to have worked. He helped himself to a third glass of brandy, which he drank off with a sort of congratulatory relish before fetching the map out of the maw of the preposterous scaled creature nearby. He handed it to St. Ives, who slipped off the string and unrolled it delicately. After a moment he looked up at Hasbro and I and nodded. "It's as we thought," he said.

Just then the door swung open and Finn Conrad came in carrying meat pies and bottled ale, and, it turned out, most of St. Ives's money. St. Ives slipped the map into his coat while Finn set down his burden, handed back the bulk of the coins, and advised the Professor (begging his pardon for saying so) not to be quite so liberal with people he didn't know, not in London, leastways, although it mightn't be a problem in the smaller towns, where people were more honest, on the whole.

My appetite had fled when I saw Merton bleeding on the floor, but it returned now in spades, and that apparently went double for Tubby, who crushed half a pie into his mouth like an alligator eating a goat, and then settled back into his chair for some serious consumption, the rest of us not far behind him. Tomorrow morning, St. Ives told us, we would take a look into the Goat and Cabbage, if Finn would be so kind as to show us the way. Finn said that nothing would give him more pleasure, and then pointed out that someone should guard the shop tonight in Merton's absence, and much to Merton's credit he said that he would be quite happy if Finn would make up the settee in the workroom, and sleep with one eye open and one hand on the shillelagh in case the rogues returned.

"Out the back door and over the wall at the first sound of trouble, that's my advice," I told him, and Hasbro echoed the sentiment.

St. Ives was doubtful about leaving the boy alone in the shop at all, now that he knew something more of the men who possessed the false map.

"The stolen item," St. Ives said to Merton," "you say it's a…*satisfactory* specimen?"

"Oh, *much* better than satisfactory, I should say," Merton said, grinning. "*Considerably* better. Not that I claim to know anything about the art of…reproduction." He had been going to say "forgery," but there was no reason to utter the word with the lad standing by. *Reproduction* said rather too much, it seemed to me at the time. Certainly there was no profit, and perhaps some danger, in Finn's knowing things he didn't need to know. St. Ives, sensibly, brought the conversation to a close.

And so we locked young Finn safely into the shop and went out into the evening to see Merton home, where we delivered him safely to Mrs. Merton, he having fully recovered his spirits, and with an extra measure into the bargain. Mrs. Merton gasped to see the bloody bandage on her husband's head, but Merton was markedly indifferent to it. "Happy to be of service," he said to St. Ives, saluting. "I'll do my part!" We assured him that he already had and left him smiling gloriously on the doorstep.

In the morning Finn was already up and working when St. Ives, Hasbro, and I returned. Tubby had domestic duties and hadn't come along, which turned out to be to our advantage, given what happened later, although I'm getting ahead of myself. Finn had shelved the fallen books, made an orderly stack of the papers, swept the place out, and was soaking the blood out of Merton's lab coat, which, he said, wanted cold water and not hot so as not to "set the stain," which was something else he had learned during his years in the circus, where he had put in his time in the laundry. "All shipshape," he told us.

We breakfasted along Thames Street on kippers and eggs and beans, and then set out with Finn walking far on ahead, which was Hasbro's idea. No one would associate the boy with us, you see, when we were in the neighborhood of the Goat and Cabbage, and I was reminded once again that there might be some danger in our undertaking. To tell you the truth, it had begun to seem more like a holiday to me. ⸺⸰

CHAPTER 3

The Goat and Cabbage

LOWER THAMES STREET from the Pool to the Tower is busy night and day, with cargo coming off the ships and going onto them, and shops open, and fishmongers hauling carts and pushing hand barrows of whiting and oysters and plaice and whelks toward Billingsgate Market, which smelled of brine and seaweed and, of course, fish. All manner of trade goods and all manner of people crept up and down, jostling in and out of coffeehouses and shops, intent on doing business or on getting in the way of other people doing theirs. I was knocked sideways by a grimacing man with an unlikely large and wet bag of oysters over his shoulder, and knocked back again by a donkey hauling a cart of herring barrels, but nobody meant any harm and it struck me as rather agreeable than otherwise to be out and about on a busy spring morning, last night's blustery cold having given up and gone back to whence it came.

In all that seething crowd we lost sight of Finn, but then saw him again, lounging against a store front, eating something out of his hand, giving the last of it to a mongrel dog and setting out again without so much as a look in our direction, the dog at his heels. Half a block farther along, I smelled a waft of pipe tobacco, Sobranie again. The tobacco isn't all that rare, but it naturally put me in mind of the tall workman in Lambert Court last night. Then I thought of the small man who had been with him earlier in the evening, and then of Merton's description of his apelike assailant and of the tall man from the pub in Poulton-le-Sands, and suddenly, like a bonk on the conk, it didn't feel like a holiday any longer as the truth rushed in upon me. The two men in Lambert Court yesterday evening weren't the navvies they had appeared to be. One had evidently stayed behind to keep an eye on us, and the other had gone down to the embankment to beat poor Merton over the head with a pipe. Hasbro's untimely entrance must have complicated things for them, and yet they had managed to remain one step ahead of us.

Abruptly I wished I had taken along the leaded cane, and I looked around, trying to catch sight of the pipe smoker while I was revealing all this to St. Ives, who narrowed his eyes and nodded at me. But I saw no one who might be our man, or our men. Soon we drew abreast of a narrow alley that angled away toward the river. Finn was just then buying a bag of hot chestnuts from a man with a kettle on wheels, and he nodded discreetly up the alley, where there hung a weather-battered sign depicting the head of a goat wearing a cabbage leaf cap.

There was nothing for it but to push through the door into the fug of the gin shop, which was busy enough for that hour of the morning. A man was singing "Pretty Mary Tumblehome" in a voice like a broken cartwheel, and there was a good deal of low talk, which staggered just a little when we walked in. It evened out again when we three trespassers had navigated the tavern and found calmer water in a corridor beyond.

There were a couple of straw pallets along the near wall of the first room off the corridor, and a chamber pot, and boxes of destitute old junk that you might see for sale in a two penny stall in Monmouth Street. Against the far wall stood a heavy oaken wardrobe with a broad, high door, considerably scarred and black with age—nothing that interested us in the least. We jibbed without a word, angling back out into the dark corridor, sailing past other dead-end rooms and none the wiser for any of it. Evidently we had come on a fool's errand.

"They'll no doubt find *us* soon enough," St. Ives said, shrugging, and he turned back down the corridor with us following, anxious to gain the street—or at least I was. But Hasbro stopped outside the room with the wooden wardrobe, cocking his head as if listening to something.

"Commodious wardrobe," he said in a low voice.

"Just so," St. Ives said. "Just so." He darted a glance up and down the corridor. "Jacky, watch the door," he whispered. "Give us a whistle if anyone appears."

But there was no need to whistle, because no one, apparently, was interested in us, a fact that had begun to seem peculiar to me. The entire mob had been aware of our entering the place. Someone, you'd suppose, would begin to wonder what we were about. I looked back to see Hasbro fiddling at the lock with a piece of wire and St. Ives endeavoring to see behind the wardrobe, which appeared to be pressed tightly against the wall, perhaps affixed to it. I wondered why the wardrobe would be locked at all, but just as the question came into my mind, the door swung open to reveal that it was utterly empty.

"Interior lock," Hasbro said, indicating an iron latch that was attached to the inside of the door, identical to and directly behind the outside latch. There was a key in it, which Hasbro removed and slipped into his pocket.

St. Ives reached in and pushed on the panel at the back of the wardrobe, fiddling with the mouldings, and very shortly the panel slid sideways to reveal a dark passageway beyond. Without an instant's hesitation St. Ives stepped through the door and ducked into the passage, waving at us to follow. I was quick enough to comply, half of my mind worrying that someone from the tavern would look in to see what we were up to, the other half worrying that they hadn't already done so.

I glimpsed a precipice ahead—stairs leading downward beyond a small landing, more or less in the direction of the river. St. Ives was already descending along a rusty iron railing. Hasbro followed behind me, swinging the wardrobe door closed, the passage instantly disappearing into utter darkness. I heard him step out onto the landing, and then the panel in the wall at his back slid into place with a clicking sound.

"Steady-on," St. Ives said from somewhere below.

There was a cool updraft, and a wet, musty smell that might have been the river itself. I heard what sounded like the roar and hiss of a boiler letting out steam. "Can you find your way, sir?" Hasbro whispered into my ear in a disembodied sort of voice.

I told him I could, and I stepped off, one foot in front of the other, gripping the railing with one hand and feeling my way along the wall like a blind man with the other, hoping that no rotten stair tread would catapult me into the abyss. Soon, however, I found that I could see tolerably well. There was light somewhere below, which brightened as we descended.

A vast room—more a cavern than a room—opened out, and we paused for a moment to take in the sight below us. The floor lay at a depth that

must have been beneath or near the level of the river. On that floor lay two strange undersea craft set on stocks, one of them evidently half built. Roundabout them lay a litter of metal panels, casks of rivets, and heavy glass sheets in wooden racks. One of the ships was the length of a yacht, and might have been completely built for all I could see in that dim light, with a shape that reminded one of an oceangoing prehistoric monster—finny appendages and convex, eyelike portholes. The other vessel was smaller, just a shell, really, of a similar craft. Some distance away stood a third craft, exceedingly strange and unlikely, a sort of elongated orb standing on bent iron legs—apparently an underwater diving chamber. It had nothing of the diving bell about it, but was altogether more delicate, built of what appeared to be copper and glass, and probably capable of independent movement, if the jointed, stork-like legs and feet were any indication.

A few feet beyond that lay a broad pool of dark water, the lamplight glinting off little eddies and swirls on its otherwise still surface, as if it were flowing eastward, perhaps a subterranean channel of the Thames, or a backwater of one of the underground rivers that transect the city—the Walbrook, perhaps, or a branch of the Fleet.

The ceiling soared away overhead, supported by arches of heavy, cut stone. There were gaslight lamps some distance up the walls, with iron ladders leading up past them to a web of narrow walkways. The walkways ran hither and yon far above our heads, linking platforms on which lay what appeared to be tools and crates, perhaps shipbuilding paraphernalia, too dim in the gaslight to make out clearly from where we stood near the base of the stairs. The platforms, evidently, could be raised and lowered: they dangled from heavy chains that angled away in a complicated, block and tackle system. The boiler and coal oven of an immense steam engine hissed and glowed beyond.

We were apparently alone in the room, and we descended the last few steps warily, the bottom stair-tread hanging a foot above the stone floor, held aloft by heavy chains suspended from above. The entire bottom flight shuddered with our movements like a ship in a cross sea. I was on the look-out for some sort of activity, and a little surprised (I speak for myself again) not to find any, especially with the boiler stoked and glowing. No one with legitimate business in this vast place would have any reason to hide. We were the intruders, after all, just as we had been intruders in the gin shop above.

St. Ives, however, didn't have the air of an intruder. He stepped down off the precarious stairway and walked eagerly to the half-built ship on the stocks. "A submarine vessel in the making!" he said, his mind instantly taken up with questions of science and engineering. He pointed at slabs of neatly stacked grey stone, weighted down by pigs of iron. The stone looked as if it had been cut out of blocks of sea foam. "Pumice," he said. "Do you see this, Hasbro? They've cut it into slices and encased it within the aluminium shell. Ingenious." He stood looking for a moment at a tub full of water nearby. Wires looped down into either end of the tub, dangling beneath floating rubber bladders with tubes running out of them. "They're producing hydrogen gas," he muttered, rubbing his chin. "I believe they're pumping it into the shell of the craft to further increase buoyancy. But what motive power? Electricity, surely, but what source…?" He went on this way, peering into recesses of the craft, talking mainly to himself, pointing out incomprehensible odds and ends, apparently having forgotten what we'd come for.

But what *had* we come for? If we were pursuing the simian man who had failed to steal Merton's map, we hadn't found any trace of him. Instead we had found a subterranean shipyard, very nice in its way, but another riddle, not a solution. I looked around warily, my mind far removed from questions of scientific arcana. I'll admit, craven as it sounds, that I was thinking of the potential for escape. Back up the stairs and into the Goat and Cabbage? The idea was almost welcome. At the downriver end of the cavern, I saw now, stood a pair of high doors, closing off an opening wide enough to cart in any sort of freight—the way in, no doubt. The wardrobe door was simply a bolt-hole.

And then something happened that was almost disorienting under the circumstances: I smelled pipe tobacco, faintly but distinctly. I looked around sharply, peering into the dim and distant recesses of the enormous room, but I saw nothing. My imagination? I heard a scraping noise from somewhere overhead, and I glanced up sharply at the walkways, where I glimpsed the small glowing circle of a lighted pipe. Someone leaned on a railing, looking down at us. He was tall man, I could see that much, and he was evidently in no hurry, but was considering us as if we were animals in a cage, which wasn't far wrong. The light was too dim for me to make out his features, but I knew well enough who he was. I saw a second man on one of the platforms now, also making no effort to hide.

"There they are!" I shouted, but my words were buried by the abrupt ratcheting, clattering sound of winches turning and of heavy chain hauled through iron rings and the whistle and gasp of steam. The entire system of chains and pulleys and winches seemed to be moving now, the cacophony erupting from far and near. The three of us turned as one back toward the stairs.

But the lower flight of steps was hovering some few feet above the floor, hauling slowly upward on its chains, already moving out of reach. We were trapped, just as I had feared. I realized with a cold start that my feet were wet. There was an inch of water on the floor now. Sluice gates—they had opened sluice gates. The dark river beyond the diving chamber had risen—was rising—and the truth, pardon me for saying it, flooded in upon me. We had been lured here, hoodwinked, the biter bit.

"The freight doors!" I shouted, probably worthlessly in that ongoing cacophony of noise, and I pointed wildly toward the distant doors and set out at a splashing run. Before I'd taken six strides, there was a hand on the back of my coat and I was stopped in my tracks, the water swirling around my ankles. I turned to see Hasbro gesturing in the direction of the diving chamber, which St. Ives was examining with a trained eye. *Of course*, I thought, wading after Hasbro, looking hastily into the maze of catwalks overhead, where the tall man still watched us. He was holding a rifle now, leaning casually against the railing as if he meant to shoot squirrels.

The ratcheting and banging ceased abruptly, throwing the room into an eerie silence but for the hissing of steam. There was a gurgling noise and a soft splashing of water as the tide rose abysmally fast—knee deep now, cold and dark as death. St. Ives had the hatch door open and was climbing in, one foot on the nearest outstretched, bent leg of the craft, his hand on an iron rung. He disappeared inside briefly, turned around, and looked out at us, leaning forward and waving me along, although I had no need of encouragement. I found the rungs easily enough, my hands made nimble by fear, to tell the truth. St. Ives ducked back into the chamber to allow me room to enter the surprisingly spacious compartment, where I slumped down on a padded bench and sagged with relief.

Hasbro's face loomed into view outside the hatch now, and I bent over to give him a hand in, hearing at that moment a small explosion—the crack of a rifle. Hasbro teetered backward off the rungs, holding on momentarily with one hand. I leaned out, grabbing for the lapel of his coat, but finding empty air, watching him tumble into the black water and disappear. St. Ives was so concentrated on the controls of the craft that he was oblivious, and I shouted incoherently at him, turning around and backing out into the open again, hunched up like a man trying to cram himself into a box, anticipating the bullet that would surely follow, and *did* follow. It glanced off the metal shell of the chamber near the side of my head, so close that I heard the ricochet along with the report of the rifle. —◦

CHAPTER 4

The Bottom of the River

HASBRO LURCHED UP out of the flood, his hand gripping his upper arm, and I let loose of the rungs and splashed down alongside him, going under for one dark, cold, horrifying moment before getting my feet under me, river water streaming into my eyes, my clothes sodden. Hasbro waded forward, putting his hand on a rung and feeling blindly to get a purchase with his foot. He climbed heavily as I pushed from below, trying to keep at least partly protected by the curved wall of the diving chamber. St. Ives leaned out and hauled Hasbro in from above, and I scrambled up after him, finding myself inside for the second time, kneeling in a pool of water on the deck, gasping to catch my breath, and too stunned and flummoxed to know how cold I was.

The hatch was already slamming shut, but there was one last report from the rifle, only a dim crack, like two stones knocked together, and the sound of the bullet pinging off the interior walls of the chamber, four rapid, distinct *pings*, and then the flattened bullet dropping to the curved floor and sliding down into the shallow pool of water. I realized, as I plucked the spent bullet up from where it lay and put it into my pocket as a souvenir, that the chamber was illuminated now, a soft glow emanating from overhead lamps, and there was the sound of a beehive-like humming on the air.

St. Ives twisted closed the latch that secured and sealed the door from within, nodded his head with satisfaction, and said, "We're carrying dry cells! She's an independent traveler!" The statements meant nothing to me, but his apparent joy bucked me up just a little. He worked at the controls methodically, manipulating levers and wheels, cocking his head with concentration. I helped Hasbro off with his wet coat, the inside of which was a marvel of pockets. After he extracted a roll of bandage and a flask of the cask-strength malt whisky that he carried against emergencies of all sorts, he worked his shirt down over his arm, exposing the wound. The bullet had scored the flesh and then had gone on its way, thank God, although there was a prodigious quantity of blood, which we staunched with the steady pressure of a wet kerchief folded into a compress. Hasbro dribbled whisky over the wound and I tied it with the bandage, making a neat job of it. I was reminded of poor Merton, beaten bloody in his own shop. We were getting the bad end of things, and no doubt about it—apparently played for fools all along.

"Thank you, Jack," Hasbro said, offering me the flask. I raised it in a brief salute and took a swallow, nearly gasping at the strength of the whisky, and then gave the flask to St. Ives, who was smiling like a schoolboy. "Oxygenators," he said cryptically, nodding his head toward the controls. "Compressed air, so it's a limited supply, but it'll do if we look sharp. Jack, you'll be on call to let in fresh air when we need it—that lever on the port side, there. But be as stingy as a landlady with it." He turned the air lever downward, and there was a sort of metallic swishing sound, air through pipes, the exhaled air tasting cool and metallic.

St. Ives took a quick drink from the flask before handing it back to Hasbro and turning again to his work. Hasbro followed suit and then slipped the flask back into his coat. I won't say that we felt like new men after the whisky, but at least not so old fashioned as we had felt a few minutes earlier. There was a constant hum and mutter and whoosh now, the chamber having become a living creature. St. Ives turned to us and nodded, as if to say, "What about *that?*" and with Hasbro attended to and apparently well, there was nothing to be done but to let St. Ives go about his able business, and I for one was happy to let him do it.

I watched the water creep up the side of the heavy glass portholes, my mind beginning to turn, trying to come to grips with what this meant, this watery entrapment. We had neither food nor drink, aside from the flask. Perhaps, I thought, we could wait until the water reached its zenith and then open the hatch, flood the sphere, swim to the surface, and try to find our way up the stairs, which might be reachable in the high water. Or might not. And of course our friend with the rifle might simply be waiting for us, conspicuously closer now on his perch overhead, which would make matters difficult indeed.

My spirits declined even further when I suddenly recollected Finn Conrad emerging from across the way last night at the precise moment that I was surveying the street. I wondered, perhaps unkindly, whether the boy hadn't simply been waiting for us, whether he was an even better actor than he was an acrobat. It was he, I thought darkly, who had led us to the Goat and Cabbage, the Pied Piper turned on its head, and him cheerfully eating chestnuts outside on the street as we witlessly filed in through the door, avidly pursuing our doom....

The thing suddenly seemed to be a certainty, and that was a damned shame. I liked the boy, and I was shocked at the level of loathing I felt for scoundrels that would lure such a likely lad into a life of dishonor and falsehood. He had been monumentally helpful at Merton's, but now that seemed evidently suspicious. Of *course* he would have been helpful, if his goal had been to lure us into the gin shop, where we would almost certainly discover the secret door, one thing leading to another. He hadn't known about the map in the armadillo's mouth, I reminded myself with some small satisfaction: the vital secret was still safe. But then I recalled Merton uttering the word, "reproduction" in his enthusiasm last night, and my satisfaction fled.

I sat there with a heavy heart, with nothing to cheer me aside from the faded glow of the whisky, which had seemed sufficient only moments ago. But I sat so only briefly, because the water outside had risen beyond the tops of the ports and I found myself looking out into the inky black of subterranean water. Lamps came on outside the craft, illuminating things, and I saw fish—eels of some sort—darting away into the darkness. The chamber tilted abruptly, as if it wanted to float, and I shifted on the seat, trying to distribute the weight so that we didn't simply fall over like a dead thing.

"Hold on," St. Ives said, opening a valve and listening, his head bent and eyes narrowed. "I think I've…"

There was the sound of water rushing into what must have been ballast chambers, and we settled on the floor once again. St. Ives tentatively began to work the several levers that rose from the deck of the chamber, manipulating the thing's legs, the chamber rising and settling, pitching backward and forward in a way that was distinctly unsettling. I thought of an upended beetle, struggling to right itself, its myriad feet utterly useless to it, but I swept the thought away, aware that we were creeping along now with a slow, ungainly gait. "A drop of air, Jack," St. Ives said, and I dutifully let in a few seconds' worth.

"Where are we bound?" I managed to ask after I had done my duty. We could hardly climb the stairs, after all, and merely creeping about the floor of the shipyard would accomplish little.

"Out," St. Ives said. "We're bound for points east. It's my idea that we have no choice but to make away with this marvelous craft. We'll borrow it, I mean to say. If we could find the owner and ask permission, we'd do it, but under the circumstances it's quite impossible, ha ha. And of course we have immediate dire need of it, which justifies our actions somewhat." He furrowed his brow and shook his head, as if this were a thorny moral issue, but it was evident that he was elated, that he couldn't have asked for a more suitable answer to our dilemma.

The elation faded into puzzlement, however, for right then the water outside our craft was illuminated far more brightly, and a large, moving shadow hove slowly past. It was the submarine that had sat on the stocks, suddenly alive now, making its way out of the flooded cavern. We watched in mute astonishment as it passed slowly by, one of the lighted portholes revealing the frozen profile of Dr. Hilario Frosticos himself, clearly having been aboard all along, waiting in the darkness. He was sitting at a desk in a cabin full of books and nautical charts, looking down at some volume as if unaware of our existence. And in the moment before he and his submarine passed out of sight into the depths, he glanced sideways into a cheval glass that sat before him on the desktop, and I saw his abominable reflection staring back at me, his ice-white visage perfectly composed and disinterested.

The lighted portholes winked out one by one, as if he were passing beyond the wall of the cavern into a subterranean sea, and abruptly we toppled forward, off the edge of the shipyard floor, descending in a rush of bubbles, swept along in a current that bore us away eastward, as St. Ives had promised. The only illumination came from our own craft now, but I thanked God for it, underwater darkness filling me with a certain horror. More eels undulated past the portholes, and a school of small, white fish, and then a corpse floated past, bloated and pale, its sightless, milky eyes staring in at us for a long moment before it was swept away in a current. It was horrible, and yet I scarcely remarked it, my mind still dwelling on the submarine and the living, corpse-like man who navigated it. Where had it gone, I wondered, and why had Frosticos allowed us our freedom, if indeed he had?

The water slowly brightened roundabout us. St. Ives switched off the lamps both inside and out, so as not to waste power. If we were tethered to a ship, he pointed out, then the ship's engines would generate abundant electricity, but we depended upon the batteries—what he had meant by *dry cells*—which were an unknown quantity. We discovered ourselves to be in the depths of the Thames itself, the water murky with silt and river filth. How far we had come in the darkness we couldn't say. Our rate of travel was mere speculation. It had no doubt been equal to that of the river, but where in the river were we?

It wouldn't do, St. Ives said, to surface in the Pool, or in some other part of the river busy with shipping, and run afoul of a ship's hawser, or come rushing up from below to tear a hole in a ship's bottom. And of course as long as we were afloat, we traveled at the whim of the current, whereas we had some hope of controlling our movements if we could find the bottom in still water. How to accomplish this feat—that was the thorny problem, although St. Ives had clearly taken it up as a challenge. We clanked into something unseen, spun slowly, and continued on our way. I let in another burst of air. Through the port I could see what must have been the remains of a wrecked coal barge slide past, and I realized that all manner of debris lay on the river bottom, most of it half buried in muck. It would have made fascinating viewing, no doubt, under different circumstances.

St. Ives allowed more water into the ballast tanks, and we sank again, settling momentarily, a cloud of mud rising around us and obscuring our sight. We found ourselves toppling forward as the river pushed against us, and it was only by flushing water out of the ballast tanks that we managed to right ourselves once more, bobbing along eastward again, careening this way and that way in a manner that was soon sickening, as if we were afloat in a laundry tub. I let in more of our precious air, which we seemed to be breathing up at a prodigious rate. Directly after that we were cast in shadow, a shadow that stayed with us for some time before passing on.

"A ship," St. Ives said, looking upward through a port. "Out of the Pool rather late." He took his chronometer from his pocket and peered at its face. "The tide is making, or nearly, if I'm not mistaken."

"Yes, sir," Hasbro put in. "Just past midday, given the moon's activities."

"Excellent," St. Ives said, winking at me.

I nodded my hearty assent, although truth to tell I know little about the tides. What I cared about at that moment was for the craft to cease its constant, rollicking, drunken behavior.

"We'll have a period of slack water soon," St. Ives told me by way of explanation. "Enough time, I very much hope, to find our way out of the river, ideally downstream some small distance, where we'll cause less of a sensation. Air, Jack."

"But when the tide turns," I said as I reached for the lever yet again, "won't that merely propel us back upriver?" I recalled the corpse that had visited us earlier. Quite likely it would continue to navigate the same shore-line, upriver and down, at the whim of the tides and with no end to its travels until it simply fell apart or was hauled in by a dredger's net.

"Absolutely," St. Ives said. "It won't matter to us, though. Don't give it a second thought."

"Ah?" I said, wondering at this. Certainly it *seemed* to matter.

"We'll be suffocated before the tide flows again," St. Ives assured me. "Almost without a doubt. There's no telling how much air we've been blessed with, but even if the tanks were full, with three of us breathing up the surplus we'll be dead as herring in a couple of hours. You can bank on it."

This silenced me, I can assure you, although St. Ives hadn't meant for it to. He was merely making a practical observation. For another half hour or more we floated and bumped and spun our way downriver, in and out of the shadows of moored or passing craft. I found that I had become unnaturally conscious of my breathing, and so I began breathing unnaturally, gasping now and then with no provocation, mimicking the wheezing of the air in the pipes. What had seemed a spacious chamber had shrunk to the size of a pickle barrel, and I fidgeted about, trying to occupy myself by peering out the ports, spotting no end of mired flotsam—a wagon wheel, a tailor's dummy, a chest half buried in silt and enticingly bound shut with heavy rope, probably containing gold coins and Java pearls the size of goose eggs, but already disappearing behind us.

"Air, Jack."

It seemed to me that the rush of air was labored now, as if the pressure were low. But I was distracted from that frightful thought when I became aware that we were slowing settling again to the bottom. River mud swirled up around us so that for a moment we could see nothing at all. St. Ives consulted a compass among a small array of instruments, and when the murk settled he pointed out a long, curved wooden beam, a ship's keel perhaps, lying half exposed on the river bottom. "That's our bearing," he said. "Along the edge of that beam. Due north."

He began to manipulate the motivating levers once again, carefully now, waiting for the muddy water to clear time and again to get a view of the sunken keel so that we could take another creeping step. We edged around impediments sideways, like a crab, and two or three times backed away from a cavernous sort of rocky pit. Twice we mired ourselves in weeds and had to tug ourselves free. The broken end of the keel was far out of sight behind us now, and St. Ives was navigating by compass alone, adjusting and readjusting our direction of travel, none of us speaking or moving more than was strictly necessary. How much time passed, I couldn't say, nor could any of us guess whether we were twenty feet from shore or sixty, whether we would creep out onto dry land, or bang up against the base of a cliff and find ourselves no nearer salvation than we ever were.

Again I opened the air valve, but the flow was feeble, a tired hiss, and the air in the chamber was distressingly thick. I tried to distract myself by watching our progress, but it was too frustratingly slow, and there was little of interest to be seen in the river, which was perpetually murky now in the slack water. Hasbro, who had either been asleep or in deep meditation, said, "I beg your pardon, sir?" and I had no idea what he meant until I heard the echo of my own voice in my ears, and I realized that I had been talking out loud, like a mad man, and with no idea what I had said.

"Nothing," I told him with the rictus of a smile. "Just musing."

"Best not to talk at all," St. Ives said.

I decided to try closing my eyes, but despite my best efforts, I couldn't rid my mind of the watery clanks and thumpings that accompanied our slow progress across the bottom of the Thames. Abruptly there came into my mind the morbid notion that I was nailed into a coffin and had been dumped into the sea, and that I was suffocating in the darkness. My eyes shot open and I sucked in a great gasping breath of air, but there was no nourishment in it, and I sat there goggling like a rock cod drawn out of deep water.

"Are you quite all right, sir?" Hasbro asked.

I nodded a feeble lie, but noticed through the port just then that bits and pieces of floating debris had apparently begun swirling past us from downriver, and that the clouds of silt were clearing much more quickly. I was filled with a sense of doom. We had missed our tide, it seemed to me, and I was persuaded that we should throw open the hatch and try our luck with the river, abandoning the loathsome chamber.... Hasbro, God bless him, handed me the whisky flask in that dark moment, and I took a grateful draft before handing it back to him.

Very shortly we began to make a certain haste over a flat and sandy bottom, and my spirits lifted. I was conscious of the water brightening around us, and up through the port I could see what looked like a silver rippling window, which must, I knew, be the surface of the river. Then the chamber was out into the atmosphere, the water level declining along the glass. We staggered ashore until we were waist deep and could go no farther. Gravity, St. Ives told us, had gotten the best of us as our buoyancy decreased, and we risked breaking our legs if we ventured onto dry land.

I swung out of the open hatch like a man plucked from the grave, and leapt down into the river as into a bath, inflating my lungs with air that was as sweet as spring water, splashing my way to shore like a frolic at Blackpool. Recalling that moment of freedom even now makes me wax metaphoric, although the memory fades quickly, and I'm reminded of how close I had come to shaming myself with my fears and my weaknesses. If I were a younger man today, with a more frail sensibility, I might revise this account, and cast a more stoic light on myself, perhaps adding a small moment of personal glory. But be it only ink on paper, that would be to commit the same fearful folly again, and with a lie on top of it. Surely there's more virtue in the truth.

We had made our way, we soon discovered, to the lower edge of the Erith Marshes, almost to the bend above Long Reach. No one had seen us emerge—another bit of luck. Three hours later the diving chamber sat atop the bed of a wagon, affixed to a swivel crane and fenced in by empty crates to disguise its shape, all of it tied down securely and covered in canvas. We found ourselves on our way merrily enough, north to Harrogate now, where St. Ives told us we would replenish the compressed air at Pillsworth's Chemical Laboratories, and then on across the Dales and around the top of Morecambe Bay for a rendezvous with Merton's Uncle Fred at his cottage in Grange-over-Sands. We were in need of a sand pilot, you see, to go along with our map and our diving chamber. We had no time to waste if we wanted to catch the tide. ⁓

CHAPTER 5

Hesitate and You're a Drowned Man

W E HELD A sort of council of war there in the wagon, mapping out our campaign so that we proceeded according to a stratagem rather than a whim. It seemed to us that the ruse with the map must have borne fruit. Surely there would have been some way for Frosticos to prevent our flight in the chamber if he suspected that we possessed the true map. He was sure of himself, apparently, and that was a solidly good thing. And yet if we were wrong in this notion, we dared not return to the Half Toad or to St. Ives Manor at Chingford-by-the-Tower, lest the Doctor's henchmen lurked about, on the lookout. We wanted simply to be quit of them, now that we had the means to make use of the map, and so we decided to make straightaway to Morecambe Bay in time to catch a particularly low tide. And yet we had some small matters of business in London, having to do with Tubby Frobisher, which I undertook to accomplish while St. Ives and Hasbro rattled away north with all possible speed.

It was an added bit of good fortune that Tubby could walk abroad without exciting the suspicions of our enemies, and could convey the tragic details of our untimely deaths to the newspapers, where he had a useful acquaintance who wrote for the *Times* and occasionally for the *Graphic*. It was reported that our diving chamber, with three suffocated bodies inside, had been washed up onto a rocky strand near Sheerness, where it was found by fishermen. The scientific community mourned: much lamented passing…eccentric genius…intrepid explorer, and so forth. St. Ives, vilified just months earlier over the incident of the burning squid, was lauded by paragons of science, and there was, Tubby informed us, talk of a bronze bust in a plaster niche at the Explorers Club.

It was all very gratifying, I can tell you. And of course before the news was revealed publicly, Tubby had looked in on Merton and then had scurried like Mercury himself down to Scarborough to alert Mrs. St. Ives and my own dear wife to the nature of the fraud. (Neither of them were quite as taken with our cleverness as they in all fairness should have been, we discovered later, especially when Tubby regaled them with his secondhand accounts of the flaming meteor over the Yorkshire Dales and the floating cattle and dead parson and other salient and half understood details.)

We knew little of this, of course, except that I had set Tubby into motion. It wasn't the first time, by the way, that St. Ives had been mourned, and I wondered whether it was a good enough ruse to further confound a man like Hilario Frosticos. But then perhaps he wouldn't need further confounding, since he already possessed what he understood to be Kraken's map. We would soon know, for better or ill.

—⁓—

St. Ives drove the wagon beneath a full moon, Hasbro and I sitting beside him, along a seldom-used dirt track that winds down from the forest below Lindale and carries on beyond Grange-over-Sands down to Humphrey Head, which was our true destination. We had ridden in secret along this same road a decade ago, engaged in a similar mission. That had turned out badly, as Tubby had pointed out, and taken all the way around we had fared scarcely better this time, at least so far, despite the success of our flight down the Thames and our subsequent hasty journey to the environs of Morecambe Bay.

The trees grew more stunted when we drew nearer the water, blown by sea winds as they were, and we found ourselves moving along at a slow pace, creaking over sea wrack and shingle covered with blown sand, the wind in our faces. The moon illuminated the road, thank God, or we might have met Kraken's fate, for there were innumerable creeks flowing out of Hampsfield Fell to the west, most of them half-hidden by dead leaves and low-growing water plants, and the place had a dangerously marshy quality to it that kept me on edge, ever on the lookout for bogs and sand pits. Several times we stopped to search out a crossing—ships timbers sunk into the mire—but midnight finally found us near the village of Grange-over-Sands.

The tide was turning by then, and we hadn't much time to lose, unless we wanted to wait another day for a second chance. But of course every hour that passed made it more likely that Frosticos would become aware of our little game with the forged map, if he weren't already aware of it. It was our great hope simply to avoid him, you see. Unlike Tubby Frobisher, we had no pressing desire to feed him to feral pigs or to anything else. We meant to keep him at a safe distance, smugly busy with his own fruitless search, never knowing that we were still pursuing the device in our own more useful way.

The moon was bright, and the broad expanses of infamous sand, cut by rivulets of seawater, appeared to be solid, with shadowy hillocks and runnels that hadn't been visible an hour ago when we had first come in sight of the Bay. It seemed quite reasonable that a person would venture out onto the sands for a jolly stroll, to pick cockles or to have a look at some piece of drowned wreckage that lay half buried off shore, only to have the place turn deadly on the instant, the tide sweeping in with the speed of a sprinting horse, or a patch of sand that had been solid yesterday, suddenly liquefied, without changing its demeanor a whit.

The opposite shore seemed uncannily near, although it must have been four miles away. We could see the scattered, late-night lights of Silverdale across what was now a diminishing stretch of moonlit water, and farther along the lights of Poulton-le-Sands and perhaps Heysham in the dim distance. There was considerable virtue in the clear, illuminated night, but an equal amount of danger, and so I was relieved when the track turned inward across a last stretch of salt marsh and away from the Bay, growing slightly more solid as the ground rose. We quickened our pace, climbing a small, steep rise, hidden by a sea wood now from the watching eyes of anyone out and about on the Bay.

Soon we rounded a curve in the track, and there in front of us stood Uncle Fred's cottage, which he called *Flotsam*. It was very whimsical, built of a marvelous array of cast off materials that Fred had salvaged from the sands or had purchased from the seaside residents of that long reach of treacherous coastline that stretches from Morecambe Bay up to St. Bees, where many a ship beating up into the Irish Channel in a storm has found itself broken on a lee shore. Looking out over the Bay was a ship's quarter-gallery, with high windows allowing views both north and south. In the moonlight the gallery appeared to be perfectly enormous, a remnant of an old First Rate ship, perhaps, and it made the cottage look elegant despite the whole thing being cobbled together, just as its name implied. The cottage climbed the hill, so to speak, most of it built of heavy timbers and deck planks and with sections of masts and spars as corner posts and lintels. On the windward side it was shingled with a hodgepodge of sheet copper torn from ships' bottoms. It was a snug residence, with its copper-sheathed back turned toward the open ocean, and the sight was something more than attractive. There was a light burning beyond the gallery window, illuminating a long table already set for visitors. Someone, I could see, sat in a chair at the table—perhaps Uncle Fred, if he were a small man.

What amounted to something between a widow's walk and a crow's nest stood atop the uppermost room, giving Fred a view of the sands from on high. I noticed a movement there, someone waving in our direction and then disappearing, and the door at the side of the gallery was swinging open when we reined up in the yard. I was fabulously hungry, and weary of the sea wind and anxious to get out of it, if only for a brief time. Uncle Fred stepped out with what turned out to be a boy following along behind him.

"The ubiquitous Finn Conrad," St. Ives said, laughing out loud to see him there. I wasn't quite so pleased, although I kept silent. I hadn't revealed my suspicions about the boy to St. Ives and Hasbro, because, to tell you the truth, I felt a little small about doubting him. If he was who he appeared to be, then I was a mean-spirited scrub. If he was an agent of Frosticos, then I was a fool, and perhaps a dead fool. But what on earth was he doing in this out of the way corner of the Commonwealth? I'm afraid I stood staring at him, dumfounded.

Finn nodded at us, touched his forehead in a sort of salute, and said he hoped we were feeling fit. "I'll see to the horses, sir," he said to St. Ives. "I rode bareback in Duffy's Circus, before they sent me aloft. Three years as stable boy." He took the reins and led the horses around out of the wind, strapping on feedbags with an easy confidence.

It turned out that Finn had brought with him a letter of introduction from Merton, in order to "set things up," as Merton had apparently put it. Finn had traveled into Poulton-le-Sands by any number of conveyances,

and then had come around over the bridge with a kindly farmer before making his way down the north side of the Bay on foot, having run most of the distance. He would have crossed the sands if the tide allowed, he said, in order to do his duty. St. Ives said that he very much believed it. I believed it, too, but his duty to whom?

Merton had been expansive in his letter, the incident at the shop seeming to be a rare piece of theatre now that he was removed from it. He laid out the details of the hiding of the map, the production of the forgery, and an account of St. Ives's eagerness to search for whatever it was that had gone down into the sands all that long time ago. There was a mention of the timely appearance of young Finn, whom he recommended without reservation. Even the armadillo made its appearance upon the stage. Uncle Fred, in other words, was *in the know*, as the Americans might say. Who else? I wondered darkly. But soon we found ourselves in the lamplit cottage looking at a joint of Smithfield ham, boiled eggs, brown bread, a pot of mustard, another of Stilton cheese, and a plate of radishes.

"You gentlemen have your way with that ham and cheese," Fred told us, rubbing his hands together as if he were even more pleased than we were, "and I'll fetch us something to wet our whistles."

"Amen," I said, my doubts abruptly veiled by the sight of the food, and it was fifteen minutes before we slowed down enough to say anything further, when Fred abruptly announced that it was time to go.

He looked remarkably like Merton, but not half so giddy. There was an edge of authority to him that made you think of a ship's captain—something that came from a lifetime of dangerous work in the open sea air, I suppose. Merton had revealed to us that his uncle had lost three people to the tide in the early days, and that he had lost his complacency at the same time, as he watched them being swept away into deep water, and he standing helplessly by. He wasn't a large man, but there was a keen, wind-sharpened look in his eye, and he was burnt brown by the sun. I found that I was heartened by his rough-and-ready presence. He listened as St. Ives told him what we meant to do, his eyes narrowing shrewdly. His nephew's letter hadn't mentioned the diving chamber, but had revealed only that we would want a pilot. It was the diving chamber that threw him.

"It's madness," he said. "You'll join the rest of them at the bottom of the sands."

"Almost without a doubt," St. Ives said, sitting back in his chair. "Clearly we need your help with this."

"You'll need help from a more powerful personage than Fred Merton," he said.

"Granted," St. Ives told him, "but Fred Merton is the one man on Earth that we *do* want. We'll trust to providence for the rest."

Fred sat silently, watching out the window, where the wind blew the sea oats and the moon shone low in the sky. "You mean to captain this vessel?" he asked St. Ives, who nodded his assent. "And you," he said to me, "you'll go along as crew?"

The question nearly confounded me. Fear, still dwelling in my mind from our previous jaunt in the chamber, showed me its ugly visage. Another moment of hesitation, and that visage would be my own. Finn was a youngster, of course, and St. Ives wouldn't consider his going along, not under these circumstances. Hasbro's arm was still tied up in a sling…. I nodded my assent as heartily as I could.

Fred stood up abruptly from the table, checked his pocket-watch, and nodded toward the door. The rest of us followed him out into the wind, which was sharply cold after the comfort of the cottage. Finn brought the horses around, an enviably game look on his face, and he clambered up onto the seat, holding the reins. We cast off the tarpaulin and saw to it that all was shipshape with the chamber and crane and the crane's mechanical apparatus—a block and tackle rig running through a windlass mechanism with a heavy crank. It was double-rigged, and would allow for the separate lowering and raising of the diving chamber and a grappling hook. Our duty if we found the box was merely to grapple onto it securely, and then to stand aside and let the power of the windlass haul it out.

"Once we're out onto the sands," Fred said to us, "the full ebb will leave us high and dry. It'll be warm work then, because when the tide returns, it'll be with a vengeance. When I say we pack it in, that's just what we do, quick like. Hesitate, and you're a drowned man. Do you hear me, now?" He looked at each of us in turn, as if he wanted to see in our faces that we would obey the command. I answered, "aye!" and nodded my assent heavily, becoming a drowned man not being one of my aspirations.

We set out at once, Uncle Fred and Hasbro in a two-wheeled Indian buggy going on ahead, and the rest of us in the wagon, with Finn handling the reins. The track along the edge of the sands was solid enough out to Humphrey Head, which is a small, downward-bent finger of land smack in the center of the top of the Bay, covered with grasses and with stunted trees growing on its rocky, upper reaches. It afforded us no shelter at the edge of the sands, either from the wind or from the view of others out and about on the Bay, and of course there was no time to concern ourselves with these "others," in any event.

The tide was still declining, and as it withdrew it revealed surprisingly deep and narrow valleys as well as broad sand flats, the water vanishing at a prodigious rate. Entire shallow lakes and rivers, shimmering in the moonlight, appeared simply to be evaporating on the night air. It was the sand flats that were worrisome, because they might be solid or they might be quick, the difference discernible only to the practiced eye of a sand pilot.

We left the buggy tethered to a heap of driftwood that stood well above the tide line, and straightaway ventured out with the wagon, Finn still driving, Hasbro up beside him, and Uncle Fred walking on ahead, prodding the sand with a pole to be doubly sure, Kraken's map in his hand. Where was I, you ask? I was already ensconced in the diving chamber along with St. Ives. As you might have discerned, I had no desire to be there, and even less now that I was within that confined space, but either my natural timidity or what passed for courage still prevented my saying so. The hatch stood open to the night air, for which I was grateful. —o

CHAPTER 6

The Undersea Graveyard

W E HAD WANDERED a quarter mile or so out onto the sands when Fred once again stopped to study the map. Kraken had fixed the location of the sunken device by lining up a blasted tree above Silverdale with a chimney pipe atop a manor house beyond it and away to the northeast. Fred walked along a line defined by the tree and the chimney pipe until he was very near dead center on yet another pair of conspicuous points, the spire-like pinnacle of a high rock atop Humphrey Head, and a stone tower on a hill off in the distance toward Flookburgh. He gestured the wagon forward, stopping it a few short feet from the edge of what turned out to be a broad pool of quicksand.

"This is what we call 'Placer's Pool,' hereabouts," Fred told us. "It's always quick, never solid. A man named Placer and his bride went down into it in a coach and four, with their worldly goods, because they were in a flaming hurry and didn't bother to hire a pilot, but left it up to the driver to find a way. The fool found it right enough, but it wasn't the way they had in mind. If your man was bound from the shore opposite to Humphrey head, then…" He shook his head darkly. "The good Lord alone knows what you'll find down there, because no one else has stepped into Placer's Pool and come back out again."

It was then that I began to grasp the obvious truth, although of course it should have been plain to me all along: we weren't plunging into a pool of water this time, but into a pot of cold porridge, so to speak. It came into my mind simply to admit to St. Ives that I'd rather be pursued by axe wielding savages than to drop blind into a pool of quicksand, but I sat there mute, trying to distract myself with the goings-on outside, looking at the grappling hook where it dangled in the grip of one of the craft's pitiful claws. My mind argued senselessly with itself—whether it would be courageous to admit my cowardice and stay topside, or cowardly to *fear* admitting it, descend into the murk, and risk going insane. There would be no opening the hatch in these waters, I told myself insidiously. I pictured Bill Kraken, hurriedly sketching his map in the moonlight, corking it up in a bottle, and heaving it end over end toward solid ground, and I very much hoped that there had been something in the bottle to drink before it became a mere glass mailbag.

But of course there wasn't a moment to lose. Fred looked at a pocket-watch, shouted, "Thirty minutes by the clock!" and St. Ives shut us in tight. We were lifted bodily by the crane, Hasbro turning away with one arm on the windlass crank as if letting down an anchor while Fred held the horses steady. The sound of their voices and labor seemed to come from some great distance as we swung out over the pool of quicksand, me gripping the metal edge of the circular bench as if it were the edge of a precipice.

"Surely the tide won't return in a mere thirty minutes," I said to St. Ives.

"No, sir," St. Ives said. "But we must agree upon an absolute limit, you see. In thirty minutes we'll either have failed or succeeded. If we succeed, they'll drag the box out bodily with the crane. If we fail, they'll drag us out."

"Good," I said. "Good." In fact I liked this very much. *Thirty minutes*, I told myself. Almost no time at all…

The myriad sounds of the living chamber rose around us, and we began to descend, St. Ives sitting there mute, attentive to his business, not a furrow of concern on his brow. I was already in a cold sweat, trying to manage my breathing, sending my mind off to more pleasant, imaginary, places, only to have it return ungratefully an instant later, not taken in by the ruse.

Now there was nothing outside the ports but brown, mealy darkness, the wall of congealed sands illuminated by the interior lamps. Our tanks were full of ballast to hurry our descent, but even so we drifted downward very slowly, the sand shifting around us, gently disturbed by our passing, with suddenly clear windows of trapped water that closed again at once.

"Two fathoms," St. Ives said. And then after a time, "Three."

"What lies beneath us?" I asked, suddenly curious. I hadn't given any thought to our destination.

"Ah!" St. Ives replied, glancing at me. "That's an excellent question, Jack. What indeed? More of this quicksand, lying on a solid bottom, perhaps, in which case we've almost certainly failed unless we land square on the wagon, because our movements through this sand would be both sightless and slow." He shook his head. "Or it might be that…" He paused now, staring hard through the port, where there had floated into view the face of a wide-eyed sheep, looking in on us with a certain sad curiosity. Most of it was invisible in the heavy sand, and we could make out only its ghostly visage. It appeared to be perfectly preserved in this dense atmosphere, or more likely only recently drowned. We seemed to draw it along downward for a moment, as if it heeded our departure, but then, like an image in a dream, it faded into the silent darkness overhead.

"Six fathoms," St. Ives said. "I believe we're descending more rapidly."

"The water seems to be clearing," I pointed out hopefully. "Do you see that broken oar?" It floated some distance away, a piece of an oar weighted down by an iron oarlock. At the depth of the sheep just minutes ago it would have been hidden from us. The sand swirled in an upward flowing current now, as if clear water were rising from beneath us. Then abruptly there was a clattering noise, something hitting the underside of our craft, and we emerged into water that was pellucid as a pail full of rain, and a sight that was utterly uncanny.

A small, upright wooden chair that our craft had apparently driven downward, now bumped and floated its way upward past the ports, and I peered out to watch its ascent. The sand layer hung overhead like a layer of thick clouds, and floating beneath it was a scattering of wooden objects, topsy-turvy chairs and tables from someone's drawing room, lost to the sands and now forever trapped beneath the heavy ceiling.

"We've come through the false bottom," St. Ives said, "at just over ten fathoms."

"The false bottom of what?" I asked, letting in a whoosh of air in through the pipes.

"The bottom of the *Bay*, Jacky. Into subterranean water. I've long suspected that there was communication between Morecambe Bay and some of the inland lakes—Windermere and Conniston Water, and perhaps north into the great lochs. There! Do you see?"

And indeed I did. An illuminated area of the actual seabed was clearly visible below us now, alive with great, feathered worms reaching out of holes in the sand, and colorful anemones the size of giant dahlias. A pale halibut, large as a barn door, arose from the bottom and winged its way into the darkness as if we had awakened it, and then a school of enormous squid slipped past, watching us with large eyes that reminded me of the face of the suspended sheep.

With a soft bump we settled into the sand, St. Ives attending to his levers, and almost immediately we were off, striding along on our crooked legs. St. Ives was surer of himself now, having honed his skills on the bottom of the Thames. "We've got about two hundred feet of line," he told me, "and so we're on a short tether. Some day we'll come back prepared to do a proper investigation…. There's something!"

There was indeed something—what appeared to be a stagecoach of the sort you might have seen on the Great North Road a century past, when coaches were more elegant than they are today. It stood upright on the sands as if it were a museum tableau—a very dusty museum. The wheels were buried to the axles, the exterior covered with undersea growths—barnacles and opalescent incrustations, decorated by Davy Jones. The skeletons of four horses were tethered to it, and there were human skeletons inside, still traveling hopefully. Household objects littered the sea floor: pieces of luggage, crockery jars, broken crates spilling out bric-a-brac, porcelain vases, an iron teapot, a fireplace screen, bottles, a heavy crystal goblet half full of sand. A small bookcase miraculously stood upright, its glass doors unbroken, the books still standing on the shelves, held in place only by the rigid leather covers, the contents no doubt having melted into mere pulp like a lesson in humility. Fishes swam around and between the lumber of objects, enjoying their inheritance.

As the chamber strode shakily through this undersea museum it was easy for me too imagine what had transpired: the passengers, no doubt the Placer family, crossing the sands in order to avoid the extra few hours of travel around the top of the Bay. The weather had been fine, the sands apparently dry and solid. But then suddenly not so solid—the wheels abruptly mired, the horses stumbling forward, sinking to their withers,

thrashing to get out, but simply propelling themselves deeper into the mire, the passengers and the driver pitching the cargo overboard—anything to lighten the load, but all efforts utterly useless except to assure the victims that their worldly goods would be waiting for their arrival at the bottom of the sea.

It was St. Ives's notion that we were within a vast oceanic cave with a perforated roof, if you will, the quicksand pits created by upwelling currents, which accounted for the suspension of the sand particles and for the firm sand flats and cockle beds in the Bay above, which lay on solid tracts of seabed. There was something immense about the darkness that surrounded us, and it seemed quite possible that this hidden, underwater world, an ocean beneath the ocean, might pass well beyond the shoreline of Morecambe Bay.

And then we saw it: Kraken's wagon, gradually appearing within our halo of light. I had almost forgotten about it, so caught up was I with the strange nature of the dead place where we had found ourselves. The wagon was settled on a solid bit of sea floor, washed by currents. There was no skeleton, thank God, but that meant only that poor Bill's bones numbered among the billions scattered across the vast cemetery that is the World Ocean. In the bed of the wagon, beneath a shroud of silt, lay the wood and iron strongbox that contained the device, whatever it was—something worth the death and injury it had engendered, I hoped.

St. Ives looked at his chronometer, and then immediately set to work with the levers that manipulated the grappling hook. On either side of the crate there were what appeared to be leather-covered chains that functioned as handles, and I watched as our mechanical arm extended, its claw reaching out with the hook.... Too far away. We crept closer, bumping up against the side of the wagon with a muted thud. Again the arm reached out.

I became aware of something then: a light in the distance, a bright, moving lamp. It looked almost cheerful in all that darkness, like the moon rising on a dark night, and it took my mind a moment to grasp the fact that it oughtn't to be there.

"The submarine!" I said, for what else could it be? No sooner had I uttered the words, than the craft turned, displaying its row of illuminated ports. I could make out the dark shadow of its finny shape. St. Ives had been correct. We were in a navigable, subterranean sea, apparently open to the pools or rivers we had encountered in the underground boatyard. Dr. Frosticos had found us.

"Can you discern what he means to do?" St. Ives asked, concentrating on his task.

"No. It's difficult to tell how far off.... Wait, I believe he's coming directly toward us now, moving slowly. Perhaps he's just seen us."

"We've got it!" St. Ives said, glancing through the port at the approaching submarine. He gave the grapple a small tug to assure that it was secure, and then tugged in earnest, and we teetered forward for one breathtaking, eye-shutting moment before we settled back onto our pins. The box slid neatly off the bed of the wagon in a silty cloud and settled on the sea floor, dozens of feather worms snatching themselves into their holes. St. Ives released the grapple, retracted the mechanical arm firmly against the hull of our craft, and began to propel the chamber a few paces off. "We'll leave the rest up to our friends topside," he said with satisfaction.

"Gladly," I said, glancing out through the port at the submarine, suspended there at a distance of perhaps 50 yards, although it was difficult to tell in the darkness. Frosticos seemed to be doing us the favor of casting a helpful light on our work.

"Keep an eye on that box, Jack," St. Ives said, looking steadily at his chronometer. "We should see Merton's hand at play right about...now." All was still for a moment, and then the box gave a jerk and began hopping and scooting along the floor of the sea, sand and sea bottom debris rising in a cloud. St. Ives nodded agreeably at me, and I couldn't help but smile back at him, our notable success having swept the fears out of my mind like yesterday's cobweb. All this time, of course, I had been doing my duty with the oxygen lever, and I noted cheerily that the air still whooshed briskly through the pipes. Suffocation, then, was still some distance off. We began our creeping, homeward progress, our real work finished. We simply had to wait our turn to be reeled in. St. Ives meant to be as directly under the crane as ever we could be, so that our ascent was unimpeded by anything but a floating chair or two.

I waved victoriously at the submarine, imagining happily that the good doctor's head was set to explode from frustration. The craft had by then begun to move away, and was circling around as if turning tail for

Carnforth in defeat. "He's showing us his back, the dog," I said to St. Ives. "Slinking away." But the submarine continued to turn in a close circle, not slinking away at all, and soon the light was aimed dead at us, its watery glow obscuring the shadow of the ship behind it. Abruptly it launched itself forward, flying at us in an increasing rush. ⁓

CHAPTER 7

The Turning of the Tide

I GASPED OUT A warning to St. Ives, who shouted, "Hold on!" at that same moment. He was bent over the controls, high-stepping our awkward craft across the sea floor now, attempting to maneuver us out of the way of the approaching submarine, which veered to remain on course. I held on with an iron grip, watching our doom hurtle toward us. The submarine easily compensated for our creaking, evasive ploys, and within moments we were blinded by the intensity of its light, and we both threw ourselves to the deck, hands over our heads, as if we could somehow protect ourselves.

The chamber toppled backward, and we were thrown together in a heap. I banged my elbow into something hard, but scarcely felt it, fully expecting the rush of cold water, the desperate, futile flight through the hatch. But there was no rush of water, and I had no sensation of our craft having been struck by anything. The light from the submarine was gone. The submarine had passed over us, and we found ourselves dragged along backward at what seemed to be a prodigious rate. It was our friends above, hauling us out bodily. We were "packing it in" as Fred had put it, right on time, and there was no dignity involved in the packing. I gripped the stanchions that supported the circular seat, and looked up through the port at the dark ceiling of our grotto, and once again I saw the flotsam held in stasis against the sands.

Then the blinding light again, and the submarine swept past, inches overhead, its dark shape passing like a great whale, and I thanked my stars that we were tipped flat, for the submarine evidently didn't dare to swim any closer to the sea floor. But my musings were shattered by a heavy jolt, and now out of the port I saw that we had bulled our way straight into the coach and four. A rain of human bones tumbled out through the window. Our retracted arm hooked into the bottom of a horse's skull, which sailed along with us like a misplaced figurehead before another jolt knocked it free. Then suddenly we were ascending smoothly, and we hauled ourselves gratefully onto the seats again, taking stock of bruises and abrasions.

We passed through the stasis layer into the murk of the sands, St. Ives letting out ballast to aid our ascent, and I reminded myself not to be quite so prematurely satisfied in the future, gloating over a victory before the enemy had left the field. Now we were clear, though. He could hardly follow us into the pool of quicksand. "Nothing broken?" I asked St. Ives.

"My chronometer, I'm afraid." He held up the shattered timepiece. "I'd rather break an arm, or very nearly. But not a bad bill to pay, all in all."

We continued to ascend in silence for another minute or two, but then abruptly stopped.

"Perhaps a fouled line," St. Ives said. "They'll be at it again directly."

But the minutes passed, and still we sat there, my mind turning in the silence. It came to me that I should make a clean breast of my long-held suspicions while I had a quiet moment. "I'm a little worried about an element of this entire business," I said.

"Out with it, then."

"We've had some good luck," I told him. "And it seems we've been clever. But consider this: what if Frosticos knew what we were about, and I mean from the beginning. That business at Merton's—knocking poor Merton on the head like that—what if it was meant to move us to action? For my money Frosticos wasn't foxed by the false map for more than a moment. He *knew* we had the original, and he intended for us to lead him to the box. He provided us the means by lending us this diving chamber. We were at the mercy of the tides once we arrived here at the Bay, and it was no great feat for him to lurk about the subterranean reaches watching for us when the time was right. Then he played a helpful light on our endeavors until we had succeeded, at which point he tried to murder us in cold blood, having done with us."

St. Ives sat thinking, but there was only one element of the theory that required any thinking. He reached up and gave us another gasp of air. "You say he wasn't foxed by the map," he said carefully. "You're suggesting…"

"I don't mean to *suggest* anything," I said, looking out into the by now thick sands, "only that we might have been played like fiddles."

"I sense that you don't want to cast any blame on Finn Conrad, but he might easily be the necessary link in the chain? His appearance outside Merton's was certainly convenient."

"It was," I said, "although it's as easily coincidental. Perhaps Merton's forgery was simply no good, and Frosticos saw through it."

"You've seen his handiwork," St. Ives said.

"Yes, but suppose Frosticos had come here straightaway by some subterranean route and had already found the map useless before our arrival, thereby suspecting it to be a forgery and lying in wait for us. When he saw us in our lighted chamber meddling on the sea floor..." I shrugged and gave us more air.

"But we've got to consider that Finn was our means of finding the boatyard and discovering this chamber. We were forced to flee in it in order to avoid drowning or being shot by men who seemed to have known we would come along when we did."

"One other thing," I said. "You were careful to slip the true map into your coat pocket, but Merton wasn't half so careful, especially with his insanely detailed letter, which he placed directly into Finn's hands before sending him post haste to the Bay."

"I find the idea distressing," St. Ives said wearily. "I don't say that I find it unlikely, just distressing."

"I've been distressed by it for the past days," I told him, "and I should have spoken up earlier. But I like the boy, and I don't want to malign him, especially when there's the chance that he's innocent. Perhaps we're as shrewd as we think ourselves to be, but it looks very much as if Frosticos has been leading us along like blind men." I watched the unchanging view through the port, worried that they were taking an infernally long time, and slightly unhappy with myself for having laid out my suspicions about Finn Conrad like a trial lawyer while insisting that I didn't want to malign him.

"For the moment," St. Ives said, "let's remember that all their machinations have been in vain. We'll keep a weather eye on Finn, just for safety's sake, but we'll not condemn him until we're certain."

"Good enough," I said, and abruptly we began to rise again, jerky and quick, and within moments we burst out into the dawn twilight, dripping watery sand, having been reeled in ignominiously, but alive. I saw straight off, however, that something was amiss.

The wagon was tilted disastrously, headfirst into the sand. Fred had untied the team, their forelegs covered with ooze, and was leading them away. Finn stood by him, but I saw that Hasbro lay over the back of one of the horses, unconscious or dead. Fred glanced back at us with concern evident on his face, and when St. Ives opened the hatch Fred shouted, "Remain *very* still, lads. Your friend's been shot. He'll live to tell the tale. There's nothing for you to do for him." He pointed up the bay before turning away.

We looked in that direction discerned movement atop a high dune not too far off the shore. It was impossible to say who it was for certain, but we had no doubt that it was our tall friend who had peppered away at us in the boatyard.

Then we saw that we hadn't, in fact, been drawn clear of the sands at all, but our legs and underbelly were still submerged. The wagon itself was half sunk, too, and Fred had evidently unhitched the team in order to save them from being drawn down with the wagon. The box was grappled to its line, and it seemed likely that the combined weight of the box and the diving chamber and we two human beings had been enough to haul the wagon down into the mire.

"One at a time, now," Fred shouted in a voice meant for the deck of a ship. "Out the door and across the wagon, lads. It's the only way. And be quick about it! Don't stand arguing." He set out toward shore.

"Out you go, Jack," St. Ives said, putting his hand on my elbow.

I shook it off. "You first. Think of Eddie and Cleo," I said to him. "And take the box with you or this is all for nothing. I'll follow."

Of course he started to protest, but I cut him off sharp.

"It's no good," I told him. "My mind's made up. So it's either out the door or shut the hatch."

Fred shouted something more from afar, shouted as if he meant it, and St. Ives shook his head darkly and swung carefully out of the hatch, reaching for the line along the side of the crane, stepping across to get a foot on the bed of the wagon. At once there was more shouting from without, and then the unmistakable sound of a rifle shot. I was thinking quite clearly and reasonably and was filled with a certain calm, and doubly determined to wait until St. Ives was clear of the wagon and the box with him.

He had his shoulder under it now, lifting it upward to take the weight off the grapple. When it was free, he carried it heavily to the rear of the wagon and set it down in order to drop to the ground. Beyond, nearly halfway to Humphrey Head now, the others swarmed along, Fred leading the horses with one hand, the other holding onto Finn's arm. I saw the boy look back at us, and Fred letting go of him for a moment to gesture for us to hurry. And in that moment Finn bolted, back across the sands toward us. Fred slapped the horses and sent them careening forward, carrying Hasbro toward high ground, and he turned and ran back after the boy. There was another rifle shot, and I saw Fred drop to the ground, but then he was up again and running.

I saw something else, too: far in the distance, out toward the broad ocean, the tide was returning. It appeared as a wall of roiling whitewater, lit by the rising sun. How high and how distant I couldn't make out, but it was moving toward us like galloping doom.

St. Ives saw it, too. He left the box on the bed of the wagon and ran toward Finn. What the boy thought he could accomplish returning to the wagon I can't say. The only answer was that he was coming to our aid at the peril of his own life, and I was filled with happiness and shame both. Even so, he had chosen the worst moment for his heroics.

I leaned out of the hatch in a fair hurry now and clutched wildly at the crane arm, managing to grab the grappling hook, looking back to see St. Ives stopping Finn in his tracks, urging him back toward shore. Holding onto the grapple, I stepped out across the three empty feet to the tilted bed of the wagon, and suddenly I was falling, the line reeling out of the unsecured windlass. I clutched at the air futilely with my free hand, landing on the sands without a shudder, plunging in knee deep. I could hear Fred shouting, and St. Ives shouting, and out of the corner of my eye I saw Finn catapult past St. Ives and run out across the sands. Fred grabbed St. Ives by the coat now and dragged him back bodily, and St. Ives had no choice but to follow. Together they fled toward shore, not knowing that I was mired and supposing that I would gather Finn up and follow.

I heard the ratchet sound of the windlass crank, and the rope, which was coiled atop the sand like a floating snake, began to retract. I held onto the grapple with both hands, otherwise keeping very still, and after a moment the line went taut, and I began to rise from the sands with the heavy sound of sucking and of gasping as my boots pulled free. I let go with one hand and reached for the side of the wagon, getting a good grip on it, kicking myself up onto the seat and clambering to the bed, where I stumbled to my knees, breathing heavily, half with fear and half with exertion. Finn had jumped down now, and was waving me on and pointing toward the tide, frighteningly close, moving in a long even mass of dark green and white.

Spurred by this sight, I leapt down, heeding Finn's admonition to run, but when I glanced again at the tide I saw that I could not. The quarter mile to shore was simply too far. Fred and St. Ives would be hard pressed to save themselves. To the north, the hillock of sand from which the doctor's henchmen had been shooting was empty. They'd seen the advancing sea and gone away like sensible men.

"To the wagon!" I said to Finn, and the two of us climbed back up onto the bed, which was canted steeply downward, its stern to the tide. Finn's face wore an avid sort of lunatic joy, as if this were an adventure rather than a death sentence. My own thoughts were equally lunatic—that the wagon might save us, and that I might save the abandoned device, which had taken a disastrous toll over the years. I was damned if we'd lose it now. I shouted at Finn to lash himself to the mast of the crane with the line from the grappling hook, and I picked up the box and staggered to the front of the wagon, where the diving chamber hung with its hatch open. I spun half around with the effort of throwing the box, nearly pitching off into the sands again, but I was dead on. It crashed through the open hatch, the ocean-corrupted case knocking itself to flinders, the device sliding beneath the seat.

When I turned around the Bay behind us was a shimmering, rapidly expanding sea, its leading edge billowing and surging forward at a height I wouldn't have thought possible, and I could do no more than throw myself down on the bed of the wagon and latch onto the crane mast like a limpet before the tide was upon us. The waters slammed into the wagon, throwing a wave of cold ocean across our backs at the same moment that it pitched the rear of the wagon upward and forward, so that it bucked like a spooked horse. I was flung into the air, but I hung on tenaciously, hearing the splintering of wood as the wheels and axle and tongue of the wagon were torn from the bed like rotten sticks. We spun around crazily, abruptly free of the quicksand, and I slammed down sideways to the deck again, aware that we were flying forward on the crest of the tide at a prodigious speed.

After a few moments, I realized that doom hadn't overtaken us after all, at least not yet, and I ventured a look around to see how things stood. What I saw was the oddest thing: ahead of us lay dry sand flats and dunes, cockle beds and half-buried debris, but beneath us the roiling tide was tossing and tearing along, now surging ahead as if to outrun us, now abating so that we moved ahead, careening along at the very forward edge of the rushing sea in a death-or-glory flight.

I heard Finn shout out loud, not a warning or a shout of fear, but one of primal joy as we sailed like maniacs up the Bay, bouncing and scudding on the current. I clung stubbornly to the crane mast, but Finn stood up and let go with one hand, holding on with the crook of his elbow, dipping and bobbing, loose-kneed and as sure of himself as if he stood bareback atop a horse, reeling around the center ring of Duffy's circus.

We were quartering across the Bay now, swept west as well as north, so that we would make a landfall somewhere above Grange-over-Sands. I espied the crow's nest atop Flotsam already behind us, and the thick trees along the marshy, lower reaches of Hampsfield Fell some distance ahead. I was cold, soaked with seawater, and blessedly thankful—even more thankful when the shoreline finally hove toward us in a rush. The wagon was thrown onto the beach by the tide, wheels forward, and we rolled across twenty feet of sandy shingle in a mad instant and straight on into the marsh, where we quickly lost momentum, slowing to a stop in a pool of dark water that sat amid the trees. The diving chamber with its prize inside was still miraculously secured to the crane, and it swung back and forth slowly like the pendulum of an enormous clock. ⟡

CHAPTER 8

Smothercated

THE MORNING WAS peacefully silent but for the calling of gulls, the cool spring sun filtered through the leaves of the tree limbs overhead, and Morecambe Bay lay as placid as a lake behind us, the tidewaters a thing of memory. It was as if we had stepped out of the tumult of a noisy ball into the silent peace of a garden.

"Stay well clear of the pool," I said, looking down at the swampy ground beneath us. The wagon settled more deeply into the mire even as we watched, as if the sands of the Bay and its marshy environs were determined to consume us. Finn leapt clear, landing on his feet, and I followed, coming down on solid ground with an ankle-numbing force.

"Look, sir! She's in a hurry now!" Finn said, pointing at the forward part of the wagon, which slipped a couple of inches deeper again, the pool emitting a soft, deadly, well-fed sigh. The canted-down, forward deck of the wagon was buried, sandy mud oozing up over the bench, the diving chamber leaning away from the crane mast.

"If we make the grappling hook and line fast around a tree," I said, "we might still haul the wagon out with the block and tackle and save the diving chamber and the box."

"I'll try for the hook," Finn said gamely, and he paced backwards several yards and set out as if to make a rash leap onto the bed. I stopped him in mid-stride. Leaping down from a height was one thing, but leaping upward entirely another.

"Perhaps a tree limb," I said, and we looked above us now. Our luck held fair, for some ten feet overhead a leafy limb reached out over the wagon.

"Give me a heft, sir," Finn said, and in an instant he was up and standing on my shoulders. He leapt, caught a lower limb, and scampered into the tree like a forest creature. I stepped back to watch him. Getting a line on the wagon would be easy enough, if we were quick about it, although hauling it out again might want the team of horses, if in fact it could be hauled out.

There was abruptly the sound of voices from somewhere very near, and in my current state of mind I thought that it was St. Ives, come to fetch us. But then I knew that it wasn't his voice, and I turned to see two men appearing from along a trail that followed the edge of the Bay—the two men I had first seen in Lambert Court, playing the part of workmen. The tall one carried his rifle; the short, simian-looking man who had struck Merton had only his ugly countenance to recommend him. They seemed as astonished to see me as I was to see them, but it was only in that regard that we were equal, for there were two of them and one of me, and there was the rifle to consider. A smile flickered across the face of the tall man, if indeed you could call it a smile, as he glanced from me to the wagon. He slowly raised the rifle and pointed it at me. I assumed that he meant to shoot me, and so I stood perfectly still, hoping that Finn was doing the same in the tree.

"What have we here, Spanker?" the tall man said.

"A hideous devil, I do believe," Spanker said. "Pity its poor mother."

"I say that if it moves it's a corpse, but if it stays still it might be of some small value to men like us."

"It's brought us the undersea chamber," the man Spanker said. "Isn't it a good 'un, returning the doctor's stolen property?"

"A peach. Sit down and have a rest, mate," the tall one said to me, "there by that tree. Spanker, twist his head for him if he gets fancy. I'll find a piece of rope to secure that wagon, and then we'll see what his friends think he's worth—a couple of quid and the odd pence, I should think."

I sat down as requested, not anxious to have my head twisted, and watched the tall man head off through the close trees. A horse whinnied in that direction, and I saw that a canvas tent and bits and pieces of gear stood some distance beyond our clearing, lost in the woods unless you knew where to look. A sort of dogcart or shay was tethered nearby them. It was a neatly hidden bivouac, close enough to the road so that they must have seen and heard us early this morning when we were rattling along toward Grange-over-Sands in our wagon. Frosticos, of course, had posted them there. How they communicated with the doctor, I couldn't say, but I recalled what St. Ives had speculated about underground waters and passages inland, and it would seem no great feat for Frosticos to surface now and then a mile or so north in the lower reaches of the River Kent, where it broadened out and entered the Bay.

I stole a casual glance into the treetops, and spotted Finn straight off, perched over the wagon among the leaves. He was anxious to be up to something, and was gesturing furiously. He pointed at me, put his hands together as if praying, and pretended to dive headfirst from his limb. I had no idea what he meant, but then he repeated the gesture, pointing determinedly at me again, and I understood: he wanted *me* to do the plunging. Apparently he had gone mad.

The tall man had by now reached the clearing in the woods, and would doubtless soon return. Spanker was paring his fingernails with a murderous-looking knife. He gave me a malicious grin, and I grinned back, the seconds passing quickly. *Trust the boy*, my misgiving mind told me, and before it could tell me anything different, I leapt forward from where I sat and threw myself bodily into the quicksand, trying to scoop my way to the wagon, but bogging down almost at once, too far from solid ground, however, to be easily retrieved.

Spanker stared at me with a look of surprised wonder on his face, but that changed to something else again when he saw Finn drop out of the tree and onto the bed of the wagon, at which moment he began to shout incoherently for his companion. I held very still, feeling myself sinking, fighting the urge to kick my feet and fully expecting to be shot. Within seconds Finn had slipped the catch on the windlass and was hauling out line, swinging the grappling hook and letting it fly out toward me over a distance of perhaps ten feet. I latched onto it, and straightaway I heard the windlass turning and began towing forward across the surface of the muck. I looked back, and saw that the tall man had returned, and that he held a coil of rope. His rifle, however, stood against the tree, and the smile still twisted his mouth.

We had no place to go. He saw that. We were making good our escape, but onto a variety of sinking ship. I reached the wagon and hefted myself over the side, the quicksand holding the wagon steady in its grip, although it was apparently sliding downward at a steeper and steeper angle, the diving chamber swinging out farther on its tether, dangling a mere foot above the surface now. In a moment it would simply be out of reach.

"The chamber," I said to Finn in a low voice, and he caught my meaning directly. Without a pause I reached far out and managed to open the hatch, drawing the chamber closer to us. I shoveled Finn through the door, and than climbed in myself, throwing out the broken remains of the strongbox before locking us in. I picked up the odd, ovoid device that Parson Grimstead had recovered from his manure pile and set it carefully on the seat. It was the size of a large loaf of bread, built of several riveted metals, brass and copper among them. Despite its having remained dry in the rubber-sealed strongbox, the brass and copper were discolored with faint lines of verdigris. One of the ends was contrived of a crystalline substance, separated from the metals by a band of ebony-like wood. The crystal was translucent, but was cloudy with striations, so that it obscured whatever lay beneath it.

"May I take a squint at it, sir?" Finn asked, and I could see no reason to deny him. We certainly had nothing better to do with our time. He picked it up, holding it by the ends and peering into the crystal. Right then the wagon gave another downward jolt. There was the sound of laughter from our two friends on shore, and the tall one waved at us in a cheerful, bon voyage sort of way. Then they set about getting a line out to us.

"It's warm-like," Finn said. "Like an egg under a hen. I wonder what it does."

It did feel curiously warm, although it hadn't a moment ago, and either the sun was shining on it so as to make the crystal glow faintly, or else it was glowing of its own accord. Certainly we had done nothing to it aside from picking it up. It was decidedly close in the chamber, and so I turned the valve to let in air, and there was a satisfying blast, although nothing like its original pressure. Soon we would have to do something decisive or else give ourselves up. Either way, it was better to do so before the chamber sank into the sands than after.

And with that thought I had a look at the controls of the chamber, wishing I had paid more attention earlier. Still and all, St. Ives had figured them out, and I supposed I could do the same to some useful extent. Straight off I found the lever that emptied the ballast tanks, and I resolutely drained them, giving our friends on shore a moment of pause. We would at least ride higher in the quicksand, I thought.

Then another thought came to me: if the line affixing the chamber to the windlass were released, we might still float. Even if the wagon sank to the very bottom of the swamp, it wouldn't drag us down with it. What had St. Ives said?—two hundred feet of line? As I saw it, the wagon was our anchor....

"I'm going to open the hatch," I said. "Can you pop out and release the stop on the windlass line so that the chamber might float?"

"Done," Finn said, laying the device on the seat. I threw the hatch open and in a trice he was out and had released the line. I was surprised by the sudden plummet of the craft—a plummet of perhaps six inches—onto the surface of the pool. Finn clambered back into the chamber and shut the door behind him, picking up the device and holding it again, as if he meant to keep it safe. I immediately doubted myself, full of the unsettling notion that we were sinking deeper into the ooze now, that the broad expanse of the wagon had in fact been our temporary security.

On shore, the tall man gave us a discerning look, but again seemed to find our activities irrelevant, as perhaps they were. They had their own line run out and around the trunk of the tree now, and Spanker, who had the build of a Navy topman, was quickly aloft. Within moments he dropped heavily to the deck, ignoring us utterly until he had secured the line to the base of the crane mast. Then he pitched the grappling hook shoreward, and the tall man gave it a turn about the tree, and Spanker moved across to the windlass, where he took the slack out of the rope. He made an effort to turn it farther, to winch the wagon up out of the quicksand, but to little avail. They had a double line on it now, though. No doubt to their mind, the chamber was safe enough. Spanker stepped across the deck toward us. He bent down and made a series of loathsome faces before silently acting out the antics of a man in the throes of suffocation, after which he shook his head sadly, winked at us, and disappeared back up into the tree.

"We're in the hopper," Finn said, "and no doubt about it. But my money's on the Professor and old Mr. Merton. They'll be along directly."

"Surely they will," I said.

"Look at this, sir." Finn said, nodding at the device now. The crystal had a more pronounced glow, from deep within, and it was blood-warm to the touch. "I believe it's woke up," Finn said. "What does it do, do you suppose?"

The term *woke up* alarmed me. "*Do?*" I asked. "I'm afraid I can't say. Professor St. Ives seems to believe that it was connected with the odd behavior of cattle, but that tells us little."

"Cattle, is it?" He gave me a skeptical look.

There was a decisive sucking noise now, directly below us, and the chamber shuddered and shifted. We held very still. I was certain now that releasing the line had murdered us, that we were sinking, and that someone—Frosticos or St. Ives—would fish the chamber out of the quicksand with two corpses inside.

But we didn't sink. We shifted and shuddered and sat still again. Then we shuddered, as if the wind were blowing, and kept on shuddering. The two on shore were eating a jolly breakfast now, with a pot of tea and two cups—all very elegant, and meant, no doubt, simply to torment us. Spanker held up a great chunk of bread and jam, raised it in a greedy salute, and devoured it. But the tall one noticed the antics of the chamber, and he set down his teacup and gave us a hard look, as if we were up to something.

And apparently we were, quite literally, for instead of sinking, we seemed to be rising. "We're off," Finn said, matter-of-factly. "It's the device, sure as you're born. Same as one of those hot air balloons, maybe."

That made no sense at all to me. How could it be *the device*? Hot air balloons? We had seemed to become one. We rose slowly, looking slightly downward onto the two on shore now. The tall man shouted something to Spanker, who climbed hurriedly into the tree, moving out onto his limb just after we had drifted past it. He glanced up at us, and he wasn't grimacing and gesturing now, but was apparently mystified and suspicious. He stepped straight off the limb and latched onto the rope, which had begun to unreel itself like a charmed serpent. The chamber rocked with his weight, and for a moment was actually descending, putting an end to our capers. Our descent quickly slowed, and for a moment we rocked lazily in stasis. And then once again we were off, as Finn had put it, with Spanker still dangling tenaciously below us, kicking and tugging.

"He's off his chump," Finn said. "Why did he go for the rope when there's a winch in easy reach?"

"He doesn't have much of a chump to start with," I said.

The craft swung and shook as Spanker struggled futilely to accomplish what gravity had failed to accomplish. And then, perhaps realizing that he was dangerously high above the deck of the wagon and that we were drifting to leeward despite the sea anchor, he let go, heaving himself toward the deck of the wagon below, the chamber canting sideways with the force of it. We looked down in time to see him turn in the air, head downward and still a couple of narrow feet from the wagon when he smashed headforemost into the quicksand with enough force to bury him waist deep, one arm trapped by his side and his legs waving, as in that painting of the fall of Icarus. His free arm and legs worked furiously, driving him downward. The tall man tore at the knotted rope (which, fittingly, Spanker had himself knotted) but he was taking far too long about it. The wind drifted us north, so that we got a better view of the scene below, and what we saw was the tall man pointlessly casting the rope at his erstwhile companion's ankles in the moment that he slipped beneath the sands and disappeared.

It was in fact a ghastly sight, despite Spanker's criminal tendencies, and the odd notion came into my mind that I wished I hadn't known the man's name. Perhaps it's not odd. I tried to think of something sufficiently philosophical to say to Finn, but the boy was already nodding his head in contemplation. "In Duffy's Circus," he told me, "old Samson the elephant sat down on his trainer, something like a tea cosy over the teapot, if you see what I mean. He was a terrible man named Walsh, and his head went straight up the hiatus. The doctor told us that Samson smothercated him dead."

I wondered in that moment, from my elevated perspective, how I had ever come to doubt the boy. My doubts had all been speculative. His actions had clearly professed his innocence and loyalty. A high regard for one's powers of logic, I told myself, can smothercate a man.

"Take a look down the way, sir," Finn said now, pointing out toward the Bay.

I took a look. It was St. Ives and Fred Merton, perhaps a quarter mile down toward Grange-over-Sands, coming along the trail by the shore. Merton carried a rifle. They had seen us right enough, floating there high above the treetops, and they stood for a moment marveling at the sight. As for us, we could see far out into the broad Atlantic, the dark line westward being the shore of Ireland, I believe, and the Isle of Man sitting in the sea in between. I opened the hatch, leaning out into the giddy breeze, and pointed downward, toward where the tall man stood at the edge of the pool in dazed contemplation. He apparently saw the signal himself, deduced that reinforcements had arrived, and set out at a dead run toward his camp, carrying his rifle.

St. Ives and Merton were wary, of course, and came along much more slowly. By the time they reached the camp our assailant had fled in his shay, leaving his accoutrements behind. From our height we could see him scouring along the road in the distance, but there was nothing at all to do about it, which was a dirty shame. Hasbro had been shot twice in the space of a few days by the same man, a man who had no motive aside from mere sport, which says something about human degradation that I'd rather not soil these pages speculating upon. Justice, I'm afraid, sometimes is not met out on Earth, or at least not that we know of. But then I'm reminded of Spanker, burrowing his way to Hell, and I find that there's little satisfaction in that sort of justice anyway.

We descended from our height after a good deal of shouted communication with St. Ives. The device—an anti-gravity mechanism that reacted quite simply to heat—bodily heat and radiant sunlight in our case—gradually lost its powers when Finn was induced simply to set it down onto the deck of the chamber. Later St. Ives speculated that the naturally high degree of heat in the manure heap on Parson Grimstead's property had been sufficient to elevate the immediately surrounding cattle. Our descent was every bit as graceful as our ascent, although far more disappointing, for I rather enjoyed the view.

As for Dr. Frosticos, he and his submarine didn't reappear, and so we had no choice but to keep his diving chamber until he called for it. We took a certain joy in the fact that he had failed in all his endeavors, and that in his last, mad rush in the submarine he had passed out of our lives again, at least for a time. —☙

The Affair of
the Chalk Cliffs

CHAPTER 1

Madness at the Explorers Club

THE MOOD AROUND the table at the Half Toad Inn, Lambert Court, that Saturday evening in spring was lamentable, despite the food, which consisted of an enormous steak and kidney pie that Henrietta Billson had five minutes earlier drawn forth from the oven and set out steaming on the table in front of Professor Langdon St. Ives, his man Hasbro, and myself—Jack Owlesby. There were grilled oysters, tidbits of cold mackerel dusted with salt, roasted potatoes and potted leeks. Dead center of the table stood a gallon of Olde Man Newt, William Billson's own ale, served at the Half Toad in wide-mouthed vessels. Mrs. Billson was just then turning a jam roly-poly on a floured board, which would be hot out of the oven in half an hour. It might be said that she looked like some variety of roly-poly herself, although it would be an insult to the woman, and so I won't say it. A half hour earlier she threatened to run a man out of the inn who hadn't any manners but was "all swank talk," and when the man said something clever to her she bent his arm up behind his neck, kicked him half a dozen times in the seat of his pants, and drove him head foremost out the door.

Now rain hammered at the windows along Fingal Street on this stay-at-home evening, the room nearly empty although there was surely no better place to be in Greater London. There were oysters on the plate and ale in the glass, but a morose Langdon St. Ives apparently tasted nothing, stabbing at the bivalves with an indifferent fork and borne down by the blue devils. St. Ives, as perhaps you might already know, is the greatest, if largely unheralded, explorer and scientist in the Western World. I know little of scientists in the Eastern World, where there might well be some Mandarin equivalent of Professor St. Ives piecing together a magnetic engine for a voyage to the moon, a chronicler like myself peering over his shoulder, sharpening a nib and rustling foolscap. But St. Ives's stature as a man of science meant nothing to him tonight, and Hasbro's subtle efforts to interest him in a slice of mackerel went unheeded; he might as well have been sitting in a cell in the Fleet Prison staring at a plate of salted oakum.

We had just that afternoon returned from Scotland, from Dundee on the Firth of Tay, where the Rail Bridge had collapsed into the firth in December of last year, three days after Christmas, taking a train with it along with seventy-five passengers. St. Ives had been a boyhood friend of Sir Thomas Bouch in Cumbria in the first half of the century, and Bouch, as you no doubt recall, was vilified by the courts and in the press for having badly engineered the bridge. St. Ives had received a letter from Bouch, imploring his help, and we had gone up to Dundee to discover whether deviltry was the cause of the collapse as much as shoddy workmanship. The submarine vessel of the infamous Dr. Ignacio Narbondo had reportedly been sighted on several occasions in the firth during that fateful month of December. By the time we arrived, however, Bouch had decamped to Glasgow, and we were left to our own devices, pursuing our suspicions up half-blind avenues that came to nothing. The authorities declared St. Ives's suspicions about Narbondo's machinations to be fantastic, worthy of the imagination of Mr. Jules Verne.

When we ran Bouch to ground in Glasgow, he had no idea that we were in Scotland. He hadn't sent any letter to St. Ives or to anyone else, and he had never heard of Dr. Ignacio Narbondo.

If our failure to forestall the ruin of Sir Thomas Bouch were the long and the short of it, the food and drink and the comforts of the Half Toad might have fetched the home stake, as the Americans say, but St. Ives was further diminished by a recent falling out with Alice, Mrs. St. Ives, who had grown weary of her husband's constant adventures. He had promised her a month-long holiday on Lake Windermere, before the summer crowds descended, but fast on the heels of his solemn promise had come word from Scotland. Honor left St. Ives no choice but to set out for Dundee to help his old friend, the holiday abandoned. Alice, you understand, agreed that St.

Ives must undertake the journey, but she wasn't happy about it, and they had parted ways in cold silence, St. Ives to Scotland and Alice to Heathfield in East Sussex to visit her niece Sydnee. This silence between her and St. Ives had lasted close upon two weeks now, and St. Ives had been deafened by it, the sun having utterly disappeared from the cloudy firmament of his soul.

Alice is a sort of paragon of wives, equally handy with a fowling piece or a fishing rod, and can quote Izaak Walton six to the dozen, as if she has the *Angler* by memory. She's as competent as Henrietta Billson to kick a man in his daily duty if he asks for it, and pardon the expression. Although the particulars of their marriage are none of my business, I'll insist that she understands St. Ives fully, and has looked with equanimity on giant squids autopsied in the larder and pygmy hippopotami occupying the barn. (A canal for the hippopotami was, I'll admit, a recurring subject of contention.) In short, she's the perfect mate for a scientist and adventurer like St. Ives. But the man's zealous sense of duty to the world and to science, admirable as it is, could try the patience of a marble saint.

St. Ives gazed at his kidney pie, nodding senselessly at our efforts to rally him, tasting his drink and setting the glass down again. Nothing useful could be done this side of Alice's homecoming. She was due into Victoria Station tonight at half past nine o'clock.

The door opened and our old friend Tubby Frobisher staggered in out of the weather, oddly taking no notice of us there in the corner. He attempted to hang up a dripping coat and hat before heading across to warm his considerable bulk at the fire, but the coat fell to the floor and the hat on top of it. I nodded to Lars Hopeful, Billson's halfwit tap boy, who fetched the garments from the floor and hung them up near enough to the fire to roast them. Tubby's usual cheerful demeanor had abdicated. He looked like a man pursued by demons, his rotund face haggard, his eyes wild, his hair apparently coifed by the Barber of Seville, who, of course, had been dead these two centuries past. His clothing was askew as well, his shirt yanked half out of his trousers, his right sleeve gaping open.

He spotted that roly-poly pudding just going into the oven, a sight that would normally lend him the giddy look of a hedgehog eyeing a worm, but he turned away as if blind to it. Then he saw the three of us sitting at our table and seemed to recall, from deep within his mind, that he had in fact agreed to meet us at just that hour—that he had no doubt come to the Half

Toad for that very reason. He veered toward us now, laboring like a dockyard lump in a side wind, sitting down heavily in a chair, where he gaped and blinked.

"What cheer, Tubby?" I said to him, but he looked at me as if I'd uttered an insult. Then, coming to himself at last, he picked up my glass and drained half a pint of Olde Man Newt in a single draught.

"I've just come from the Explorer's Club," he said, shaking his head darkly and setting the glass down hard. His face was plowed with deep furrows, and he gave us a look that was heavy with meaning, although I was damned if I could make it out. St. Ives sat deathly still, not so much as acknowledging Tubby's pronouncement, his own mind still traveling in a dark country. I signaled Hopeful to bring along another glass, since Tubby had seized upon mine. "I believe that I momentarily witnessed the end of civilization," Tubby muttered.

"I trust that you comported yourself with dignity," I said to him, filling both our glasses from the pitcher.

"I did not," he told me, evidently serious. "Dignity wasn't in it. It was the most extraordinary thing. The strangest turn of events."

"More extraordinary even than dignity?" I asked. "Pray tell us what happened. The champagne ran short? Duel in the bookroom?"

"I'll tell you what it was," he said, "although I still doubt myself. I went out of my mind, quite literally, and when I stepped back into it I found that I had taken a cutlass off the wall and hacked the head from that stuffed boar in among the potted plants by the gallery window. I was dead certain that it was attacking me, and I laid it out with a single stroke. I vaguely recall singing "The Sorrows of Old Bailey," looking down at the decapitated monster and wondering why it didn't bleed. I admired that boar. Attacking it was unconscionable."

"Tubby Frobisher *singing*? That's bad, very bad," I told him. "Whisky might account for it."

"Whisky be damned!" he shouted, glowering at me. "I'd had nothing but a cup of hot punch. There was *no* accounting for it—that's what I'm telling you, confound it. The entire *room* was in the same straits. Lord Kelvin was smoking three clay pipes at once while balanced on one leg atop a divan, and that French somnambulist whose name never fails to escape me was setting in to shoot the pipe out of his mouth with a pistol. He had already blasted a vase full of crocuses to smithereens. Secretary Parsons was accusing some harmless old blighter of being the Devil, shouting that he would cut out his liver and lights with a sharpened spoon. You've never seen such a thing—utter chaos and uproar. Every man a raving lunatic, living geniuses reeling and chattering like gibbon apes."

Tubby had grown red in the face, half bonkers again simply recalling the scene. I could see that he was deadly serious, but even so I was again on the point of saying something droll when I noticed that St. Ives had awakened from his deep stupor.

"You say that every man jack of you went mad?" he asked. *"At the same instant?"*

"That's just what I say, Professor. Tomorrow it'll be in the news. No way to keep it quiet, what with Admiral Peavey pitching furniture off the balcony and shouting at people on the street below to clear the buggering decks. Bedlam reigned. Utterly scandalous behavior for two or three minutes. Then the spell lifted like a curtain and we were all of us left gaping at each other, begging pardon right and left." Tubby gobbled three oysters in rapid succession, washed them down with the ale, and then carved out a piece of kidney pie. "God bless an oyster," he said, heaving a great sigh.

"And the people in the street—they were unaffected by this…fit?" St. Ives asked, his eyes alive for the first time in two days.

"I can't quite say," Tubby told him. "There was no sign to the contrary aside from a general uproar, but perhaps that had something to do with the flying chairs."

"You mentioned that cup of punch," Hasbro put in, speaking in his customary, even tone, as if Tubby had been talking about the price of wool. "I wonder whether someone hadn't put a chemical into it. May I attend to your shirt cuff, sir?" Tubby noticed then that he was dragging his unlatched cuff through the mackerel, and he allowed Hasbro to swab it with a napkin and button it up. He took stock of himself then, and made a belated effort to smooth down his hair with a dab of fish oil.

As I said earlier, Hasbro is St. Ives's manservant, his factotum. They'd been comrades in arms time out of mind, and had traveled together to destinations that beggar description. Hasbro has saved St. Ives's life more than once, and St. Ives has returned the favor. He's a tall man, Hasbro is, well turned out, with a long face and a demeanor that rarely changes its atmosphere. He's a crack shot with a pistol, and I've seen him reef and steer as if he were Poseidon's nephew. His notions about punch and poison were sensible. Everything about the man was sensible.

"Poisoning might explain it," St. Ives said, although he didn't seem convinced. "Lord knows what it would be, given that the effects were transitory and apparently immediate. Some variety of plant extract, perhaps. Datura might do the trick, in the form of a condensed tea brewed from the roots. But what would account for the sudden cessation of effect? Dosage? Surely everyone hadn't consumed the same quantity, and of course no two men are constructed alike." He forked up a dripping lump of kidney and seemed to eat it almost happily now, his mind revolving on the trouble at hand rather than the trouble soon to be awaiting him at Victoria Station.

"But *all* of us?" Tubby said. *"The staff as well?"*

"Who's to say the staff hadn't been lapping up the punch?" I asked. "They're not immune to the attraction of warm spirits on a cold evening. For my money Hasbro has put his finger on it. The mystery is solved."

"*Half* the mystery, perhaps, even if it is the case," St. Ives said. "The other half is the more vital."

"Which other half?" I asked.

"Whose hand is behind the outrage, and, of course, why?"

He seemed to grow distracted, as if something had come into his mind, and he cocked his head curiously. For a moment I waited for him to advance some further, enlightening theory, but the clock spoke the hour, and we set in to eat in earnest, time being short. With food going down his gullet Tubby seemed to have forgotten his embarrassment, and agreed with me that he had been fortunate to hack the head off a stuffed boar rather than off the shoulders of Admiral Peavey. After the third glass of ale he was laughing about the entire business, brandishing his stick and insisting that I act the part of the boar for the general amusement of Billson's patronage. I declined. Mrs. Billson set the roly-poly pudding on the table and sliced it, the currant jam leaking out in a purple river, and it seemed to me that all our troubles could be put right by a kidney pie, a pudding, and a pint of ale. —⌀

CHAPTER 2

The Commercial Traveler

TEN MINUTES LATER we went out into the rainy night beneath umbrellas, considerably improved in spirit, although soon St. Ives fell into an anxious silence again, the awful moment approaching. Hasbro and Tubby walked on ahead, which gave me an opportunity to say something useful to my friend. "Throw yourself on the mercy of the court," I told him. "That's the smoothest path when it comes to making up with wives. Fewer thorns and clinkers if you take that route. I can't claim experience, but I've read widely on the topic. Common sense supports my argument."

"I intend to do just that," he said. He walked along in silence for a time, and then said, "If Alice will have me back, I'll…"

"Don't talk rubbish," I said, emboldened, perhaps, by that pudding. "Have you back from *where*? She hasn't sent you away."

"Not yet she hasn't," he said with sad defeat in his voice. "Not yet."

"Then pray do not compound the problem by anticipating any such thing. Pardon my saying so, but you sell her short. Thinking evil sometimes invites it, and the opposite, too. I suggest that you start by assuming on Alice's better nature, and your own, for that matter. You couldn't simply leave Bouch to twist in the wind, after all. Alice knows that."

He gave me a long stare and then nodded his head. "You're in the right of it," he said, "although that's precisely what came of our ill-fated trip to Dundee. I'll beg her forgiveness, though, and then steel myself for the onslaught. Perhaps it won't come. We don't deserve them, you know."

"Wives, you mean?"

"Yes. Few men are worthy of the women they marry."

"Tell her just that thing. Give her a chance to agree with you. That should cheer her up immensely."

We continued in that vein of chat for some time, oblivious to the activities roundabout, until we were vaguely surprised to find ourselves on Victoria Street, the broad arch of the great railway station looming before us. Coaches and dogcarts clogged the boulevard, and rattled away in either direction, and there was a great noise of people coming out of the station and going in, the entryway illuminated by gas lamps flickering in the damp wind. We still had our umbrellas hoisted, although the rain had mostly stopped without our realizing it. I can't imagine that I had said anything to St. Ives that was worth more than two shillings, but perhaps I had distracted him from himself, which was something.

Hasbro and Tubby had already entered the station, and we steeled ourselves and walked into the bustle and clamor of the crowds, the hissing of locomotives, and the smell of wet wool and engine oil. The hour had come, and Alice's train along with it, rolling slowly into the station at that very moment, its journey at an end. The doors opened, and people descended to the platform, scores of people, from Croydon and Tunbridge Wells and points south, making their way out toward the street past heaps of luggage. For the space of some several minutes we were certain that Alice would momentarily appear among them. Then the crowd dwindled, and the platform cleared. For a time there was no one, until one last harried passenger got off—a commercial traveler by the look of him—carrying a portmanteau and with a head like a pumpkin and eyes like poached eggs. That was the end of the exodus. No Alice.

"Gents," the commercial traveler said to us when he hove alongside and dropped anchor, "I'm in the timepiece line." He took his portmanteau in both hands and shook it, four metal legs telescoping from the bottom. A hidden drawer sprang out, revealing a velvet-lined compartment full of tolerably dusty and tarnished pocket-watches. He smiled in a toothy and unconvincing way, his shop set up on the instant and open for business.

St. Ives had fully expected something unpleasant this night—longed for it, even—but Alice's non-arrival was beyond his ken. He stood blinking, completely at sea, loosed from his moorings and apparently unaware that the timepiece salesman stood before him, wearing worn tweeds and grinning into his face. Tubby was not unaware of the man's presence, however, and he said, "Shove off, mate," in a tone calculated to be understood.

"Of course," the man said. "I can see you gents are preoccupied. I… Say!" he said, suddenly bending forward and gaping at the professor. "Ain't you that chap St. Vitus? Wait! That isn't it! St. Ives! I knew I'd get it! I had the good fortune of perusing your likeness in *The Graphic*, sir, some months back. Story about a sort of enormous skeleton…? On the riverbank, I believe it was, out in Germany. I'm honored, sir." He thrust out his hand, looking admiringly at St. Ives. Then, slowly, his visage took on the air of commiseration. "Asking your pardon, sir," he said, more quietly now, "but you ain't waiting for a *Heathfield* traveler, are you? You look worn down by care, as they say."

"What do you know of Heathfield travelers?" I asked him. I'll admit that I didn't like the look of him, although I myself had written the account published in *The Graphic* concerning our exploratory trip down the Danube the previous year, from which we had returned with a giant human femur and a lower jaw set with teeth the size of dominoes. At least our watch salesman had the good sense to have read the piece.

"Only that there weren't no Heathfield travelers aboard, mate," he said in my direction. "Not tonight there weren't. The train went past Heathfield like a racehorse. Scarcely slowed down."

"Why would it do such a thing?" Tubby asked. "Damned strange behavior for a train."

The man hesitated for a moment, and then looked around conspiratorially. "They're keeping it on the quiet," he said in a low voice. "Mum's the word down south, don't you see? Some sort of *contagion*, apparently."

He had St. Ives's attention now. "Contagion?" the Professor asked. "What variety?"

"I don't know the particulars," he said. "But I'll tell you that in my way of business I talk to some…interesting people, so to say. And one of these people let on that the village was one great Bedlam, the entire population picking straws out of their hair and crawling about on their hands and knees. Madness by the bucketful. Mayhem in the streets. I wouldn't have stopped in Heathfield for anything for fear of getting a dose of it. And mark my words, now that I know what I know, tomorrow morning I'm going back home to Hastings, and you can be certain it'll be by way of Maidstone, and not Tunbridge Wells."

St. Ives seemed to reel at the news, and Hasbro put a supportive hand on his arm. We all gave each other a look, what with Tubby's story of the recent horror at the Explorers Club still fresh in our minds.

Wait!" the man said. "Don't tell me you've got a loved one in Heathfield, sir?"

"His own wife," Tubby said.

"Good Lord, sir! You'd best get her out, and no delay."

"Anything more you could tell us, then?" Hasbro asked him, keen for information.

"Well, sir," the man said, dropping his voice again, "you didn't hear it from me. But seeing as who you are, and that you're worried for your poor wife, and rightly so, I'll be straight with you. Like I said, the village is closed down tight—roads blocked, soldiers patrolling. If you go down that way by rail, as perhaps you must, you'd best get off at Uckfield and make your way to the village at Blackboys. This chap I know, my sister's gentleman friend, I'm ashamed to say, who does some work in the sneak thief and housebreaking line when he ain't poaching, reckons that a man could find his way into Heathfield through the forest—past the coal fire pits alongside of Blackboys there. It's easy pickings in Heathfield with the village in an uproar, is what he told me. 'In through the front door and out again with the swag'—them was his very words. You'll say I should have him jailed, of course, given what I know, but that's not my way. What a man tells me in confidence is just that, if you understand me. Now, do you know the open country around Blackboys?"

"Tolerably well, yes," Tubby put in. "I've got an uncle in the smelting way at the Buxted Foundry. Produces railway steel for the Cuckoo Line. He's got a house there in Dicker. I've hunted my share of grouse in and about Blackboys."

"Then you know something of the place." He nodded, as if relieved to hear it.

"Why would this…acquaintance of yours chance going into the village at all?" I asked skeptically. "Never mind the authorities, it's the contagion I'm thinking of."

"It's a brain fever, you see. This fellow I'm talking about has fixed himself a cap out of those great heavy gloves they wear at the kilns. Lined with woven asbestos, they are—*amianthus* some call it. Split open and pulled down over the ears, it'll keep out the lunacy molecules like leather keeps out the wind. If you're in the mood to go into Heathfield, he's the fellow you'll be wanting to see down in Blackboys. People call him the Tipper. He's a small man, not above so." He held his hand waist high. The man was apparently a dwarf. "He's not unacquainted with the Old Coach Inn, there on the High Street. If you look him up, tell him you're a friend of Peddler Sam Burke. Give him this." He dipped into a pocket in his coat then and pulled out a card with his name on it: "Sam 'the Peddler' Burke: Watches, Jewelry, and Pawn."

And with that he once again became the man "in the timepiece line." He said loudly, "No one fancies a pocket-watch, then? Very fine works. Austrian made." But he was already folding up the portmanteau, knocking the legs back in, having lost interest in us. He walked off toward the ticket counter without looking back.

"My God!" St. Ives muttered, knuckling his brow. "Here it is again. Madness springing up like a plague."

Tubby gave me a hard look. "Poisoned punch, forsooth!" he said.

"Should we send to the Half Toad for our bags, sir?" Hasbro asked St. Ives, who nodded decisively.

"If you'd like another hand," Tubby said to Hasbro, "I'm your man. I know the way of things down there, and I've always got a bag packed and ready. I'll bring my blackthorn stick, if you follow me."

"A generous offer, sir. There's a late train south—an hour from now, I believe."

"I'll need half that," Tubby said over his shoulder, already hurrying toward the street, bowling through the slow-footed like a juggernaut.

"I'll fetch the tickets," I said, and went along in the direction taken by the Peddler, who had apparently purchased his own return ticket and gone about his business by then. I'll admit that I wouldn't have given him two shillings for one of his "Austrian-made" timepieces. His consorting with thieves didn't recommend him, either.

The man behind the glass sat on a high stool, reading a newspaper. He glanced up at me without expression. "I'm looking for a gent," I told him, the idea coming into my mind at that very moment. "He might have got off the last train. Large, round head, sandy hair, red-faced. He generally dresses in oatmeal tweed, perhaps a little on the shabby side. He might have tried to sell you a pocket-watch before buying a ticket to Hastings."

"You're three minutes late," he told me. "Your man's out on the street by now. And you mean Eastbourne, and not Hastings. He bought a ticket on tonight's train, the Beachy Head Runner."

"Beachy Head?" I said stupidly. *"Tonight's train?"* He scowled just a little, as if I'd accused him of a lie, and so I sensibly let the matter drop. Perhaps the Peddler had meant Eastbourne by way of Hastings. Perhaps he meant anything at all. Probably he was the fabulous liar of the world, about as genuine as his timepieces.

An hour later the four of us were bound for East Sussex on the very train that the Peddler himself had bought a ticket for, although I hadn't seen him board. Good riddance to bad rubbish, I thought. In Eridge we would abandon our train for a seat on the aptly named Cuckoo Line, into Uckfield, where we'd strike out overland on foot toward Blackboys if it was too late to hire a coach. With any luck, the mysterious contagion would evaporate, as it evidently had at the Explorers Club, and our sojourn would amount to nothing more than wasted hours.

I was deeply asleep, my head bumping against the window, before we were out of London.

———

WHEN I CAME awake in the dim coach, we were sitting dead still, the night outside dark and lonesome. For a moment I had no idea where I was or what I was doing there, but the sight of my sleeping companions brought me to my senses, and I sat in the lovely silence for a time and gazed out the window. I saw that I was looking out on a heath, and I could distinguish a line of trees in the distance, and a star or two in the sky, which was full of scudding clouds.

It came into my mind that I'd soon have to find the necessary room, which was situated aft. I arose quietly and made my way down the aisle, passing into the darkness at the back of the car, and trailing one hand along the wall to steady myself, expecting at any moment that the train would start forward and pitch me onto the floor. Abruptly I ran out of wall, and my hand fell away into a void. I lurched sideways, temporarily off balance, and at once heard a shuffling noise and was abruptly aware that someone— a shadow—was standing near me, hidden by the darkness. A hand gripped my arm, I was pushed sideways so that I spun half around, and before it came into my mind to cry out, I was knocked senseless. —◦

CHAPTER 3

The Journey South

J ACKIE!" A VOICE said, sounding distant and dreamlike. It occurred to me that the name was my own, or had been in some dim, earlier life. Soon after I recalled that I had eyes, and I opened them and squinted up into the worried face of Tubby Frobisher, who looked down at me, holding his blackthorn stick in his hand. My first thought was that Tubby had beaten me with it, but on second thought it seemed moderately unlikely. The train was moving along now, slowly picking up speed.

"I knocked the bugger sideways," Tubby said to me. "Broke his wrist for him, I warrant you. But he leapt out the carriage door straightaway and disappeared. A railway thief, no doubt. The man had his weapon raised to strike you again, by God, but I put an end to his filthy caper."

I managed to sit up now, but reeled back against the wall, shutting my eyes at the sudden spasm of pain in my skull. On the floor beside me lay a piece of rusty iron pipe wrapped in greasy newsprint that smelled unhappily of fried cod. There was a spray of blood on the newsprint—my blood, I realized. I scrabbled weakly in my coat pocket and discovered that my watch was missing, and of course my purse with it. To put it simply, I'd been bludgeoned and robbed. By now my assailant had no doubt gone to ground in Ashdown forest through one of the common gates.

If I could have felt anything past the pain in my head, I would have felt like a fool, a richly deserving fool. It was no secret that railway thieves booked passage on the South Eastern Railway for no other purpose than to waylay nighttime travelers at carefully chosen spots along the track. East

Sussex is full of forests and empty heath, you see. There's no point in stopping the train to give chase, or to report the incident at the next station, because there's damn-all that anyone can do to put things right. In that part of the country, railway thievery is perhaps the safest line of work there is, unless you're unfortunate enough to run into Tubby Frobisher and be laid out by a blackthorn stick.

Tubby helped me back to my seat, where my companions voiced a general concern. St. Ives probed the back of my head and announced that my skull wasn't crushed. I'd been dealt a sort of sideways blow, to my great good fortune, he said, due to my falling away from the man even as he struck me. To my mind my fortune would have been considerably improved at that moment had I been spared the entire experience.

"What's this now?" St. Ives asked, looking at the newsprint-wrapped pipe, which Tubby had brought away with him.

"The weapon," I muttered stupidly, but then I saw that he didn't mean the length of pipe, but rather the newspaper. He held it up gingerly and unfolded it—the *Brighton Evening Argus*, it turned out to be, from two days past. It was the story on the front page that interested him, and he read it in silence for a time and then laid the newspaper down and looked away. "Of course," he muttered and shook his head tiredly.

Hasbro picked the *Argus* up again and said, "Might I, sir?" St. Ives nodded but said nothing. The salient bits of the remarkable story went thus: A merchant ship, the *India Princess*, out of Brighton, had driven up into the shallows below Newhaven and had stuck fast near where the River Ouse empties into the Channel. She was hauled free when the tide had risen the following morning, with tolerably little damage done to the hull or cargo. Virtually the entire crew had drowned or disappeared, and that was the puzzler. The ship wasn't wrecked. There had been no storm, no foul weather. As remarkable as it might be, they had apparently leapt or fallen over the side shortly after the ship had rounded Selsey Bill, several miles from shore, the lot of them shouting and carrying on like candidates for head nutter at Colney Hatch.

The ship's boy, the sole known survivor of the tragedy, had been asleep, and had awakened when he heard the ruckus. He reported that a fit was even then upon him. He found himself laughing hysterically at nothing and then reeling in sudden terror when his old uncle, dead three years earlier, dressed now in knickers and wearing a fright wig, descended the companionway, grinning fearsomely. In his terror the boy had rushed straight through the apparition and up the companionway to the deck, only to see the first mate and the captain, wrapped in apparently bloody pieces of sail canvas, dancing a hornpipe on the railing. The cook was beating time on an overturned tub, wearing a swab on his head, his face garish with rouge. Other members of the crew staggered about the deck singing and groaning, tearing their hair, jigging in place to the strains of a phantom fiddler. As the boy watched, the two dancing men lost their balance and pitched straight overboard into the sea. The cook, his eyes whirling, picked up the kettle and advanced upon the boy coquettishly, mouthing insanities and beating his head with an enormous galley spoon. His nankeen trousers and shirt were stained with bloody red streaks. The boy trod backward in fear, stepped into the open hatch, and plunged to the lower deck, where he was knocked insensible.

When he came to consciousness he found that the entire crew had disappeared, although the boats were still aboard. His own fit had passed away, and the ghost of his uncle with it. The deck was scattered with trash and overturned kegs. The cook's tub and most of the kitchen tools were thrown about, a cleaver imbedded in the mast. Someone had painted a grinning moon-face on the mainsail, making a general mess of the deck with red paint so that it appeared as if a bloody battle had taken place. Finding that the ship was adrift, the sails flapping, the boy did his best to take her into Brighton, but was at the mercy of the winds, and couldn't manage it alone. The fates favored him, however, because the ship ran on up the Channel, going aground on sandy bottom without disaster. He made his way into Newhaven where he reported the incident, and was immediately taken up on suspicion of having engineered the thing himself. The following morning the drowned bodies of the captain and the cook washed ashore near Littlehampton, their costumes confirming the boy's strange tale. It was a mystery comparable to the recent case of the *Mary Celeste*, and the maritime authorities were at a loss to explain it.

"Well now," Tubby said when Hasbro had finished reading the piece. "Here's another outbreak of lunacy—the third. To my way of thinking the third of anything smacks of a plot, unless this *contagion*, as they call it, is carried on the wind and weather."

"Yes indeed," St. Ives muttered ambiguously, and then he disappeared down into himself again and fell silent, apparently deep in troubled thought. "A plot," he said a moment later. "Poor Alice." Then he said, "A word with you, Hasbro," and the two of them huddled together and spoke in low voices, Hasbro nodding in solemn acquiescence to whatever St. Ives was telling him. I could make out little of what the Professor said beyond his asking Hasbro whether he recalled the death not long past of Lord Busby, Earl of Hampstead, or the Earl of Hamsters, as the press laughingly referred to him. The rest of the talk was mere muttering. It seemed a little thick to me that I was left out of the conversation, although Tubby didn't apparently mind, because he was asleep.

The train soon arrived in Eridge, and we abandoned her for the Cuckoo line to Uckfield, all of us but Hasbro, that is. He mysteriously boarded a London-bound train without so much as a by-your-leave the moment that we climbed down onto the platform. The four of us were now three.

"Hasbro is returning to Chingford to fetch along something that I hope we won't require," St. Ives said. I waited for the explanatory sentence that would surely follow, but it didn't come. It would in the fullness of time, of course, but it was damned strange being left out of things. I was leery of playing the Grand Inquisitor, though, and anyway was too tired to speak. We had been traveling for days it seemed, with only that brief respite at the Half Toad, and the hours had heaped up into a heavy weariness. Tubby was snoring again directly we got underway, and despite the pain in my head I sank toward sleep myself, caught up in a recollection of the shocking condition of Lord Busby's two-days-old corpse when we'd found it.

Busby had been engaged in experiments involving the production of various rays, both visible and invisible, created by the use of large, precious stones. The stones, to the value at tens of thousands of pounds, had been stolen along with his papers and apparatus at the time of his murder. Scotland Yard suspected that he was in league with certain Prussian interests, who were financing his experiments, and St. Ives was of a like mind. The Prussians, perhaps, had simply taken what they wanted when Busby's work had born fruit, and for his efforts had paid poor Busby in lead, as they say.

I tell you this now because my mind is fresh, and because it has a bearing on our story, but there in the train car, at the edge of sleep, I didn't care a brass farthing about Busby one way or the other, given that the man was a traitor, or had been setting up to become one. Take a long spoon when you sup with the devil, I say. In short, I faded from consciousness and slept the sleep of the dead until the train stopped in Uckfield well past midnight.

ABOUT OUR TEDIOUS trek into Blackboys I'll say little. There was no transport to be had in Uckfield, and so, the weather being moderately clear and the night starry, we optimistically set out along the road, hauling our bags in a borrowed handcart. An hour into our journey the sky clouded over and it began to rain in earnest, and despite our umbrellas we were soon soaked through, the mud up to our withers. I was in a bad way by then, leaning heavily against Tubby on the lee side.

News of the peculiar shipwreck had by now changed the general view of things, putting an edge on it, as the knacker would say of his knife. Something was afoot that apparently had little to do with a mere prank involving poisoned punch at the Explorers Club. Tubby, game as ever, was enlivened by the nearness of our goal, and was edgy with the desire to push on into Heathfield immediately instead of bothering with Blackboys, and the Tipper be damned. Probably the man was off robbing houses at the moment anyway. It was common sense, Tubby said, that the raid had best be carried out in the early morning hours, when vigilance slept and darkness was an ally.

But I wasn't up to the task. Tubby's idea was that I could bivouac well enough in one of the huts near the coal pits, while he and St. Ives slipped into Heathfield and made their way to the niece's cottage, situated, as it was, on a country lane. The relative isolation of the place would tip the whole business in our favor. They would fling Alice into the back of a hay wagon, and the niece in with her, and spirit both of them out of the village, by stealth, bribery, or main force. They would gather me up and run south, going to ground at Tubby's uncle's place in Dicker.

I was a wreck by then, and far too weary to object. A dark hut near the coal pits would be a welcome thing even if it were crawling with adders, so long as it was dry. I half thought that St. Ives would agree with Tubby, time being of the essence, but about that I was wrong. Instead of seizing the moment as Tubby advised, he reminded us of the asbestos caps, and it was those hats that carried the day, since there was no going into Heathfield without them. He honored us for our loyalty, he said, but it was the Tipper or nothing.

And so it was an hour before dawn when we fell in through the door at the Old Coach Inn on the High Street and roused the innkeeper, still in his nightcap, and moderately unhappy that he'd been deprived of his last hour of sleep. It was wonderful, though, to see what money can do to improve a man's spirit, for he took ours happily enough in the end, and, being short of accommodations, stowed us in two closed up, empty rooms with pieces of dirty carpet on the floor to serve as beds. We'd slept rougher, though, in our time, and the rooms were at least dry. The Professor took one of them, and Tubby and I the other, ours having the added luxury of a solid shutter across the window to block out the day.

Once again I fell into the arms of Morpheus without so much as a heigh-ho. It was several hours later that Tubby arose to heed the call of nature, stumbling over me in the darkness and nearly crushing my hand. I cried out, as you can imagine, and that was the end of sleep. A morbid sun shone through the chinks in the shutter. We rapped on the door of the adjacent room, but apparently the Professor was already up and about. Tubby and I put ourselves together and hastened out into the inn parlor to find our friend, who had solicitously let us sleep—odd behavior under the circumstances, it seemed to me now. The clock began to toll the hour: nine o'clock.

St. Ives was nowhere to be seen, and in fact the inn parlor was generally empty of people. Somehow the journey down the hall from our room had reminded my head of that iron pipe. There was the smell of rashers and coffee leaking out of the kitchen, which on any other morning would suggest the smell of heaven itself, but which gave my stomach an unhappy lurch. I sat down heavily in a chair by the hearth. "I'm all right," I said to Tubby. "It'll pass."

"Of course it will," Tubby said, a little too cheerfully. "That piece of pipe would have knocked the sense out of any other man alive, but you haven't any sense to begin with, Jack, and that's what saved you." He bobbed up and down with silent laughter and then headed toward the door, meaning to look for our companion. But the door swung open in that very moment, nearly banging into him. A boy of about ten crept in—the stable boy, as it turned out—and stood looking from one to the other of us, twisting an envelope in his hands as if he were wringing out a towel. He was a long-faced lad with a shock of hair that stood up on his head as if he had taken a fright. He touched it to his forehead by way of a greeting.

"Begging your honors' pardon," he said, "but is one of you Mr. Owlesby? Mr. Jack Owlesby?"

"One of us is," I told him. "In fact, I am the very man. Who might you be?"

"John Gunther," he said. And without another word he handed over the envelope, which bore my name across the seal: Jack Owlesby, Esq. I could see at once who had written it. St. Ives's curious back-slanted script is unique. "The man told me to give it to you personal, sir," John Gunther said, "when it was nine by the clock, and to show it to no one else. And I was to give you these." From his pocket he took three guineas and handed them to me. "And now I've done my job and done it fairly, sir."

"So you have, John," I told him, and he stood there goggling at me until I said to Tubby, "Be a good fellow and give Mr. Gunther a token of our esteem, will you Mr. Frobisher? My purse was stolen by blackguards last night, as you might recall."

"Of course," Tubby said. "You can consider it a loan, Jack." He handed over a coin and the boy turned happily toward the door, nearly stumbling into the innkeeper coming in, who cuffed him on the back of the head, cursed him for a slow-belly, and reminded him of his duty. My brain must have been creeping along in sluggish way, for it was only then that the certainty struck me: St. Ives had gone on without us into Heathfield. I bearded the innkeeper before he could take his leave. —◌

CHAPTER 4

A Day at the Inn

S T. IVES APPARENTLY hadn't slept at all, but had sneaked out at dawn and roused the innkeeper again. He had asked about the Tipper, and although the innkeeper had warned him against the man, St. Ives set out down the road in the direction of the Tipper's shack with a sleepy John Gunther to show him the way.

"That must have been three hours ago," I said incredulously.

"Nearly to the minute," the innkeeper said, and then he went on to tell us that John Gunther had returned shortly with the missive, but with instructions not to rouse us, but to wait until we'd come up for air. And so it was done. The innkeeper had seen to it. He went out again, promising breakfast and coffee, which sounded distinctly more palatable to me now than it had only a few minutes earlier.

"He's left us in port," Tubby said, slumping into a chair. "And by design. He could as easily have sent the boy back at once to rouse us. For God's sake, man, read the letter, and we'll know why."

I tore it open straightaway, although there was no hurry, as it turned out. "Tubby and Jack," the letter read. "I'm going on into Heathfield without you. I ask your pardon for my deceit, but I can tell you that there is nothing else to be done. I've made a ruin of things in every possible way, and it's my business to sort things out if I can. With the idea of departing at first light, I paid a visit to the Tipper, where he lives below the miners' houses at the bottom of the High Street. The man was unhappy to see me, but he was game enough when he had three of my guineas in his pocket and more promised.

He resolutely refused to lead anyone but me into Heathfield. The entire company is out of the question, he maintains, with the roads and paths guarded as they are. He has been in and out twice in the past two days, and it was a close business—work for a cat, he said, and not an elephant.

"Of course I didn't tell him what I was about, and he affected not to care, so long as he received six guineas in all. When we reach our goal, I'll release him from his obligation. He's agreed to return to the inn, find the two of you, make his report, and receive the second payment, which I've entrusted to John Gunther, the stable boy, who is a good lad. By that time, God willing, I'll have thwarted Narbondo's plans and Alice and I will be making our way south to Dicker to look up Tubby's uncle."

I heard Tubby gasp at the mention of Dr. Narbondo's name, but I read on without pause and with precious little surprise:

"When you've paid the Tipper his due, you'd do me a service by leaving straightaway for Dicker yourselves, for we've got further business to attend to in the south. If we're not there by sunset this evening, then I'll leave the two of you to your own devices.

"Many things have become clear to me, Jack, and it's high time that you and Tubby know all. It was Ignacio Narbondo himself who sent the false missive from Dundee, luring us north. I did him the foolish service of dawdling for two weeks, scrutinizing the nonsense that he himself had planted for the very purpose of manipulating me. And it was Narbondo who murdered Busby and stole the gems and his apparatus, suspicion naturally falling to the Prussians. To put it simply, I fear that Narbondo has made use of Busby's Second Ray—a madness ray. I cannot explain the effect of the ray, but I suspect that the gravitational distortion of the energy's waveform provokes a complimentary distortion in the activity of the brain. You'll recall that Busby's portable laboratory was often set up on a prominence. The old Belle Tout Lighthouse at Beachy Head might answer. If it does not, then the device might well be set up within the cliff itself, perhaps in a cavern, where the chalk walls would facilitate the acceleration of the ray, which I fear is impervious to the horizon. That would explain the curious matter of the Explorers Club. Narbondo's submarine vessel has been sighted often enough near Eastbourne...."

"Narbondo!" Tubby said, unable to contain his loathing any longer. "I'll give that bloody reptile a taste of my blackthorn stick this time. See if I don't!"

"Pray that we have the opportunity," I said, waving him silent.

"You recall the experiment with Busby's sapphire propulsion lamp," the letter went on, "the way the crystal structure of the sapphire was destroyed in a single use. This is much the same, except that the lamp that transmits the madness ray makes use of an emerald. Even Narbondo's coffers cannot support the continual destruction of emeralds, and I suspect that the three trials have cost him dearly. Busby had discovered a way to dissolve the emerald in acid, and then reconstruct it under high heat, so that the crystalline lattice would be perfect, impervious to the degenerative effects of the device. In short, Narbondo will want this fortified emerald, which Busby gave to me for safekeeping, although I fear that there is no such thing as safekeeping.

"Busby was in great fear for his life there in Scarborough. I was to return the emerald to him in a fortnight if his fears were unfounded. Alas, they were not. Clearly it took Narbondo some time to discover that an unfortified emerald would deteriorate, but Busby's notes *must* have mentioned the existence of the fortified emerald, and, I suspect, mentioned my name along with it. If not, then Narbondo would have no need to involve me at all. To the contrary, he would have a free hand with things, and the Crown, perhaps the planet, would be at his mercy. Hence my sending Hasbro to Chingford to retrieve the fortified emerald, which is the most valuable card in our hand. But in the end it must be destroyed, even if it means my own destruction. Narbondo can be tempted by it. It will draw him out. *But he must not be allowed to possess it.* If I'm taken, the ransom demand will shortly follow. I've tarried long enough. *Sharp's the word!*"

This last was heavily underscored, with a blot of ink at the end where the tip of the nib had snapped off. The four of us who had set out from Victoria Station just a few hours ago were now two.

"Feedle-de-de," Tubby said, immensely unhappy. "Clearly he shouldn't have gone into Heathfield alone, not with this much at stake. *Elephants!*"

"Surely that wasn't directed at you," I told him. "It was meant to be a what? A metaphor, not an insult."

"I know that, you oaf. What I mean to say is that the venture *wanted* an elephant. He should have seen that. It was damned reckless of him not to. What's this business of the lure and the prey?"

"For my money," I told him, "it means that Narbondo fabricated a letter from Thomas Bouch to draw St. Ives north to Scotland. Then, discovering that Alice had fortuitously gone on to Heathfield, he orchestrated this uncanny outbreak of madness, understanding full well that St. Ives would race straight into the heart of danger upon his return."

"*Orchestrated it*? So this entire thing was a ploy? What about the business at the Explorers Club, and the ship run aground? What does that have to do with St. Ives?"

"Nothing and everything," I told him. "I'd guess that they were merely trials. Narbondo effected them from out on Beachy Head. Do you know that our watch salesman bought a ticket last night on the *Beachy Head Runner*? I did a bit of sleuthing there at Victoria Station, after you'd gone home after your things."

"Is that right?" Tubby said. "The blithering pie-faced devil. I should have beaten the man where he stood. But of course you're neglecting the fact that scores of people bought that same ticket. We did, for instance, at least as far as Eridge."

"As did the railway thief." I said, everything coming clear to me now. "It fits, don't you see? Narbondo wouldn't want an army of us in Heathfield. Given another couple of minutes and your railway thief would have tumbled me from the car, hidden himself once again, and knocked you on the head as well, or Hasbro, when one of you came along. Robbery was convenient, but perhaps it wasn't the motive."

"And that's why the blighter was setting in to finish you off when I dealt him that blow," Tubby said. "He'd already taken your purse, after all. There was no point in murdering you for mere sport."

"No point at all," I said.

"One might say that he was attempting to hack the legs off the elephant before it lumbered into Heathfield."

"There's perhaps more truth than poetry in your phrasing, but it's as you say. There's a good chance I owe you my life."

"As well as the half crown I gave the boy just now."

"That was no half crown," I said, calling his shameless bluff. "I clearly saw you give the boy a shilling."

"God's rabbit!" Tubby said. "I'll need that breakfast directly. My big guts are eating my little guts, and without salt." As if his command were a wish on a genie's lamp, breakfast arrived, interrupting our parlay.

Maddeningly, there was nothing for it but to wait. St. Ives had declared it necessary. The absence of asbestos caps declared it necessary. The two of us would sit on our hands in Blackboys and be satisfied with our lot, hoping to God that the Tipper would appear, and quickly, although to my mind it was a long shot. Like as not the Tipper was just another rum mug in the employ of Ignacio Narbondo—another person for St. Ives to knock on the head if he were to prevail in Heathfield.

We idled away the balance of the morning browsing through the books in the inn parlor. I made inroads into Southey's *Life of Nelson*. Tubby dipped into Andrew Marvel's *Bachelor*, perpetually interrupting himself to look out of the windows with an expectant squint in his eye. Now and then he stood up, grasped his stick, and flailed away at an enemy that only he could perceive. Hours later, after endless rounds of two-handed Whist and flagons of tea, we ate a roasted duck stuffed with potatoes while watching ever more intently for the door to open and the Tipper to walk in and announce himself. But although the door did just that off and on, and any number of people walked in or walked out, there was no sign of the Tipper. We whiled away the last hour of daylight at a table near the fire over a beaker of port, the rain still falling, half a dozen people sitting around the parlor taking their ease.

The inn door slammed opened, and, as you can imagine, we both looked up sharply. Once again, it wasn't the Tipper. It was Alice, looking like a wildly beautiful Ophelia, her dark hair windblown, her dress and coat splashed with mud, a haunted look in her eyes. In her hand she clutched what could only be one of the asbestos caps. She gaped at the two of us, cried out, "Oh, Jack!" and fell to the floor in a dead faint. —๑

CHAPTER 5

Treachery in Heathfield

THAT SAME MORNING, while the sun was still low on the horizon and Tubby and I slept, St. Ives followed the Tipper into the woods. It was nearly dark beneath the oak trees and the Scots pine. Steam rose from the wet leaves and needles that covered the forest floor, creating a ground fog. St. Ives carried an asbestos hat, but the Tipper told him that until they were on the very outskirts of Heathfield itself, the cap was of no value to him. In Heathfield it would be priceless. He declined to respond to the questions St. Ives put to him. He had been paid his fee to take St. Ives into Heathfield, he said, not to palaver like a jackdaw.

Soon the ground itself grew black with coal dust, and the forest opened onto a heath as blighted as the Cities of the Plain after the hail of brimstone. There were mountains of coal dug out of the pits, which descended some 150 fathoms into the depths of the earth—deep enough, the Tipper pointed out, to bury a mort of corpses. Rusting coal tubs lay roundabout, and ruined iron machinery, and heaps of firebrick, fabricated by the hundreds of tons to be shipped off to smelters, and all of it covered with black dust where the dust wasn't washed off by the elements.

The coal pits were quiet, it being the morning of the Sabbath, but there was a low hovel with smoke coming out of a chimney, with a stream that flowed alongside it, the water running black. The Tipper led St. Ives on a circuitous route, behind the pallets of firebrick and outbuildings, wary of the watchman in the hovel. They crossed the stream on a foot-bridge, the morning growing darker rather than lighter, and before long a spewy sort of rain started in. The Tipper vowed that if he had known that the weather would turn on them, he'd have asked for something more than six guineas for his trouble. Out of fairness, he said, the Professor should pay him the rest of his fee at once, and not compel him to wait for it, since the result was the same in either case, and if they were discovered and pursued, it was every man for himself. If he were captured, he would be three guineas to the bad.

"Aye," said St. Ives. "But a man with something to look forward to is likely to do his work more cheerfully, and not retire early from the field. And in the situation you describe, I'd be the one who's three guineas to the bad, wouldn't I?"

The Tipper lapsed again into silence, and they went on, into the forest once more, leaving the coal dust behind them. Near Heathfield, the fog rose again around their knees, with here and there patches of it ascending into the treetops. "Pray this fog ain't washed out by the rain," the Tipper said. "A fog is perfect weather for a lark like this."

His prayer was answered, for the fog grew heavier as the minutes slipped away and they neared the point where they'd don the caps. The Tipper slowed, held out a restraining hand, and whispered, "Steady-on!" And then, when all was still, "Listen!"

There was a distant mutter of voices, not the lunatic voices of a village gone mad, but of reasonable men, several of them. How close they were, it was impossible to say. The fog hid the world from view and obscured sound. The Tipper turned to St. Ives and in a low voice said, "So much as a quack from your lordship, and I'm gone, do you hear me? You'll not see me again. I'll go back after the payment that's waiting for me in Blackboys and tell your friends that everything's topping. You'll be on your own."

"Agreed," St. Ives said, and the Tipper muttered something about it's not making a halfpenny's difference who agreed with what. They moved forward carefully, keeping hidden, until they could see a road ahead, the fog blowing aside to reveal a small company of red-coated soldiers sitting beneath an open canvas tent.

"Lobsters," the Tipper whispered. "Up from Brighton, no doubt." He nodded toward a dense birch copse some distance farther on, which ran right up against the road. "That's where we cross into Heathfield proper. Put that cap on. Pull it low over your ears. If you lose the cap, you'll lose your wits with it, although you won't know you've lost either of them, if you ken my meaning."

St. Ives donned the cap, which was indeed cobbled together from a pair of gloves, the fingers rising atop like the comb of a rooster. He tugged it firmly down over his ears, deadening what little sound was left in the quiet morning. He had no real understanding of the science involved in the caps, although he suspected that the answer lay somewhere within the note-books of Lord Busby. More to the point, he wondered how the Tipper could have discovered the efficacy of the asbestos cloth. He couldn't have, of course. Even if the gloves were ready to hand, it wouldn't have come into his mind to sew them into a cap. The Tipper was clearly in the hire of some-one who had knowledge of such things. Busby being dead, that someone's identity was obvious.

When would the betrayal come? St. Ives wondered, watching the Tipper scuttle on ahead toward the stand of birch. Soon, surely. He felt for the bulge of the pistol tucked inside his waistcoat. Then he reached into his vest pocket and drew out a hastily written letter addressed to Alice. He hadn't had time to write what he meant—couldn't find the words to say it. But if it were necessary, and if the fates were willing, he could get the pitiful attempt into Alice's hands even if he were captured, and she might at least win free and remember him for who he had always meant to be, paving his marriage with good intentions.

He crumpled the letter into his vest again, where it would be within easy reach, and then hastened forward to where the Tipper stood a few steps back from the edge of the road. The two of them might be hazily visible through the fog when they crossed, although for the moment they were hidden from view. The Tipper mouthed something incomprehensible, but made his meaning clear with a gesture. They crept out into the open, looking carefully north, and for a moment they caught sight of the soldiers again, mere shadows in the murk, before slipping into the forest on the Heathfield side of the road.

St. Ives experimentally tugged his cap away from his ear, and instantly, as if the space within his mind had been occupied by a ready-built dream, he had the strange notion that he was at a masquerade ball. He had never been a dancer, and he loathed costumes, but now he was elated at the idea of taking a turn about the floor. He saw Alice approaching, although she was a mere wraith, which didn't strike him as at all odd. She carried a glass of punch, seeming to float toward him atop a shifting bed of leaves. He could see forest shrubbery through her, and an uncanny white mist roiling behind her like smoke. Something was happening to her face. It was melting, like a wax bust in a fire.

He yanked the cap back down, pressing his hands tightly against his ears. Now there was no Alice, no masquerade. The madness had slipped in like an airborne poison as soon as the door had swung open, and then had evaporated when the door had slammed shut. And yet despite the cap there seemed to be some presence lurking at the edge of his mind, some creature just kept at bay, but straining to be loosed from its bonds. As they neared the village the capering presence in his head became more insistent. He began to hear small, murmuring voices that rose and fell like a freshening wind. Quite distinctly he heard the voice of his mother saying something about a piano. He imagined himself sitting happily on the parlor floor of his childhood home, dressed in knee breeches, watching a top careen around in a wobbly spin, its buzzing sound clear in his ears.

It came into his mind that his cap might be inferior, that it might be compromised somehow. The Tipper seemed to be sober enough. St. Ives compelled himself to put up a mental struggle, recalling algebraic theorems, settling on Euclid's lemma, picturing prime numbers falling away like dominoes. He added them together as they ran, tallying sums. A bell began to ring, in among the numbers, it seemed to him, but then ceased abruptly, replaced by the sound of a fiddler, the fiddling turning to laughter, the numbers in his mind blowing apart like dandelion fluff. He forced himself to think of Alice, of himself having gone away to Scotland on his fruitless mission while she journeyed south, possibly to her doom.

The branch of a shrub along the path lashed at his face, sobering him further. He saw a cottage ahead through the thinning trees now, recognizing the blue shutters. On beyond the cottage lay the broad heath from whence the village got its name. The Tipper had taken St. Ives straight to the cottage, despite its remote location: clearly he knew the way well enough. He stood just ahead now, his finger to his lips.

The fog had deepened, and not an imaginary fog. St. Ives could smell it, the damp of it on the stones of the cottage, the musty leaves. It recalled the holidays of his youth, spent in Lyme Regis. Memories of seaside vistas wavered pictorially now on the fog itself, like images in a magic lantern show. He reached out to take hold of them, thinking that he might literally hold them, and he was saddened when they passed through his fingers as mere mist.

The Tipper was grinning at him, as if enjoying St. Ives's mental unmooring. He put his fingers to his lips and whistled, and out of the fog came Alice herself, not at all a wraith, but solid now, walking slowly as if mesmerized. Her eyes were distant, gazing out on heaven-knew-what. The sight of her brought St. Ives instantly to himself. A man walked behind her, holding onto a clutch of fabric at the back of her dress and wearing one of the asbestos caps.

Then she quite apparently saw St. Ives, for she shook her head as if to dislodge the cobwebs and focused on his face in apparent amazement. This partial return to the waking world seemed to stagger her, and she stumbled forward, nearly falling. The man behind her hauled her to her feet again. St. Ives saw then that he was none other than Sam Burke, the Peddler, dressed in his familiar tweeds.

The Tipper suddenly loomed in front of St. Ives and, quick as a snake, his empty hand disappeared inside St. Ives's waistcoat and reappeared with the pistol in it. He stepped back, shrugging. "This'll do just as well as the three guineas," he said. From behind the corner of the house a third man stepped into view, his right arm tied into a sling. In his left hand he held a pistol of his own, which he pointed at Alice, no doubt as a message to St. Ives, since Alice seemed to have gone out of her mind again and was indifferent to it.

A wave of anger washed the confusion from the Professor's brain, and he threw himself forward, hitting the surprised Tipper a heavy backhand blow that knocked him down. The pistol flew from his hand, but St. Ives ignored it. Without pause he snatched the Tipper's cap from the man's head and shoved it into his own waistband. He clutched the Tipper's neck with his right hand and lifted him bodily off the ground so that he hung by his own weight, his feet kicking, his mouth opening and closing like the mouth of a fish drawn from deep water. The one-armed man still pointed his pistol at Alice. He stepped forward now, shaking his head at St. Ives, and in that moment St. Ives knew that the man wouldn't shoot either of them. The pistol was a bluff.

St. Ives made a sudden lunge forward, carrying the Tipper with him, clutched to his chest, the Tipper biting and lurching insanely, a low, gibbering nose uttering from his mouth. Pivoting on his right foot and spinning halfway around, St. Ives hurled the Tipper like a sack of potatoes at the man with the pistol, both of them going over in a heap. He reached into his vest and drew out the note that he had written earlier that morning, and then, rushing toward the Peddler and Alice, he yanked the Tipper's hat from his waistband, shoved the note into it, and with both hands pulled the cap down over Alice's head and ears, turning sideways in that same moment and bowling into the Peddler, knocking him backward and clubbing at his head with his fists.

The Peddler grappled him, strong as an ape, reeling back against the wall of the cottage. He heard Alice shout something—no sort of madness, but something sensible—and he shouted back at her, "Run! Run!" at the top of his voice, holding on to the Peddler, pressing his thumb into the man's throat, compressing his larynx. And then his own cap was snatched off his head, and there was a shout of triumph in his ear. Abruptly he heard fiddling and laughter on the wind, a cacophony of wild noise. There was a gunshot, fearfully close, and he saw Alice running, the one armed man pointing the pistol and firing it over her head and into the trees. St. Ives looked back vaguely at the man he was throttling, confused now, and saw with horror that the man wore the contorted face of his own father.

St. Ives reeled backward, releasing the man's neck. Smoke seemed to him to be pouring out of the windows of the cottage now, taking the form of grinning demons as it roiled into the air. The world was a reeling inferno in the moment before he was struck in the back of the head and darkness descended upon him. —◦⸱

CHAPTER 6

Alice's Story

MOMENTS AFTER HER collapse on the floor of the inn parlor, Alice revived, and of course we helped her to her feet and into a chair. For a time she sat there with her eyes closed, catching her breath and her sensibilities, still clutching the cap. When she opened her eyes again they had a steadier sort of look in them, as if she had returned in spirit as well as body and mind. From inside the cap she drew out a crushed piece of paper, then threw the cap angrily into the corner of the room.

Tubby made straightaway to our table to fetch a flagon of tea and a cup. She drank the tea down gratefully, and then after another moment's rest, happily took a glass of port. She thanked the both of us, looking somewhat recovered, but in no wise happy.

"We've been waiting all day for word of St. Ives," I said to her anxiously.

"I've got all the word there is," she told us, "and none of it good."

―◦∿◦―

THE MADNESS THAT had possessed her for the past three days had diminished when St. Ives put the asbestos cap upon her head, and had evaporated utterly when she was well clear of Heathfield. Of the madness itself, she recalled that some of it was wonderful, some of it horrifying, but the memory of it was already fading from her mind, as if it had been a waking dream, even now only a memory of a memory.

Some few days previously she and her niece Sydnee had been strolling through the village, where the spring Cuckoo Fair was just then getting underway. The streets were awash with people, with dozens in the costume of St. Richard and with feast booths set up and a great deal of merriment that the weather couldn't dampen. The legendary cuckoo was on display, looking something like a large pigeon that someone had waxed artistic with. The two of them had stopped to hobnob with the bird, when suddenly, without warning of any sort, although Alice faintly recalls a high-pitched keening in the air, the world, in her words, "tipped sideways." On the instant the feast day merriment turned to mayhem. She found herself sitting in the road, with the odd certainty that she was the literal embodiment of the Heathfield cuckoo. She remembered chuckling out loud there in the street—not laughing, mind you, but chuckling like a hen on a nest—convinced that her dress was woven of feathers rather than merino wool.

She recalls Sydnee wandering off, snatching at the air as if trying to catch a will-o'-the-wisp, and in the days that followed Alice never once saw her niece again, or didn't know her if she did. Those days might as well have been moments or years, her sense of the passing of time having abdicated. She somehow found her way home to the cottage, where she conversed with hobgoblins and wraiths, although the hobgoblins might simply have been the Tipper and his cronies.

She fell silent for a time after telling us this, and then in a smaller voice said, "I left him there. I simply fled. It was what he wished—what he commanded. And yet it was cowardice on my part. There was a fallen pistol that I might have reached, had I acted instead of standing there stupefied. There was also that horrible man aiming his own pistol at me. He was injured, though. His arm was in a sling. I might have prevailed over him." She stared into the purple depths of the port. "I fled through the woods, right into the midst of the soldiers at the blockade. I had removed the cap by then, and at first they assumed I was insane, and perhaps I still was, a bit. I told them that a man had been assaulted, because I didn't know what else to call it, but they were in no haste to venture into Heathfield. I bid them good day and quite coolly walked away into the woods and came here, every step of the way thinking I should turn back, regretting that I had left St. Ives in such peril."

"By God they would have shot you, too, Alice, if you had," Tubby told her sensibly. "You must see that. Your value to them was to draw St. Ives into Heathfield. Once you had, you were worth nothing. Jack and I would have been sitting here playing Whist while the two of you disappeared out of existence. But here you are, alive and well, *precisely* because you weren't rash. Now we three can put our considerable shoulders to the wheel."

"You're wrong," she said. "They allowed me to go. They want something, and they believe that I might provide it for them. They wouldn't have hindered me."

"Perhaps," Tubby said. "But in any event you were better out of it. And they wouldn't have *had* to kill you. They'd simply have had to remove your cap. You couldn't have prevailed against them. The three of us might, however."

I half listened to Tubby's assurances, but I had been shocked to stony silence by Alice's pronouncements. St. Ives taken? It was almost too much for me to grasp, even though I had feared that very thing. There were indeed three of us, but clearly there was only the one cap, and no time to find the elusive "wheel" that we were to put our shoulders to. I couldn't abide waiting. I strode to the corner full of bloody-minded thoughts and plucked up the cap, looking out the window toward the edge of the forest, which was dark now. There was no question of the identity of the man with his arm in a sling, nor any question of his being a cold-blooded devil. Alice had described the third man: clearly the Peddler, but at that moment I didn't much care if he was Beelzebub in a dogcart.

Tubby saw what I was up to with the cap straightaway. "Don't be unwise, Jack," he said, taking me by the arm. "Alice has just escaped from that mire of human scum. There's no sense in your wading back in."

"There's but the one cap," I told him, as if that justified my going alone or at all.

"And there's no telling how many of the villains are at work. St. Ives sees things far more clearly than either of us. Now that the prey has fallen into the trap, they'll almost certainly return to Beachy Head. The battle of Heathfield was lost, although thank God Alice was not. Your visiting the scene of the battle can't come to anything useful. At best it's a mere delay. We'll do what St. Ives asked and take the battle to them, by heaven. It wasn't but half an hour ago that you were telling me the same thing. Listen to yourself if you won't listen to me, but listen to yourself sober, for God's sake, and not drunk on anger."

There was of course a great deal of sense in what he said, although I still couldn't see more than a red glimmer of it. But then Alice prevailed upon me to read the message on the folded piece of foolscap that she had found in the cap—apparently the first of the two messages that St. Ives had written out that morning, for the nib of the pen was still sharp.

"Dearest Alice…" it began, and what followed was the plea of a man whose hopes were defeated. His first concern, you see, was to put things right between the two of them. But Alice's tears as we silently read the note made it clear that she had no idea that things had gone wrong, no earthly notion of the Professor's misery, the ebbing of his hope, as if he believed that love was as shifting and transitory as the tides. What strange things we convince ourselves of when the shadows descend upon us!

In short, the first part of the note, written hastily in the darkness of the early morning hours, is none of our business here.

"Follow the track east into the sun," the message read. "Across the road and some two miles farther on, you'll find the coal pits, which Tubby Frobisher tells us consumes a considerable acreage. It's his invaluable knowledge of the area that I depend on here. The path that skirts the pits will come out of the forest directly behind the Old Coach Inn, Blackboys, where Tubby and Jack will be waiting. If I'm taken, my guess is that it'll be to Beachy Head. Narbondo's goal is ransom, not murder, although murder might follow the ransom, as it often does. If you're reading this, then I'm no longer the captain of my fate. Adieu, Alice."

That was the long and the short of it, although the "adieu" was preceded by another profession of his love, as if the first wasn't convincing. There was an irony at work here. Alice had been driven mad by the machinations of a human monster, and St. Ives had rushed impetuously into danger to rescue her. Now their roles were reversed, and it was Alice's turn to play the hero, for she wouldn't be talked into returning home to Chingford under any circumstances, despite both Tubby and I bringing the cannons of logic to bear upon her flank, so to speak. Alice had a single contentious desire, and that was to find St. Ives and to bring him out of bondage alive.

The mention of the fortified emerald brought up more questions than it answered, so we left Alice to read the note that John Gunther had brought to us that morning, and set out down the hallway to fetch our bags. In a little over an hour there was a southward-bound mail coach that would take us on into Dicker, and the three of us were determined to be on it. We would spend the night at Tubby's uncle's house, find Alice some suitable accoutrements, and lay out our plan. However it fell out, the three of us would not go quite so impetuously into the environs of Beachy Head as St. Ives had gone into Heathfield. —⌘

CHAPTER 7

Ransom

I T TOOK BUT a moment to ready ourselves for the trip south. The coach sat in the yard, the coachman eating his supper inside. We had forty minutes of waiting, and were determined not to stand idle. There was no telling what we would find at Beachy Head or along the way, but it might easily be further outbreaks of madness, in which case we wanted for asbestos caps, which meant paying the Tipper's residence a visit. Tubby insisted that with a little luck we might manage to burn his shack to the ground, but Alice wasn't keen on the idea of gambling away the higher stakes by engaging in irrelevant pleasures, nor was she keen on remaining at the inn while Tubby and I went off on the errand. The Tipper wouldn't be there, we assumed. Surely he wouldn't be so brazen as to return to Blackboys, knowing that Alice had escaped and that the two of us waited at the inn.

We went out then, the night blessedly dry and with a shred of moonlight. In the stable we found our young friend helping the coach horses to bags of oats. He leapt up like a jack-in-the-box when he saw us and asked could he be of service. Perhaps Tubby *had* given him a half crown, for he was singularly anxious to oblige us. We asked merely that he describe the Tipper's shack, which he did with particular care.

"It's a low hovel of a place," he said, "that sits alone at the bottom of the road near the forest. There's a pile of old trash you'll see alongside, and the door is half a-hanging. One of the great rusty hinges is broke-like, and the top of the door is fixed with a hook and eye. It's a lazy man's dodge, and a bloke could find his way in easy enough by setting a pry bar into the gap or knocking out that hook."

"I see that you're a sharp one, Mr. Gunther," Tubby said, giving him a wink. "Will you do us another service now?" The boy replied that he would, anything we required, all the time goggling at Alice. "Don't mention at all that we've been round talking to you," Tubby told him. "And if anything out of the way happens at the Tipper's shack tonight, perhaps you'd be good enough to know nothing at all about it or about the three of us either."

"I ain't heard nothing," he said, making a key-turning motion in front of his lips. "I hate the bloody Tipper. Nothing but cuffs and curses from the likes of him, and him a bleeding midget, begging your lady's pardon."

"And don't let the mail coach go on without us," Tubby said, giving him another half crown, which he accepted gleefully, it apparently being his lucky day.

With that we left our bags in his care and went along down the High Street in a singular hurry, but silent as phantoms, past two blocks of miners' cottages, with more set behind them in rows. The village was quiet on the damp Sabbath evening, people staying indoors, which was to the good if Alice had some sort of mischief on her mind. She has as much pluck as does St. Ives, although she is, if I might say it, far easier to look at than the Professor, who is growing tolerably craggy as the years pass. Alice has what might be called a natural beauty, which strikes you even if she's just come in out of a storm or from mucking about in the garden. She's moderately tall, very fit, with eyes that are just a little bit piercing, as if she sees things, you included, particularly clearly. Her dark hair is perhaps her best feature—perpetually a little wild and refusing to stay pinned down, something like the woman herself. I write all this in the interests of literary accuracy, of course. My own betrothed, Dorothy Keeble, a beauty of a different stamp, would tell you the same about Alice, who has become her great good friend.

The Tipper's hovel sat conveniently alone, a good distance below the rest of the village, partway down a grassy decline: our good luck, for we wouldn't be easily heard or seen. It was just as the boy had described it, right down to the junk pile and the badly hung door with its makeshift hinge, which you could see easily enough in the moonlight that shone on the front wall. We were crossing the last patch of ground when we saw a glim of light inside the hovel, right along the edge of a curtain, as if someone had opened the slide on a dark lantern to see what he was about.

"*Here's* a bit of luck," whispered Tubby. "He's sneaked back after his swag, I'll warrant, before clearing out. I'll just see to the front door, and you two go around to the back, eh? He'll have a bolt-hole. No doubt he'll make for the woods."

We set out without a moment to spare across the wet grass, thankful for the curtains on the window, which would hide us as well as they would hide the Tipper, if it was him mucking around inside. Tubby of course carried his blackthorn stick with him, but I had no sort of weapon, and neither did Alice. There in the weedy trash, however, lay a serendipitous length of rusted pipe, which I snatched up in passing. Despite my rough treatment aboard the train, the idea of similarly bashing anyone with a length of pipe didn't much appeal to me, although the idea of the Tipper slipping away from us appealed even less, and I was determined to do the useful thing.

We had scarcely taken up our position outside the rear door when there was the crash of the front door coming down, a shout from Tubby, and the sound of running feet. I raised the length of pipe and was moving forward when the door flew open and the Tipper hurled himself down the several wooden steps, wearing a slouch hat and carrying a canvas bag. He was clearly intent upon making for the safety of the woods, which would have been easy enough if it were only Tubby in pursuit. I stepped in front of him, however, crouching down, drawing back the piece of pipe like a cricket bat. He endeavored to slow himself, but gravity had helped impel him down the steps, and now the hillside was doing the same. He rushed at me headlong, swinging the canvas bag and slamming me on the shoulder with it, knocking me sideways. I swung my piece of pipe as I fell, clipping him neatly on the back of the leg behind the knee. The bag flew out of his hands, sailing away toward Alice as he sprawled forward. Alice picked the bag up, and the thing was done.

Tubby came out then, puffing and blowing like a whale. "Looks like a pawnbroker's shop inside," he said.

Miraculously, despite his tumble, the Tipper still wore his slouch hat, which Tubby plucked from his head now, cuffing him twice across the face with it. "You're in the presence of a lady, you goddamned rascal," he said, and then he sailed the hat away down the hill, where it settled over the top of a moonlit stone. The Tipper looked at us hatefully, a human bomb about to detonate.

Alice tugged open the drawstrings of the bag and peered inside, reaching in and pulling out two of the asbestos caps and tossing them to me. "Sydnee's silver," she said, taking another look. "Tableware and candelabra." She reached inside and drew out a clasp purse, which she snapped open. "Jewelry—Sydnee's jewelry—and a good lot of coin. Here's my broach, too, and my necklace...."

"You *crawling* piece of filth," Tubby said to the Tipper, raising the blackthorn stick menacingly. The Tipper cringed away, certain that he was about to be pummeled, but Alice sensibly shook her head at Tubby.

"Into the house with him," she said, "quickly."

In an unwise moment I latched onto the Tipper's coat, twisting it in my fist and yanking him to his feet. More quickly than I could follow, he snatched a dirk from a scabbard in his boot and took a swipe at my arm, tearing through the sleeve of my coat. I felt the blade slice through skin, a sharp pain, and a wash of warm blood on my forearm. In my surprise I let go of the handful of coat and reeled back, sitting down hard. The Tipper lurched away toward the woods again, running like a hare. Tubby swarmed past me in pursuit, but it was an uneven race, and by the time I had joined in, gripping my bleeding arm, the Tipper had already disappeared into the shadow of the forest.

Tubby returned, looking immensely unhappy. I could do nothing but apologize, although of course there was no point in it. None of us had seen the dirk, after all, and it might have gone even worse for one of us if things had fallen out differently. "I'm all right," I said, when I saw Alice's anxiety. I pressed my coat and shirtsleeve hard against the wound and gave her my best smile.

In we went without another word. The Tipper's lantern was still lit, sitting where it had sat when Tubby pried open the door, which hung out across the threshold now, aslant the bottom hinge. The place was littered with stolen goods—porcelain objects, bric-a-brac, paintings, furs and other garments. The Tipper had been a busy little thief. How he intended to flee with the goods I can't say, unless he had a cart waiting somewhere. Perhaps he had returned merely to take out the coin and the jewelry and meant to leave the rest. We didn't have time to puzzle it out, for we couldn't brook any delay. Our mail coach would soon be standing idle on our account, and we had an aversion to calling attention to ourselves and even more of being left behind.

We dressed the wound on my arm with gin and with a silk scarf as a bandage and went out through the back door again, shutting it after us, Alice carrying the canvas bag. I felt first rate, I can tell you, despite my sliced-up arm. We had put our hands on the swag and had two more caps into the bargain, should we need them. We hadn't ended the Tipper's depredations, but we'd taken some of the wind out of his sails—real progress, it seemed to me, and the whole job hadn't taken a half hour.

The coach waited in the yard, the horses stamping and whinnying, the wind out of the south with the faint smell of salt on it. John Gunther stood with our luggage looking anxious. When he saw us he hurried across, holding out what appeared to be a stiffish envelope. Alice took it from him.

"A man give this to me directly you went down to the Tipper's," the boy said. "He was an ugly article, with a head like the moon."

"Dressed in brown tweed?" I asked him.

"That's the one."

"The Peddler!" I said to Tubby as Alice slipped a largish photograph out of the envelope, tilting it toward the gas lamp to see it clearly. Something came over her face then, and it seemed to me that she went as pale as she had been when she had walked into the inn an hour ago. She steadied herself and handed me the photograph, which reeked of chemicals. It was of Langdon St. Ives, lying in a wooden coffin. At first I thought he was dead, and I simply couldn't breathe, but he was not. He was evidently mad, his eyes opened unnaturally wide, as if he were staring at some descending horror. His forearms were raised, his hands half closed so that they appeared to be claws. At the bottom of the photograph, in a scrawl of grease pen, were the words, "Belle Tout Light. Eleven in the morning. Bring the stone."

The meaning was clear. They hadn't sent the message with Alice when they allowed her to flee from Heathfield, because they intended to underscore the demand with the photograph, which was a hellish obscenity. They had made a tolerably quick business of it—anticipated our movements, too, as we stumbled about imagining ourselves to be acting, when in fact we had inevitably been acted upon.

I tipped the photograph into the flame of the gas lamp until it blazed, burning down to my fingers before I dropped it to the cobbles of the courtyard and ground it beneath my heel. My recently elevated mood had vanished. I regretted letting the Tipper get the better of me. I regretted Tubby's having prevented me from going into Heathfield alone. I regretted not having been at the Inn when the Peddler delivered the photograph. The night was suddenly a hailstorm of regrets. I told myself that I might yet see the whole crowd of villains hanging from gibbets, but it was cold comfort.

Alice very calmly asked John Gunther if he would do us one final service. She even managed to smile at the boy, who was staring at my bloody coat sleeve now, apprehension in his eyes. After our departure, Alice told him, he was to fetch the constable and say that he had been out taking the air when he'd seen someone coming out through the Tipper's door, which was broken from its hinges, and making away downhill. She put another coin into the boy's hand, and he nodded reassuringly. The three of us turned to the coach, as impatient as the coachman to be on our way. Our business in Blackboys was at an end. The authorities would find the leftover swag before anyone else thought to loot the place. When sanity returned to Heathfield, as it perhaps already had, the Tipper's victims might at least recover what they'd lost.

The three of us climbed into the empty coach, which swayed as if on heavy seas as Tubby hoisted himself aboard. The driver hied-up the horses and away we went down the road toward Dicker, rattling and creaking along. The moon was high in the sky now, and the forest trees along the roadside shone with a silver aura, the wind just brisk enough to move the branches. —

CHAPTER 8

On the Side of the Angels

S T. IVES ABRUPTLY came to himself, waking up fully sensible, but with no idea where he had been a moment earlier. Now he lay in the back of a moving wagon that smelled of hay, and in fact he rested comfortably enough on that substance, looking up in the faint light at what was apparently tightly stretched canvas. His hands and feet were bound, although the rope that connected his ankles had some play in it, enough so that he could hobble if he had any place to hobble to. He could recall the scuffle at Heathfield, and Alice's flight, but precious little else since then, aside from a suspicious memory of having met the Queen, who had taken the form of an immense jackdaw wearing a tall golden crown. Other memories flitted through his mind—a trip to Surrey in a cart drawn by a pig, a flight over London on an enormous bullet fired out of a cannon on Guy Fawkes Day, a descent into the depths of hell where he held a long conversation with a crestfallen devil who looked very much like himself. He knew that he had been insane and that he was now in the hands of his enemies, but whether for hours or days he couldn't say. Nor could he tell in which direction the wagon traveled, only that they moved at a moderate pace, bumping and jostling along over an ill-maintained road.

After a time the driver reined in the horses, and all was momentarily still. St. Ives closed his eyes, feigning sleep. The gate of the wagon clattered downward, and as the night wind swirled in around him there was the swishing sound of the canvas being drawn back. The wagon dipped on its springs as someone climbed aboard, and then there was the sharp reek of ammonia under his nose, and his eyes flew open involuntarily. A voice said, "That roused the bugger," and immediately he was dragged bodily off the back of the cart and dumped onto the ground, still bound.

For a moment he lay there, wary of being kicked, but the men—the Peddler Sam Burke and the man with his arm in a sling—walked off and left him to his own devices. He sat up, grateful to breathe clean air, and looked up through the trees at the moon riding at anchor amid a flotilla of stars, which told him that they were traveling south. *Beachy Head*, he thought, smelling the sea on the wind now. It was pretty much the same moon that had risen last night—only a few bare hours having passed since he had been taken. They weren't on the Dicker road by any means, but were on a broad sort of path through the forest, little wider than the wagon.

In a small clearing nearby, his companions had set up a low table, with a Soyer's Magic Stove alongside it, the wick already lit. The Peddler was just then filling a kettle with water, which he set on the stove, and then from a basket he took out candles, a teapot and cups, a loaf of bread and a piece of what looked like farmhouse cheddar, all of which he set out on the table, arranging it neatly, as if he took particular pleasure in what he was doing. He lit the candles and nodded with satisfaction.

The other man watched him with a derisive scowl. "A man would think you were a miserable sodomite with those pretty ways of yours, Peddler," he said.

"Some of us are what they call civilized, Mr. Goodson," the Peddler told him. "My old mother was particular about serving tea. She had the idea that it was proof positive we were descended from angels rather than the much-lamented apes. 'I'm on the side of the angels,' she'd say, taking out the china teapot. She didn't have the pleasure of knowing you, of course, Mr. Goodson. You might have changed her mind for her. Cup of tea, Professor St. Ives? Rather later than is customary, but we make do in our crude way."

St. Ives saw no reason to answer.

"Ah, I forgot that you were bound hand and foot, Professor. Not at all conducive to holding a teacup. We might untie our captive friend's hands, Mr. Goodson. Loop a noose around his neck first, however. Then you can lead him into the trees so that he can relieve himself in Mother Nature's waterless closet. The tea should be steeping by the time you return. We'll give the Professor something more fortifying—a restful glass of brandy, perhaps."

"Get your old mother to lead him into the woods," Goodson told him, nearly spitting out the words. Then he stepped across to the short-legged table, picked up the entire cheese, and took a great bite out of it, spitting the chunk into his hand and setting the cheese back down. He stood there chewing like a cow and glaring at the Peddler, who calmly removed a long clasp knife from his pocket, opened it, and sliced off the ruined corner of the cheese, which he flung over his shoulder. He flipped the open knife neatly into the air, moonlight glinting off the blade, and let it fall onto the table, where it stuck quivering.

"The Doctor would particularly appreciate your cooperation, Mr. Goodson. Indeed he would. He's a generous man, the Doctor—a generous man. No one moreso when good work's been done." The Peddler looked steadily at Goodson, who seemed to be reconsidering his ways. After a moment he swallowed what he was chewing and walked unhappily to the wagon, where he drew out a length of rope. His arm being in a sling, he awkwardly tied a slipknot into the end of it and then stepped across and dropped the loop over St. Ives's head before drawing the noose tight. Then he untied the Professor's hands, all the time staring into his face with a dark look.

"Up you go, cully," he said, hauling on the rope, and St. Ives had to scramble to his feet to avoid strangling. For all that, he was grateful enough for the short jaunt into the trees, and for more reasons than one. He looked out for Mr. Goodson to let his guard down, and he meant to cause him some real harm before the Peddler could join the fray. But the man had the rope wrapped half a dozen times around his good hand, and would without a doubt keep St. Ives on a long tether, pulling him taut at the first hint of a false move. With his feet hobbled, the Professor would have little chance of prevailing, but even so, he watched for his chance, determining to force the issue while the odds were close to even.

When they returned to the clearing again, the Peddler was standing at the wagon, pouring brandy into a cup. He nodded cheerfully at St. Ives. "Night-cap, Professor? Best you drink it while your hands are free. There's more dignity in it."

Clearly the question was meant as a command, and St. Ives took the cup as if he were happy to oblige, tasting the brandy before consuming it, the bitter flavor of chloral nearly making him spit. "Cheers," he said, and he pitched the brandy into the Peddler's face, spun around so that he was facing Goodson, and grabbed the line, yanking Goodson forward and off balance, slamming him on the nose with his knee, hard enough so that the man's head snapped back and he fell, the rope still wrapped around his hand. St. Ives was dragged forward, despite yanking savagely to free himself. The Peddler's arms wrapped around his chest just then, and he was lifted bodily off the ground, getting in one last boot-heel blow that caught Goodson in the forehead.

Goodson got up more slowly the second time, blood flowing from his nose. "Hold him still, Peddler," he said. Securing the coil of rope even more tightly around his hand, he drew back his arm and hit the Professor savagely on the cheek, the rope cutting into his flesh. He would have struck him again if the Peddler hadn't turned away.

"Fetch the funnel," the Peddler told him brusquely. "Give the rope to me." He set St. Ives down, took the line from Goodson, and quickly tied St. Ives's hands behind him again, so that his hands were tethered to his neck now. He pushed him back toward the bed of the wagon, still squinting his eyes against the sting of the brandy that St. Ives had flung into his face. "You'd best sit down of your own accord, Professor, or I'll let Goodson have his way with you. That's it. Now lie down on the straw there." He bound the Professor's feet tightly now, doing a neat job of it, then walked over to where the cup had landed in the dirt and picked it up. He took a satchel from Goodson, from which he removed a bottle of French brandy, followed by another small bottle, clearly from a chemist's shop, and a funnel with a long tube. He knocked the cup against the side of the wagon by way of cleaning it, and then poured brandy into it along with a heavy dose of chloral. St. Ives lay there looking up at the moon again, weighing the odds without any real hope. Resistance was useless. Better to bide his time. When the Peddler told him to open his mouth, he did it. The Peddler was middling accurate with the funnel, sliding it neatly into the Professor's throat and pouring the contents of the cup into it, and even though the liquor bypassed his tongue, St. Ives nearly gagged on the fumy bitterness of the chloral.

The gate came back up, the canvas was drawn back across, and he found himself once again lying in darkness, his head throbbing with pain, listening as if from a great distance to the sounds roundabout, of night birds and teacups and the racket of the table being stowed. He moved his jaw, relieved that it wasn't broken despite the pain, but almost anxious now for the chloral to take effect. The wagon set out once again, and very soon the St. Ives was slipping into a drugged darkness, thinking with the last remnants of his waking mind that his companions were somewhere very nearby, that Alice was with them, safe. ─◦

CHAPTER 9

Dry Bones and Clinkers

WE CAUGHT SIGHT of Tubby's Uncle Gilbert's house when we were halfway up the yew alley—a vast sort of Georgian pile with three tiers of windows. The ground floor looked large enough to house a company of marines, and smoke billowed from the chimney, which was a happy sight. There was a pond, too, with the moon shining on it, and a boathouse and dock with a collection of rowing boats serried alongside. "Uncle Gilbert is a boatman of the first water," Tubby told us, laughing out loud at his own pitiful wordplay.

Barlow, Uncle Gilbert's butler, let us in with great haste, as if, impossibly, he had been expecting our arrival. Uncle Gilbert himself met us in the vestibule, leading us into a stately, oak-paneled room with coffered ceilings and stained glass windows depicting knights and dragons. Hasbro himself sat in a chair, drinking whiskey out of a cut glass tumbler, and when he saw us his face fell. He couldn't help himself. He had been full of the same hope and unease that Tubby and I had felt waiting for the Tipper at the Inn at Blackboys: he had banked on the thin chance that St. Ives would be with us. But now hope was dashed, and you could see what was left of it in his eyes. That changed, however, when he saw Alice. Something good had come of the day after all. Hasbro looked done up, as if he had traveled night and day to rendezvous with us, which in fact he had, having come back down by rail on an express to Eastbourne and then back up again to Dicker, arriving only a half hour ago.

There arose a gleam of optimism in my own mind, for the company was gathered together at last, the elephant reassembled, the waiting mostly over. I'm told that it's common among soldiers and sailors to feel both a sensible fear and a fortifying elation before going into battle, and my own emotions confirmed it that night. There was a great fire of logs burning in the hearth, which was sizable enough so that a person might step into it without stooping, if one wanted to be roasted alive. There were oil lamps lit, and the room shone with a golden glow, our shadows leaping in the firelight. The walls were hung with paintings of birds and sailing ships. It struck me that I couldn't remember having been in a more pleasant room with better companions—if only St. Ives were there. Already I was fond of Uncle Gilbert, who might have been Tubby's older twin, if that were possible, but with his hair disappeared except upon the sides, where it stuck out in tufts. The old man was in a high state of pleasure and surprise at Tubby's arrival, for he had himself been made uneasy by Hasbro's revelations. His pleasure was heightened considerably when he got a good look at Alice.

"Ravished, my dear," he said, bowing like a courtier and kissing her hand. "Simply ravished. You're a very diamond alongside these two lumps of coal." He gestured at Tubby and I. Then he shook my hand heartily, apologized for having called me a lump of coal, compelled me to admit to the truth of the insult, and then apologized again for having nothing but dry bones and clinkers to feed us. If he had known for certain that we were coming, he said, he would have slaughtered the fatted calf.

Barlow hauled me away at that point to see to my arm, which needed a proper cleaning and bandaging. He gave me one of his own shirts, my own being a bloody ruin, and he took my coat away with him to see whether Mrs. Barlow could put it right. Mrs. Barlow was at that moment apparently looking after Alice's needs. We were being looked after on all sides. I had the distinct notion that the earth was growing steadier on its axis after having been tilted this way and that for the past weeks.

I found my companions in the dining hall where they were just then sitting down to gnaw on the bones and clinkers, which turned out to be bangers and mash running with butter and gravy, cold pheasant, cheese and bread, and bottles of good burgundy. Barlow had already taken the corks out of three of the bottles, and the glasses stood full. You can imagine that we fell upon the food and drink like savages, Alice included, pausing only to answer Uncle Gilbert's myriad questions. He cocked his head at what we had to say, nodding seriously, cursing the man who had hit me on the head, astonished at the machinations of Ignacio Narbondo, who, he insisted, needed a good horsewhipping before he was bunged up in an empty keg with a rabid stoat and set adrift. He knew the Tipper, he said, from his hunting forays around Blackboys. Gibbet bait, he was. Vermin. A worm. Gutter filth. "We'll settle him," he told me, nodding heartily and tipping me a wink. "We'll hand him his head in a bucket." He seemed to be as worried for the Professor's health as we were, as if the two of them were old friends.

His use of the word "we" made me uneasy. I mentioned to him that we would be out of his way before dawn, which meant getting precious little sleep....

"Of course I'll come along," he said. "You'll need another stout hand when you beard these rogues." He stood up from his chair and crossed to the wall, where he took down a saber, cutting at the air with it and skipping toward a great, mullioned, oak chest full of crystal objects as if to hack it to pieces. I thought of Tubby beheading the stuffed boar in the Explorers Club. I was fond of Uncle Gilbert, as I said, but he was distinctly excitable. My refusing him outright, however, wouldn't have been gentlemanly, so I rather hoped that Tubby would come up with something to put him off the scent.

"You knew the Earl of Hamsters, didn't you Uncle?" Tubby asked as Barlow poured more wine into our glasses.

"Lord Busby, do you mean? I did indeed know him. We were at Cambridge together, you know, before we were sent down over a misunderstanding involving the fairer sex, ha ha. Pardon me," he said to Alice, "not half so fair as you, my dear. Anyway, I regretted it immensely, of course, but I mend quickly, and I was never any kind of scholar. I'm afraid it went ill for poor Busby, who was a frightfully sensitive man. Every small insult struck the man like a blow. The press made game of him, with the Earl of Hamsters comments, although he did have capacious cheeks. He had a trick of packing them full of walnut halves and then eating them one by one when we were in chapel. He saw nothing humorous in it, do you see. He simply didn't have to share them with the rest of us that way, or crack the nuts during sermon. Poor Busby had a run of ill luck after the scandal, and became a variety of scientific hermit. I felt badly when I read that he'd been murdered. What has he to do with our mission?"

I told him what I knew—about the Prussians, about Busby's experimental rays that were said to be impervious to the horizon and therefore monumentally dangerous, about the man's palpable fear when I met him, like a mouse expecting the imminent arrival of a snake. At that time he had been holed up in the top floor of a hotel on the hillside looking down on Scarborough Bay. It was a den of prostitutes and panel thieves, but he was attracted to the hidden passages. Everything in his laboratory was set up on an ingenious scaffolding of stout wooden crates, and could be packed up and spirited away on the instant.

I had witnessed the workings of the sapphire ray on that occasion—a propulsion ray generated by a device that Busby referred to as a 'transmuting lamp.' Light bounced around inside a cylinder containing the sapphire until it was released as a narrow stream of blue light—'disciplined radiation,' as Busby would have it, although the phrase conveyed little meaning to my mind. The ray had sent a glass paperweight hurtling from where it sat on a table in front of the lamp, out through the open window and down into the sea. It plunged into the depths without so much as a visible splash, and was (for all I know) driven into the sea floor. The crystal structure of the sapphire was destroyed in the process, broken down, Busby told us, by 'imperfect hydrothermal synthesis,' although why the phrase has lingered in my mind I can't tell you. Mother nature's stones, to put it simply, were of inferior quality. It had been a costly little experiment (the expense apparently borne by the Prussians) and one that quite surprised the Professor. I didn't have the scientific wit to be surprised by it.

We agreed to meet again the following day. St. Ives, I believe, wanted to confront him on this issue of the Prussians, to talk sense, as they say, but Busby, perhaps anticipating some such thing, was gone from the hotel, lock, stock, and barrel when we returned. I was entirely ignorant of Busby's having entrusted St. Ives with the fortified emerald, and quite rightly. It was a monstrous thing in every sense of the word, a thing best kept secret. A short time later St. Ives and I found Busby dead in the upper deck of a folly tower in North Kent.

Uncle Gilbert shook his head in both sadness and astonishment. But he was as keen as a schoolboy to know about the emerald, and his eyes grew wide when Hasbro drew it out of a drawstring bag and set it on the table. It was a vast thing, and I say that as a man who himself came into the possession of an enormous emerald some few years back, which I've set into a broach as a wedding gift for Dorothy Keeble, my intended. Busby's manufactured emerald dwarfed my own. It fit neatly into the palm of Hasbro's hand, but only just. It was oddly flattened and faceted, evidently not cut for beauty's sake. There was something about it that was almost malignant, like a poisonous toad, or the proverbial ill wind that blows no good. Alice, I noticed, didn't care to look at it. Hasbro slipped it back into its bag.

"What can you tell us of the lighthouse, Uncle?" Tubby asked, gnawing on a pheasant bone.

"That it's a damned treacherous light," he said. "Hard to see. It's on the bluff, invisible when you're coming down from Eastbourne 'til you sail halfway around Beachy Head. In a sea mist, you don't know where you are. Captain Sawney was the keeper until recently. Drunk as a lord most of the time and asleep the rest, but he kept the lights topped off with oil and his wicks trimmed. You'd think he'd have fallen downstairs hauling oil up to the light or cleaning the blasted glass, but he didn't, the poor sod. He walked off the cliff one night in a mist. They went out to look because the light went dark for want of oil and found the Captain on the rocks below with his head bashed in, the crabs eating him. There's nothing on the beach below the headland but a ledge of shattered chalk. It comes down, you know, great masses of it some years."

"Uncle Gilbert knew Cap'n Sawney on account of the birding," Tubby said. "Beachy Head is a famous place for birds."

"Quite right," Uncle Gilbert said. "There's a sort of cow path that winds around from East Dean. First rate birding on the South Downs and along the cliffs. Eagle owls, long ears, whooper swans, merlin. A blind man could see two-dozen varieties in a day with half an eye open. Captain Sawney kept a log, pages and pages of observations. God knows what came of it. Used to wrap fish, probably."

"There's a new keeper, then?" Hasbro asked.

"Some three months or more. I've been down that way twice now that the weather's warmed up, taking a turn on the Downs with the binocle, but the new man won't come down. Captain Sawney always liked a chat. It gave him a chance for a whet, you see. Didn't matter what time of day. He'd bring the bottle and two glasses down with him. I'd sometimes haul along a fresh bottle myself and leave it with him in order to buy my round. If there was weather, I'd go up for the view. Many's the time we watched ships beating up the Channel in a storm. He always wanted to know what I'd seen in the birding line, and if there was anything new. He was fond of owls…."

His voice fell, and he saw something in our faces now. "They murdered him?" he asked after a silent moment. "He didn't fall? He was *pushed?*"

"Quite likely," Alice said. "I'm sorry."

"Then this new man…he's in league with your Dr. Narbondo? They put their own man in?" He didn't wait for an answer, but nodded darkly. He looked at his hands, opening and closing them. "It's late," he said, all the vigor gone out of his voice. "I want some rest. I suggest that we lay things out in the morning. I've an idea of how we might come at them." He nodded decisively. "We'll learn 'em," he said. "See if we don't."

The pheasant had been reduced to a skeleton, the wine drank, and the cheese and bread lay in a general ruin. Uncle Gilbert was quite right. There was nothing left to be said that would do us half so much good as a few hours of restorative sleep. As I rose from the table I wondered what "come at them" might mean, and what Uncle Gilbert intended to learn them. —꩜

CHAPTER 10

Go On or Go Back

MORNING FOUND US on the Downs, or at least it found three of us there, Alice, Hasbro, and I, hidden in the shrubbery that covered the hilltop just west of the light, eating sandwiches out of a basket put up by Barlow and drinking tea out of an ingenious traveling teapot. There was the twitter of birds and the morning sun through the leaves, and away off shore a schooner ghosted along, appearing and disappearing through a rising sea mist.

I watched the lighthouse through a pair of Uncle Gilbert's birding glasses. Five minutes ago a heavy, large man, most likely the keeper, had stepped out onto the encircling balcony carrying a telescope to take a look over the Downs as if he anticipated someone's arrival. There was smoke rising from the chimney of the attached cottage, and a light beyond the window—someone else waiting inside, perhaps. Maybe several someones, unless the keeper kept lamps burning even while he was out. He had lamp oil to spare, certainly.

White mist drifted through on the breeze off the Channel, obscuring the lighthouse and the edge of the cliffs now. When it cleared, Tubby and Uncle Gilbert appeared, coming along the path from the direction of Eastbourne like Tweedle-dee and Tweedle-dum. Tubby used his blackthorn as a walking stick and Uncle Gilbert leaned on what I knew to be a sword cane, and not one of the cheap varieties made for show. This one had an edge on it and a certain amount of heft. Both men wore walking togs and carried birding glasses, the very image of well fed amateur naturalists taking advantage of the morning quiet. Uncle Gilbert stopped in his tracks, pointed skyward, clapped his glasses to his eyes, and watched a falcon turning in a great circle, drifting away northward. Tubby wrote what appeared to be an observation into a small note-book. A curtain of mist drifted between us again, and for a moment I saw nothing. When it cleared, they were halfway along the path to the lighthouse itself, Uncle Gilbert pointing up at the light, then at the schooner out in the Channel, apparently explaining nautical arcana to his nephew.

The plan proposed by Uncle Gilbert was simple: he and Tubby would chat up the lighthouse keeper on the off chance that he would let them take a look upstairs. Uncle Gilbert wasn't a stranger to the Downs, after all—the keeper would suspect nothing. A jolly peek at the light wasn't much to ask. The man's allowing it wouldn't demonstrate his innocence, but we would know something about the location of Busby's lamp, at least in the negative. And if the keeper wasn't amenable? They would persuade him, Uncle Gilbert had said, laughing at the word. But the whole thing must be done by eleven o'clock if Hasbro was to heed the ransom demand and give up the emerald at the lighthouse. If they failed to produce St. Ives, then he would give up nothing, but would look to his pistol.

Tubby knocked on the door of the cottage now, and they stood waiting. Then he knocked on it again, with his stick this time, and they stepped back in anticipation. But the door remained shut, the window curtains still, the smoke tumbling up out of the chimney. They went on around to the door of the lighthouse and treated it in a similar fashion, stepping back so as not to crowd the keeper if he opened it, which he did, directly.

He was a swarthy, heavy man in a Leibnitz cap. I could see through the glasses that he was scowling, as if he had perhaps been awakened by their racket. Uncle Gilbert gestured at the Downs, perhaps explaining what the two of them were up to, and then up at the light. The keeper shook his head, seemed to utter something final, and stepped back inside, shutting the door after him. Tubby turned as if to walk away, but Uncle Gilbert didn't follow. He stood looking at the door, studying it, and then smote it hard several times, the handle of the sword cane held in his fist. The sound of the knocking reached us an instant later.

"Here's trouble," I said to Alice and Hasbro, who could see well enough what I meant. Uncle Gilbert held the cane before him now, his left hand on the scabbard, his right gripping the hilt. "We'll have to act if we lose sight of them in the fog," I said, "or if that cottage door opens."

"Not the three of us," Hasbro put in. "I have a revolver, after all. I'll lend them a hand, but you two should remain hidden."

"Yes," Alice said.

Hasbro removed the velvet bag from his pocket, drew out the emerald, and sank it in the teapot, fastening down the lid afterward. "No use taking it into the fray," he said.

Tubby turned now and said something to Uncle Gilbert, apparently trying to draw him away. Our battle, after all, wasn't with the lighthouse keeper, although perhaps Uncle Gilbert's was. Perhaps he meant to strike a blow on behalf of Captain Sawney.

The lighthouse door swung open again, and the keeper strode out onto the little paved porch, closing the door behind him. He held a belaying pin in his fist. Tubby walked back toward them, stepping behind his uncle, who was talking and gesturing, his voice rising. The keeper pointed with the pin, as if telling them to clear out. Then a wisp of fog blew through, and when it dissipated everything had changed. Uncle Gilbert was sprawled on the ground, on his back like an overturned tortoise, and Tubby had drawn the blackthorn stick back to strike a blow. There was incoherent shouting as the keeper rushed at Tubby, ducking under the blackthorn. The keeper clipped Tubby on the side of the head with the belaying pin, but Uncle Gilbert had crawled to his knees by then, blood running from a wound on his forehead, and he delivered the keeper a great blow on the back of the head with the sheathed sword. And thank God it was sheathed, because if it had not been the man's head would have been split like a melon, and although dead men tell no tales, as they say, there's no virtue in collecting specimens.

The keeper pitched forward, and Uncle Gilbert struck him again, hard, and snatched the cane back for the third blow, the sheath flying off the blade now, end over end. Tubby parried the sword blow with the blackthorn to save his uncle from the gallows, but the keeper scrambled to his feet more nimbly than I would have thought possible and attempted to hit Tubby another savage blow on the side of the head, although it caught him on the shoulder as Tubby twisted away. Hasbro was up and out of the blind now, running down the slope toward the lighthouse, vanishing in the rising fog, which sailed through heavier this time. Right before the curtain closed, however, I saw the door of the cottage fly open, and a man—a small man—come out at a dead run. It was the Tipper, wearing his slouch hat, turning up like a bad penny. I scanned the downs with the glasses, trying to sort things out but hampered by the wall of mist. Then I saw him briefly at the very edge of the precipice, where he disappeared like a goblin over the ledge as if he meant to scramble down the face of Beachy Head and swim across the Channel to France.

"I'm following him!" I said to Alice, which would be senseless blather if she hadn't seen the Tipper emerge from the cottage. I crawled out the back of the copse to open ground and ran toward the cliff, slowing down when I neared the edge, wary of suffering the fate of Captain Sawney. I looked back toward the lighthouse but made out nothing, although I could dimly hear the sounds of the struggle. I could see perhaps thirty feet downward through the mist, and straightaway spotted the shadowy form of the Tipper as he made his way along what was apparently a narrow trail cut into the chalk. From far below came the muffled sound of the swell washing in over the rocky beach, but I couldn't see it, which was just as well, because I meant to follow the Tipper downward, and I wasn't keen on the view.

It was then that I saw a length of three-inch line below and to the right, the color of the chalk of the cliffs and nearly invisible. It was affixed to a heavy iron ring-and-bolt driven into the rock, a holdfast that allowed for a person to climb downward in comparative safety. It had been there for some time, for it was weather-frayed and there was rust on the bolt. I waited until the Tipper was safely out of sight, and then stepped onto the narrow trail, which was steep, but fortunately clear of loose debris. I didn't tarry, but intended to remain just out of sight in the fog, which meant keeping one eye on what I was doing and another farther down the path in case the Tipper came into view.

I scuttled down sideways, hanging on to the rope carefully, all the time watching and listening for the Tipper. I had made my way perhaps fifty feet from the top of the precipice, when the wind gusted and the fog cleared utterly. I found myself looking down the edge of the cliff, which was unnervingly sheer, the sea moving over the shingle nearly five hundred feet below. My head spun with sudden vertigo when I saw that moving water, and I threw myself into a crouch against the cliff face, grasping the hand-line and closing my eyes. When I opened them again, the fit having passed, the Tipper was gone, although he might still be somewhere on the trail farther below, hidden by an outcropping.

I heard a scrabbling sound above me, and there was Alice, coming along downward with considerably more grace and agility than I had shown. She clutched her dress out of the way with one hand and held onto the line with the other, and within moments she stood beside me. "He's vanished," she said, apparently referring to the Tipper. "I assumed you meant to follow him, so I decided to do the same. He'll lead us to Langdon."

"What of the emerald?" I asked.

"The emerald doesn't interest me, Jack. It only interests Doctor Narbondo. My husband is my sole interest, but he doesn't interest Narbondo at all, except as a means to an end. When the end is achieved..." She shrugged, looking out over the sea as if St. Ives were somewhere beyond the horizon.

"We'll find him," I said, starting downward again while the weather was clear. The trail doubled back toward the east, although some distance ahead it was apparently blocked by a great slab of chalk that had slipped from above and which stood precariously among a litter of boulders. The hand-hold ended there, bolted to the slab. Perhaps it started up again beyond. If the Tipper had seen us above him when the fog lifted, he might easily be waiting for us, hiding behind the great rock. It would be a simple thing for him to reach out and give us a hearty push when we edged around it, and us with nothing to hold onto but sea air.

But Alice made it clear that it was go on or go back for the two of us, and she was clearly in no mood to go back. We approached the great slab warily. The trail was littered with a scree of chalk and flint now, which chattered away downward with each step. The Tipper would certainly hear us approaching if he were hidden up ahead. But now that we were closer, I couldn't for the life of me see how he could have climbed past the slab, unless he were some variety of ape, for it thrust out over the ledge that it stood on, almost in defiance of gravity, the cliff face angling inward below it.

It wasn't until we were two or three steps from it that we saw the dark crack of the cavern mouth, which would be completely hidden from above and below both. It lay behind the slab itself. From out to sea, it would appear to be merely a long shadow cast by the slab and the overhanging cliff. But it was a cave mouth right enough, and we stood looking into the dark interior in utter silence, listening hard but hearing nothing but the calling of gulls and the sighing of the ocean below. —෴

CHAPTER 11

Uncle Gilbert Parlays with the Lighthouse Keeper

THE BLOW THAT felled Tubby was the last that the keeper would strike, for as soon as Tubby no longer stood in the way, Uncle Gilbert stepped forward and skewered the man in the shoulder, wrenching out the sword and drawing it back, watching the belaying pin clatter to the paving stones. The keeper's face had a stupefied look on it, his doom writ plainly on Gilbert's face.

"Greetings from Captain Sawney!" the old man shouted, and swung the sword at the keeper's neck, lunging forward to throw his vast weight into the blow. But the keeper wisely dropped to the stones, sitting down and rolling sideways, and the sword passed harmlessly through the air, spinning Uncle Gilbert half around. The keeper scrambled away crablike, lurching to his feet and grasping his shoulder, backing away onto the meadow and turning to run before the old man was after him again.

It was then that Hasbro loomed up out of the fog, holding the pistol. Tubby was just then coming round, his face awash with gore, as was Uncle Gilbert's, who stood there panting for breath, his chest heaving with exertion. After a moment he walked the several steps to the fallen sheath and once again turned his sword into a cane. Tubby heaved himself up with an effort, and they made their way to the cottage, the door standing open now.

"By God someone's come out of here while we were busy," Tubby said. "He must have been hidden by this bloody fog."

"Perhaps," replied Hasbro, who looked into the interior warily, his pistol at the ready as they entered. It was a single, open room, with a fireplace dead center in the opposite wall, burned-down logs still aglow. A bedchamber stood off to the side, built as an open, lean-to closet with a curtain half drawn across it and a long cord hanging down alongside to tie it back. The door of a privy opened into a second closet, the door ajar, revealing that the small room was empty. There was a narrow dining table with a pair of chairs standing beneath a window looking east, an upholstered chair near the hearth, and a sideboard with plates and cups that stood beside an iron stove. A bowl and pitcher sat on a three-legged table, with a towel hanging alongside. Shoved into a corner sat several open wooden crates stuffed with excelsior. Nondescript pieces of brass and iron poked out of the stuffing.

"There's your evidence," said Uncle Gilbert nodding at the crates. "Our man here is an assassin, or I'm King George."

Hasbro stepped across to the curtain that half-hid the bedchamber, drawing it back slowly, his pistol at the ready. No one was there. Someone had been in the cottage earlier, but whoever it was had fled like a coward rather than to take the keeper's side in the battle.

"Take a seat in that chair, my good fellow," Tubby said, gesturing at the stuffed chair with his blackthorn. The keeper sat down heavily, still holding his shoulder, although there was no longer any apparent flow of blood.

Hasbro put away his pistol in order to take a look into the top crate, which yielded short lengths of glass and metal pipe of various dimensions and what appeared to be a three-sided mirror that filled the palm of his hand. The words "Exeter Fabricators" were burned into the wooden slats of the crate.

"That's as has to do with the light up topside," the keeper said, jerking his head upward. "Property of the Crown."

"Property of Lord Busby if you ask me," Uncle Gilbert said. "But we'll get to the bottom of it in due course."

Hasbro nodded. "Indeed," he said. "I'll just be off, then, if you gentlemen have everything in order. My companions will be wondering what I'm about. You'll want to take a look at the light, perhaps? If the device is still there, you'll do well to dismantle it, but I don't hold out much hope. The rendezvous, then?"

"Just so," Tubby said. "We'll be out of the way when the time comes."

With that Hasbro stepped through the door and disappeared into the mist.

Uncle Gilbert looked out after him for a moment and then closed the door quietly. "We both need a swab, Tubby," he said, and he walked to the three-legged table, poured water into the basin, and dipped the towel into the water, wiping the drying blood off his face while peering into a mirror that hung on the wall. Tubby stood by, ready to cave in the keeper's skull with the blackthorn if the man invited it. Then they traded places and Tubby washed himself, the keeper looking back and forth nervously, first at one and then the other.

"Do you mind if a man has a pipe of tobacco?" he asked.

"Which man would that be?" Uncle Gilbert said to him. "There are only two of us here, and neither of us has the habit."

The keeper looked at him blankly. "I just thought I might..."

"Ah!" Uncle Gilbert said, leaning heavily on his cane. "Your use of the word 'man' confounded me. But I suppose that even a dull-witted reptile like yourself might have learned to stuff a pipe. By all means, then."

The keeper removed a briar from his coat pocket, all the while looking nervously at Uncle Gilbert. The old man's face was a grimacing mask as he watched the keeper load tobacco into the bowl and tamp it down with a ten penny nail, setting the pipe between his teeth and producing a Lucifer match from his vest. He lit the match on his shoe sole and put it to his pipe. Uncle Gilbert whipped the sword cane upward then, knocking the pipe out of the man's mouth. It clattered away onto the floor, spinning to a stop near Tubby's foot. Tubby picked up his blackthorn and smashed the heavy end against the pipe, shattering the bowl into pieces and cracking off the stem. "It'll draw like a chimney now," Tubby said, nodding heartily and hanging the towel on its hook.

"Knock him into the Channel if he moves," Uncle Gilbert said. With that he strode toward the bedchamber, unsheathed his sword, and hacked through the cords that hung next to the curtain. He returned with the pieces and set about tying the keeper into the chair, the man dead silent, his eyes moving from Tubby to Uncle Gilbert and back again, full of loathing and fear.

"Be a good lad and stoke up that fire, Tubby," Uncle Gilbert said heartily. "We'll want it as hot as the hinges of Hades after we've had a look upstairs at that light. We'll see whether our fellow here can sing." He grinned into the keeper's face. Tubby piled split logs onto the dog grate and the fire swept up around it, throwing sparks up the chimney. The two men filed out through the door onto the meadow again, hurrying around to the lighthouse door and stepping inside the vestibule.

Several more of Busby's crates lay on the floor, empty but for tangles of excelsior. The spiral stairs wound away upward, and the two set out, climbing slowly, Uncle Gilbert wheezing but coming along manfully. The great lights burned with good lengths of wick, the oil recently topped off. There was a broad balcony that ran around the outside, and they stepped out onto it, seeing immediately that a platform had been set up there in the open air, bolted to the railing for the sake of stability. Atop the platform stood what appeared to be a large and very finely calibrated compass, vast as a barrow wheel, with a rotating face. There was a second platform fixed above it, studded with bolts and with a confusion of gears and a crank for the purpose of tilting and swiveling. The second platform was empty. But the debris in the crates downstairs had made the thing clear: Busby's ray-producing lamp had almost certainly been moored to this second platform, where it could be aimed like a precisely-manipulated cannon.

They descended the stairs and went out onto the meadow again, the spring sun having melted away most of the fog now. The morning was wearing on. Uncle Gilbert threw the cottage door open in order to have a telling effect on the lighthouse keeper, who back pedaled with his feet, as if to scurry out of range.

"Thrust that poker into the fire, Tubby!" Uncle Gilbert cried. "We'll melt his eyeballs out like jellies, the lying dog!" He laughed hard into the keeper's face, then stood back and regarded him through squinted eyes. "Say your prayers, my man, if you have any to say. It was you who murdered Captain Sawney. You'll admit it before we're done with you."

"Captain bloody *Sawney?*" the man said. "I didn't know the man. You're daft!"

"He was your predecessor, you lying toad!" Uncle Gilbert said. "The man you threw down the cliff."

"*Down the cliff?* I was sent out by Trinity House, by God! I was second man at the Dover light, and they sent an agent up from Eastbourne to fetch me. I was told that Cap'n Sawney had come a purler off the top of the Head, and I was filling in, temporary like, till I passed the trial. I swear on my old mother's grave!"

"What's your name, then?" Uncle Gilbert asked, abruptly pleasant and smiling.

"Stoddard. Billy Stoddard, your honor."

"Billy, is it? Sounds like a name for one of the lads, doesn't it? Fancy a murderer with a pleasant name like Billy. Scarcely stands to reason. How's that poker coming along, Nephew? Hot?"

"Red hot, I should think," Tubby said, holding up the glowing iron.

"Isn't that grand! We'll start with his eyeballs then. He's got two of them. When the first one bursts it'll give him a chance to consider his ways, like the Old Book advises. Ever see a sheep's eyeball burst when the head's on the boil, Billy?"

The man sat gaping at him.

"It swells up first, you see, to twice the size. Then it pops right out of the socket and splits open like a banger on a griddle. The French are fond of an eyeball. They eat them with periwinkle forks. I'm told that a well-turned sheep's eyeball has the consistency of mayonnaise, but a distinctly muttony flavor, which doesn't surprise one. I'll take it now, nephew, before it cools down. We'll want the full sizzle."

Tubby handed it over gingerly, more than slightly ill at ease. Uncle Gilbert seemed to have come unhinged—an unfortunate state of affairs for the keeper.

"Clutch a handful of his hair, Tubby, and hold fast," the old man said. "He'll make a mighty by-God effort to fly when the poker slides in past the eyeball. It'll take all your strength. If he pulls away, though, it'll fry his brainpan, and he'll be no good to us nor anyone else, the poor sod."

Tubby did as he was told. If Uncle Gilbert had gone off his chump and actually meant to burn the man's eyes out, he would pull the keeper over backward in the chair....

Squinting at the smoking end of the poker, the old man inched it toward the keeper's face, regarding him with a wide-eyed, sideways stare as if concentrating utterly on his task. "Hold him still now!" he cried.

Tubby held on tightly, bracing the toe of his boot against the chair leg.

The keeper shut his eyes tight and cringed away as best he could. "It's better to save the eyelid, Billy," Uncle Gilbert shouted into his face. "But if you don't care for it, it's not my lookout. Latch on, now, Tubby! His time has come!"

"Jesus, Mary, and Joseph!" the keeper shouted, and then began to gag, his head rotating on his neck as if he were augering a hole in the sky.

"I believe he's swallowed his tongue," Uncle Gilbert said matter-of-factly. He handed the poker to Tubby with instructions to put it back into the fire. The keeper looked up now, one eye open, gasping for air. "Now, my man, what do you know of the death of Captain Sawney? Mark me well, you'll by-God tell us or you'll go out eyeless onto the Downs like a beggar man!"

"Not a bloody damned thing, mate," the keeper gasped out. "I swear to you. They told me that he'd gone off the top of Beachy Head. Trinity House give me a trial. Half a year at half keeper's pay and a tight-knit little cottage—better than second man at Dover, says I, and down I come with my kit."

"And yet here you are tied into a chair, Billy, close as a toucher to losing your eyeballs and the good Lord knows what all else. You assaulted the two of us on the porch outside when we asked you a civil question, and you've got these wooden crates full of Lord Busby's goods. It doesn't stand to reason that you're innocent, Billy."

"Lord Busby! I don't know him neither. And they ain't mine, them crates. Them others brought that trash round, don't you see? Them damned scientists. They set up shop up in the lighthouse. They give me a few quid, maybe, to watch out, but murder…? I swear to God it ain't in me to kill a man."

"You gave it a try not long back when you laid us both out with that belaying pin," Uncle Gilbert said.

"You was a-beating of me!"

"Who was in the cottage, then?" Tubby asked.

"A bloke. Just a bloke. One of them as I told you."

"What sort of bloke? What's his name? Quick-like!"

"The Tipper they call him. He's a man does odd jobs for the others."

"Which others would that be, Billy?" Uncle Gilbert asked.

"There's three that I knows of besides the Doctor, him what set up the device."

"The Doctor is it?" asked Tubby. "The Doctor came and went? Left you to mind the shop?"

"Just so. Past few days."

"They must be bivouacked somewhere nearby then."

"Eastbourne, I'd think…" the keeper started to say, but Uncle Gilbert shook his head into the man's face to stop him.

"It won't do, Billy. They didn't flog up and down from Eastbourne. It doesn't make sense. I don't call it a *damned* lie that you're telling us, but it's some such." He shook his head tiredly. "Well, as the poet said, red-hot pokers doth make falsettos of us all."

"He'll *do* for me, don't you see!"

"*Who* will, Billy?"

"*The bleeding Doctor.* You don't know him. I can see that. If you knew him you wouldn't be using me so. You'd ken what I'm up against."

"I ken it well," Uncle Gilbert said. "I can see it with my own eyes. You're tied into a chair and I'm about to burn your deadlights out. What's not to ken? But you've already peached on the Doctor, don't you see, Billy? He'll know you've been a-talking with us. There's precious little the Doctor doesn't know. If I were you I'd say what *I* know and skedaddle. They're always looking for hands on the docks in Eastbourne. A two-year cruise might answer. Difficult for a blind man to find a berth, though…."

"By God that's *just* what I'll do," the keeper cried. "I don't half like this work, and I don't half like the Doctor. Ask me a question and I'll tell you fair, but I didn't kill no Captain Sawney."

"Where's the Doctor's lamp, then? Quick."

"They took it away. Middle of last night it was. Experiment was finished, they said. They cleared out, the lot of them. Then the Tipper, he showed up two hours ago and said he was done up, said he would take a bit of a nap, and I let him have his way. No harm in a nap."

"Where are they, then? Where'd they clear out *to*? No nonsense now. Tell us and you walk away whole."

The keeper sat thinking for a moment, as if making up his mind, and then he began to speak. —❧

CHAPTER 12

The Window on the World

W E WAITED, STANDING there on the face of the cliff, not talking, but listening. Certainly the Tipper had slipped into the cavern and vanished. He had fled the lighthouse to avoid running afoul of Tubby, and it was unlikely that he thought to lure us into the darkness to waylay us, because he didn't know we were there. I looked at my watch, surprised to see that the morning had nearly flown. It was half ten o'clock—another thirty minutes until the rendezvous at the light. "Whither?" I asked.

"We'll give him another minute or two and then follow him into the cliffs," Alice said. "He'll lead us to something. It's our good luck that he ran off into the woods in Blackboys."

I hope so, I thought. "What about the others—Tubby and Uncle Gilbert?"

"They're grown men," she said. "They'll get along well enough."

Gulls wheeled around us, and small seabirds flew out of crannies in the chalk and flew back in again. Birds of prey rode effortlessly on the drafts rising from below. Uncle Gilbert could have named them all, no doubt. The sea wind blew ever more freshly, straight through one's clothing. To the west the Seven Sisters stretched away, and below us the swell washed in. On the horizon a low brown haze might have been the coast of France.

We slipped into the darkness of the cavern and waited again, allowing our eyes to grow accustomed to the twilight. We were in a high room—a sort of chalk rotunda with a window letting in sunlight high above, which illuminated a domed ceiling. As the moments passed I became aware of a general movement roundabout me, the cavern apparently alive with crawling and flying things. Moths of great size flitted through the air, and chitonous insects scurried away across the floor, which was littered with what were apparently bones, perhaps fossilized bones, and a rubble of flints and sea shells. Water dripped here and there from above, running in dark rivulets downhill along a dim passage, apparently along the edge of the cliff itself. Some forty or fifty feet farther another wash of sunlight shone through yet another window in the wall.

Alice set out across the cavern toward the passage, with me following as quietly as I could, although the rubble on the floor rattled and scraped as we trod on it. The second window stood at head-height, appearing to be a natural fissure in the rock. Someone had chiseled it larger, however, and the chalk was nearly white where it was newly exposed. The walls of the passage itself were grey, however, with black blotches and streaks of red, and here and there veins of quartz and flint. The stream ran heavier in its channel, fed by further streams where surface water filtered through from above, having dissolved the chalk over the long ages.

We passed into darkness, stepping into the surprisingly chill stream more than once and soaking our shoes, the passage leading ever downward, sometimes steeply. The air had grown stale, but I got a scent of salt air suddenly, and rounding a corner I saw another window, nearly level with the floor this time and providing scant illumination, but enough so that I could see that the passage turned again ahead, and then again after that. On we went, time ticking away. It seemed to me that we might easily have passed beyond Beachy Head proper, into one of the Seven Sisters, and that soon we would come level with the Channel itself if we continued downward at the current rate.

In time, however, the passage leveled off. We saw a tiny flame hovering in the darkness ahead of us, surrounded by a golden aura. When we drew near to it, I could see that it was a large lantern, sitting in a carved-out niche. It must have held a couple of pints of lamp oil, which meant that someone routinely filled it to keep it alight—someone who might be making his rounds at that very moment, lurking nearby. There was nothing for it, though, but to go on, ever on the watch for movement in the far shadows or for the sound of footsteps. Another lantern glowed beyond the first, and I could see that the floor of the cave had been swept clean now, as if we had arrived at a habitation. Chunks of chalk had been pushed up against the far wall in a heap, with a wheelbarrow upside-down atop it. On our right-hand side an arched doorway stood open, through which light glowed. Like the windows along the seaward passage, the doorway had apparently been enlarged, which accounted for the chalk pieces in the rubble heap. At first all was quiet, the air deathly still, and then there was the sound of movement, clearly coming from within the lighted room.

I shrugged at Alice and nodded at the doorway. She nodded back at me, and at once I stepped in front of her and walked silently forward. If one of us were going to stick our head into the lion's den, it would be me. I wafered myself against the wall, craning my neck to see past the edge of the door. What I saw was my own rather murky face looking out of what was apparently an illuminated mirror that framed the front of a wooden wardrobe cabinet.

I admit that the unexpected sight confounded me, although the confusion vanished when I saw that there was another face peering at me from out of the glass—the grimacing face of Dr. Ignacio Narbondo, who sat atop a wheeled stool, his back to the door. He regarded me without the least show of surprise. I gestured at Alice, still hidden behind me, waving her away, praying that she would vanish back into the darkness. Then I walked calmly into the Doctor's presence as if I had been invited.

I was aware in that moment of how few times I had actually set eyes on Narbondo, and then most often from a distance. He was one of those men who keep to the shadows, living in out-of-the-way places in the countryside, or inhabiting low dens deep in the rookeries of the Seven Dials or Limehouse. He was largely unknown to the police—the sort of evil genius whose machinations are carried out by men easily manipulated by greed or fear. He was gnome-like in feature, and middling small in stature, although he was rather stout and was as pale as a frog's belly. There was something bent about him—something you saw at once, or rather felt. I don't refer to his being a hunchback, which is neither here nor there, but to something hellish and inhuman in his demeanor, some fell presence that made him appear to be a leering devil. One could easily imagine Narbondo taking pleasure in flaying small animals, but the idea of his drinking a cup of tea or a pint of ale with any relish was impossible. A dog would cross the road to avoid him.

He sat there regarding me now, not seeming in the least unhappy to see me. "I'll show you a wonder, Mr. Owlesby," he said simply, gesturing at the mirror.

I realized then that the oil lamps that stood in niches around the circular room were unlit, and yet the room was illuminated with a pale glow, the light emanating from disks of glass set into the chalk of the ceiling, looking like full moons. Somehow he had contrived to pipe sunlight far back into the cliffs as if it were water. Aside from the stool and the cabinet that supported the large mirror, the room was empty of furnishings. Broad tubes, apparently made of copper, descended from the ceiling into the wooden closet, the door of which, as I said, was the mirror itself. In front of Narbondo stood a ship's wheel affixed to a complication of gears and levers that evidently worked whatever mechanical contrivance was housed in the wardrobe.

The reflection in the glass, as I said, was of inferior quality. My features were vague, and seemed almost to ripple, as if I were looking back through a haze of heat rising from hot summer pavement. But then I saw moving shapes in the glass, and my eyes looked to a point beyond the shimmering surface, where, to my vast amazement, there was a scenic view of the surface world—a ghostly view, as if some of its substance had evaporated during its journey through the periscope. I saw a line of trees that were certainly the edge of the South Downs woods, and below them, across an expanse of meadow, our own copse, where lay the emerald in the traveling teapot and my half-eaten sandwich. And out of that copse, as I stood there watching, strode Hasbro himself, just then putting his watch into his vest pocket.

Narbondo turned the ship's wheel, exactly as if he were navigating a vessel across the empty Downs, following Hasbro's progress. The lighthouse and cottage swung into view, and beyond them the edge of the cliffs and the sky over the Channel. Hasbro stopped before the door of the cottage, raised his hand, and knocked on it. The hour of the ransom was upon us. The door opened, although the dim interior hid whoever stood within. For a moment all was frozen. No doubt someone was speaking, but of course I could hear nothing. Then Hasbro took half a step backward, turned toward the cliffs, and toppled over slowly. A man stepped out of the interior of the lighthouse and stood for a moment looking down. He held a revolver in his hand. It was Sam Burke, the Peddler. He bent over, rifled Hasbro's pockets, and removed what he wanted. Hasbro shifted then, trying to sit up, and the Peddler drew back the revolver and clubbed him on the side of the head before dragging his now-limp body in through the door. After a time he stepped back out and closed the door behind him.

And then, strangely, he waved at me, or at us, very solemnly, before setting out across the Downs in the direction of the cliffs, disappearing out of the scene, which was now merely a picture postcard view of the Belle Tout Light. The horror of what I had witnessed was accentuated by its utter silence—a dumb show of viciousness.

"What do you think, Mr. Owlesby?" Narbondo said. "You've just witnessed what amounts to a small scientific miracle, given that you and I are three hundred feet beneath the earth's surface. It's the wonder of the ages, is it not? And all accomplished with mirrors, like a circus illusion."

I stared at him in stony silence, which he apparently took as an invitation to explain himself further.

"I envisioned a sort of Momus Glass," he said, "but looking outward and not inward. The mirror itself wasn't difficult to construct, but the necessity of tunneling through chalk was something else again. I contrived a mechanical mole to burrow to the surface, and then built a copper chimney set with highly polished mirrors of various shapes and magnifications. It's a toy, really. But one gets weary of spending time in caverns, you see, and longs for a view of the outside world. The sad case of Tennyson's Lady of Shalot comes to mind...."

"The Peddler knew he was being watched," I said. "Why did he wave at us? Was that a mere pleasantry? Mockery, perhaps?"

"It meant simply that he had done his duty."

"We had seen as much."

"No, we had not seen as much. What we saw was merely the initial step—the shooting of the man Hasbro. The Peddler was constrained from killing your man outright, but he could scarcely allow him his freedom. As you saw, he dragged him indoors, where he was to see to his wounds before binding him into a chair. Now mark this: in the room with him sits an infernal device with a simple clockwork mechanism. There is quite a lot of explosive, enough to demolish the lighthouse and to alter the contour of Beachy Head. If I'm at all unhappy with the quality of the emerald, we'll let your man sit there until the device detonates. Ideally he won't bleed to death in the mean time."

I turned on my heel and lunged through the door, possessed of a cold fury. There were tools atop the rubble pile. I would beat him to death with a shovel like the vermin that he was!

But two men stood without, and I nearly hurtled into them, one of them—the Tipper—tripping me up so that I sprawled on the ground. The other was a man I hadn't seen before. He wore his arm in a sling, and quickly I deduced that he must be none other than the railway thief. In his free hand he held a pistol. I found that I wasn't attracted to pistols, especially in the hands of my enemies. I stood up slowly, surreptitiously looking around, wondering about Alice, relieved that she was nowhere to be seen. The Tipper appeared to be amused to see me, no doubt full of hubris at having once again prevailed over me.

"That'll do, gents," Narbondo said. He lurked behind me in the open doorway, his face in shadow. "If you'll allow me to borrow your weapon, Mr. Goodson," he said, "I'll escort our bold Mr. Owlesby to the room where his companion is taking his ease, and the two of you can finish conveying our cargo to the ship. We sail with the tide."

Mr. Goodson did as he was told, and the two of them walked off silently. I was left alone with Narbondo, who gestured with the pistol, the two of us setting out at once along a down-sloping passage, its mouth nearly invisible in the heavy shadows. Soon, however, lantern light illuminated the passage, and I could see easily enough. This part of the caverns was apparently a warren of rooms and tunnels, most of them dark, although twice we passed lamp-lit rooms heaped with casks and crates, as if the place had been a smugglers' lair. It would have been vitally interesting at any other time, but my mind was fixed variously on Alice and on making a play for the pistol.

Narbondo followed behind me, fairly close. I could almost feel the weight of the pistol against the small of my back, as if it, too, emitted some sort of physical ray. I envisioned turning, batting away the hand that held the weapon, slamming the Doctor bodily into the wall. I determined to do it and steeled myself for the assault. But I had thought too long about it, for the tunnel steepened now, becoming a narrow stairway cut into the chalk. The cavern wall on the right abruptly disappeared, and we descended into a vast, open room, the floor a hundred or more feet below us, so that any quick, erratic movement might have precipitated me into the abyss.

Again sunlight shone through natural windows in the chalk walls high above. There was an updraft of air now, heavy with the smell of the ocean and sea wrack, and I heard what sounded like the relentless surging of the waves. I caught sight of birds winging across the open expanse, darting and flitting as if snatching insects out of the air. We were in a monumental sea cave, the floor of which was a pool of dark water. Small waves washed across the surface of the pool, breaking against tumbled rocks. Alongside a wooden dock lay Narbondo's submarine vessel, and even in the dim twilight of the cave I could see a glint of light from its portholes and the shadow of its dorsal fin. It seemed clear that Narbondo was waiting only on the fortified emerald in order to be underway, and when he gained his objective he would disappear into the vast oceans, surfacing at will to rain down literal madness on some unsuspecting corner of the world.

The flight of stairs ended on a natural outcropping of the chalk, chiseled flat to make a sort of landing some twenty feet in length and width. A second flight of stairs descended from the landing to the bottom of the sea cave, another fifty feet below. Immediately beside us stood wooden door, barred with a length of oak. On the door, hanging on pegs, were four of the Tipper's asbestos caps, looking incongruous in that vast, subterranean place.

"I'll ask you to step away from the door, Mr. Owlesby," Narbondo said, speaking in a polite tone that increased my desire to strangle him. "You have the look of a desperate man about you. If you'd like to hobnob with your friend the professor, you'd best don one of these admirable headpieces. If, on the other hand, you take it into your mind to bolt down the stairs, I might or might not shoot you in the back, but I can assure you that you'll next see your friend singing in the heavenly choir. And for goodness sake, keep that infernal device in mind. It's very much on the mind of that poor trussed up fellow topside. If all goes well, perhaps you'll have an opportunity to do the man the favor of saving his no doubt invaluable life. In short, the fate of your friends very much rests in your capable hands, so pray do not be foolhardy."

I stepped away, just as he asked, taking him entirely at his word. He removed one of the caps from its peg and tossed it to me. I put it on and watched as he tugged one tightly down over his ears, holding onto the pistol and gazing at me steadily, and all the time half smiling, as if he found the business slightly amusing. "I'll thank you to open the door and to step inside now," he said.

I dutifully lifted the bar out of its holdfasts, set it aside, and swung the door outward. Within lay a largish room. Again there was a window in the chalk, a stiff breeze from off the channel blowing through it, stirring the dust on the floor. On a wooden platform stood Busby's lamp, the lens shining mistily with a dim green glow. Behind it lay an array of jars and wires—the Bunsen battery that I had last seen in Busby's loft in Scarborough. Atop a small table were vials and bottles of various chemicals. To the left of the door a long sort of bench had been cut into the wall, and on it sat the open wooden coffin that I had seen in the photograph at the inn. St. Ives lay within it, his eyes closed, the lower half of the coffin lid fastened down. I could see movement behind his eyelids, as if he was dreaming, and his face was enlivened almost theatrically with rapidly altering emotions. His eyes jerked open and he uttered a quick gasp, and then they closed again, and his entire body seemed to twitch.

"Stand closer to your friend, if you will, Mr. Owlesby," Narbondo said. "It takes only one hand, you see, to manipulate the lever that increases the power of Busby's cleverly contrived ray, which leaves my other hand free to hold the pistol. You're perhaps aware that the emerald, which lends this lamp its pleasant green color, is very nearly played out, as they say. It's effective in close quarters, but now quite useless over distances. Its power is ebbing even as we speak. Still, it should provide us with some entertaining and edifying sport. I'm quite aware, by the way, that the stone recently delivered to our friend the Peddler might be a fraud. Professor St. Ives wouldn't be so easily persuaded to hand over the genuine article. That's why we esteem the man so highly, is it not? No, sir, I anticipated complications, betrayals, perhaps even opportunities. Now, purely in the interests of science, note the effect of the ray as I increase the power of the lamp."

The Professor's face contorted and twitched more rapidly now. He cried out, gasped heavily, and tried to sit up, although the coffin lid pressed downward on him, and he could do nothing to help himself. His eyes flew open, revealing a look of absolute, unutterable, maniacal terror, and he cried out in a tormented voice, his mad eyes sweeping blankly over my face.

Narbondo's expression, to the contrary, was alive with evident delight, as if he were witnessing a droll scene at the theatre. He licked his lips and narrowed his eyes, nodding his head slightly as if very well satisfied. And yet he was not entirely distracted, for he held the pistol steadily, aimed straight at me.

St. Ives shrieked now, and I could hear his feet hammering against the coffin lid and his teeth clacking together. He looked at me again, and I saw in his eyes, God help me, a flicker of recognition and a silent plea. Without a thought I turned and lunged toward Narbondo, thinking to put an end to his depredations once and for all. There was the shattering sound of the pistol firing, magnified in that small space, and I felt rather than heard myself scream in fear and pure animal loathing. —⟋

CHAPTER 13

Complications and Opportunities

IT TOOK TUBBY and Uncle Gilbert ten minutes of careful searching to find the cut in the hill where the keeper had alleged that the mouth of the cave was hidden. A dense stand of shrubbery disguised it, but someone had hacked a passage behind it, leading around a corner of rock to the low opening in the hillside. If they hadn't been told where to look, they wouldn't have found it, so completely was it hidden by shrubbery. They stood in the shadows now, taking stock, bushes crowded up against their backs, when they heard a voice coming their way from within the cave—someone apparently singing. They turned hastily and hurried back around the way they'd come, going to ground behind a heap of boulders. The singing—a fine tenor voice—grew louder, and the Peddler himself strode into view, walking jauntily downhill in the direction of the lighthouse like a happy man on holiday.

"Shall we follow him?" Uncle Gilbert whispered. "We can lay him out with the blackthorn, pitch his body off the cliff, and be done with another one of these villains."

"I suspect that he's off to the ransom, Uncle. If we knock him on the head, the greater plan goes awry."

"That's damned unfortunate. His head badly wants crushing."

They watched the Peddler make his way to the cottage, open the door, and step inside. He wouldn't find the keeper at home, for the man had already been hurried off in the direction of Eastbourne with his spare trousers and shirt tied up in a bindle. The keeper's absence might be a suspicious thing, but it couldn't be helped.

They returned to the cave mouth, listened for a moment, and then stepped into the near-darkness across a litter of leaves and sticks.

"No quarter for them," Uncle Gilbert said in a low voice. "That was my old dad's way. He fought at the Battle of the Nile, you know, and don't I wish I could have been there. I'd have knocked a Frenchman or two on the head. Perhaps one of these villains is a damned Frenchman."

"Certainly there'd be more glory in it," Tubby said, not feeling quite so brash as his uncle. He set out, endeavoring to see through the gloom, Uncle Gilbert coming along behind, the two of them walking ever downward into the nether regions of the earth, sometimes in the light of oil lamps, sometimes in darkness.

In due time they saw a brighter light ahead, coming from within what was apparently a room off the passage. There was the scuffling and banging of what sounded like someone laboring over heavy crates, and then two distinct voices, one of which said, "Blast your blasted arm," which was followed by "Bugger off," from the other one. A moment later the bottom corner of a large trunk appeared in the doorway, followed by the wheels of the upright, two-wheeled trolley that it rested upon.

Tubby and Uncle Gilbert stepped back into the shadows, watching as the Tipper himself appeared, pushing the first cart, which held a Saratoga trunk that towered over his head. A second trunk followed, this one pushed by the railway thief, whom Tubby recognized on the instant. He was turned nearly sideways so that the trunk and cart rested against his good arm, like a man shoving open a door with his shoulder. Soon they were out of sight around a bend in the tunnel.

"I say we come upon them from behind while they're discommoded by those trunks," Uncle Gilbert said.

Tubby nodded, but his uncle was already setting out, his statement being more in the line of an order than a suggestion. The two of them crept along like sneak thieves in a dark house. The passage straightened, and there ahead, quite close, stood their prey, the railway thief struggling with his burden, and the Tipper berating him. Tubby glided forward, the blackthorn stick at the ready, which was a good thing, for the Tipper looked back just then, saw him, and gave a shout, which was his undoing. Tubby swung the stick at his head, and the Tipper ducked forward, trying to get out of the way, but he caught the full weight of the club between the shoulder blades. He was driven forward, his forehead rebounding audibly off the corner of the heavy trunk. Uncle Gilbert had waded past Tubby now, his sword cane raised, calling on the railway thief to stand down. The man elected to flee. He hadn't taken three steps, however, before Uncle Gilbert drew back his arm and cast the sword cane like a whirligig at his knees, the weapon whistling as it flew. The man somersaulted forward in a tangle of arms and legs and lay for a surprised instant on his face before trying to rise again. Tubby was too quick for him, and the man found himself looking at the upraised blackthorn. He held up his good arm to fend off the blow.

"It was me that did for your other arm," Tubby said to him, "you crawling piece of filth. Do you deny it?"

"No sir," the man said unhappily, withdrawing his raised arm and tucking it sensibly away under his side. He made no further move to rise.

The Tipper was just then coming round. He stood up, staggered two paces toward the wall of the tunnel, and then collapsed again.

"Come my good fellow," Uncle Gilbert said to the railway thief. "Lend us your one good arm, and we'll let you keep it. Let's have a look inside that Saratoga trunk that our tiny friend was trundling. Jump to it, now."

Puzzled, the man crept to his feet and threw open the lid of the Tipper's trunk, which was filled with carefully stowed bottles of wine, waxed cheeses and cured meats. "Our good luck," Uncle Gilbert said, his eyes greedy. "To the victor go the spoils, eh nephew?" He gestured with his cane. "Stow the lot of it against the wall there, my man. Break so much as a bottle and it'll go rough for you."

He set about unloading the freight, piling it carefully against the wall, until the trunk was empty. The Tipper had come round again. He stood up unsteadily, holding onto the edge of the empty trunk with the look in his eyes of a man about to bolt. Before he had a chance, Uncle Gilbert bent forward and pushed him, and the Tipper toppled over into the trunk with a shout, the lid slamming down over him. Uncle Gilbert sat on it in order to do up the latches and fasten the two heavy leather belts that girt it, and just like that the Tipper found himself lying in the darkness of a locked Saratoga trunk. He continued to shout and to pummel the sides until Tubby whacked on the lid half a dozen times with the blackthorn.

"Now you, mate," Uncle Gilbert said to the railway thief. "That one's yours. I've taken a liking to you, and I give you my warrant that we'll return in due time to set you free—such freedom as you deserve, that is. As for the Tipper here, I have a notion to cold storage him in that room back yonder. It's tolerably dry down here, and he'll stay fresh as a pharaoh for the next century or two."

"You want me to get into the bleeding trunk?" the man said.

"As you value your neck," Uncle Gilbert told him. He unsheathed his sword and took a vicious swing in the man's general direction, and in a trice he was unloading the second trunk, which was filled with much the same sort of delicacies as the first—no doubt intended for Narbondo's larder aboard the submarine.

"In you go, then," Tubby said. "Easy does it." They stood on either side of him, crowding him into it, throwing the lid down and fastening it.

"They'll be tight as bugs here until we return," Uncle Gilbert said loudly, for the sake of the two prisoners. "And if we don't return they'll be dead men." He laughed out loud, claimed happily that he hadn't in his life had such sport as this, and shook Tubby's hand on a job well done.

———

HASBRO AWAKENED TO find himself bound into a chair—the very same chair that the keeper had been bound into a scant hour earlier, and with the same lengths of curtain line. He quickly found his wits and deduced that his wounds were perhaps more bloody than dangerous, and that the problem lay not in the bullet or possible concussion, but in the infernal device that sat like a toad on the floor some three feet from the chair in which he was tightly secured. It was a simple thing of wires, a clockwork mechanism, and a large bundle of explosives, and it ticked loudly in the quiet room. The face of the heavy clock was imprinted with a grinning moon. Inserted into one of the eyes was a copper peg, which must surely complete an electronic circuit when touched by the minute hand of the clock, which, it seemed to Hasbro, was moving in its revolution surprisingly quickly.

His first wild instinct was to raise the front legs of the chair in an endeavor to hop bodily backward, wanting to distance himself from the device. But although he succeeded, he quickly gave up on the effort, for the device was evidently large enough to blow the cottage and the lighthouse to pieces, and distance would avail him nothing without freedom and an open door.

He struggled now with the bonds, but they were cleverly tied, and his actions simply drew the knots tighter. There was a clasp knife in his pocket—he could feel its weight—but unless he could free either of his hands, it was useless to him. He bucked in the chair, coming down hard on one of the rear legs, which snapped off, tilting him slowly over sideways so that he slammed down onto his side on the floor. If it had been a front leg, it would have freed one of his feet, and he might yet win free, but as it was he could no longer bring any leverage to bear, and his struggles simply propelled the chair in a feeble circle, so that he ended up staring once again at the bomb.

He was weakened, too, by loss of blood or concussion, and it came into his mind that if he lost consciousness he was a dead man. He calmed himself by force of will, moderating his breathing, clearing his mind, and then very carefully he went about the process of testing each of his bonds in turn, distracted all the while by the maddening ticking of the clock, the seconds and minutes slipping away. Freeing a foot would avail him little, and so he attended to his wrists and arms, certain that force would work against him, and that subtlety and patience might prevail.

Time passed, although how much time he couldn't say. He found it necessary to stop more and more often simply to rest, and finally the desire to sleep came over him, subtlety and patience having invited it. His determination had leaked away with his vital fluids, and it was only with the very last vestiges of his consciousness that he heard the door behind him creak open and a gruff voice asking, "What the bloody hell is this now?" ——

CHAPTER 14

The Battle in the Sea Cave

AT THE SAME moment that the gunshot stunned my ears and I threw myself witlessly to the ground, I felt a spray of blown-apart chalk pepper the back of my head, and I realized that the bullet had gone wide, had struck the wall behind me. Narbondo corrected his aim in the heavy, ear-ringing silence that followed, gesturing me to my feet again. He began to utter something, but before the first words were out of his mouth, a shadow filled the doorway, and there stood the Peddler, an evil looking truncheon in his hand, what's sometimes called a "slung shot"—a heavy iron shot with a flexible handle, meant to kill or maim.

"I heard the gunshot, Doctor..." he started to say, and then he saw me standing there, my face still drawn with shock. "Good day to you Mr. Owlesby."

I said nothing. There was scarcely enough space in the small room for another person, and so he remained there in the doorway, digging into his pocket and removing the drawstring bag that he had taken from Hasbro. He handed it across to Narbondo, who fished out the large green stone from within and held it up between his eye and the window. Then he laid it on the table top, picked up a stoppered bottle of some sort of chemical, opened the bottle, and with a glass rod dipped out a droplet of the liquid and touched it to the emerald. A faint wisp of smoke rose from the surface. Narbondo shook his head sadly and swept the emerald onto the floor beneath the table, as if it were worth nothing.

"Mr. Burke," he said, "I suggest that you either don one of the asbestos caps or retire from the scene so that we can continue our experimentation. You've carried out your work admirably, and I thank you for it. I'll make my thanks more tangible in due time, but at the moment I intend to put Busby's interesting device to further tests. Professor St. Ives has made himself a willing subject, and it's time that we put him through his paces, as the quaint saying goes. You might want to adjust your cap, Mr. Owlesby."

The Peddler turned to leave, and in that very moment there was the sound of a heavy thud, and the man was precipitated bodily back into the room, sprawling on the floor, blood flowing copiously from his scalp onto the white chalk. Alice stepped into the doorway now, holding the oak bar from the door. There was cold murder in her eyes. She looked at St. Ives, lying blessedly still now, and then at Doctor Narbondo, who still held the pistol, which apparently meant nothing to her.

There was a long silence as she stared Narbondo down, and I believe that I saw doubt in his eyes for the first time. She reached into a pocket in her waist now and withdrew the fortified emerald, which she had clearly fished it out of the teapot before following me down the cliff, intent upon bringing it to Narbondo herself, choosing to be the one to decide its fate and the fate of her husband.

Narbondo and I stared at the emerald in her open palm, the silence heavy in the room, the world waiting. Then, breaking that almighty silence, there was the sound of a distant, very powerful explosion, and beyond the window I saw a perfect storm of birds flying skyward, and the air was rent with their calling.

"Alas," said Narbondo, shaking his head sadly. "I'm afraid that we've tarried too long with our experiments, and..."

"He's murdered Hasbro," I said to Alice, interrupting him. "They lured him to the lighthouse, locked him in, and detonated an infernal device."

"Of course," she said, her voice steady. "His baseness knows no bounds. It's a Devil's bargain, giving him the stone, and I choose not to bargain with the Devil." And with that she calmly and deliberately flung the fortified emerald, square through the center of the window. It glinted for a green moment in the sunlight and then soared out of sight, bound for the depths of the Channel. Submarine or no submarine, Narbondo would never in life find it.

"Well done!" Narbondo said, affecting his usual bonhomie. But his voice was pitched too high, so that he sounded rattled. He looked down at the Peddler, seeming to notice him for the first time, and he lost himself in a sudden, tearing rage and kicked the man savagely in the back of the head. The pistol shook in his hand, and when he aimed it in my direction, I took a step backward. Narbondo bent at the knees, groping for the cast away emerald beneath the table. He slipped the emerald into his pocket, and then awkwardly picked up Busby's lamp, yanking it loose from its wires, all the while watching us, murder in his eyes.

"Out, you go," he said simply.

Alice dropped her oak club. Narbondo wouldn't give her a chance to use it a second time. He was a careful man, was Narbondo. He had been surprised once, but that would be the end of it. We were at his mercy.

"Downward," he said simply, and I set out down the long steep flight of stairs that led to the moored submarine. I knew but one thing—that I would not allow Alice to board that submarine while I had any life left in me. Soon enough we stepped down onto the boards of the dock. Away to seaward stood the sheer wall of the cavern. There was no sign of an opening of any sort, but seawater was perpetually sucked out from somewhere beneath the wall, and then, after a moment, it swept back in again, the submarine rising and falling on the surge. The entrance to the sea cave, then, lay hidden beneath the surface of the sea.

Narbondo, ever vigilant, fiddled with the latching mechanism on one of the porthole panels on the side of the metal ship, swinging open the panel. I stepped in front of Alice, crowding her back toward the stairs. "See to St. Ives," I whispered.

"Silence!" Narbondo croaked.

But instead of silence there came a growing clamor from above, where Tubby and Gilbert heaved along downward, already halfway to the landing outside the room where St. Ives was held prisoner. From out of that room, as if on cue, staggered the Peddler, truncheon in his hand. Hearing the clatter above him, he turned stupidly and lifted the truncheon as if the mere sight of it would give Tubby pause. But pause wasn't in it for Tubby. Inertia carried him down the last few stairs, and he was swinging the blackthorn even as he came along, cracking the Peddler on the shoulder with twenty stone of moving weight behind the blow.

The Peddler would have been knocked into a cocked hat, if there had been one, but there was not. There was empty air at the edge of that precarious landing. He endeavored to catch himself, wind-milling his arms like a man in a play before toppling over the edge. We watched him fall, shattering himself on the rocks in shallow water, the ocean washing in around him, crabs scuttling away to safety. Tubby stopped just short of the brink and leaned heavily against his stick. But already Uncle Gilbert was rampaging down the stairs, death or glory in his eyes, his sword unsheathed. I saw Narbondo's pistol rise to stop him, and I sprang forward, clipping Narbondo's arm near the elbow. He fell backward with a grunt, the pistol clanging on the metal of the ship and dropping into the dark water. He rolled sideways, back into the vessel, and then sprang to his feet like an ape and reached out to claw at the hatch in order to yank it closed. But he was hindered by Busby's lamp, which he still held on to. He was desperate to salvage it, everything else having gone completely to smash in the last three minutes. It was Alice who sprang forward and snatched if from him, yanking it away viciously. He let out a wild groan, feinted as if to climb out onto the dock again, then slid back into the bowels of the submarine, slamming shut the hatch despite my endeavoring to stop him.

We busied ourselves in trying to find a way in, thinking to haul Narbondo out by his boot heels, but there was nothing to do but hammer on the sides of the submarine as it sank slowly into the dark water with an upsurge of bubbles. There was a humming noise, and lights sprang on within, shining through the portholes and illuminating in the water around it a garden of waving waterweeds and darting fish. Slowly the vessel glided forward and downward, and within moments the lights winked out as it passed from the cavern into the open ocean. —◦

The Last Word

WE RELEASED ST. IVES from bondage straightaway, Alice naturally taking charge. She was solicitous, but left St. Ives his dignity—no fawning over him, only a few tears, her emotion passing away quickly, but enough of it for St. Ives to take heart. You could see the change in his face, the lifting of the clouds that had darkened his sensibilities that distant-seeming night at the Half Toad. Although he managed to accompany us without aid, he obviously knew little of where he was or how he had got there. We trudged tiredly along, Uncle Gilbert regaling us with the tale of the taking of the keeper and of persuading him to give up the location of the hillside cave, and then of persuading the Tipper and his crony to climb into Saratoga trunks, which Uncle Gilbert suggested be trundled down onto the dock now in order to be cast into the sea.

Neither Alice nor I had the heart to say anything about the explosion, although the truth would soon be known—sooner than I anticipated, in fact. The great periscope mirror was of vague interest to St. Ives in his still-fuddled state, although it was of monumental interest to me, for there in plain sight stood the Belle Tout Light and the keeper's cottage, perfectly whole.

The cottage door opened even as we watched, and out walked the keeper himself, looking back and apparently saying something through the open door. He carried a crate full of items that he had apparently looted from the cottage and lighthouse.

"Forsooth!" Uncle Gilbert cried. "The villain returns! We should have burnt his eyes out when the poker was hot! I mean to say…" He glanced at Alice and left off sheepishly.

"I'm persuaded that it's Hasbro's good luck that he *did* return," I said. And it turned out to be true, which we discovered when we followed Tubby and Uncle Gilbert out through the cave into the midday sunlight of the Downs. The keeper, having been ignominiously chased off by our friends, had sneaked back to the cottage to recover a purse of money from beneath a hearthstone. One can only imagine his surprise when he found Hasbro tied into an overturned chair and the infernal device ticking away, getting ready to blow the entire place to flinders. In a desperate effort to save his hidden loot, he had fetched the device out through the open door and hurled it off the cliff, apparently setting off the bomb, which did no more than frighten the sea birds. Then he had prised up the hearthstone, retrieved his purse, filled a crate with odds and ends, bid Hasbro a good day, and went away again.

It was we who untied a grateful Hasbro. Tubby's figurative elephant had been knocked about, but was happily reassembled. St. Ives showed signs of recovery, and so to enliven him further we repaired to the cavern, where we made a brilliant lunch of the would-be contents of Doctor Narbondo's larder, including several bottles of superb wine—I can't recall quite how many. The rest of Narbondo's considerable stores eventually found their way to Uncle Gilbert's house, small payment for services rendered. As for the Tipper and Mr. Goodson, we took them along down to Eastbourne, secure in their Saratoga trunks, where we left them in the care of the authorities.

—∿∿∿—

Several weeks later, after Alice and St. Ives had returned from their holiday on Lake Windermere, we revisited the Downs on a balmy, early summer day, only to discover that the hidden entrance to the cavern had collapsed in what appeared to have been an explosion. Boulders of shattered chalk littered the ground without, and the once-dense shrubbery was blown to leafless, broken sticks. We walked out to the edge of the cliffs, where we discovered that the hand-line down the face of Beachy Head had been cut away as well. Determined to see the adventure through, we made our slow and treacherous descent along the narrow trail, only to discover that the great stone that had sheltered the cleft above the Channel had fallen inward—more likely *drawn* inward, if that were possible—blocking the entrance so effectively that the cavern had become the domain of sea birds and bats and other creatures small enough to find their way in through cracks and crevices. Narbondo had evidently returned to Beachy Head, either to make his fortress secure or to destroy it.

We spent the remainder of the morning scouring the Downs near the copse where we had hidden on that fateful morning, searching for the lens of Narbondo's fabulous periscope. It was a wonderfully sunny day, and yet there was no telltale glint of sunlight on glass. The lens must have had a clear view of the Belle Tout light and the meadow roundabout it, and so must have been in plain sight, and yet it was maddeningly undiscoverable. After a time the idea came into my mind that we must be looking at the lens but not seeing it, the victims of a master illusionist. I was possessed by the uncanny certainty that we ourselves were at that very moment being observed in our fruitless meanderings—that somewhere in the depths of the chalk, Dr. Narbondo was even then gazing into his mirror, his hands on the spokes of the ship's wheel, his mind revolving upon schemes of revenge. —◌

The Adventure of
the Ring of Stones

For Deuzie and Kydd
This tale of the sea...

The Voyage of the *Celebes Prince*

*I*N THE YEAR *1843, I, James Douglas, signed on to the hired clipper* Celebes Prince *out of Portsmouth, bound for Hispaniola. I was rated ship's boy, twelve years old that very week. We were to return with rum, sugar, and bath sponge, as easy as kiss-my-hand if the wind was fair. The* Celebes Prince *was what is called an opium clipper, and I knew well enough that she was a smuggler, but I was a boy with few scruples in that regard, and the Captain treated me well. The first mate told me the Captain had a boy my age who had died, fell from the maintop and hit his head on a carronade, and that meant something, I suppose. I could use a sextant, and I knew the night sky as well as any man aboard, barring the Captain, who was a right seaman but a dark, bloody-minded man in most regards, with a taste for Port Royal rum that would have done for him if he'd lived long enough.*

We soon picked up the variables and logged a hundred-forty sea miles a day, straight down into the northeast trades and in among the Caribbean Islands. We took on rum and sugar and bath sponge in Santo Domingo, filled our water, and weighed again, the Captain having a fear of the yellow jack, which was mortal that season. Two sponge fishermen came along, dark brown men. I was told that they were the last of the Taino Indians, who had mainly died out on Hispaniola. One was deaf from his time spent in deep water, and the other didn't seem right in the head. What use we had for sponge fishermen I couldn't say, our hold already being full of that item.

We were bound for home, I thought—a fast run if our luck held— Portsmouth or thereabouts, perhaps a handy cove first where we could offload the rum. The second morning I awoke at eight bells in the dark and went on deck. We were at anchor, rolling on a moderate swell. Just to starboard lay an island, a rocky coast with surf running, although there was a likely bay sheltered by a long reef where a ship's boat might lie at ease. Even in the darkness I could see a mountain in the center of the island, where smoke was rising—a volcano, I thought, although I had never seen one. There was no beach, just the black mouth of a sea cave and cliffs, very steep, rising away on either side. I could see the water boiling over the reef in the moonlight, no doubt a dry reef when the tide fell. The air was clear, and the stars shone, and without a thought I fetched the instrument and took a reading, curious how far we had sailed in the night, Santo Domingo being 18 degrees north and a little under 70 degrees west. Nearly 200 sea miles was my answer, although it was mere curiosity at the time. The island had a name, but I won't write it here, nor utter it neither.

We rowed across to the cove four hours later in the launch, at eight bells in the morning watch, four pulling on the oars, including me. I could pull middling well for a boy, and the Captain favored me. Those left aboard the ship were to fire the bow chaser as a warning if there was a sail in sight, for we didn't want company. The Indians sat in the stern. No one spoke, and there was never a man more intent than the Captain on what he was about, although what it was I didn't yet know. He carried two pistols on his belt, and it was the pistols and the silence that put my mind to working, and the more it worked, the more it turned on treasure—something on the bottom of the sea, which called for the sponge fishers. Anyone could see that the Captain was half gone in rum, even at that early hour. His flesh stank of it. Mayhaps he hadn't slept and had finished his bottle waiting for the sun.

We rowed into the cove, protected by the reef, which stood out of the water now, and the sea cave open before us. The roof of the cave was a rough dome fifteen feet above our heads, with sea birds nesting along the walls and a great lot of noise. There was sea wrack and flotsam that had washed into the cave, the dark water below ink-black, how deep I couldn't say for the darkness in the cave. We put the anchor over the side, and played out fifteen fathoms of cable, which told the tale.

There we sat, not a word said, and everyone in main fear of the Captain, who was in a state. It was still dim in the cave, despite the sun in the east. The Captain took out his pocket-watch now and then to see the time slip past, until he tipped me a wink at last, and said, "Stand by, Mr. Douglas, and you'll see something," although he seemed to be talking to himself. No sooner were the words out of his mouth than a ray of light shone into the cavern from a window in the east wall, a jagged crack like a half-open mouth, that hadn't seemed to be there a moment before. The ray of sunlight played upon the water, the sea floor coming visible, the water as clear as air. Straightaway I saw a long, black shark deep down, then two and three, circling. The sponge divers saw them, too, and didn't much like the look of them, for the two of them were going over the side. "They're nought but gammon," the Captain told them, but it was the brace of pistols that he used to persuade Indians overboard, for there was no time to spare, only a short period of sunlight, and then darkness in the cave until the following day, when the sun crossed the window again.

There on the bottom, fifteen fathoms deep, lay what looked to be a giant great pearl that a man would need a barrow to move. It rested within a ring of white rocks that seemed to have been carefully placed, although that scarcely seems possible, and so was protected from the surge that rolled into the cave and might have washed the pearl away otherwise. Sea fans passed over it in the current, and then moved back, so that you could see it again plain. It couldn't be a pearl, of course, not that size. "Ambergris, Mr. Douglas," the Captain said, nodding at me as we watched the Indians kicking hard for the bottom, hauling themselves down the anchor cable hand over hand. They let go the cable and swam to the prize, the two of them grappling with the great ball, lifting it from where it was settled. It was later that I was told that ambergris weighed little. Indeed, it floated on the surface unless it was very old and dense, as this was. Up they came, quicker than you would have thought, but followed by one of the black-bodied sharks, three times the men's length. It seemed to brush the two of them in passing. They let loose of the burden, and so it fell. The two of them broke the surface empty handed, having been under for three full minutes. The Captain cursed them for the loss and glanced at the light shining through the crack, which glowed yellow now as if the sun was peering straight through.

The bosun said that we should have brought a rope and a net, and that we might try again tomorrow morning. It was dead obvious he was right, but rum had dimmed the Captain's mind, and the ambergris had been a secret of his own keeping. "Be damned to tomorrow," he said, and sent the Indians down again, although they would have climbed into the boat but for the pistols. Two more times they tried and failed, the sharks showing little interest now. The water was growing dimmer. The fourth attempt very nearly fetched the prize, *although it was in that moment, when they were on the bottom, that we heard cannon fire and saw the smoke from the chaser. It was plain that something was dead wrong with the* Celebes Prince. *The ship was shaking like a dog throwing off water, and she canted to larboard as if driven over by a heavy gust of wind, although there was no wind. There was no explaining it, not from where we sat in the sea cave.*

The Captain stared at the ship, shaking his head sharp, like his mind was adrift and he was trying to call it back. Up came the Indians from the bottom, the great pearl wedged between them, hauling themselves one-handed along the anchor cable, the boat dipping with the strain of it. The bow chaser fired again. The Indians neared the surface, bubbles rising from their nostrils. I saw what the two of them didn't see—the black shadow rising behind them. One of the two—the deaf man, I believe, was jerked downward. Blood clouded the water, and the ball of ambergris fell away into it once again. I saw the man's face in the last moment, the horror on it plain, his severed leg crosswise in the shark's mouth, the fish's brethren rising from the depths, either of them big enough to knock the launch cockeyed if they had a mind to.

The second Indian's head broke the water. He was empty handed, his eyes full of fear, and him gripping the anchor cable like salvation itself. The Captain held his sheath knife in his hand, and without a word he cut the cable, and the Indian fell back as the launch moved away with the surge. "Leave him!" the Captain shouted, cuffing the bosun on the side of the head when he leant over to clutch the man's hand. The Indian swam two strokes toward us, his death written on his face. On the instant his body flew half out of the water as one of the sharks took him, the huge mouth and teeth cutting him in half at the waist, a bloody spray spattering the boat, which nearly capsized, the wave thrown up by the shark's lunge washing us farther toward the cave mouth. The cave was fast falling into darkness now, and we bent to the oars, watching the sharks as they fed. I saw the man's torso jerk again and again as it was butchered, and then the sun rose another notch, and the light went out of the sea cave, and we were in the cove again and very soon in the open ocean, leaving one horror for another, or so it seemed to me.

The Celebes Prince *leapt upon the sea now, like the bodies of the Indians had done. The mainmast went by the boards, and the sails and rigging fell across the deck, as if she had been shattered by the first blast of a hurricane. And yet we could see nothing of any enemy. The ship was caught in the grasp of some great spirit, which was destroying it as violently as the sharks had destroyed the two sponge divers. The bosun tied onto the seizing and hauled himself up the mainchains, the Captain at his heels and the rest of the men following. There was a vast creaking and rending of timbers from the ship, and the sound of screams and shouting. I stood alone on the pitching deck of the launch, full of stony fear, the memory of those butchered divers still before my mind's eye.*

During the pull back to the ship, I had seen that to the north lay cloud drift over what must be an island, and it came to me now to leave the ship to its fate, which I could not alter in any event. As soon as it entered my mind to do so, I slipped the knot and sat on the thwart, taking the oars in my hands, in a moderate hurry now that I knew what I was about. Before I was thirty yards from the ship, however, there sounded a vast cracking, the Celebes Prince *listed to starboard, and as God is my witness, the bower anchor itself pierced the side of the ship near the waterline. I mean to say that it smashed straight through the hull, like an arrow through straw. I set out rowing with a will, and when I was perhaps a half mile away, thinking to reach the island, I saw the ship cant sideways again, stay there, and start to settle. In three minutes she was drawn under.*

I knew in my heart that I must go back in order to pick up survivors, but I could not. I knew also that the island with the sea cave was cursed, and the sea around it haunted. I made landfall on the island before night and drew the launch up a stream out of the jungle, setting it upside down for a snug roof, and there I lived for a time before a ship put in for water and I was saved. I made up a lie, left the launch behind, since it didn't fit with the lie, and found myself in Santo Domingo, living there for three months before taking ship for Portsmouth once again, a year and two months after setting out. By then the sea cave and the destruction of the Celebes Prince *had come to be very much like a figment to me, and at night I dreamt of sea fans waving over that ball of ambergris, and the sharks circling, and the water red with blood.*

I set this account down in my own hand and gave it of my own free will to my friend Reginald Sawney when I set out for home. Whether any but me came away from the wreck of the Celebes Prince *I never learned. I take my oath that what I write here is true.*

—James Douglas

PART I

Captain Sawney's Log

CHAPTER 1

Ambush at the Half Toad

A WEEK FOLLOWING THE Snow Hill Massacre, which had rocked Smithfield and all of London, I found myself once again at William Billson's Half Toad Inn, Lambert Court, along with the brilliant Professor Langdon St. Ives and his man Hasbro, who had traveled with St. Ives these many years and was more friend than factotum. We were waiting on Tubby Frobisher and his eccentric and fabulously rich Uncle Gilbert, the two of them a worrisome quarter of an hour overdue. Tubby was coming down from Chingford, and Gilbert up from his mansion in Dicker, the old man anxious to communicate with us face-to-face. It was he who had summoned us. The mails weren't to be trusted, Gilbert had told us, and we were to destroy the missive that called us to the Half Toad.

We were well used to Gilbert's fancies and had done as he'd asked, ascertaining from the summons that he had in mind a sea voyage of some four weeks duration, the destination a well-kept secret: somewhere in the Atlantic, given the brevity of the voyage, but whether to the high northern latitudes or to the tropics we knew not. His privately-owned, ocean-going steam yacht was moored at the West India Docks. Our curiosity piqued, we had come along to the Half Toad, dunnage in hand, St. Ives evidently relieved to be active once again after a long period of hibernation.

Nearly a year had transpired since the terrible business of the Aylesford Skull, during which time St. Ives had gone to ground in Kent, playing the role of the gentleman farmer. He had seen to the building of an oast house on his and Alice's considerable property during that mild fall and winter, and in the spring to the planting of a cherry orchard. The breezes of early summer, however, generated a certain nervous energy in the man, the old wanderlust rising in him like a tide. He had been denying nature, of course—something that Alice understood all too well—and it was she who insisted that he agree to Gilbert's voyage. Meanwhile, she and the children and my own betrothed Dorothy toddled off to Scarborough for their annual summer visit to Alice's aged grandmother, leaving the running of their acreage in Kent in the hands of the admirable Mrs. Langley, old Binger, the groundskeeper, and young Finn Conrad.

Foot traffic in Smithfield was uncommonly sparse this evening, and there were few customers, the bloody murders having cast a shadow over the neighborhood that hadn't lifted yet. But it was all the better for our clandestine meeting with Tubby and Gilbert. Billson, who had the physical properties of a blacksmith and the mind of a natural philosopher, was cooking with a keen eye and a generous hand, turning a multi-armed spit that skewered two dozen of Henrietta Billson's fat sausages, the drippings basting three plump pheasants on another spit directly below, the fire sizzling happily. Billson had just served out delicate mounds of lobscouse as a kickshaw, molded in tiny pie dishes and swirling beneath a cloud of steam redolent of nutmeg, juniper berries, and corned beef. Billson subscribes to the odd habit of serving lobscouse with a brown onion sauce, by the way, which I heartily recommend, the entire business, lobscouse and sauce both, thickened with pounded ship's biscuit that had borne the government stamp—an inverted arrow—before Billson pulverized it with a belaying pin.

Billson had been a sailor, you see, in the years before he married Henrietta and purchased the Half Toad. Indeed, he had brought an immense, carved, wooden toad home with him from the West Indies—a fanciful ship's figurehead, the ship itself having been blown to flinders, turning the toad into a missile that had very nearly done for Billson when it splashed down like a meteor not three feet from his head. But the toad had meant his salvation, for he had clung to it through the long night, the rest of the crew dead, the ship sunk. The heroic amphibian now looks out from its perch above the door on Fingal Street, its broad mouth set in a mysterious smile that brings to the well-tempered mind Leonardo's *Mona Lisa*, and never more evidently than after one has consumed two quarts of Billson's best ale, Old Man Newt.

I had just put a share of it away, the three of us having decided to whet our appetites and whistles while we waited for Tubby and Gilbert. I was admiring in a happy reverie the old oak wainscot, the etchings by Hogarth that adorned the wall, and the pheasants on the spit, my mind idle but well satisfied. Lars Hopeful, the halfwit tapboy, had renewed our jug of ale, and the window behind us stood open, letting in a grateful evening breeze. The bell of St. Bartholomew the Great began to toll just as Mrs. Billson was putting a bread pudding into the oven, which would come out again, hot and with buttered rum set aflame, when we had need of it later in the evening. I recall having turned to the window at the sound of the bell, looking for the crenellated tower of St. Bartholomew over the rooftops, when there came the sound of a wild curse, a pistol shot, and running feet.

We all leapt up, doubly alarmed because of the recent murders. I leaned out through the casement and was astounded to see Tubby Frobisher himself chasing a man out of Lambert Court—a swarthy, heavy-set man, although not so heavy as Tubby, who was milling along with his blackthorn stick gripped in his hand, very much like an enraged hippo and wearing an old Bollinger hat with a vast, bowl-shaped crown skewered with peacock feathers. There was blood on the fleeing man's coat from a wound in the shoulder—no doubt a bullet—although it wasn't apparently slowing him down.

I went straight out through the window onto the sidewalk and gave chase, my fork in my own hand, not knowing that St. Ives and Hasbro had also gone out, although through the inn door. A four-horse carriage blocked my path, followed by a man driving a gaggle of ill-natured geese, and by the time I had navigated the carriage and the geese and set out again, I had lost sight of Tubby, who had apparently followed his prey into a byway behind Long Lane. I raced into that same byway in time to see Tubby's man turning into a narrow alley just as a second man—an ally, no doubt—stepped out from behind a brick chimney and tripped Tubby up. Tubby sprawled forward, his blackthorn spinning away, the man raising a cricket bat into the air in order to crush Tubby's skull with it.

I sang out, "Stand, or I blow your head off!" and charged straight at him with the tines of the fork gripped in my fist. I had no pistol, of course, but there was some chance he had heard the earlier pistol shot or had seen the bloody wound in his companion's shoulder and would take the fork handle for a pistol barrel. In any event, he hesitated, considered the quickly closing distance between us, looked in vain for his companion, and abruptly ran off, easily cowed, thank God.

I ranged up beside Tubby, who was crawling to his feet. The sight of the fork handle set him to laughing, his sense of humor easily overcoming his gratitude and any lingering distress from the sight of that upraised cricket bat. He dusted his hands off, shrugged his shoulders, fetched his blackthorn and his fallen hat, which had rolled away like a cartwheel, and the two of us walked back to the inn, Tubby hypothesizing that the man had taken me for a cannibal when he had seen the fork. "You put the fear into him, Jack," he said. "The horror of being eaten is one of the primal instincts. There was stark terror in the man's eyes when he fled." He banged his Bollinger hat against his thigh, handed his cudgel to me, and smoothed the hat's peacock feathers with his fingers.

A reply to his comment about the fork would merely have compounded Tubby's wit, or what passes for it. "Your Bollinger is somewhat past the fashion," I told him, deciding to insult his hat, which was scandalously stained and beaten. "I admire it immensely, of course. It's…seasoned. Some might say 'stained' or disreputable, but not I. A man's hat is his own business."

"I won't sell it to you, Jack, even if you beg. It's my lucky hat. The peacock feathers are from the royal flock, by the way. I doubt you've ever seen such a radiant, sapphire blue. It brings out the color in my eyes, I believe."

We came in through the door of the Half Toad. Our friends, including Uncle Gilbert, were sitting once again at the table by the window, Gilbert just then draining a glass of ale while wiping the sweat from his brow with a kerchief. He stood up, relieved to see Tubby apparently unscathed, and he shook my hand heartily, saying, "Well met, Jack." Then he shifted his Gladstone bag from what had been my chair, waited for us to sit, and filled our glasses from the jug.

"Yes, sir, it was indeed an ambush," Gilbert said to St. Ives, apparently having begun to tell the tale before we arrived. "Thank God I brought my pistol; we might have been dead men else." He nodded heartily. "You see, I recognized the man, as did Tubby—Billy Stoddard by name, the stinking reptile. The two of us bearded him in his den not two years ago, at Beachy Head, as perhaps you recall."

"The lighthouse keeper from the Belle Tout Light?" I asked, realizing that it could quite easily have been that very villain's back that I had seen vanishing down that byway.

"I'll never forget his face," Gilbert said, "a pig's bladder with poached grapes for eyeballs. I should have done him the service of taking his head off at the shoulders and presenting it to him on a plate when I had him tied into a chair at Beachy Head. We could have pitched his body over the cliff, serving him out like he did to poor Captain Sawney, God rest him."

"I didn't have the pleasure of meeting this Billy Stoddard," St. Ives said (and in fact St. Ives had lain comatose within a cavern in the chalk cliffs themselves when the temporary lighthouse keeper had fled away along the bluffs).

"Perhaps Stoddard meant to repay you for infamous way you used him," Hasbro said.

"No," Gilbert assured us, shaking his head again by way of punctuation. He leaned forward, smiling now and looking around like a conspirator. "I'm perfectly certain that he wanted...the *thing*...the reason I summoned you here," he whispered.

We nodded, although we only half understood. The fact of the summons was obvious, the reason not at all.

He opened the Gladstone bag, in which lay his pistol, clearly visible, and withdrew a small, leather-bound journal, much worn and rimed with salt. He turned to a random page, which appeared to contain a tally of bird sightings that his birding friend Captain Sawney had totted up, perhaps from his aerie in the Belle Tout Light in the years before he had fallen (or had been pushed by Billy Stoddard) to his death from the top of the cliff. Gilbert opened the book briefly to the title page now and held it out for us to read. It bore the legend, "Hispaniola, Reginald Sawney, 1844." It was indeed a birding log, but compiled forty years previously in the Caribbean, replete with dates and tallies and species: the purple gallinule, the sandhill crane, the snowy plover, coots, crakes, egrets, guinea fowl, and dozens of others. Why anyone would endeavor to ambush two stout men in order to steal a birding log was a mystery—a mystery that Gilbert Frobisher understood full well, the answer to which apparently lay in the palm of his hand.

"No doubt you gentlemen believe this log to be innocent enough," Gilbert said. "What would you say, Jacky? Are you a bird fancier?"

"Certainly," I told him, "well roasted and served with potatoes and spring onions."

He winked at me and laughed, the recent violence no longer troubling him. The smile, which revealed the pleasure he took in his superior knowledge, reminded me absolutely of Tubby, as did his vast girth, the difference between them having to do with Gilbert's advanced age—past sixty, although strangely hearty despite the years—and the absence of hair atop Gilbert's head. They might have been twins otherwise.

"I'll admit to seeing nothing of great value in it," Hasbro said, after Gilbert had closed the book and returned it to the bag, "although surely it would be of interest to a naturalist. The islands of the Caribbean must be a very treasure trove of bird species."

"And of other treasures, gentlemen, I assure you," Gilbert said in a low voice. "Treasures that beggar the imagination."

He sat back in his chair and fell silent, looking with vast pleasure at the utterly appropriate pheasants now arriving at the table, already cut into pieces, along with sausages, roasted potatoes, long beans with butter sauce, and a heap of crispy salmon fritters as a sort of relish, fish and fowl together being recommended by Henrietta, generally at removes, although in this instance our hurried schedule warranted the lot of it served up at once. There were bottles of burgundy as well, and more of the onion sauce, this batch heavy with the smell of sage.

Gilbert was evidently happy to keep us suspended while he ate. He knew absolutely that the word "treasures" was now uppermost in everyone's mind, reigning there just as Gilbert reigned over the table. The old man set about his pheasant as if he'd been two years at sea, picking up a leg and slathering it with onion sauce, then forking up an unctuous sausage with his free hand, so that he might have both appendages working at once, in the manner of an octopus. Gilbert and Tubby are trenchermen of the first water, you see—a vast emptiness within the two of them crying out to be filled, a process that reminds one of shoveling sand into a sinkhole. The bottles went round, the potatoes and long beans and sausages vanished from their dishes, and Henrietta Billson heaped more into them and brought new bottles to the table, whisking away the old. It was the loaves and fishes come again.

I was emboldened, finally, to fill the glasses ostentatiously in order to propose a toast: "To our venture, gentlemen, whatever it might entail, and may we discover what it entails some time this side of the grave."

We tipped the glasses back, Gilbert grinning at me and nodding. He picked up a drumstick and sucked the last fragments of meat from the bone. Then he put his head out the window to have a cautious look around before pulling his head back in and drawing the casement closed behind it. Gesturing at me with the drumstick, he asked, "What do you know about whales, Jack? The sperm whale? The cachalot?"

"I've read Mr. Melville's book," I told him.

"Then surely you're the learned man of the world. Did Mr. Melville expound upon..." and at this juncture he once again surveyed the room before dropping his voice, "...the phenomenon of *ambergris* at all?" We all leaned in closely now, our supper quite forgotten, the word having fetched our attention, as he well knew it would.

"The account of the substance was the subject of a brief chapter, as I recall," I told him. "I remember that it forms in the belly of the whale and is excreted from time to time in hard lumps, often loaded up with the beaks of squid. It's thought that perhaps the beaks are the irritant that gives rise to the production of the substance."

"*The beaks of squid!*" Gilbert said, nodding ponderously. "Just so. No doubt that's valuable information, Jack, for the man who fancies such a thing as a discarded squid beak. But the perfumeries, what do they pay for the substance itself, and never mind the beaks? By the ounce, let's say. None of your infernal, recently excreted filth, Jack, but ambergris washed and tumbled by the salt sea and the ocean winds until it has the appearance of a pearl. Dense enough to sink to the bottom of the sea, by God! The French eat it, you know, although there's precious little that a Frenchman doesn't eat. Imagine a great globe of it, if you can, three or four times the size of a man's head." He held his arms apart, stretching them wide by way of illustration, squinting at the lot of us. "A vast ball upward of thirty inches in diameter, lads, and as round as the moon. Imagine, if you will, the whale from whence the phenomenon was ejected, a whale well beyond a hundred feet in length, a vast great leviathan, which, if it desired, could swallow enough Jonahs to make up a dinner party very like our own, and with room left over for Balaam and his talking ass, by God. What would you say to that, Jacky? Can you place a *value* on such a thing?"

Gilbert waited, and he might have waited forever for all of me, for I had no idea. "A bloody great heap of gold ducats," I said to him.

He sat back in his chair and smiled with amusement. "What a fellow you are, Jack. Pray tell me, what constitutes a *heap*? Define your terms."

"Hundreds of thousands of pounds," Hasbro put in, getting to the heart of it. "Many hundreds. There's no precedent for such a thing, however—not as you describe it. The perfumeries would never see the item, if it existed. It would be in the hands of a fabulously wealthy collector. Only a man with an uncommon fortune could afford to keep it."

"Indeed," Gilbert said, nodding slowly. "Unless it's the man who finds it and takes it in the first place, eh?" He winked heavily. "Oh, it exists, right enough, lads; so it does. Now, shall I tell you the secret of Captain Sawney's log?" —◦

CHAPTER 2

Trouble in Pennyfields

THERE WAS A rumble of heartfelt assent when Gilbert uttered his question, to which the old man shook his head and responded by saying, "Presently, but not here. No sir. You'll have to be patient. We'll miss our tide if we don't look sharp." He shoved the log into his bag again, snapping it shut.

"God help us..." I started to say, when Henrietta Billson appeared with the flaming pudding and a bottle of cognac. We pledged each other's health, shoveled more food into our mouths, and had no sooner licked our plates clean like greedy dogs than a private coach reined up outside, the letters GF in gilt paint on the doors. Gilbert threw open the casement, waved his napkin at the cadaverous driver, pressed a sum of money into Henrietta's hand, and bundled the lot of us through the door, gripping his pistol and looking roundabout himself savagely, anxious, it seemed to me, to blow someone's head off.

We rattled away toward the river, the coach burdened with our persons and our baggage, through dark streets that were very much awake in the summer moonlight. I felt as if I had been taken up by the press gang: summoned to the meeting at the Half Toad and then ignominiously shanghaied before the pudding had completed its plunge into my gullet. The coach slowed its capering pace in order to avoid running down the pressing throng as we descended through Limehouse—Lascars and Chinese and Arabs in colorful dress, the prostitutes and the destitute dressed in rags, the sailors just back from foreign shores and kicking up Jack's-a-dying with their pay.

Low lodging houses lined the road, phantom courtyards lying within a mephitic gloom, and here and there a sputtering gas-jet to enliven the night, illuminating wastes of broken tile and brick, villainous gin shops, and opium dens. A black reek poured from chimneys, the smell of it mingling with the stink of fried fish shops and the conflicting odors of the hundreds of thousands of tons of goods in the warehouses above and below ground: tobacco and spirits, sugar and molasses, tar and cordage. The entire neighborhood—buildings, ramshackle and tilting away on either side and darkened by soot and dirt and poverty—was colorful in a way to make Hogarth shudder.

The carriage turned off West India Dock Road, proceeding along a narrow street through Pennyfields where it drew to a premature halt adjacent to a general shop, so called, in front of which was a clutter of old iron, kitchen debris, broken wooden chairs, and rags hung from hooks. Some short distance down stood a down-at-heel public house with the 'Jolly Tar' painted on a sign hanging over the door—not intentionally ironic, I assumed.

"God's rabbit, Boggs! What is it?" Uncle Gilbert shouted when the carriage remained still. He opened the door and peered out. Our coachman, a narrow cockney man with a long face, was trading hard words with someone unseen. Within moments all of us were out of the carriage and looking on. A dead cow utterly blocked the road, its master, a man in a filthy apron, was explaining that it had collapsed there and died and that he couldn't shift it without help. The story was highly unlikely, since the cow stank, and its legs were thrust out from a bloated midsection. Despite that, I had no suspicion of a threat until I saw St. Ives and Hasbro signal to each other, followed by the issuance of Gilbert's pistol.

Some distance in front of us stood the forests of masts rising from the docks. Black smoke tumbled from the chimneys of steamships, for the tide was making and there would be great activity for the next two or three hours. I could see moonlight on a sort of canal just forty feet away. We were very near our goal, and it occurred to me, rather stupidly, that we were hearty enough to haul our own dunnage the next hundred yards and leave the coachman to deal with the cow.

No sooner had the thought entered my head, than the owner of the cow simply bolted, disappearing through a nearby open door. None of us were foolish enough to follow. Gilbert swiveled this way and that, pointing his pistol, looking for trouble. Tubby gripped his blackthorn as if he meant to use it, and Hasbro had drawn a pistol of his own from within his coat. There were footfalls behind us now—four men coming at a run—and more footfalls and what sounded like the banging of a pan from an alley on our right. The coachman climbed down onto the pavement, standing next to Gilbert, who aimed a pistol back down the road as if to shoot past my head, compelling me to drop to the street. There was a loud report and a flash of fire from the muzzle. As if by magic the four men had vanished into the warren of courtyards and passageways. The open door of the Jolly Tar swung shut with a bang. Someone called out a warning—Tubby, I believe—just before a heavy object struck the road very nearby, glass shattering—a wooden crate of bottles. I looked up to see a man ducking away from the edge of a balcony three stories up. Hasbro blew a splinter from the balcony rail, but the man was already gone. There was momentary silence, and then a shout from the alley—someone crying out "Heave away!" and then a dark shape flying into our midst, a round, black bomb with a sputtering fuse. Tubby scooped it up in his broad hand as if it were a grapefruit and pitched into the canal, where it exploded with a wet, whooping report, sending up a small geyser of water.

The foot traffic on the road had entirely melted away. Save for the sounds of nearby shipping there was a silence that was heavy with menace. The five hundred pounds of dead Guernsey cow still lay in the road. In the lull I looked about me for a weapon, as did St. Ives, both of us hurrying to the heaped debris in front of the general shop, the door of which was now shut tight. I grasped the long, cast-iron handle of a loaf-shaped bread pan, and St. Ives plucked up a three-legged chair and a bent fireplace poker. Immediately there came another onslaught, as if the ambuscade was written out in scenes and choreographed for the stage: four heavily muscled bruisers wearing the striped jerseys of stevedores. They were perhaps the same men whom Gilbert had shot at, having come round in front of us now, their faces hidden by kerchiefs. We stepped out to meet them, the cow a barricade between our two groups, Hasbro and Gilbert holding their pistols in plain sight. Our four assailants would have been madmen to carry out an assault against five armed men, six counting our carriage driver, who stood flicking his buggy whip, the tip snapping.

Tubby hefted his blackthorn and shouted, "Come on, you bastards, if you're not shy." But the four attackers, such as they were, stopped dead, and then feinted this way and that, cutting silly capers on the road before dashing away, two each in either direction. I was very much afraid that Gilbert would shoot them down like dogs, but he was blessedly too sensible to commit murder unless there was some defense for the crime.

I heard the sound of something landing on the road behind me, and thinking of bombs, I spun around, fear closing my throat. What I saw was a small man bolting away, carrying Gilbert's Gladstone bag, which the man had pilfered from within the coach while we had been distracted by the raree-show on the street. I shouted, and pitched my bread pan at the man, the long-handled piece of iron flying straight as an arrow at the back of his head. Unfortunately it was impeded by gravity and clanged uselessly to the street. Tubby and I set out in pursuit, but Gilbert whistled us to a halt and waved us back.

"Your bag…" Tubby started to say to him, but Gilbert shook his head at us, and patted his coat.

"I've foiled the blighters again," he said upon our return. "Let them have the bag, eh? Why not? There's not a damned thing of value in it. Their antics were a mere diversion, you see, except for the infernal device, which was a penny squib after all—nothing taken away from your courage, Tubby. Great bravery, I call it, or perhaps an act of consummate foolishness, which it would have been had it blown your head off, ha ha!"

The flight of the small man apparently signaled the end of the threat. People reappeared on the pavement, looking around warily at first, and then more boldly when it became clear that the danger had passed. The door of the Jolly Tar opened once again, and the night resumed its normal debauched course. I fetched the bread pan and returned it to its place, along with St. Ives's chair and poker. A slatternly woman scowled at me from the door of the shop, and I gave her three shillings by way of rent money before I set out to help my friends move the impossibly heavy cow.

A crowd soon gathered to laugh at us and to offer ribald suggestions. Our exertions led to the issuance of insects from various of the cow's orifices, which fueled the public mirth until Gilbert had the brilliant idea (at the hazard of being robbed on the spot) of producing a handful of sovereigns and offering one to each and every man who would rally round and shift the beast so that the carriage could move on. There followed a great heaving and scuffling as the cow was edged away into the gutter and pitched violently up onto the pavement so that it blocked the door of what was either a desperate sort of boarding house or a house of prostitution or both at once. A pudding-faced woman shouted curses out a window on the third floor and was ridiculed for her efforts. She disappeared, then shortly reappeared, generally increasing the hilarity when she emptied a chamber pot onto the heads of two men who were entirely innocent of the outrage with the cow, and who had just come out from the Jolly Tar. Gilbert didn't look up, but quickly doled out coins. The throng dispersed, the great bulk of them returning to the pub amidst much hooting and calling for drink.

We crawled back into the coach, twenty minutes wasted, and traveled the small distance to the moonlit docks, where we found the *Nancy Dawson*, out of Eastbourne, lying at anchor, our home for the next four weeks. I was surprised at how commodious she was. I knew that Gilbert was as rich as a sultan, but I was surprised even so. The ship bore a mainmast (complete with a crow's nest) and a bowsprit as well, as if she had descended from the days of sail, which in a sense she had. She had three steel-walled holds separated one from the other with impregnable bulwarks, each of the holds entirely removable from the ship via the dockyard's cantilever crane, so that it might be set on the dock and unloaded through a cargo door. It was Gilbert's own invention, which he anticipated would bring him a million pounds sterling as soon as the patent was secure. He meant to put them to the test, he said, when he had the leisure to load a cargo of sufficient weight. The decks of the *Nancy Dawson* were a-bustle with activity, steam rising lazily from the stack, engines rumbling.

"Who might you be?" Gilbert asked a man in shirtsleeves who stood on deck at the railing, watching the lighters ply to and fro across the water, unloading the ships that couldn't come in to the crowded docks.

The man spit a wad of tobacco over the side, doffed his cap, and said, "George Beasely, if it please your honor. First mate."

It didn't seem to please Gilbert much at all. "Have we met?" he asked.

"Just this present moment, sir, and happy I am to make your acquaintance. I'm sent up from Eastbourne—Mr. Honeywell's draft, me and five other good men. Came up by rail, we did, and set about readying the ship instanter."

"Honeywell's draft, is it? Right-ho. And where is Captain Deane, then?"

"Drunk as Davy's sow and snoring in his bunk, sir, no judgment implied. He was brought aboard this past hour on a stretcher. Belike he'll come into his senses after a fortnight of sleep."

Gilbert looked dark for a moment, as if he might clap the Captain in irons or tie him to the grating in order to give him a taste of the cat. But the cloud passed, and, as the last of the baggage came aboard, he said, "Cast off the lines, then, Mr. Beasely. We haven't a moment to lose. And look sharp for villainy. There are those that would discommode us if they could."

"Aye, aye, sir," Beasely said. "Villainy it is, sir."

There were shouted orders, a good deal of stamping about by the several deck hands, and within minutes the ship moved beneath us as we were towed into the offing on the flood tide, out into Limehouse Reach as the Isle of Dogs rotated away behind us, the West India Docks disappearing from sight. We made our way through the shipping in the Pool, which to my view was a very chaos of feverish activity, demanded twice a day by the holy tide. Gilbert Frobisher strode back and forth, generally getting into the way, his pistol in his belt. He spoke to several of the crewmen whom he apparently knew, and he asked others their names, doing his best to be agreeable. I heard him laugh out loud several times, his spirits lifting now that the ship was underway, the great adventure begun at last.

I stood at the stern railing with a view of both banks, watching the constantly changing vista and the debris swirling past on the Thames. I thought of Dorothy, who I would marry if this voyage turned out to be as prosperous as Gilbert implied, and whom I had taken leave of some few hours ago. It was disorienting, I can tell you, leaving the great city behind in such wild haste when we had been aboard for a scant quarter of an hour. But wild haste was Gilbert Frobisher's idea of sensible precaution, and Gilbert Frobisher was Commander of the *Nancy Dawson*, and had come into his own at last. —◦

CHAPTER 3

All is Revealed

T HE CHART ROOM of the *Nancy Dawson* bears a passing resemblance to the interior of Uncle Gilbert's wonderful mansion in Dicker: oak wainscot, bow windows, Turkey carpets, and oil lamps mounted on ingenious, roundabout swivels that cast a golden haze over a long table laid out with charts of the Caribbean Sea, our destination. An enormous speaking trumpet stood atop the charts like a conical paperweight, painted with depictions of undersea marvels, fish and lobsters and whales and crustaceans all circulating through and around a rampant octopus, intricately drawn. There were upholstered chairs (upon which we sat), bookcases, bottles of whisky, brandy, and rum, paintings of birds and ships, and a row of large-throated, brass voice pipes corked with whistles.

They were ingenious devices, the voice pipes: a whistle would blow, one would uncork the appropriate pipe and bend an ear, and a cheerful conversation would ensue—a chat, say, with the bridge or the engine room or with the Captain himself if he weren't drunk in his bed. If the ship foundered and took on water, the corks, or rather stoppers, would prevent the sea from flooding the ship via the pipes.

All in all it was a room in which one could plan a campaign or be happily imprisoned, whichever suited. The starboard windows looked out onto the right bank of the Thames, where the lights of Allhallows had recently drifted past, Southend visible to larboard. The ship rocked on the swell, feeling the surge of the North Sea proper, the Nore lightship growing visible in the distance. I very much felt England slipping away like a receding dream as we were swept along by the great river and by the tide of Gilbert Frobisher's enthusiasm.

The old man, a consummate bachelor with no wife to refine him, dusted the edge of his hand with a great heap of snuff and inhaled hugely through his flared nostrils, eyes watering. He staggered, caught himself, and let fly an immense, shattering sneeze. He dusted the brown wash of spilled snuff from his coat front before tasting the cognac that he poured from a large, cut-crystal decanter. He subsequently poured a generous dram into the several glasses sitting before us, glinting in the lamplight. Looking at us with a piratical squint, he raised the decanter in a general toast and said, "This is old Baccarat glass, gentlemen, one of the few heavy-bodied pieces, very much sought after by the antiques dealers and weighty enough to use as a weapon. This was my grandfather's decanter, and I'll drink a toast to the man, by golly. He was a good 'un—turned out of Eton for shameless conduct in 1756—the theft of this very decanter from the provost's rooms!—and died a hero at Pondicherry three years later on the bloody foredeck of the old *Tiger*, mowing down Frenchmen with a saber! Cheers!" He drank off a great gulp, as did we all, and God's grace to his dead grandfather.

"I trust that you gentlemen are in no tearing hurry to fall into your bunks, for the tale I mean to recount will take some time in the telling, and I'll want to be thorough. Most of what I have to say will be new to you."

He drew Captain Sawney's birding log from within his coat and held it up as if it were a piece of evidence. "This log, which those cutthroats have attempted to rob me of twice tonight, came to me by way of a man from Trinity House named Elliot Benson. Benson is a purser by trade, who keeps a tally of wicks and drums of oil and the lighthouse keepers' stores along the south coast. On one of Benson's monthly visits to the Belle Tout light, Captain Sawney gave Benson this very log and cautioned him to keep it safe. Benson was to give the log to me, Sawney told him, if anything untoward happened, for I was Sawney's only living friend. Benson agreed to do so, although he was mystified: Sawney might as easily have given it to me himself on my next visit to the South Downs. Benson was doubly mystified several days later when the Belle Tout light went dark for want of oil and they found Captain Sawney's shattered body on the beach, his head like a bashed neep."

Gilbert removed his spectacles and wiped his eyes with a kerchief before tasting his cognac again. "Very shortly the reprehensible Billy Stoddard, the very devil who attacked Tubby and I on Fingal Street this evening, came round to Trinity House in Eastbourne. He was second man at the Dover light, he said, and was looking for a better position. He had heard of the tragic death of Captain Sawney, and could take over instanter. *Of course he had heard of Sawney's death*, the infamous villain, for it was he himself who had pushed Sawney from the cliff! Why had he committed the crime? I fully believe that Stoddard knew of this log and of its secret, and that Sawney had refused to give the log up when Stoddard demanded it of him. Stoddard assumed that the log was hidden somewhere roundabout the lighthouse, and he wanted the leisure to search for it. A few days earlier he would have been correct in his assumption, but Benson had the log now, and Stoddard was all to seek.

"On that dark morning at Beachy Head, after Tubby and I gave Stoddard a sound thrashing, he went straight down to Eastbourne and served his notice. It was then that he asked boldly about Captain Sawney's effects, whether there might have been a book, a birding log lying about. Sawney had promised it to him, Stoddard said, the lying pig. Benson wisely told Stoddard that there was no such thing, and Billy Stoddard went away with his hands empty.

"Two months later, after a tour of the lights along the southern coast, Benson brought Captain Sawney's log to me in Dicker, and I'm mortal certain that Billy Stoddard followed him, and that he's been on the trail of the log ever since—*hot* on the trail, as the American would say, for he nearly had the prize twice this very day. But by God he *does not* have it, and he *won't* have it, and if I have my way I'll see him swing from a gibbet for the murder of Reginald Sawney."

Gilbert looked at us darkly and thumped his knuckles on the table. The bow of the ship rose precipitously at this instant, as if the force of his blow had depressed the stern. The ship shuddered for a moment before dropping into the trough of the swell. I was surprised to see through the broad windows the lights of a sizeable city off to starboard—Margate, perhaps, unless we had already rounded the North Foreland; I had no sense of the speed at which we traveled. The White Cliffs would tell the tale when we reached the Strait, but I wouldn't be awake to see them.

"Now here's the long and the short of it," Gilbert said. "Because I'm a birding man, I found Sawney's log interesting, but for the life of me I couldn't at first fathom its mystery. I laid the log aside and neglected it again until two months ago when I had the leisure to attend to it in earnest. What I found then was passing curious."

He opened the log now, turned to an early page, and indicated with his finger a letter that had been crossed out—the first letter B in the entry that read 'Black bellied whistling duck.' "It was a simple error immediately rectified, one would suppose," Gilbert said, "and yet as you can see, there is no discernible error at all, for the identical letter was rewritten at once. Three pages later there were two corrections of the same sort, the E in egret and the N in night heron, each letter marked out and then restored. I began to look for similarly marked out letters, and very quickly discovered the simple message hidden within the log: 'Beneath the palm,' the message read—three words comprising fourteen lined-out letters. But *what* was beneath the palm? And *which* palm? I was defeated. I pitched the log onto the desktop as if it were a playing card, thus."

To illustrate he did just that thing with a flick of his wrist, the log slapping down alongside the decorated speaking trumpet and spinning atop the heap of charts. Gilbert waved his hand at it and laughed aloud. There, embossed on the leather cover of the thing, was a simple palm tree, worn flat with rubbing, but visible.

"Watch carefully, gentlemen," Gilbert said, as if he had been born for the stage. He produced a straight razor, flicked it open, and slipped the keen edge of the blade sideways into the leather cover of the log, then prised apart what was in fact two thin pieces of leather bonded around the perimeter, forming a hidden compartment between. With his thumbs he worked the glued edge loose, retrieving from within three folded sheets of thin vellum, closely written on both sides. He carefully pressed the pages flat, donned a pair of spectacles, and read aloud the very tale with which I began this account: the story of young James Douglas and his ill-fated journey to the island beyond Hispaniola aboard the *Celebes Prince*.

When he had read it through, he folded the vellum carefully and replaced it within its leather sandwich. From out of the desk he produced a brush and a small glass jar of hide glue with which he carefully dabbed the edges of the leather before pressing the two pieces together again. The birding log, message restored, disappeared once again into his coat.

I for one had little to say. It was an entertaining bit of theatre, but aside from that ball of ambergris, the wild tale of James Douglas was horrible in every regard, a catalogue of bloody violence and death, the story of malicious, unseen spirits that had torn a large sailing vessel to pieces and brought about the death of its crew. I could see no evidence to suppose it was factual aside from the "oath" at the conclusion. I was bold enough to say so at the hazard of doubting the old man. But my doubt didn't trouble him in the least.

"The tale sounds like a vast exaggeration, surely," he said. "This boy, this James Douglas, admitted that it seemed very like a dream to him. Perhaps some element of it *was* a dream: the destruction of the *Celebes Prince*, for example. Clearly he feared that his flight from the battle was craven. A mad-doctor might suggest that he sought to mitigate his guilt afterward by inventing terrifying evil spirits. But we must all of us admit that the account of the sponge divers and the ambergris has the ring of authenticity. And keep in mind that the *Celebes Prince* would not have moored off that island if there weren't some profit in it. I'll reveal that my perusal of Lloyd's records shows that the ship was owned by one Jerome Watley, of Bristol, and was lost in 1843 while cruising in just that part of the world."

Tubby, having noted my hesitation, said, "It's an adventure, Jack, at the expense of a few weeks' time. Who cares for the odds? You don't calculate the odds before crossing the road, and yet every day a dozen people are run down like dogs. I for one mean for us to have a look into that sea cave as well as another glass of this capital brandy."

"Hear him!" Gilbert said, reaching for the bottle. "And mark this, Jack: Billy Stoddard and his ruffians are believers, and they are not fanciful men."

The truth in what he said hit home, although it did nothing to rid me of my misgivings. When I searched my mind I discovered that a part of me very much believed in James Douglas and in that ball of ambergris. But if his story were true, then we were tempting fate in our reenactment of the disastrous voyage of the *Celebes Prince*.

Hasbro was inscrutable, a role he played to perfection. Tubby seemed to be in a high state of anticipation, smacking his lips over the cognac and looking at the rest of us in a madcap sort of way. St. Ives regarded Gilbert openly, and broke the silence by saying, "There are a mort of islands, unless I'm mistaken, in a 200-mile radius around Hispaniola. James Douglas fixed the location with his sextant, but he apparently neglected to note the coordinates in his account, leaving something in the neighborhood of 125,000 square miles of ocean in which the island might hide itself."

Gilbert smiled at us in a satisfied way, looking from one to the other, nodding his head. "Exactly what I myself feared, sir. But it didn't stand to reason that Douglas would omit the most vital detail. Without a careful latitude and longitude, the tale is so much air. And so I set myself to scrutinizing the log itself in order to seek out the answer. When I struck upon the yellow-breasted crake—*porzana flaviventer*—my suspicions were aroused. Sawney had allegedly seen the bird's eggs in its nest a prodigious number of times—an *unlikely* number of times. Or else he had made an error, perhaps reversed the numbers—confusing the eggs and the crakes, as it were. 'Which came first, I asked myself, the crake or the egg?'"

He laughed out loud at this witticism and paused for effect before going on. "But Captain Sawney was not given to error when it came to birds, no, sir. Rest assured, Professor, that this is no wild goose errand, ha, ha! No one but I knows the coordinates, and so it will remain until we drop anchor off the island. At present, suffice it to say that we've charted a course in the general direction of Hispaniola on the old Spanish Main. What lies waiting for us on the sea bottom is a mystery to be solved two weeks hence, if the weather treats us with respect."

We rose as a body, all of us longing for bed after the food, drink, and excitement of the evening. Only Uncle Gilbert seemed fresh. He had set out to astound us with his revelations and had very much succeeded, and he insisted now that we lay our hand atop each others' hands and recite the old, 'One for all and all for one,' oath of the Musketeers—harmless enough, except that it was Gilbert Frobisher to whom we were swearing an oath, it seemed to me. Ah, well, I thought, turning toward the door, God bless the old man and the fabulous ball of ambergris, which, if we had any idea of finding it, must have lain passively on the floor of the tumultuous sea forty-one years since the destruction of the *Celebes Prince*.

My enforced cheerfulness was altered, however, when I noted something that gave me pause. I pointed at one of the voice pipes, dead center in the row of them. For some reason it was not corked with its whistle. The stopper had been removed and balanced at the outermost edge of the speaking trumpet, which angled upward at something like 45 degrees so that one could give it the ear with a mere nod of the head. The India-rubber flange, which made it watertight when the stopper was fitted into the trumpet, must have provided enough friction to keep it stationary despite the roll of the ship.

"This has all the earmarks of a plot..." I started to say, but St. Ives shook his head to silence me. He picked up the stopper and whistle and thrust it back into its aperture, thus making certain we'd no longer be overheard, if in fact we had been.

"Perhaps you're correct, Jack," said St. Ives when it was safe to speak again. "This was quite possibly an *intentional* oversight meant to allow someone to overhear our discussion."

"I'm *certain* that's not the case," Gilbert said. "Of course it isn't. We're aboard ship, after all, with a hand picked crew. This is no doubt a completely *innocent* oversight."

"Hand picked by whom, sir?" Hasbro asked, cutting to the chase in his unadorned fashion. "There was mention of a Mr. Honeywell, who was kind enough to send out Mr. Beasely, the mate. Do you entirely trust Mr. Honeywell, sir?"

"Absolutely, my good fellow. To the death. Honeywell has been a great good friend of mine these past two years. He was kind enough to facilitate the purchase of this very ship when I let him know I was in the market for just such a vessel. He undertook to have her refit, applying himself diligently. It was no mean task, neither. His father was a whaler, you know. Died at sea. Dragged to his doom by a sperm whale when Honeywell was a mere lad."

"Out of an idle curiosity," I asked, "how many of the crew are *not* from Honeywell's draft?"

"I see what you're about, Jack—safety in numbers, you're thinking. I put it at nine, all men I knew from my yachting days in Eastbourne, including the Chief Engineer, Mr. Phibbs, who's as loyal as a limpet, as are his mates. You need have no fear, Jack, not of the crew nor of Mr. Honeywell. I stand by my friends, Jack, and I count both you and Lucius Honeywell among them.

I considered protesting, but St. Ives followed at once with another attempt, although Gilbert had begun to take on a stormy appearance.

"I apologize for this inquisition, sir, but did Honeywell know of your destination?"

"Only in the most general way, Professor. I might have mentioned Hispaniola, I suppose, but certainly not the name of the island."

"The island was not named in Douglas's account, if I remember correctly," I said. Gilbert smiled at me and pointed at his temple, where the name of the island apparently resided. No doubt he had discovered it as he had the coordinates—in a bird's nest.

"And did your conversation with Mr. Honeywell run to whales and whaling?" St. Ives asked. "I mean no offense to your friend, sir."

"No offense taken, I assure you. Our conversation did not rise to the level of particulars, Professor, at least as regards the matter that's concerning you. I was in need of a diving bell, however, and it was Honeywell who procured one, although the request itself would have conveyed little. The device is currently struck down into the hold. Lucius Honeywell, I'll say again, is without peer as a gentleman and a man of business."

"A diving bell," St. Ives said. "Quite a sensible item, given Mr. Douglas's description of the death of the two sponge divers. Mr. Honeywell has made himself invaluable, it seems."

"Exactly what I've been telling you. He's a good man, is Lucius Honeywell, and a happy one, as long as he's well-paid for his services."

"And yet bad men might have imposed upon Mr. Honeywell," Hasbro said, hanging on like a terrier to the dark thread of the conversation.

"Honeywell is too shrewd by half," Gilbert told him, dismissing the notion with a wave of his hand and very apparently tired of the conversation. "If Honeywell recommends Beasely, then Beasely is a good man as well, as are the others who accompanied him. I could scarcely have found a full crew otherwise—not of seasoned men."

"Mr. Honeywell particularly *recommended* Beasely to you, then?" Hasbro asked. But of course Mr. Honeywell had not. Gilbert hadn't any idea who Beasely was when we had come aboard.

Gilbert sniffed. By now he'd had enough of our doubts. St. Ives assured him that we had every faith in Mr. Honeywell, although the Professor's eyes implied a different story. Slightly off keel now, figuratively speaking, we went off to our various staterooms to sleep.

My own room, quite commodious, was as elegantly fitted-out as was the chartroom, including a small mahogany bookcase that was stocked with likely looking volumes, some of them impressively dusty and ancient. I chose a weighty tome that expounded upon the pelagic fishes, with fin and scale and bone structures illustrated, accurately measured, and convincingly depicted. Caught up at once in the marvels of the deep, it took me a good sixty seconds to fall into the abyss of sleep. ⟋⟍

PART II

Blood and Mayhem

CHAPTER 4

Morning Fog

I WAS JOSTLED AWAKE in the early morning by a man holding a pistol, the muzzle of which was perhaps two feet away from my forehead.

"Out you go, mate," he said to me, and gestured with the pistol. There was the sound of the ship's engines, and it felt as if we were moving, although it might have been the heaving of the sea, and there was nothing but fog outside the window. It was daylight without a doubt, but the world beyond the ship was invisible. Morning had come quickly.

I climbed out of bed wearing my nightgown, stupid with sleep. There was the ship's bell once again, clanging a warning through the murk. Only moments earlier I had been oblivious to it. The man with the pistol was familiar to me: I'd seen him working on deck when we weighed anchor, a man with a heavy, walrus mustache and wearing a striped jersey, a battered felt cap, and with a ragged looking scar across his forehead and a half-shut eye, the result of the same wound.

"You'll want your trousers, I'll warrant," he said.

Indeed I would, whatever my fate. I pulled them on under my night gown and did the same with my shoes before he grew impatient and waved me up the companionway. Out we went into the morning mist, the sea just visible below when the swell washed down the side of the ship. St. Ives and Hasbro were on deck guarded by three men with rifles and pistols, Beasely among them, his pistol in his belt, and so much for the helpful Mr. Honeywell. Beasely clutched Captain Sawney's birding log in his hand. I took my place beside my friends, began to speak, and was told by Beasely to shut my gob or he'd shut it with a bullet, something I was inclined to believe. Tubby stumbled out onto the deck then along with Gilbert, whose face was a confused muddle.

To my mind there was nothing confusing in any of it. Honeywell's draft had been made up of pirates. Utterly missing were the crewmen I had noticed during the trip down the Thames—the men whom Gilbert had evidently known. Where were they? Dead in their bunks? Locked into the hold? Pitched overboard? I was moderately certain that I recognized two of the pirates now as having been among the men who capered in the road beyond the fallen cow, despite the balaclavas that had covered their faces. No doubt their goal had been to obtain the birding log if they could. If not, then they would put into play the more devious plan of taking it away from us on the high seas. Gilbert had foiled their chance in Pennyfields, and so we now found ourselves in this desperate strait.

There was a brief break in the fog, and I could see Lizard Point some distance to starboard. I had seen it quite clearly when I sailed to Bayonne on my cousin's yacht some two years earlier. Perhaps I was wrong about our exact location, but it was certain we must still be in the Channel if there was land to starboard at all.

"Line the fat men up against the railing," Beasely said. "Billy says that he owes them the favor of murdering them. The rest of this lot can swim for it, lucky bastards."

I was apparently one of the lucky bastards, if drowning passed as luck. I wasn't a strong enough swimmer to survive in the cold waters of the Channel, and, given the still-foggy morning, the chance of our being seen by a passing boat was nil, barring a miracle. I noticed now that there was a pirate on a raised platform above us. He stood behind what appeared to be a dozen or so rifle barrels lined up side by side and mounted on a sort of swivel. I hadn't seen such a thing before, but I knew that Gilbert Frobisher was fond of weaponry, and this was certainly an innovative specimen—a variety of machine-gun, obviously. Gilbert had no doubt envisioned using it to dissuade pirates, but that was another well-laid plan gone to smash.

Two men, both carrying pistols, waved the Frobishers toward the railing, staying well away from them. Tubby was in a dangerous state, I could see that well enough. He would not die passively, and neither would

Gilbert, who had recovered from his muddle and glared roundabout him like an adder. I looked for my chance, but there was nothing but suicide in every direction. Would I allow Tubby Frobisher, one of the great friends of my existence, to be blown over the railing with a machine-gun? No, I would not. I was a dead man in any event. When Tubby acted, I would follow suit, and damn the consequences. St. Ives seemed coiled and ready, and I wondered fleetingly if thoughts of Alice and his children would give him pause. I myself thought of Dorothy and was happy she knew nothing of this, and I wished to hell I weren't in my nightgown.

"Say your prayers, you grass-combing lubbers!" Beasely cried out, his voice croaking with a sick passion. The pirates' eyes were on Tubby and Gilbert, anxious to see what the weapon might do to them, the filthy swine. I forced myself to watch, for looking away would lessen my chance of being of service to my friends, but my mind was turning upon the question of the coordinates of the island. Was this a bluff, I wondered, to compel Gilbert to reveal the island's whereabouts?

It was then that I saw a grizzled looking facsimile of a man climb over the railing carrying a wine bottle, apparently having come out of the sea, although he was bone dry. He was bearded like a goat and dressed in long woolen underwear and woolen stockings. His shirt was stained from what must have been a bout of violent puking, and his eyes were red-rimmed, his grey hair hanging lank around his shoulders. God knew who he was, Old Man Ocean, perhaps. I kept my eyes steady and held my breath as he raised the bottle in his hand—a full bottle—and swung it at the head of the pirate who stood at the gun, swung it hard, as if he were intent upon hitting something some distance farther away, and the violence of the blow exploded the bottle against the back of the pirate's skull with force enough to knock him entirely over the gun and onto the deck, where he lay unmoving.

I realized that I had been hit on the cheek with flying glass, but I scarcely felt the blow, or the spray of wine that accompanied it. The pirates turned as a man, the lot of them shocked into momentary inaction, and the newcomer—our bedlamite savior—stood alone at the weapon and swiveled it toward Beasely and the two men who stood with him. The three bolted, scuttling and diving away. If they had leapt to the railing beside Tubby and Gilbert, they might have saved themselves, at least for the moment, but they were too confounded by the sight of that insidious looking gun. I saw

Tubby garrote the nearest pirate with his forearm and elbow and lever him straight back over the railing and into the sea, which was to the man's great good luck, for at that instant there came a rapid series of explosions from the barrels of the gun. Beasely was shockingly cut to pieces, as was a pirate who fled toward the stern. Another pirate jerked three times as the bullets hit him, but still he managed to leap overboard. Someone latched onto my arm and yanked me downward, and I very nearly lashed out with my fist before I realized that it was St. Ives, and that my friends were clearing away, back along the edge of the galley, Tubby dragging Uncle Gilbert along by main force. There was another burst, and then abruptly the firing ceased, and yet we stayed where we were, listening to a deep silence, save for the shouting from someone out on the sea and the ghastly whimpering of a pirate who lay on the deck with his leg nearly severed.

Time had been passing with uncanny, dreamlike slowness, although the blood running into the collar of my nightshirt, the growing pain along my cheek, and the ringing in my ears were real enough. The grey-haired spectre of a man stepped away from the gun and spat over the side. He nodded at Gilbert—not by way of a greeting, but as if to say, "Do you see what comes of playing pirate?"

Although he stood not two feet from me, Gilbert's voice made its way only dimly into my ears: "It's Captain Deane, by God," he said.

And that was our first introduction to the mad Captain Deane, necessarily a brief introduction, for I quickly found myself helping to carry the wounded pirate below decks—three of us, actually, Hasbro and I taking his head and feet, St. Ives supporting his leg, which was pouring blood. The sickbay was a disused cabin with an operating table, a chest full of medicines and another with surgical instruments, although we had no surgeon to speak of, barring Hasbro. I knew that Hasbro had skill in that line, but had no idea how much skill. I held the insensible man flat against the table lest he come-to while Hasbro removed the leg, cutting the flesh, sawing the already shattered bone cleanly, and then sewing away like a tailor, aided by St. Ives, both of them working proficiently and steadily while I sweated and sickened at the reek of blood, passing out before the deed was finished.

I found myself lying upon the deck, staring at the ceiling, and was given a glass of brandy to help my stomach and spirits by a seaman in a bright red cotton shirt and wearing a crushed bowler hat with a curved brim, which was discolored by dirty grease. He turned out to be Phibbs, the Chief Engineer, sent down at the behest by Mr. Frobisher to make sure I wasn't dead. The wounded pirate still lay on the table, and the ground below it was awash with blood. I saw the rise and fall of his chest. The severed leg had disappeared.

The ship's bell began to clang as I poured the brandy down my throat. I thanked Phibbs and stood up much improved, climbing to the deck where several hands, recently released from the place they'd been locked away, had evidently been swabbing the decks, scouring the blood away with water and sand. They stood at the railing looking to larboard now, the fog having lifted, just a thin mist like cloud drift remaining. A square-rigged sloop lay some distance away, rolling on the swell. It had lowered a boat, which had picked up two of the pirates, both of them lucky to be alive. Three dead men floated some forty or fifty from the *Nancy Dawson*, and the severed leg half as far away. The boat was just then drawing up alongside the sloop, the men within it making haste to gain the relative safety of the larger craft, where the villain Billy Stoddard stood at the railing as bold as Satan, regarding us. I counted six cannon, with two men at each. The guns couldn't sink us, perhaps, with our iron hull, but they could cut up the cabins easily enough—or the crew if we remained on deck—and if a well-aimed shot dismounted Captain Deane's machine gun, we couldn't reply in kind, which would be a great danger if they decided to board us when the fog returned.

They would need the wind in the right quarter to accomplish that, however, whereas we needed nothing more than several tons of coal and a scoop shovel, both of which we possessed. We could do as we pleased, and I saw that we were drawing away from each other already, or rather we were drawing away from the sloop, under power. The sloop was apparently quite willing to be quit of us. 'Live to fight another day,' I thought. I'd had enough fighting, to tell you the truth, on this day or any other. Gilbert sat in a deck chair, trying to look game, but appearing ten years older now than he had appeared to be last night when he was regaling us with the story of Captain Sawney's log. He was no Captain Ahab who would chase his nemesis across the seven seas. His one goal was to fish up that ball of ambergris, and he was satisfied to be moving westward once again.

———∿∿∿———

"SHE'S A NORDENFELT gun, is what she is," Captain Deane told us, somewhat drunkenly, as we ate what Gilbert alleged was a light midday meal: toasted cheese to whet the appetite, beef in red wine with lardoons of bacon, a gratin of lobster, heavy with mushrooms and grated cheese, and a blood pudding that I won't dwell on here. The peg-legged cook, an old Scotsman whose unlikely name was Lazarus MacLean, and who had been a sail maker in his youth before his leg was taken off by a cannonball, was lavish with all things unctuous. It was one o'clock in the afternoon, and we were long out of sight of land, the sky blue above us, the swell moderate, and the decks shipshape aside from the holes blasted into various structures by the infamous Nordenfelt gun, a prodigy of modern warfare. The carpenter would soon put it right, however. We could hear the sound of his hammering and sawing even as we worked through the various dishes.

Captain Deane and Gilbert Frobisher wore the masks of comedy and tragedy between them. Captain Deane had awakened that morning to find himself locked into his cabin, from which he had extricated himself in the eleventh hour in order to come to our bloody rescue. The villain Beasely had become the biter bit, and Captain Deane and the Nordenfelt gun had done the biting. The Captain was the hero of the hour, and the fact of his previous night's drunkenness had become a decided virtue. Gilbert, on the other hand, was morose. The birding log was lost: far better had it been destroyed. And perhaps it had. Perhaps Beasely had flung it over the gunnel in his death throes, in which case it lay on the bottom of the ocean, and no great loss. Or perhaps one of the survivors had rescued it, in which case... The coordinates of the island were safely lodged in Gilbert Frobisher's head. What was lodged by now in Billy Stoddard's head was a mystery.

Captain Deane mixed another bowl of shrub, a pleasant enough summer drink, although I had been watering mine, being desirous of remaining sober at least into the evening. The Captain was criminally liberal with the rum, and he grew more voluble with each glass, his face developing a ruddy glow as his features sagged. "The gun can shoot three thousand rounds in just a trifle over three minutes," he said. "Aye, gentlemen, and can keep on shooting them, if there's bullets enough and the barrels don't melt. At close range..." At this point the carpenter and his mate were silent, and we heard the keening of the one-legged pirate, who had awakened and discovered what had befallen him. After a few moments he fell blessedly silent.

Captain Deane shook his head. There was no pressing need for him to continue, for we had seen what his gun could do at close range. "He can take out a cook's warrant if he ain't dead," Gilbert said, referring to the pirate. "Lazarus MacLean stands witness to that."

We rose together from the table now, the swimming remnants of the blood pudding encouraging us to take the air. And it was taking the air that occupied most of my waking hours for the pleasant, unvarying days that followed, during which time I submerged myself in the cephalopoda, and was thrilled, as you might imagine, when we found ourselves in tropical waters at last. On that first dark night the one-legged pirate died of his ghastly wound, despite Hasbro's careful attention. He had never reawakened after that long, mournful howl. We wrapped him in a sheet with pig iron at his feet, said a prayer over him, and slid him through the scupper into the sea. Our island was near at hand, Gilbert told us. We would make landfall tomorrow evening, half our journey complete.

Some distance north and east of Hispaniola, hours before dawn, I arose and wandered out alone into the warm night air. The sliver of moon sailed just above the horizon, and the sky was a wonder of stars. To my vast surprise, the dark ocean was abruptly illuminated, as if Neptune had switched on a thousand small, moving lamps, and I stood dumbfounded at the railing as we motored slowly through a vast school of luminescent squid. We soon left them behind, a golden cloud just beneath the surface of the sea, and I returned to my cabin in a strangely wistful mood, wishing mightily that Dorothy were beside me. —◦

CHAPTER 5

The Spirit of the Island

THE DARK, VOLCANIC smoke rising from the nameless island was visible against the blue sky long before the island itself arose from the sea. When it did, it was revealed to be little more than the volcano standing alone in the vastness—its coal-black side rising steeply along the eastern shore, but cut away along the western edge, where it became a bowl enclosing a riot of jungle growth. We motored around the island as the sun declined, and cast our anchor on the leeward side, in the shade of the mountain, grateful for the cool of evening. There was the smell of brimstone on the air, unpleasantly sulphuric.

A deep rumbling was audible when the ship's engines were throttled, sometimes loud rumbling, sometimes muted, and I at first took it to be the sound of the distant surf breaking over the reefs. St. Ives suggested that it was the uneasy muttering of the active volcano, and he pointed out the orange glow of a thin line of molten lava that wormed along a high ridge, something I had mistaken for the last rays of the setting sun. As darkness descended there was a vivid spewing out of glowing embers and sparks that made flaming trails across the sky, very much like fireworks on Guy Fawkes Night, and the sides of the mountain were alive with fires, flaring up and then slowly dying as they cooled. In time the mountain fell quiet. The embers winked away, the night was silent aside from the distant sound of the surf, and the island became a deep black shadow against the stars. The stream of lava had flowed over the edge of the cone now and was tracing its way down the mountainside at a leisurely pace, immolating forest trees along the edge of the bowl.

Gilbert had deliberately dropped the anchor out of sight of the sea cave. We would look into it tomorrow morning at the appointed time, he said as we stood at the rail. "It wouldn't do to appear greedy," he told us. "It's my idea that the ravenous desire of the Captain of the *Celebes Prince* offended the spirit of the island, and that the Captain and his crew paid for the insult with death and disaster."

"The *spirit* of the island?" I asked, failing to mask the doubtful tone in my voice.

"Yes, indeed," Gilbert said, gesturing at the night-dark island and tipping me a wink. "There are more things on earth, Jacky, than are dreamt of in your philosophy." It was nonsense, of course (not the bit from Hamlet, but the very idea of irritated spirits) but then most of us believe in some sort of nonsense, much of it more pernicious than this. His belief, after all, wouldn't call the spirit into being, or so I hoped.

"This is a stoutly built craft, Jack," Tubby put in. "What do you say, Uncle? We haven't placed our lives in the hands of pig iron and knacker's glue, I daresay?"

"No, sir," Gilbert said, "we have not. The *Nancy Dawson*'s hull was reinforced with steel H-beams of the highest quality during her refitting. Rolled steel, gentlemen—the Bessemer process, but triple-refined. I won't commit the stupidity of making needless claims in the event that the fates are listening, but she won't fail us. No indeed."

For a moment I was afraid that Hasbro would mention Honeywell again as regards the refitting, but he did not. He merely nodded his head in appreciation. There was a brief spurt of glowing cinders from the mountain now, which called on our attention.

"Will you reveal the name of the island?" St. Ives asked. "It would do no harm, perhaps, to utter it aloud now that we're anchored off its very shores."

"No harm indeed, Professor. She is known as Santa Lusca, although you won't find the name on any charts, I assure you. I've made a study of it." He pitched the butt of his cigar into the sea at this juncture, which was followed immediately by the soft splash of a fish rising to feed.

"I don't recall seeing Santa Lusca in the hagiography," Hasbro said. Perhaps Santa *Lucia*...?"

"Not a bit of it. The island of Santa Lucia lies amid the Lesser Antilles, some distance to the south and east. Santa *Lusca* it is. She's a pagan saint, I shouldn't wonder, and in this part of the world, all the more potent."

The electric deck lights were illuminated at that moment, shockingly bright, and the island disappeared from our view. Immediately there sounded the loud wheezing and clacking din of the great, fat, steam crane, manipulated by Phibbs, who, to my amazement, had begun the process of hoisting into the air a rectangular piece of the superstructure of the deck, something over twenty feet in length and half as broad. On it sat objects covered with tarpaulins that were fastened down with battens. The craft—for that's what the thing was—swung out over the railing and descended toward the calm sea, where it was warped in alongside the ship and drawn tight against fenders made of canvas bags filled with cork. The whole process was wonderfully efficient, and I was reminded that it was easy to underestimate Gilbert Frobisher, who had been a stupendously successful magnate in the smelting business and was a great authority on birds. There was no reason to assume that he was incompetent in the current venture. Before the *Nancy Dawson* had sailed from Eastbourne, he'd had Phibbs and his men enact this very exercise until they were utterly efficient. Two men removed the battens and canvas now, which revealed a ship's wheel, a boiler, oven and engine, and a second, smaller crane. It was nothing less than a motorized, twin-screw scow, built along the lines of the common lighters that swarmed around the London docks.

A broad deck-hatch, moments ago hidden by the scow, swung back on its iron hinges, revealing the diving bell standing in a section of the lower hold. In its turn the bell rose at the behest of the crane and was swung over the side and deposited neatly onto the scow, which settled a strake but bore the weight effortlessly.

"The bell is built on the principles of the Edmond Halley design, if I'm not mistaken," St. Ives shouted over the noise.

"Yes, sir," Gilbert replied as we walked aft. "The fresh air is driven into it by a Porter-Allen engine designed on the latest principles, with a reserve engine by way of safety. But it will amaze you, Professor, to learn that the bell is fabricated out of aluminium—built at the Carnforth Ironworks at no little expense. It's comparatively light, which is its primary virtue, but can descend to a hundred fathoms without danger."

"And it's fit out with windows all the way around," Tubby put in, "for the amusement of the passengers, which, by the way, will not include me. I'd sooner do battle with an elephant than descend beneath the surface of the ocean."

"I'm ashamed to say that I share Tubby's phobia," Gilbert said. "But I'm happy to say that the sharks mentioned by James Douglas are similarly disinclined to leave their watery world." He looked at me over the top of his spectacles now. "You need have no fear that they'll clamber into the bell with you, Jack."

There was more such talk over food and drink in the chart room, with the renewed rumbling of the volcano and the clatter of work on deck as an intermittent backdrop. Gilbert regaled us with further descriptions of his removable holds, the broad, top hatch of the mid-ship hold weighted with the bulk of the scow. "I have half a mind," Gilbert said, "to fill the hold with Jamaican rum in the spirit of the *Celebes Prince*, but I'll forego it if we fetch up that ball of ambergris. I'm not a greedy man, after all." And then, after a pause, he said in a loud voice, "*Mark me, lads. I am not a greedy man, nor ever was.*" He winked then, having foxed the fates.

The fabled spirit of the island was very much on my mind as I lay in my bunk that night. Through the cabin window I could see the volcano spewing embers, the slopes alive once again, the bright orange leaping and jumping, the stream of molten lava having increased to something like a river.

—⁓—

Dawn saw us anchored along the steep eastern shore, with the dark mouth of the sea cave clearly visible in the morning twilight, just as James Douglas had described it. The ocean was serene, or something like it, with only a slight surge lapping against the reef that sheltered the small bay. I had the uneasy feeling that something was pending, however. The breeze blew out of the northeast, rippling the surface of the ocean. The volcano rumbled ominously and belched smoke and ash along with showers of glowing cinders and stone. I've never been to war, thank Heaven, but it seemed to me that we were in the last moments of preternatural calm before a great battle.

Gilbert and Tubby joined me at the railing now, Tubby carrying a basket of sandwiches and a metal flask of strong, hot coffee, which went down gratefully with the makeshift breakfast, the remainder of which I was under orders to give to St. Ives, already busy within the diving bell. Tubby wore his ridiculous Bollinger hat with the peacock feathers. Gilbert was in a rare state, his face lit by the rose tinted sunlight, giving the appearance of a bemused devil. He chased a mouthful of bread and meat down his gullet with a swig of coffee and said to me, "It's a fitting morning for the work we do, Jack, the ocean easy on the one hand, and the island uneasy on the other. It's the sort of balance that's much sought after in the Orient, where the lowest scullery boy is a philosopher. I envy you, Jacky, surely I do, sailing into the midst of glory aboard the scow while I languish aboard ship. That sort of glory is very nearly gone out of the world."

His words were punctuated by a frightful explosion from the volcano, which blew out a patch of rock the size of a rugby pitch, enormous boulders flying far out into the ocean, sending up plumes of water like a pod of whales. A wide river of lava poured out of the breech in the mountainside and flowed downward toward the sea. "Let's pray that the mountain doesn't throw stones in our direction," I said with an uneasy laugh, my mind damning all glory to hell.

"These volcanoes are perpetually up to such capers," Gilbert said. "I've studied the creatures. They disgorge a bit of their innards to relieve the pressure, you see, rather like a good vomit after a heavy meal. She'll rest easier now. You can depend upon it, Jack." He smiled unconvincingly and looked at his chronometer. "We should be about our business, however. I suspect that we haven't seen the last of our friend Billy Stoddard. It would have been best if we had simply rammed the sloop when we met him off the Lizard, but there had been too much slaughter, and it wasn't in my heart to do it—a weakness, perhaps. But there'll be no such weakness if he makes a second attempt. No, sir. In three hours time I intend to leave this corner of the ocean. I mean to stop in Kingston tomorrow evening in order to look up a woman I knew in my youth, a Miss Bracken, very comely, or once was. I don't speak biblically, of course, when I say that I *knew* her, although if my luck is in perhaps that'll change, eh?"

He mopped his brow with a kerchief, for the morning was already warm. "Once you lads are moored beneath the island, Jack, Phibbs will extinguish all lamps, and you'll wait for the sun in the darkness, just as in Douglas's account. There's less chance of…attracting unwarranted attention that way." He winked, turned about, and descended via a portable companionway to the deck of the scow, which was crowded. Tubby and I followed him, the phrase *unwarranted attention*, circulating in my mind. I was suddenly anxious to be underway, if only to get the thing done. Waiting has never agreed with me.

Phibbs stood ready to cast off. Gilbert shouted something to him, took a look around, nodded with apparent satisfaction, and went back up the companionway to the deck of the steamer. Hasbro, wearing duck trousers rolled up at the ankles and a straw wide-awake hat, shoveled coal into the furnace, which was pouring smoke. There was a ruckus on the deck of the steamer, where four pike-carrying crewmen warded off imaginary boarders. Captain Deane's head was just visible above the Nordenfelt gun, as bloody-minded in his way as the pirates had been.

I saw St. Ives through one of the bell's windows, the bell itself hanging suspended from a davit on the end of the crane, tethered by chain along which ran an air-hose, which would be our source of both fresh air and pressure, although if all went well we would scarcely need more than a modicum of fresh air; either the ambergris would be there or it would not be. A speaking tube ran along beside the air-hose. From the bottom of the bell descended a large, globe-shaped mechanical claw, which opened now and descended into the sea. Up it came again, closed up and dripping water, and then opening and closing again as St. Ives familiarized himself with the controls of the device. The talons of the claw, if you will, were heavily padded in order to protect our prize. Below the bell, set into the deck of the scow, lay a round sheet of glass through which I could see fish swimming below—no doubt a way for Phibbs to find the ambergris in order to position the bell atop it.

The lot of us were taking a myriad of things on faith, it seemed to me, but at this juncture there was no more sensible way to take them. In for a penny, in for a pound, I thought—many tens of thousands of pounds if you were Gilbert Frobisher. I said a temporary adieu to Tubby and then hauled myself into the bell by way of a short ladder, which I pulled in after me, and sat on the padded leather seat, my feet on the foot rail and the mechanical claw hovering just above our foreheads in the top. Attached to the walls were two long, brass viewing tubes, devices that would allow one to see directly beneath the bell, where, for want of a window, the view would be least clear. It was cool and damp, the atmosphere having a muffling effect on the ears and also on the mechanical noise of the engine. St. Ives and I could hear each other clearly.

"Do you suppose it'll be there?" I asked him.

"I do not," he said. "It's wildly implausible that it could have found its way back into the stony depression that had been its home. Once the Indian divers dropped it, it would have been at the mercy of the surge and the tides and very soon swept out into the open ocean. Little do I care for amber-gris, Jack, although certainly it's a curious phenomenon. As for its value, however, purchasing and fitting out the *Nancy Dawson* in this extravagant manner must have consumed far more than the treasure is worth, even if it still lies where it lay forty years past, which beggars possibility. We're simply men on a holiday, I'm afraid."

Abruptly we were underway. The bell gave a lurch, and I grabbed onto one of the holdfasts at the edge of the window to my right as we swayed on the davit. "I'm of a like mind," I told St. Ives, "and now that we're here on this holiday, or better yet, fool's errand—I don't speak of Gilbert Frobisher, mind you—I find that I don't like it a bit. I'm not a superstitious man, but there's something damned odd about this place, or perhaps simply damned. The volcano doesn't account for it."

"I take your meaning, and of course James Douglas felt the same thing."

"He was a mere lad, however," I said. "I'm supposed to have outgrown such fears."

"Nonsense," St. Ives told me. "Over the past year my own mind has been quite altered from its formerly rational view of things, and I find that I now have a higher regard for much of what we mistakenly call superstition. Do you recall the name of this island?"

"Santa Lusca," I said, "not to be confused with Santa Lucia."

"The name is in itself interesting. I've seen it now and then in accounts of this part of the world, many of those accounts evidently fabulous. Gilbert's notion of an island spirit has some basis in local legend, although perhaps he's unaware of it, but is merely giving voice, as you are, to a sensation that he cannot define."

The dark, half-circle of the cave was drawing closer, sunlight sparkling on the small bay before it, although the sky was growing hazy with smoke and ash from the volcano. The *Nancy Dawson* lay at anchor some distance behind us now—farther than I would have thought possible in such a brief span of time. "Of what *basis* do you speak?" I asked.

"Local tales, apparently of native origin, concerning a large sea creature referred to as a 'Lusca,' quite feared by the natives of these islands. There's an improbably deep trench cutting through this part of the ocean, you know. No less a luminary than Lord Kelvin himself took soundings in the vicinity of Andros Island some fifteen years ago. He played out 2,000 meters of weighted piano wire and failed to find the bottom. I've often wondered what might live in the never-ending darkness of those abyssal depths. Megalodon, perhaps, or plesiosaurs, or cephalopods of a size that one sees only in dreams."

"You dream of cephalopods?"

"Regularly, however..."

Our conversation ended abruptly, for we ourselves were cast into darkness, the sea cave swallowing us. An electric lamp on the bow switched on, illuminating the cavern and irritating the sea birds nesting in the walls, although their protests were mostly lost in the engine noise. Phibbs and Tubby lowered anchors fore and aft in order to stabilize the scow, an easy enough task given the utterly calm water, and then Phibbs extinguished the bow light in order to avoid attracting the attention of...what?

We settled down in the twilight to wait out the sun. Before two minutes had passed, the island shook bodily, and a shower of rock pinged off the bell just over our heads. I could see the silhouettes of Phibbs, Tubby, and Hasbro hurrying to clear away debris, tossing chunks of rock over the side. It seemed as if the great god Lusca might dwell in the heart of the island rather than in the deeps of the sea.

To distract myself I searched for and discovered the window in the rock wall of the cavern. It glowed faintly, but with a slowly rising intensity as the sun made its way up the sky. The men on deck were more than mere silhouettes now. We were moving at last: the bell swung out over the side, paused, and then swung back a trifle. We gazed downward at the water, into which we would soon plunge, but I could make out little beneath the surface. After another long moment we jerked into downward motion, descending slowly. Cool, tinny smelling air whooshed into the bell, and very quickly seawater climbed the interior wall as if to drown us, which was more than a little unnerving.

St. Ives was as placid as a clam, however. "There it stops," he said, nodding downward, and I saw that it was true—the water had had apparently reached equilibrium and had ceased to rise, at least for the moment.

Both of us removed the viewing tubes from their mounts and dipped the broad end into the water, the sea bottom springing into clarity through the lens. As we descended I watched the living sea beneath us, the play of sunlight over the shifting landscape, the fading of colors in the depths. Fishes swam around the coral growths and volcanic rock—parrotfish and grouper that I recognized from the books in my cabin. Clouds of bright blue damselfish darted in and out of the corals along with yellow seahorses and black triggerfish. Several immense barracuda—nasty looking characters, pirates to a man—regarded us from a distance. A queue of foot-length squid hovered below the bell, their enormous eyes watching us carefully. They shifted away in a body in order to give us room as we passed, never looking away from us but rotating together to keep us in sight. And then, on the instant, they wheeled around like a flock of starlings and shot away into the distance, as if on an urgent errand.

We were thirty feet from the sea floor when we saw it: Gilbert Frobisher's ball of ambergris, perfectly immense. —⌒

CHAPTER 6

The Treasure Trove

ELOW US, JUST slightly outside the circumference of the bell, stood several giant sea fans, waving in the slow current, exposing and then hiding the great ivory ball of ambergris, just as James Douglas had described it.

"Four feet to starboard," St. Ives said into the speaking tube. We scarcely felt the shift, but found ourselves drifting until we were directly over our prize, at which point St. Ives called, "Stop." We halted perhaps six feet from the seabed, above the white coral stones and sea fans that surrounded our prize. My eyes, as you can imagine, were on that ball of ambergris. Gilbert hadn't exaggerated its size or the lustrous purity of its ivory color. It lay within the stones like a small moon that had fallen from the heavens.

"It's found its way back to its nest," I said, noting that the ring of stone around it looked very like a purposefully constructed enclosure.

"Curious, indeed," St. Ives said, the implausible having come to pass. "It shares the nest with other foreign objects, if I'm not mistaken."

"A broken cutlass," I said, spotting the encrusted blade and pommel lying next to the ambergris. "And a mantel clock with the face of a moon." The clock looked as if it might have been plucked out of a captain's cabin yesterday. Beside the clock lay a small, iron-bound chest, open and half full of sand with what appeared to be a crystal sugar basin partly buried. Unlike the cutlass, the sugar basin had apparently only begun to be encrusted with sea life, although clearly it had sat on the sea bottom longer than the clock. Impossibly, the basin was crammed full of the heads of Punch and Judy dolls, the paint having faded and chipped, but the heads still recognizable to anyone who has seen a puppet show.

"I believe that I make out the blade of a halberd," St. Ives said, "no doubt several hundred years old, and mingled with items that might have been added to the collection a month ago."

"Just so," I said. "*Collection* is the salient term. Very like a child's treasure, combed from the sea floor. What do you make of it?"

"I can make nothing of it, Jack. There is no rational explanation."

"The irrational then?"

"Some sentient creature has collected these things and deposited them here for safe-keeping."

I couldn't argue with the idea, although it was profoundly strange and unlikely. To my surprise I discovered that my doubts and fears had quite fled away, replaced by an avid curiosity. My admiration for Gilbert Frobisher had arisen a considerable degree. "Clearly we must take the ambergris," I said, "but to my mind we should let the rest of the collection lie."

"Agreed," St. Ives said. "I very much wish that we had brought something to leave in exchange. This feels like common thievery." He manipulated the retractor now, the claw opening and descending toward the ambergris. He worked with immense patience and concentration, not trusting entirely to the India rubber pads, and having no desire to chip so much as a fragment from the ocean-washed orb. The claw closed over it at last, and I let out my breath, which I hadn't realized I'd been holding. The claw retracted, simple as you please, and rose back into the bell, sucking sand and debris from the sea floor and exposing further treasures that had been hidden by the ambergris, including a number of human skulls, although the lot of it was immediately obscured by the swirling sand and languidly moving sea fans. The entrapped ambergris passed before my eyes, hanging suspended at last within the dome. The venture had gone forward with uncanny smoothness.

"We've got it," St. Ives said into the tube, with a tone of excitement that was slightly more elevated than one would expect of a man on a holiday. Up we went, the sea bottom receding below us.

"Here's to success," I said, nodding at St. Ives. In that moment a great, long shadow crossed the window, and I instantly regretted my words, which were rash in the extreme. The shadow revealed itself to be the dark bulk of a hammerhead shark, startlingly heavy of body and perhaps nineteen or twenty feet long. It nosed into the ring of stones, shook itself, and moved on. Was it the owner, I wondered, of the strange treasure? And what would it do when it discovered that the collection had been disturbed? I realized then that the air was darkening again, the sun having crossed the window and moved on.

"We've an interested shark, Mr. Phibbs," St. Ives said into the speaking tube, and almost at once we accelerated in our ascent. The shark angled downward again, swimming away from us, and then turned and came lazily back along the sea bottom. The surface of the ocean seemed to me to be appallingly distant, and very quickly it disappeared from view, the cavern having fallen into twilight.

"Certainly we're safe within the bell," I said, at a point when the creature was nearly below us. It gave a sharp jerk, and then rushed upward at an incredible speed, its eyes visible on the tips of the strange, flattened hammer that was its head. I let out a cry, jerked my feet from their perch on the foot rail, and flung them onto the seat, wafering myself against the wall. St. Ives did the same, just as the monster burst from the water, its head and upper body virtually filling the center of the bell, its great jaws snapping, its mouth lined with serrated teeth. Its hammer-like nose banged against the brass claw, knocking the ball of ambergris upward. St. Ives threw up an arm to steady it—grace under pressure, it seemed to me even then—and the shark fell away backward.

We soon found ourselves dangling in the air again, safe at last, still rising, the sound of the engine filling our ears after the undersea silence. There was a powerful rumble then, masking even the engine noise, and once again the air was full of debris clattering against the aluminum shell in which we sat. We swung inward, and Phibbs set us down jarringly on the deck, where things were moving forward in a terrible hurry. Already the anchors were coming in, and Hasbro once again shoveled coal into the orange mouth of the furnace, working in a determined hurry. Phibbs, who was signaling our success to the ship with a colored flag, apparently meant for us to remain in the bell, where we were comparatively safe and out of the way. The scow set out, its wake roiling over the rocks of the cavern behind us, sea birds fleeing away overhead, and we were out into the open air and daylight, such as it was, for the smoky sky was the color of a bruise now. Rock tumbled down the steep cliffs, flinging up spray when they struck the sea roundabout us.

Another good vomit, I thought, Gilbert's bit of nonsense coming into my mind. It would be a near-run thing if the volcano were seriously sick at the stomach, which it surely seemed to be. The tide was particularly low: the shelf of rocks that protected the bay stood three feet out of the water, which was stained an odd sepia color now, the sun glaring through the cloudy reek of the volcano, which was spewing stones, cinders, and ash as if it were engaged in a battle. Fortunately for us, the discharge was mostly on the windward side, although God knew how long our luck would hold.

I watched one such explosion very near the headland, marveling at the force of the thing, although my attention immediately shifted when the bowsprit and top-hamper of a sloop sailed into view—Billy Stoddard's sloop that we had last seen disappearing into the fog—pelting along on the freshening wind now, barely avoiding the shower of rock flung from the volcano. I looked out toward the *Nancy Dawson*, which was apparently moving away from us. "Where on earth are they going?" I asked aloud, with rather more emotion than I intended.

"I believe that Gilbert means to engage the enemy," St. Ives said, "and is endeavoring to bring the Nordenfelt gun to bear on their flank. Or perhaps he means simply to run them down, although he risks being boarded in the process. He has a great amount to lose at this juncture, and we're in a suitably empty tract of ocean. He can sink the sloop out of hand and no one the wiser."

St. Ives and I sat entombed within our bell, mere onlookers as the scow set out to sea. Phibbs, of course, had no idea of allowing the pirates to take us, which would interfere with Gilbert's designs. There was a hellish, foreboding cast to the air now, and the sea roiled roundabout us, waterweeds and dead fish upwelling from the deeps. I wondered at Gilbert playing monkey games with the sloop when the more fearful enemy was the volcano itself, or so I thought in my ignorance.

The sloop fired the cannon in her bow, a spray of spark and smoke that was a mere popgun against the volcanic turmoil. Where the ball fell I couldn't see, but it didn't bother the *Nancy Dawson*, which was more distant by the moment, maneuvering so as to use her motive power to advantage. The sloop had run clear of the island now and had the sea room to do some maneuvering of her own. It was dead clear that she meant to pass between the scow and the *Nancy Dawson*. The scow was slow, and the open deck left it utterly vulnerable to the sloop's guns. Either Gilbert must take the sloop very soon, or the sloop would take the scow with its five hostages and its ball of ambergris…

And then the sloop stopped dead in its flight as if she'd run headlong into an invisible wall. Her masts swayed dangerously, righted themselves, and then for a long moment she simply stood still in the water before careering forward once more. Simultaneously her bow twisted away to port and the foresail was torn away along with a mass of rigging. She jerked to a stop once again, although she wasn't still by any means, but shuddered and quivered bodily, the sea churning roundabout her. "She's struck a reef!" I said to St. Ives.

"No, by Heaven!" he said. "Look there, at the foremast. The bane of the *Celebes Prince*! Pray to God that Gilbert sees it!"

What I saw—and there was no disbelieving it—was a great tentacle rising from the sea, twenty, thirty feet and still rising, followed by a second tentacle, like undulating tree trunks. The spirit of the island, a giant octopus—monstrously large—had been stirred from the its lair in the hidden depths of the sea. The first tentacle wrapped itself around the foremast, the second gripped the bowsprit. There was the sharp sound of rending timbers, and the bowsprit snapped off like a matchstick, followed immediately by the foremast, both of them cast into the sea along with spars and sails and rigging in a tangled mass. The cannon in the bow was swept away in turn, rolling off the shattered foredeck on its carriage, the iron weight of it hauling the floating debris under the surface.

The volcano blasted out another salvo of glowing rock now, and several flaming chunks fell onto the deck in the center of the sloop. The mainmast and its sails simply burst into flame from the intense heat of the molten rock. Men leapt from the deck as the monster hauled itself up the port side of the ship, so that we saw its great, domed mantle rising until its enormous eyes were revealed. I saw Billy Stoddard then—a brave man in his way, although a monster himself—exhorting four crewmen to rally round, to train a cannon on the beast. But the creature that threatened them was inconceivably massive, a living horror, come up out of the depths of Lord Kelvin's bottomless trench, perhaps disturbed by the erupting volcano, perhaps out of anger at the meddling of human beings within its domain. The cannon were pitiful things, and the fearful pirates abandoned them and leapt over the starboard rail into the midst of flaming wreckage and almost certain death. Alone on the deck, Stoddard was driven toward the bow by the heat, which must at any moment ignite the powder room and destroy the ship.

The octopus swept the deck one last time with a departing tentacle. Debris flew, the burning mast tilted and fell, and the retreating tentacle plucked up Billy Stoddard by the neck where he stood teetering indecisively over the sea, raising him high into the air. A second tentacle gripped Stoddard around the waist, and the monster quite simply tore his head off, a spray of blood flying from the severed neck. With a curl of its tentacle, the octopus tucked the head beneath its mantel, rearing back and grasping it in its terrible beak, and then crushing it and swallowing it before disappearing into the sea carrying Stoddard's headless corpse.

Very shortly it reappeared, clambering up onto the reef that sheltered the bay and the sea cave, uncomfortably close to our scow. The creature sat watching us. Gravity flattened its great mantle, which looked something like an immense, drooping balaclava now. It clutched the headless Billy Stoddard as if he were a turkey leg, and, with a look of great relish, tucked Stoddard into its open, yard-wide beak, and snipped him in half at the waist, his innards spilling out as the torso disappeared into the creature's maw.

Horrified, I looked away, just as the sloop exploded in a shower of shattered spars and timbers, the blasted hull quickly sinking as we watched, leaving only floating debris and the tip of the mizzenmast with a ragged scrap of black pennant still attached to the wreckage and marking its grave. The octopus finished its supper, slithered backward off the reef, and disappeared into the sea. —☙

CHAPTER 7

The First Wonder of the Natural World

W
E MOTORED AT full speed toward the *Nancy Dawson* now. Gilbert had apparently witnessed the destruction of the sloop, and the steamer was lying to, waiting for us. The great crane swung slowly out over the side, making ready to haul us in. Gilbert stood beside it shouting through the decorated speaking trumpet from the chart room and waving us on, unnecessarily exhorting us to make haste. Captain Deane sat at the Nordenfelt gun, swiveling this way and that, on the lookout for the reappearance of the monster.

The death of the sun had cast the world in a perpetual, hellish twilight, which lent the morning a doomful air. My mind was fixed on the wild fear that the octopus would take us next, we having meddled with its ball of ambergris and otherwise disturbed its treasure. It could pluck up the bell with the tip of a tentacle and root us out of the interior like worms from a piece of fruit. Unlike the shark, which seemed to me to be a deeply stupid, vicious creature, the octopus had a distinct gleam of intelligence in its eyes, and perhaps even the semblance of a soul, I thought, given the sentimental business of the thing's keepsakes.

Phibbs took us in neatly, running in alongside the *Nancy Dawson* and tying on. Tubby descended the companionway to help Hasbro attach the cables that would allow the shipboard crane to winch us aboard in a package. Air was still blowing into the bell, making a low whistling noise, and there was nothing for St. Ives and I to do but sit with contrived patience. The waiting was short, however, for the sea began to move and shift, and although the view into the depths was occluded by the smoky shadow that hid the sun, we perceived the dark bulk of the octopus rising from below. St. Ives shouted a warning through the speaking tube, but it was unnecessary, for Gilbert had spotted the thing too, and was very nearly dancing with anticipation on the deck and pointing downward. He appeared positively boyish, as if he *welcomed* the thing's appearance.

Hasbro and Tubby looked down into the sea momentarily. Stalwart lads that they were, however, they straightaway continued their work, which was nearly finished—as were we all, I thought.

"It's a colorful way to die," St. Ives said, knowing what I was thinking.

"True," I said, trying to maintain something of the same spirit. "We'll have uncommonly strange things to chat about in the afterlife."

The tip of a great tentacle appeared then, seeking and then touching the deck of the scow. Another tentacle followed, the two together latching on with vast great suckers. The octopus meant to clamber aboard, perhaps, which was in some small way preferable to destroying us out of hand as it had destroyed the sloop, although it would quite possibly carry us under with its weight. We tilted to port as the octopus hoisted itself upward, and we kept on tilting until half the deck was awash. Tubby stood stock still several feet from the railing, watching the beast rise, higher and higher, until one of its immense eyes stared straight into Tubby's face, the creature regarding him brazenly. There arose from the sea another tentacle, moving wonderfully slowly. With an almost stupefying gentleness it lifted the allegedly lucky Bollinger hat from atop Tubby's head. Thinking of that nest of bric-a-brac in the sea cave, it came to me that the octopus coveted the hat, and I was suddenly fearful that Tubby, who knew no fear, might try to take it back.

"Hold your fire!" Gilbert shouted through the bullhorn, his voice audible even within the bell. Captain Deane had swiveled the Nordenfelt gun around and brought it to bear on the octopus, which had risen high enough out of the sea so that the top of his mantle could be blasted to pieces without endangering Tubby, who made a small bow to the creature, shook his head decidedly, and removed the hat from the tentacle, replacing it atop his own head and tapping it down with the palm of his hand.

The octopus gazed at him a moment, as if pondering whether to take the hat and the head along with it. But now the creature swiveled its great mantle toward Gilbert, fixing him with its awful gaze. Gilbert held his hand up, palm forward, in a ridiculous gesture of goodwill. There was a smile on his face, meant to be welcoming, but even from my vantage point it was stiff—the bluff smile of a man facing a firing squad. Yet another tentacle rose from the sea, wandering upward toward him, the octopus treating him with something like a high regard, just as he had treated Tubby despite Tubby's intransigence with the hat. All Englishmen, it seemed to me, must look very much alike to an octopus, but Tubby and Gilbert, who reminded one of the Tweedles, no doubt appeared to be the twin embodiment of the generous fat man, an image that was evidently pleasing to the octopus. The tentacle touched Gilbert's face, and still he didn't flinch, but was smiling more authentically now, the naturalist in him enthralled by this desperately strange experience. I thought of Miss Bracken, waiting in Kingston, blessedly unaware that she had a rival.

I'll admit to the strangeness of that notion, but there was something in the evident regard that the creature had for Gilbert that put it into my mind. Once again the tentacle was in motion, as the octopus carefully plucked the speaking trumpet from Gilbert's hand and held it close to its own vast eye, peering at the thing. Did it recognize the image of the rampant octopus painted on the cone? I prayed that it did, that it would suppose it to be evidence of our high regard for cephalopods, perhaps that we worshipped them as well as dreamt about them.

The speaking trumpet traced lazy circles in the air, held aloft by the waving tentacle as the creature gazed steadfastly at Gilbert, who casually bent forward to unhook a Jacob's ladder that hung from the railing of the *Nancy Dawson*. The lowest rung fell to the deck of the scow, as if Gilbert meant for the octopus to make use of it. He reached into his vest now and withdrew his pocket-watch, dangling the shiny object before the octopus, and at the same time taking four deliberate steps backward—not fearful steps, mind you, but evidently purposeful.

He shouted something at Phibbs now and gestured him forward. Phibbs, for his part, threw both his hands in the air as if out of frustration or disbelief. He climbed boldly to the deck of the *Nancy Dawson* without protest, however, not five feet from the quivering bulk of the monster, and made his way slowly to the big crane where he sat down and was still. It was clear that Gilbert intended to lure the octopus aboard the ship, Heaven alone knew why. It seemed clear that the beast either coveted the pocket-watch or was mesmerized by it, for its attention didn't stray, not even when Phibbs started the engine of the crane in a cacophony of smoke and noise. The octopus, its gaze fixed on Gilbert, pulled itself upward now, and the steamer listed to starboard. Gilbert traced elaborate gestures with his free hand, pointing back and downward in the direction of the mid-ship hold, which would shortly (I prayed) be covered by the hull of the scow, for we were already lifting into the air, unerringly manipulated by Phibbs's chugging machine. Gilbert stepped backwards carefully, the watch dangling from its chain, and the octopus crushed the railing as it swarmed bodily onto the open deck, shedding cataracts of seawater. Captain Deane sat stone-faced at his gun, not moving a muscle, although his hands were locked onto the trigger mechanism.

Gilbert moved along the steeply pitched deck now, gesturing at the massive octopus to follow him, which it did, smashing the foredeck cabin, dragging unknown tons of tentacles after it, one of which swept the Nordenfelt gun straight overboard and Captain Deane along with it before the startled man could react. The creature's tentacles made loud sucking noises against the deck. It advanced with a gliding, graceful manner, however, eyeing the remainder of the crew, who stood in a knot well back toward the stern, watching the dappled creature in fear and wonder.

And then Gilbert disappeared from sight, and I was certain for a brief moment that he had been snatched from his feet by the octopus.

"He's darted into the hold!" St. Ives said.

"Has he?" I asked. "Why on Earth would a man do that with a giant octopus at his heels?"

But the question was moot. The octopus was even then disappearing below decks, apparently into the mid-ship hold. Like its diminutive cousins, it could slither its great bulk through strangely small apertures, ironing itself out on one side of the opening and then expanding again on the other.

"He means to trap it below," St. Ives said, his voice revealing a certain amount of awe and astonishment.

"Gilbert has gone mad," I said.

"I agree with you there, although I believe I can guess out his intentions. Watch the knot of men aft now."

Those very men were already moving fast toward the hold, where they slammed shut the broad, steel panel doors, effectively sealing Gilbert's fate.

"Gilbert means to imprison the beast in the hold," St. Ives said. "He has great faith in his H-beams. I agree that it's madness. He didn't achieve his current station in life, however, by being timid. I'll wager that he's a shrewd hand at piquet."

The crewman had cleared away by now, and the scow settled into its depression, adding its weight to the top of the creature's cage. Very shortly Phibbs raised the bell from the deck and we were released into the reeking air, which smelled of brimstone, and I was reminded that although the octopus was at least temporarily sequestered and Billy Stoddard in its gullet, the volcano still threatened us. Gilbert reappeared from a companionway forward, looking done-in, as did Captain Deane, who had swum round to the Jacob's ladder and was now dragging himself aboard.

There was an enormous, belching explosion, and once again rock rained down and a great cloud of ash blew skyward, straight into the air until the trade winds caught it and shifted it to the southwest. It took me a moment to realize that it was mid-morning, which I had forgotten, what with the stupendous occurrences and the layer of ash and smoke that hid the sun. Phibbs hastened toward the engine room, followed by Captain Deane, and very soon we were moving away from the island, making toward the clean air of the open sea.

Gilbert had outwitted the beast when it followed him into the hold. He had gone straight back out through the open door of an interior bulwark with the octopus close behind, and then had slammed the heavy door shut behind him, shooting the bolts and praying that the monster wouldn't simply tear the door from its hinges. But no such thing had happened. The octopus was so far responding in a blessedly civilized manner, and the slightly delirious yawing of the ship as our speed increased was simply a matter of the creature's great weight shifting about as it inspected its dark lair. Gilbert had bet his ship—and our lives—on a throw of the dice. His luck, as he had put it, was in.

As for Kingston, Jamaica, Gilbert concluded that he hadn't the leisure to look in on Miss Bracken. "We've all heard the old saw about the woman in every port," he said to me as we walked into the chart room to dine, "and for some lucky dogs it comes tolerably close to the truth. But a giant octopus is nowhere as easy to find, not by a long sea mile."

There was perhaps more truth than poetry in what he said, and I was happy enough to acknowledge it, for I was longing for home and had no interest in Jamaica or Gilbert's capers with Miss Bracken. The great ball of ambergris rested in the middle of the chart room table, sitting securely within a double ring of braided rope, which brought to mind the rock nest in the sea cave.

As you can imagine, our afternoon conversation had much to do with the morning's perils and successes, returning often to the fearful creature below—its surprising agility in the open air, its uncanny ability to sense human villainy, which it apparently hated, its apparent fondness for Gilbert. Of particular interest was the obvious intelligence of the beast, and the childlike pleasure that it took in trinkets. It seemed entirely likely that it had been the keeper of the great ball of ambergris forty years ago, when James Douglas was a lad. We wondered at the age of the creature, and what ancient oddments we might find if we were to search through its possessions. If the octopus was in fact the fabled Lusca, namesake of the island, stories of which hearkened back to antiquity, then its continued existence suggested that giant octopuses enjoyed prodigiously long lives. We had all heard of koi fish, of course, which lived in excess of two hundred years, and of giant tortoises that crept through the passing ages on a single-minded search for edible shrubs. Our octopus, however, beat them all hollow. To the last man we feared for its health, for it seemed as much human as beast.

"There are sweetening cocks in the each of the three holds," Gilbert told us reassuringly as lunch was brought in, including steaks cut from the wings of red-devil squid, fried and sauced with lemon, caper berries, and brown butter. I wondered if the octopus had smelled its cousins being sautéed in the galley, and whether it would object in some violent manner. But the octopus was quiet in the cool darkness of its stateroom now, and although we were heavily laden, we were making a good fourteen knots atop a placid sea. "We can let in any amount of clean seawater through the cocks, as well as pump out the bilge," Gilbert told us. "The creature will be quite content, bless its heart."

"Until it becomes aware that it's been shanghaied," I put in.

"It'll thank us for transporting it to a civilized corner of the globe," Tubby said, draining a glass of bitter. "Did you allow the fellow to keep your chronometer, Uncle? It seems only fair, to my mind, after luring him aboard with it."

Gilbert nodded. "It would have been kind of you to give the poor thing your hat, nephew. But you were always tight-fisted. I was compelled to give up the watch in order to distract it while I barred the door of the hold. It was a Breguet chronometer, I'm sorry to say, and not a cheap, pinchbeck ticker. The octopus, which I believe is a member of the fairer sex, by the way, quite likely won't mark the difference, alas."

"The telling of time means little to a cephalopod, I'm afraid," St. Ives said, "although this one seems to be something of a philosopher. But inform us, sir, what will be the creature's fate, given that it survives the voyage?"

"That, gentlemen, has everything to do with an inspired thought that came to me when I communed eyeball to eyeball with it there on the deck. I fully expected my imminent death, but I find that my most brilliant ideas occur to me when I'm up against it. My old business partner Lord Bledsoe has long had the idea of constructing a great, public vivarium on the mouth of Yantlet Creek, just beyond the London Stone. It would house oceanic creatures of all sorts, their environment perpetually renewed by the tide pushing up the Thames—God's own sweetening cock, one might say. It would be a scientific endeavor for the most part, with the public to pay the expense. No less a personage than Alfred Russel Wallace sits on the Planning Committee, as does Lucius Honeywell, I might add."

There was an awkward silence as he looked from one to the other of us, a silence I interrupted by asking, "These men are in need of a giant octopus, then?"

"That's exactly what they're in need of, Jack, although they don't know it yet. But by God I mean to tell them, by telegraph at the soonest opportunity, so that they'll make ready for its arrival. We'll bill the creature as the first wonder of the natural world. London will be drained of its population, every man, woman, and child hastening downriver to see it. You could do worse than to buy land in and around Allhallows, gentlemen, in order to establish an inn. You'll never want for lodgers."

He laughed out loud, passed around the jug of beer, and proposed a toast to the octopus, which we drank happily. The creature was stirring again, its movements giving the ship an unpleasantly strange and uneven motion. I gazed out through the stern window, musing on the notion of success: *For whosoever hath, to him shall be given*, the Bible tells us, and certainly it seemed to be true. Gilbert would return from his voyage doubly successful. His name would be written in the history books and when all was said and done—and given that the octopus remained healthy—his net worth was likely to surpass that of the Queen.

Gilbert revealed, by the by, that the rest of us would share in the riches when the actual profit of the voyage was calculated—something that a gleeful part of my mind considered now: what Dorothy and I would do with our newfound wealth. But it was an unlucky thought, and I clapped a stopper over it. The morning had quite worn me out, and I soon grew weary of Gilbert Frobisher's incessant bonhomie. I began to wonder, as silly as it sounds, whether our great passenger might simply die of heart sickness despite its iron constitution. Yantlet Creek, I thought, would be a sad prison for such a stupendous, curious creature, and I wished to God we had taken the time to load its treasures into the bell, in order that it might take some pleasure in them while it spent its remaining days imprisoned.

Alas, there was nothing to be done about it. The *Nancy Dawson* had sunk the island with the setting of the sun, although the fire-lit cloud that towered away above it would remain visible until black night and distance obscured it at last. —☙

PART III

The Joyful Return

CHAPTER 8

Low Water Along the Thames

TWO WEEKS LATER we found ourselves once again in
the West India Docks. A storm was pending in the distance, rain
clouds stacked one atop the other on the horizon and moving toward us
out of the east on a freshening wind. But at present it was high noon on a
summer's day, seagulls wheeling in the sky and the great city cheerful and
welcoming. The tide was at its nadir, the muddy banks of the Thames broad
and glittering in the temporary sunshine. Mudlarks of all ages slogged
through the filth hoping to find lost coins, but generally digging out bits
of coal and iron and the occasional tool dropped over the sides of ships by
workmen, the toil earning them a few shillings from a day's wretched work.
Even they looked picturesque, however, beneath the summer sun, or so it
seemed to me. St. Ives, Hasbro, and I had agreed happily enough to provide
an audience during the unloading of our great passenger, which had been
alive some few hours past, although worrisomely sluggish.

The octopus had fallen silent very soon after Gilbert, on the advice
of St. Ives, had turned off the sweetening cock pumps when we passed
St. Mary's Bay in the mouth of the Thames. The river water at that point
contained too little salt, St. Ives said, and might poison the creature out of
hand. He had no knowledge of the physiology of the giant octopus, but it
was better to err on the side of prudence. It had been slow going upriver
into London, the shipping heavy, the tide dropping. Now the creature
was uncharacteristically still, as was Gilbert, who fingered the stethoscope
around his neck, perhaps considering the very real possibility of discovering

six tons of stinking dead cephalopod that would have to be chopped apart and shoveled out through the cargo door.

The transfer of the portable hold to a barge, and the towing of the barge back downriver to Yantlet Creek, was to be done with the greatest felicity. Gilbert had offered a three-pounds reward to each and every one of men doing the unloading if it were accomplished within forty minutes' time. We were to make use of the immense, cantilever crane on the West India dock to pluck the mid-ship hold bodily from the ship and set it onto the barge, an undertaking that was proceeding apace now that the scow had been lifted from its place within the deck by the shipboard crane, the diving bell still sitting on the scow's deck. Gilbert's scientific friends would meet Gilbert and Tubby at the barge's ultimate destination, where the craft would be scuttled so that the sweetening cocks could be restarted and the creature once again bathed in revivifying salt water.

The ship's carpenter had crated up the ball of ambergris in a deceptive wooden box marked "Somerset Players: Footlights." Once the barge was underway, St. Ives, Hasbro, and I would accompany the box to Threadneedle Street, to deliver it to Bank of England guards to be stowed in a deep vault. I, for one, was anxious to be quit of the ambergris and the octopus both, and I meant to dine at home with Dorothy in two hours' time. I anticipated the happy surprise on her face when I walked in, my face burned brown from my weeks on the open sea.

The ambergris box sat on deck at the moment, covered in a decorative cloth. Gilbert's Baccarat decanter and several glasses sat atop it. Old Lazarus MacLean had contrived a length of bunting on the homeward voyage, cut and sewn into the shape of a line of octopuses, each holding onto another's tentacle, a twelve-foot length of it decorating the railing. The loose arms of the creatures flapped in the breeze in a lively fashion. MacLean was a man of many talents, and he stood now in his kilt and Tam o' Shanter, cradling his instrument, ready to pipe Gilbert down the side of the ship.

The great crane, standing squarely between the South Dock and the Export Dock, began to belch steam and coal smoke while uttering an immense cacophony of wheezing, shrieking and clattering. It latched onto the braided steel cable that connected the huge eyebolts on the four corners of the hold, and the container slowly rose into view as we held our collective breath. Crowds had gathered to watch out of mere curiosity by now, having no idea of the contents of the container, which would not be revealed to them in any event.

Gilbert waved at the onlookers from his position on the foredeck, encouraging their attention. History was being writ large, if only they knew it. Up rose the steel box, swaying ponderously. It traveled out over the dock and descended toward the barge on the opposite side. Down it sank until it sat atop the barge, which settled a full two-feet, farther than that at the stern, the deck nearly awash. Lazarus McLean wheezed into a rousing rendition of "Brown-haired Maiden," and a half dozen of us, McLean and Phibbs included, tossed off a dram of whisky and flung our glasses overside onto the Thames bank, to the happy surprise of the nearby mudlarks. Gilbert descended to the dock and crossed to the barge, followed by Tubby, who wore his Bollinger hat, the feathers shining in the sun. Tubby turned and waved farewell to us once he was aboard.

Gilbert strode straight to the side of the great box and put the mouth of his stethoscope against it, listening intently. He shook his head unhappily and touched his hand to the side of the box, which was no doubt heating up like an oven in the bright sunlight. He said something sharp to the crew of the barge, which cast off the mooring lines without wasting a moment, for they were as anxious for their reward as Gilbert was anxious to revive the octopus. The barge was abruptly underway, a tugboat towing it out into Limehouse Reach and away downriver.

The rain clouds were moving briskly toward us now, and one could see the dark tracings of heavy rain showering down in the distance. It was a remarkable sight, the day having turned into a metaphor, divided as it was between darkness and light. Persuaded to hurry by the pending rain, we fetched our dunnage and loaded it onto a coach-and-four driven by the selfsame cadaverous but stalwart cockney who had stood by us in Limehouse four weeks past—Boggs was his name. I had scarcely thought of the man in the weeks since, but I was heartily glad to see him again. We heaved the valuable crate in upon a seat in the interior, climbed in after it, locked the coach doors, and set out, the three of us alert for troublemakers, of which there was no sign. Billy Stoddard and his pirates were beyond the pale, but the inscrutable Lucius Honeywell was still at large. Gilbert had never given up his faith in the man. But as Hasbro had pointed out that first evening in the chart room, bad men might have imposed upon Mr. Honeywell, and to my mind it was equally likely that Mr. Honeywell had imposed upon Gilbert Frobisher, who was canny in business, but who had a fierce sense of loyalty to his friends, or to those he considered his friends. Hasbro held his loaded pistol in his lap, prepared to use it if we were threatened. I've never liked a pistol, loaded or otherwise—very like a poisonous adder, to my mind—although Hasbro's facility with a revolver had saved my life on more than one occasion, and so I'm happy enough that he doesn't scruple to carry one.

It was troubling that Gilbert had telegraphed his biological friends, informing them that we were carrying the first wonder of the natural world. Honeywell would naturally assume that we had returned with the ambergris into the bargain, thereby surmising that Stoddard and his villains had failed. If so, he might easily cut some new variety of caper. I reminded myself, however, that I was quit of the octopus and would soon be quit of the ambergris. The back of my hand to Mr. Honeywell, I thought, and I was in a cheerful enough mood as we rattled along through Wapping, following the river past the Tower and the Pool of London under a lowering sky, watching out for the barge when we got a rare glimpse of the river and thinking to wend our way along Thames Street to Blackfriars, and then up past St. Paul's and down again via Newgate and Cheapside. Thames Street skirts the Embankment at Blackfriars, which gave us a last grand view of the river and the south shore. It was there that we saw the barge itself, fast aground on a mud bank and sunk to its withers in muck, the tug straining to tow it clear. It would be hours before the river rose again and floated it free.

St. Ives signaled to Boggs to halt the carriage, and the man reined in the horses while there was yet open ground along the pavement. It was a near run thing, though, and the left rear wheel banged hard against the curb, the wagon wobbling to a stop. A richly appointed landau carriage, following behind us with two or three passengers inside and two men up behind, swerved aside to avert a collision, the coachman bawling out insults. We shoved open the door and climbed out, happy to be alive. The wheel was still on the axle, but was evidently knocked crooked on the hub—the least of our troubles, it seemed to me. St. Ives removed the pistol from his coat and handed it to the driver. "Guard the box within, Mr. Boggs," he shouted. "There'll be a generous reward if the contents come through unscathed." Boggs nodded darkly, rainwater falling from the brim of his hat, and touched the handle of his whip to the golden initials embossed upon the door, as if to say that he knew his master and would do his duty.

A nearby set of stairs descended to the river some forty yards upriver of where the barge had grounded. We hastened in that direction, and from the top of those stairs we watched the furious activity on the deck of the barge, Gilbert gesticulating and shouting, while several men, Tubby included, were gathered at the forward cargo doors. There were idlers watching along the embankment and standing along the upriver edge of Blackfriars Bridge, hoping that the barge would provide something in the way of amusement.

A long delay might mean the end of the octopus, and I was full of regret for the great beast and for having taken it away from its beloved tropical waters in the first place. It was an act conceived as much in the spirit of greed as scientific inquiry, and Gilbert would pay the piper, as would the poor octopus. I felt done up, but I reminded myself that St. Ives, Hasbro, and I could not shift the barge half an inch. Our particular charge was to proceed to Threadneedle Street with the ambergris, and the sooner it was secure, the better.

The doors of the container were just then swinging open, however, the men backing away, taking shelter behind the heavy steel panels. Tubby and Gilbert stood squarely in front of the now-open box, looking into the dark interior, Tubby caparisoned in his lucky Bollinger hat. The long moments ticked away, and the sky grew dark, and then darker yet, in mourning for the death of the octopus, I thought. And then with a suddenness that took my breath away, the tip of a tentacle whipped out from within the box, wrapped around Gilbert's chest, just beneath his arms, and plucked him bodily from the deck. A second tentacle snatched the Bollinger from Tubby's head and then knocked him neatly over the side. He landed on his fundament in the mud as the octopus issued forth from the hold, not only alive, but evidently in dangerously high spirits, waving the decorated speaking trumpet aloft as if it meant to harangue the crowd upon the bridge. There sounded a crack of thunder, and the rain came pelting down. The octopus seemed to expand in the liquid air, as if drawing nourishment and energy from it, and it swiveled atop its trunk-like tentacles, taking in the view of Thames-side London like the pagan god that it was, and not much liking what it saw.

The crew of the barge, to the last man, leapt overboard, sinking ankle deep in sludge, their shoes sucked away as they waded heavily ashore toward our set of stairs or else launched themselves into deeper water in order to swim to safety, which was perhaps unwise, given the nature of the threat. The mudlarks, well used to the ways of the river and mud, moved more quickly, looking back at the octopus in stunned disbelief. The people atop the bridge also very apparently understood the enormity of the thing that confronted them, and amid wild shouting and pushing they moved in a mass down onto Thames Street, fleeing from the creature's sight. Very quickly people were running past us along the embankment, shouting for constables, crying out that it was the leviathan of old, come to lay waste to the city. A considerable number—young men and boys, mostly—remained despite the rain and the danger, taking up positions behind lampposts and climbing into trees in order to watch the fun, as if those objects would protect them from the creature's wrath.

St. Ives was already leaping down the stairs toward the river, past the muddy, rain-bedraggled crowd that was coming up in the opposite direction, some on their hands and knees, gasping for breath because of their exertions. The octopus stood—so to call it—on the empty deck of the barge now, its drooping bulk draped over the sides. It pulled Gilbert to its breast as if he were an infant. Gilbert's hands were pressed against the flesh of the creature's tentacle, his own eyes looking up into the massive, dark orbs of the octopus. Tubby, having struggled to his feet, waved his arms now, shouting for the octopus to put his uncle down, by God, but the beast ignored him utterly, having chosen Gilbert as its particular favorite and forgotten Tubby's very existence. It slithered its massive bulk off the edge of the barge into shallow water, carrying with it the speaking trumpet and Tubby's hat, Gilbert's Breguet chronometer dangling on its chain from the very tip of one of the great tentacles.

Aided by Hasbro and me, Tubby clambered up onto the granite landing where we stood, the rainwater sluicing mud from his trousers and shoes, just as a pair of constables descended from above to stand beside us in openmouthed disbelief as the octopus moved glidingly downriver toward the black disk that opened above the river into the granite wall of the embankment: the open mouth of the Fleet sewer, out of which cascaded a torrent of water. The octopus sheltered Gilbert and its treasures from harm as it pulled itself up the embankment wall, the torrent washing over it. Within moments Gilbert Frobisher was carried away into the darkness.

"What in the dear Lord's name…?" one of the constables asked the other, his eyes still wide with astonishment.

"It's the Kraken of old," the other said, "come out of that there box. It'll plug the Fleet like a wine cork. Come on, Bob. We can do naught standing here." And with that they hurried back up the stairs and out of sight, paying us no mind at all.

"I intend to follow the flaming son of a bitch," Tubby said, referring, I believe, to the octopus. He looked about himself as if he were ready to leap back into the Thames mud. Of course it was utterly impossible that Tubby could force his way through the torrent that poured from the circular opening in the embankment wall, even if he could climb up to it, which he could not.

"We're hampered by the torrent here," St. Ives said, putting a hand on his shoulder. "We'll want an intercepting sewer at a higher elevation."

"The Ludgate crossing, perhaps, in Dean's Court," Hasbro said to him, the lot of us turning toward the stairs. "The Oxford Street channel is too distant."

"Aye," said St. Ives, "Ludgate it is. It's conceivable that we might get in ahead of the monster rather than merely following it, given that it's traveling northward."

"And do what?" I asked, as we were ascending, but the answer never came, for at that moment a pistol shot rang out, and then another. As the street came into view we saw that our coach had moved out onto the road and traveled some distance farther down. Boggs was laying about himself on all sides with his whip, St. Ives's smoking pistol in his other hand. A man lay dead or wounded on the street. Another clung to the handhold on the side of the carriage as the horses shied and the carriage lurched on the pavement, its wounded wheel canting from side to side. Two men tried to drag the horses up the little byway called Puddle Dock while evading the coachman's lash. A fifth man climbed across the top of the carriage, apparently having gotten up over the bags secured to the rack behind. All of this we perceived by the time we had completed our ascent of the embankment.

We raised a shout and ran forward as the man climbing up beside Boggs jerked the whip from his hand and pitched it away. Boggs turned in that same moment, aimed the pistol, and shot his assailant dead through the forehead, the man sprawling away, even as the villain atop the coach clutched Boggs by the hair and the shoulder of his coat and flung him bodily from his seat, immediately sliding down onto the bench and snatching up the reins as his two uninjured companions leapt clear of the horses and climbed into the coach. In the very moment that we drew near it set out at a rapid clip despite the wobbly wheel, up Puddle Dock toward Queen Victoria Street with its maze of cross streets and byways, where it might easily disappear.

I saw then that the landau carriage that had swerved past us sat now along the curb, some fifty feet up Puddle Dock. A bearded man wearing a *pince-nez* and a Homburg hat peered out of the window, looking back. Aside from the driver he was alone in the coach, although he hadn't been a few minutes ago.

"Look there!" I shouted, pointing in that general direction. "Lucius Honeywell, by God!"

It was a guess, of course, but calculated. Tubby Frobisher and I set out at a run, but before we had crossed to the pavement, the broken-wheeled coach rattled past the Landau, which angled out onto the roadway and followed along behind it, both conveyances disappearing around the bend in the road. All of this occurred in a matter of moments—a shorter time than it takes to tell it.

We turned back, toward where poor Boggs lay stunned on the road, Hasbro and St. Ives feeling for a pulse and prodding the swelling lump where he had hit his head. Boggs was apparently comatose, and so after a brief powwow we left him with the very capable liverymen at Apothecaries Hall and hastened north up Puddle Dock on foot, the rain lessening now. We were bound for Dean's Court, where the aboveground entrance to a cross-channel of the Fleet sewer stood. There it would be possible to clamber down an iron ladder to the sewer proper without being drowned in the process.

Tubby was in too much haste, however, to be happy with the plan. "When we find our way into the sewer," he asked as we hastened along, "which way then? Up or down?"

"I don't know," St. Ives said. "Perhaps we'll discover the answer on the walls of the sewer—some gelatinous sign that the creature has passed through. Unfortunately the river sewers are in fact a warren of tunnels and cross tunnels—channels that run east toward the Walbrook and west toward the Tyburn, not to mention downward from one level to another. There's also the possibility that the creature will find the sewer gasses intolerable and be compelled to return to the river."

"Then God help Uncle Gilbert," Tubby said, with an uncharacteristic note of despair in his voice. It came to me that Tubby stood to inherit his uncle's lavish estate, and yet would cheerfully die to save the old man's life, a fact that redoubled my own determination to be of use to him, although every passing moment diminished our chances of finding Gilbert in time to save him. —⌐

CHAPTER 9

Pursuit

LTHOUGH UNDER OTHER circumstances Queen
Victoria Street might be the natural route along which the two
coaches would flee, at the moment it was at a standstill in the heavy
weather, and it seemed to us mildly unlikely that the coaches would intentionally mire themselves there. We pushed between the carriages and up
St. Andrew's hill, where our supposition was proven correct. A crowd of
onlookers was gathered around Gilbert's coach, which lay crippled on its
side in the street, the wheel having come off and careened through the
window of a butcher's shop. The landau stood abandoned behind it, the
horses skittish, left to their own devices. The box containing the ambergris,
of course, was no longer inside the fallen coach, but had been carried away
by the three villains, who had fled on foot. They were rough men, we were
told, and no one had interfered with them except the irate butcher, who had
been knocked down for his efforts. No one knew what had happened to a
man in a Homburg hat and *pince-nez*. No one had seen him.

We set out again at a run, very shortly issuing out onto Ludgate Hill at
the north end of Dean's Court, where lay a heap of brick and a tree that had
been snapped off several feet above the pavement, all of it lying in a pool of
water that still leaked out of a great hole broken into in the wall. A mangled
iron grill that had blocked the entrance to the sewer lay some distance away.
We had found our octopus, it seemed, or at least the ruin it had left behind.

St. Paul's Churchyard stood dead ahead, the great cathedral beyond.
There was a hubbub in the direction of the cathedral clock tower, people

making a din and pointing skyward. We saw it then, the octopus itself, rising up between the two towers directly behind the statue of St. Paul, which was dwarfed by the great beast. It rested the end of one tentacle around the saint's neck, as if considering whether the head was a useful trophy. With another tentacle held onto Gilbert Frobisher, the man very evidently alive, for his head swiveled as he peered roundabout him and then bent his shoulders forward in order to look below. Tubby waved heartily at him, let out a bark of laughter, and cried, "He lives!" in a voice husky with relief.

The octopus had been careful to preserve Gilbert's life thus far, but although it clearly had a regard for Gilbert, it could know nothing of architecture and engineering. The massive Portland stone in the heavy outer walls of the cathedral supported the great weight that stood atop it now, but its roof timbers were another matter, should the creature venture farther from the edge. I envisioned the destruction of the great cathedral, the smoking ruin that would be a consequence of our having meddled with Mother Nature, stealing away one of her grandest and most fearsome creatures and blithely bringing it home to lay waste to London.

People were issuing from within the cathedral now, hurrying through the great portico and down the stairs, ushered out by constables and church workers in a state of confusion. Nothing that they had been told could have prepared them for the truth, which was revealed when they looked back and upward into the rainy sky, where the tentacles of the inconceivable creature waved like branches in a stiff wind. The octopus moved away along the wall toward the bell tower now, where it stopped again, reaching upward with a long tentacle and effortlessly snapping off the golden, pineapple finial from atop the tower. A keepsake? I fervently hoped so. The finial was massive, and I recalled that the octopus had thrust an anchor straight through the hull of the *Celebes Prince*…

Again it moved off, disappearing from our view behind the massive structure of the tower. People roundabout us shifted away, back across the churchyard through the drizzle, hoping to keep the octopus in view.

"Hark!" said St. Ives, and he pointed toward the lawn beyond the clock tower, where a knot of onlookers stood pointing skyward and gawking. One of them sat upon the wooden crate that bore the ball of ambergris, and standing beside him were the other two ruffians who had taken the coach.

We set out directly in the direction of the clock tower, making a circuit of it in order to come in behind our men unawares. The man sitting atop the crate stood up, hoisted the crate to his shoulder, said something to his friends, and the three of them walked away up the south side of the cathedral toward New Change Street and Cheapside. We followed at a quick trot, unseen still, closing the gap between us and them as we approached the east end of the cathedral. There was a din from the direction in which we had come, a hundred voices exclaiming, the octopus cutting capers, no doubt. One of the three men hearing the noise, looked back, saw us closing in upon them, and shouted.

He was too late, however, for Tubby broke into a furious sprint and bowled straight through the man who had shouted, knocking him hard aside and latching onto the one who held the crate, grappling him like a great bear. The third man simply ran away like a horse in the final stretch, easily outdistancing us and disappearing into the traffic that clogged New Change, many of the carts and carriages abandoned, people standing in the road, gazing at the cathedral roof.

The crate tumbled as Tubby's man was borne down, and it broke open against the edge of the waist-high wall that runs along the edge of the cathedral garden. Hasbro threw himself forward even as it was falling, and caught the ball of ambergris in a flying leap that would have done an acrobat proud. His weight, however, tore loose a small stretch of spear-shaped iron pickets that topped the wall, and he rolled bodily into the garden. He was up again immediately, holding the uninjured ambergris, blood flowing from a long gash on his forehead, where a flap of skin and scalp was torn open.

"Here's one for Mr. Boggs!" Tubby shouted at his prisoner, and then cuffed him hard on the back of the head and pushed him sprawling onto his hands and knees. Before he could arise, Tubby skipped forward and kicked him on the backside. The man fell onto his face, but immediately scrambled crabwise to his feet and hurried off at a hobbling run, looking back in amazement at the great ivory ball that Hasbro held in his hands. For a moment I thought that Tubby would run him down a second time in order to continue abusing him, but there was more vital work to do. All three of the villains had won free, which gave none of us a moment's pause. St. Ives hauled a handkerchief out of his vest pocket and carefully closed and swabbed the wound in Hasbro's scalp, and Tubby offered up his own kerchief, which was something more in the nature of a small awning, and which St. Ives tied as a bandage around Hasbro's head while I held onto the unlucky orb.

We set out directly, back toward the Ludgate side of the cathedral in order to see the way of things above. The din of the crowd had increased, and hundreds of people jammed the pavement now. A party of Fusiliers endeavored to hold the mob back, but in fact the mob was held back in the interest of the strange view high above them. People pointed skyward past hundreds of black umbrellas, and although I was as wet to the skin, I prayed that the rain would continue, for it was the rain, I was sure of it, that kept the octopus alive.

The creature had ascended partway up the great dome by now, to the level of the Whispering Gallery, where I had gone as a child with my mother, an intrepid climber. The Whispering Gallery stood some two hundred and fifty steps above the floor of the cathedral. The climb had winded me as a boy, despite my boundless energy. The octopus was still moving upward resolutely, holding Gilbert to its breast and clutching at the Corinthian columns that girdled the lower reaches of the dome, hauling itself toward the Stone Gallery now, moving with surprising delicacy, the columns standing solidly under its weight, at least so far.

The mass of people roundabout us were in high spirits, and resembled an audience watching an open-air play at the fair. A boy approached shouting, "Brollies!" and carrying a sack of down-at-heel but serviceable umbrellas, of which we purchased three. Another lad was doing an enviable business selling second-hand opera glasses and tin telescopes. Costers pushed their carts around the perimeter, peddling hot coffee and sweets and hot-cross buns, which were bought up by the wet and shivering. A man nearby offered competing odds whether Gilbert would be crushed or eaten at the hands of the monster, and I cast him a vicious look, which engendered a happy wink. The man was more than half drunk, and offered six-to-one odds in favor of the eating. He didn't want for punters.

Tubby was deaf to all of it. His entire being was concentrated on the octopus and its passenger. The creature had ascended beyond the Stone Gallery and was creeping across the dome itself, its monstrous tentacles gripping and releasing, the sensitive tips darting here and there as it felt the terrain above. It settled atop the flat bit of eave that runs around Golden Gallery, sitting side-saddle, as it were, wrapping a single tentacle around the gilt ball beneath the pinnacle cross itself. And there it came to rest, three hundred sixty feet above the churchyard, tentacles splayed out over its heavenly throne, waving its pineapple scepter. Gilbert Frobisher sat atop one of its knees, it you'll allow me the term. Astonishingly, he now held the speaking trumpet and wore Tubby's Bollinger hat, which was surely a sign of the octopus's good will. The beast peered out toward Camden and Lincoln's Inn Fields, surveying what it perhaps believed to be its domain. Its immense, drooping mantle hung behind it like a half-inflated balloon. The sky roundabout it was a riot of pewter clouds that stood stock still in the windless heavens.

"I'll need that ball of ambergris, Jack," Tubby said, his voice clipped and terse. "If you gentlemen have no objection, I'll assume responsibility for it from this point hence." He took it from me before any of us had responded, and then removed his coat and wrapped it around the ball, tying the sleeves tightly to make a bundle.

"Perhaps two of us should carry the ambergris on to Threadneedle Street for safe keeping," St. Ives said to Tubby. "It's a matter of little more than half a mile."

"I mean to return it to its rightful owner," Tubby said, "as ransom for my uncle." He shook his head sharply, his face fixed in a determined squint.

St. Ives nodded, although his eyes revealed his doubts. "It's conceivable that such a plan will work," he said. "The creature is much attached to the globe, having guarded the thing through the years. It dearly loves a trinket of any sort, and to my mind your ball of ambergris is the real prize."

"Bartering with the creature has the distinct advantage of being our only option," Tubby said. "It's the sole form of diplomacy that the octopus understands. I looked into the depths of its eyes when it first confronted me, and I saw what I believe to be a rational being looking back out at me. It took my measure before it took my hat. I mean to parlay with it."

"I adjure you not to go alone, Tubby," St. Ives said to him. "I'll accompany you."

"I honor you for the offer, Professor, but I don't want for company. There'll be two aloft as it is, two Frobishers. A third man cannot help, nor can a fourth, neither. If our nabob takes it into its mind to descend, or,

God help us, to fall…" He paused for a moment and then shook his head sharply. "We'll want allies on the ground." And with that, the thing had been decided.

Tubby set out in the direction from whence we had come five minutes previously. I thought hard for a moment before I said to St. Ives and Hasbro, "I'll accompany him whether he likes it or not," and before St. Ives could utter anything sensible to me, I handed my newly-purchased umbrella to a woman standing beside me, and then turned on my heel and set out, hurrying to catch up to Tubby and half expecting St. Ives to call me back—perhaps hoping that he would.

"It's madness, Tubs," I told him when I drew up to him. "Sheer lunacy." I was more than a little doubtful about Tubby's climbing those endless stairs. His monumental strength was inarguable, but like the fearsome and powerful hippopotamus, his endurance was not boundless.

"We'll chat about it afterward, Jack, or else we will not. Simple as that."

"It'll mean two dead. Perhaps you didn't see what that creature did to Billy Stoddard, but I can tell you that it turned my stomach. It has a fondness for Uncle Gilbert, but…"

"He's my uncle, Jack, and I love the man dearly—more than the octopus loves him, I dare say, and the octopus is right fond of him. If it were Dorothy in the grip of the monster, you would surely do the same."

"Yes, I would. I'll come with you, then."

"It's because of my fondness for Dorothy that you will not."

It was a compelling argument, although I made up my mind to deceive him whether he liked it or no. "So be it," I lied, following along beside him with no idea of turning back.

We arrived at the spot where we'd had our brief battle with the three thieves, beyond which stood a door half hidden by shrubbery, one of three that were evident in the long wall. The ill-fitting door was locked. It rattled, but it wouldn't open. By now the interior of the cathedral would be empty of people, and even if there were someone left inside, knocking would avail us little. The nearby street, however, was not empty of people, some of whom were looking in our direction, perhaps taking us for burglars who meant to profit during the distraction. Tubby handed me the balled-up coat, hurrying the several yards to where Hasbro's forehead had sheared off the fence pickets. He picked up a connected trio of iron spears and returned.

"Step aside, Jack," he said, wedging the spearheads into the door between the jamb and the knob. Without a word he heaved himself against them, straining forward as if he meant to shift the entire cathedral in the direction of Ludgate Hill.

It was then that I saw against the dark sky to the southwest, two dark, elongated dirigibles—almost certainly warships from the Naval Air Vessel Yard at Greenwich. A single, smaller dirigible accompanied the warships. Without a doubt they were headed in our direction, which didn't bode well for the octopus. There was a splintering sound, a spray of black paint and rust from the bending iron bars, and with a loud crack the door flew open, revealing a small landing with stairs descending, the small room illuminated by gas-lamps.

"Hells bells," Tubby muttered. "I want to go up, not down." He tossed the pickets aside, however, snatched the orb out of my hands, and stepped in. I glanced behind us and was surprised to see the red coats of a dozen Royal Fusiliers coming round the building from the west. When I turned back, anxious to enter before the soldiers spotted us, the door was already slamming in my face. I threw my shoulder against it and pushed it open far enough to cram myself through, surprising Tubby, who looked as if he meant to pitch me straight out again.

"Hurry!" I said to him. "They're after us!" And they might have been, surely.

Tubby set out without a word. There was no time for debate. There was no locking the door, either, for the heavy brass bolt lay on the floor, screwed to a great splinter of wood. Down we went, not looking back, until we reached the bottom of the stairs, where we found ourselves in a broad room with a mosaic floor: the crypts, utterly abandoned, the cool air heavy and still. There was no human noise at all, but there was an ominous creaking from overhead, roof timbers straining, perhaps, from the great weight settled upon the dome. Near a high window stood the tomb of Sir Christopher Wren, who had designed the cathedral so many years ago—his greatest work in a life of great works, threatened now by an enormity that Wren could not have imagined, unless he too dreamt of cephalopods.

Tubby forged ahead as if he would leave me behind if he could, which he could not. The crypt gates, thank God, had been left unlocked, and we were through them in an instant, Tubby skipping up the stairs toward the cathedral floor with a boyish abandon. We emerged in the quire, which smelled of furniture oil and stone, and hurried past the great, silent organ, soon finding ourselves beneath the dome, where our real work would begin. The spiral stairs stretched away above us like the interior of an enormous seashell, into which we would climb until we were within the encircling tentacles of the octopus. In the sunlight that shone through the windows above us, a haze of dust was settling, almost certainly being ground out of the mortar that cemented the stones of the dome. In my mind I commanded the octopus to rest easy.

Up we climbed, putting one foot ahead of the other, as they say, quickly rising to the level of the high, arched windows. From that vantage point we could see that the dirigibles had drawn near, the warships following one after the other, the smaller dirigible at a lower elevation. There were guns mounted on the gondolas of the warships, although of necessarily small bore, since the airy ship would scarcely stand the recoil of a large caliber ball. Nordenfelt guns? I thought of the maniac Captain Deane, and the strange and murderous joy that illuminated his face when he sat at his gun. Weapons, like all tools, were meant to be used.

The view disappeared as we moved ever upward. I was breathing heavily now, my legs burning with the strain. I counted steps in order to ignore the gasping for air and the protesting muscles. Tubby had slowed considerably, which was wise if it were intentional, since continued haste might simply burst his heart in his chest.

"Shall I carry the burden?" I asked of his back, and received a vague shake of the head for an answer. I didn't have the breath to argue.

Up we trudged, scaling the walls of the great dome. I kept away from the edge for safety's sake, and watched Tubby's broad back rising before me, step by mesmerizing step. Above us, on the curved ceiling, stood the frescoes of saints and prophets going about their collective business with nary the thought of octopi; below us, dizzyingly far away now, lay the great compass rose, a double cephalopod in its own right, set into the floor of the nave. Its sixteen tentacles indicated the four corners of the earth and sundry points in between. I contemplated the meaning of the signifying, many-armed symbols above and below, the octopus as the living symbol of the compass rose, and I tried to call into my mind the gist of the Hopkins poem. "Glory be to God for dappled things," I muttered, distracting myself from the toil of the climb. And wasn't the giant octopus one of God's dappled creatures? I began to see why such a creature of wonder, a thing of octo-symmetrical grandeur and with the eyes of a prophet, might easily come to be both worshipped and feared.

Tubby tripped and fell forward now, jerking me back to the present moment. He went down hard on his knees, grunting with pain but managing to hold the ambergris ball aloft, the second time today that it had been saved from ruin. He remained there for a long moment with his head bent forward.

"I'll take it, Tubby, for God's sake," I said, coming up behind him, hearing his breath wheezing in and out.

"No, Jack," he said, and mumbled something unconvincing about duty and honor. Then pushed himself up onto his pins and we moved upward again, soon arriving at the Whispering Gallery, where we paused to look out over Ludgate and the river in the distance. Far below, St. Ives and Hasbro still stood at their post. St. Ives held a pair of opera glasses to his eyes, and seemed to be watching for our arrival, but whether he could see us or not I had no idea. There was a buzzing in the air like bees now, quite distinct, and we set out around the wall of the gallery to take in the view until we saw what was making the noise—the dirigibles, propelled by electromotor engines, quite close now. The two warships were still at a higher elevation, and it appeared as if they would pass overhead, intent upon studying their quarry from above. The smaller dirigible, however, piloted by a man either intrepid or impetuous, had descended toward the cathedral as if to have a closer look, and was approaching from the east.

We were off again, having gotten our fabled second wind, the arrival of the dirigibles putting a troubling spin on things. The wearisome steps, narrower now, fell away behind us. We attained the dizzying height of the Stone Gallery—376 steps, I've since learned—which is an open-air gallery. We lost not a moment sightseeing, however, but pushed ever on, Tubby's breath coming out of him in a wheezing roar like a broken bellows. Up we climbed and ever farther up, the sweat pouring down my face as we ploughed along. At long last we ascended to the Golden Gallery, the present domain of the Great God Octopus and the shaky pinnacle of our long journey.

We stepped out into the open air, onto the little bit of balcony that encircles the Gallery. Across the balustrade was draped a glistening tentacle the girth of an ash tree, but with a double row of suckers, their color and shape reminiscent of the bells of iron tubas. The air was warm and still and wet, as if the octopus had trailed tropical weather along with it from its ancestral home. Tubby heaved great restorative breaths while unwrapping the ambergris pearl. He pitched his coat over the side so that it fluttered away groundward like a butterfly. Tubby was all in, coats be damned, caught up in a state of dangerous determination.

With an ear-shattering peal the great bells in the south-west tower began to toll, including the sixteen-ton bell known as Great Paul. I pressed the palms of my hands against my ears as Tubby recoiled, reeling from the noise of the vast pealing. It was not near the top of the hour, and so it seemed likely that it was an effort to frighten the octopus from its perch. The bells did little to agitate it, however, and I wondered whether it could hear at all; certainly it had no apparent ears. Its tentacles rose and fell, the golden pineapple swinging past our heads like a pendulum. By crushing ourselves against the balustrade and craning our necks backward, we could see the beast's vast bulk stretching away skyward like a hillside with two great, staring eyes. It bent forward, contemplating us as we stared upward at it, the rain in our faces. It knew Tubby, but it did not know me, and it could not guess that I held it in high esteem. The octopus twisted now, looking to the right and left, its wary eyes revealing a dawning understanding of the untenable nature of its circumstances, or so it seemed to me.

The two warships had quite disappeared, which could mean only that they were now hidden from our view by the dome. They would have the wind at their backs upon the return, which would improve their ability to maneuver. The small dirigible had descended to a point nearly level with the peak of the cathedral, and for a moment it seemed to be stopped in the air, framed by a backdrop of moving clouds, grey through the rain. The octopus shifted its great bulk, evidently intent upon meeting its nemesis straight on. It hefted the golden pineapple as if biding its time.

Despite the pealing of the bells I heard Tubby shout the word "Fools!" for his mouth was six inches from my ear. He stepped away, shaking his fist at the dirigible, bidding it be gone with broad gestures and holding the ambergris tight against himself with left hand and forearm.

The craft veered slightly now, whirring ever closer, and I could see that a camera was set up within its gondola—two, three cameras. The idiots were risking all—including Gilbert, Tubby, and I—for the sake of a pho-tograph, although in truth it would be a photograph very nearly worth someone else's dying for. The clanging of the bells was tremendous now, masking all other sounds. The people in the streets below stood stock-still, all eyes turned upward, the center-point of the dark afternoon being the misplaced octopus and its hostage and the two fools who had climbed into the heavens to parlay with it. Tubby held up the ambergris pearl, offering it to the beast, trying desperately to attract its interest, but its attention was riveted on the dirigible, its eyes shining with a fearsome intelligence.

The craft began to swing past now, coming dangerously near. I could see the pilot's face clearly, his eyes wide as he watched the octopus, his hands on the spokes of the ship's wheel. The craft drew up beside us, a bis-cuit toss away. Three arms thrust out through the gondola windows, each holding a platter on a long handle, each of the platters sheltered beneath a tin umbrella that was affixed to its handle, either to shelter the plates from the elements, or—if the plates contained incendiary chemicals, which seemed certain—to protect the hydrogen-filled gasbag that floated above.

The bells abruptly ceased to peal, and in the strange silence Tubby and I bawled uselessly at those aboard the dirigible to leave off. I could clearly see the cameras on tripods now and the humped shadows of pho-tographers beneath black drapes. Within the gondola there was a quick, triple glare—clutches of lucifer matches being lit—which flew straightaway like tiny meteors toward the plates heaped with chemicals, some of the matches winking out or falling away, but a number striking home. Bright, white, fizzing fire erupted from the plates, a cloud of vapor roiling out from beneath the umbrellas. The manufactured light cast a demonic glare upon the octopus and the top of the cathedral, and illuminated Tubby's horrified face, as it must have illuminated my own. Ground magnesium, I thought, no doubt mixed with gunpowder so that it burned with that particular hellish light. The octopus, which had gazed with relish at the inferno of a burning ship, was unfazed, and seemed to be peering curiously into the glass eyes of the several cameras.

The dirigible veered away, its mission apparently successful, when an errant gust of wind blew it sharply back toward the dome. With a suddenness that must have been a mortal surprise to those within the gondola, the octo-pus lashed out with the golden pineapple, smiting the fragile wooden vessel, shattering the rudder and sundry wooden struts and planking. Immense splinters of wood pin-wheeled away, pieces of rudder and gondola raining down over Cheapside as the three platters of shimmering magnesium, each trailing long showers of white fire, fell into the churchyard, blessedly far from the gathered throng. Several of the flying splinters tore through the fabric of the balloon, and the crippled dirigible wheeled farther around, ragged bits of India-rubberized cloth flapping like bedsheets. Cameras tumbled out, following the rest of the debris when the stern of the ruined gondola lurched downward, several of its mooring lines having been torn loose from the balloon. I could hear the cheering of the crowd, which dearly loved a spectacle but possessed the bestial stupidity of the crowd mind, and apparently didn't fathom the carnage that would have occurred if the dirigible had exploded overhead, or been knocked completely to pieces.

The crippled dirigible, without steerage now, drifted across the city at the pleasure of the wind, descending in the direction of Hampstead Heath, the rear structure of the gondola smashed away, the whole thing hanging askew. Two men looked out, mouths agape, as they held on to their broken wooden cage with both hands and regretted their sins.

The octopus craned its immense neck backward now, watching the approach of the two warships, which had lowered an immense, coarsely woven, weighted net, the rope heavy enough to be made out against the sky. It looked very much like the ratlines and shrouds of a sailing ship, which was quite likely just what it was. It was clear that they meant to ensnare the octopus in order to pluck him from the dome, and Gilbert Frobisher into the bargain. A circle of hot air balloons, dozens of them, kept the net evenly suspended, very much like the glass fishing floats of Norwegian cod fishermen. Lead weights hung below every other balloon in order to draw the net shut when it was released.

Gilbert clung to his own encircling tentacle like a vigorous limpet, having by now caught sight of the two of us standing twenty feet below—his first glimpse of possible salvation after two frightful hours of captivity. He shouted through the speaking trumpet at the octopus, although the beast, which had been deaf to the great bells, was scarcely likely to heed his suggestions, whatever they were. The octopus peered downward at us, however. Tubby held out the ball of ambergris once again, like Atlas hoping to deliver himself of his burden, but still the octopus spurned him.

I heard Gilbert's voice ringing out from above. He was shouting through the speaking trumpet, aimed downward at the two of us now. It came to me that he was saying goodbye, and my heart fell. "My love to you, Nephew!" he hollered at Tubby. "And my great good wishes to your Aunt Leticia in Cork! Make sure she wants for nothing!" And then to me he shouted, "Fare thee well, Jack! You've earned this keepsake!" Carefully, using both hands, he lobbed the speaking trumpet down to me, and I caught it just as the two leading ships hove into sight above us. The rain beat down now, making it almost impossible to look upward, and yet Tubby refused to retreat, but stood holding the ambergris beneath the open sky, his legs wide-set. I believe that he fully intended to be caught in the net, which loomed overhead above us, to ride to glory with his uncle and the octopus in order to see the thing through to the end: great bravery, as Gilbert had put it a month ago on that fateful night in Pennyfields, or else an act of consummate foolishness.

But it wasn't to be. Two tentacles descended now, one of them holding Gilbert. I realized with a wild surge of relief that the octopus had made up its mind to free the old man. I swear that I read its intentions in its eyes despite the rain and the chaos. The dirigibles hovered over us, the net drawn tight, the engines backing and filling, so to speak, keeping their stations. The wind had fallen off, something that was favorable to the vessels. They would act quickly.

I set the speaking trumpet aside and raised my arms to aid in Gilbert's landing, but at that crucial moment I glimpsed a movement directly to my left—a surprising thing, for I had quite forgotten the world beyond our aerie. In the shadows behind me loomed the striding figure of the man wearing the *pince-nez* and the Homburg hat—assuredly Lucius Honeywell, his arm outstretched, a revolver in his hand. Before I could react, there was a loud report from the pistol, and to my horror, Tubby spun half around and pitched forward, shot in the shoulder. He teetered against the railing, pivoting there as the weight of his upper body threatened to carry him over.

I leapt at Honeywell, who turned the pistol on me while still moving toward Tubby, clearly intent upon securing the ambergris ball before the octopus could retrieve it or it fell into the void. His distracted shot was wild, and I caught his wrist with my right hand, throwing my hip into his midsection and bringing him down, pinning him to the deck. Tubby wrenched himself away from the balustrade with an effort of will, his shirt already soaked with blood at the shoulder, and he sat down hard on the deck, falling forward over the ambergris ball in order to entrap it. Gilbert settled decorously beside him, the tentacle drawing away, the octopus parting company with the two objects of its greatest affection. Gilbert cast a vicious glance at Honeywell, as if he would murder him on the spot, and then set about attending to his injured nephew.

Honeywell erupted suddenly, thrashing beneath my weight, spittle flying from his mouth as he roared and bit like an ape. On the moment he had ceased to be the consummate gentleman and man of business, as Gilbert had styled him. His enormously costly machinations had fallen apart. His head jerked toward my own as he endeavored to bite me, and I raised my fist to knock him senseless, but before I could strike the blow I was swept bodily aside by the wet, rubbery weight of an immensely heavy tentacle. Honeywell endeavored to rise, the pistol still gripped in his hand, but the very tentacle that had pushed me aside grappled him around his chest, pinning his arms, his feet kicking like those of a man hanging from a gibbet. His hands opened involuntarily, the pistol clattering to the deck as the golden pineapple whipped downward out of nowhere, out of the sky, and smote Honeywell's wide-eyed head from his shoulders, the head flying out over the churchyard and into the mob, which scattered screaming. The octopus flung Honeywell's headless body away like a bit of trash, and I watched it fly off through the branches of a tree along New Change Street.

Popping and cracking noises sounded from overhead now, and a fear swept through me that sharpshooters in the great gondolas were endeavoring to murder the octopus. But it was not so. Their rifles were trained on the balloons that buoyed the net, and which popped one after another, the net descending, the dirigibles hanging overhead so close that they blocked my view of the sky. The net fell over the mantle of the octopus, ensnaring four or five tentacles as it was drawn closed by the lead weights, which thumped against the dome. I fully expected the octopus to secure itself to the pinnacle of the cathedral, perhaps endeavor to pull the dirigibles out of the air. Surprisingly, it released its grip and clutched at the net instead, giving up its protracted struggle.

The two great dirigibles hauled the octopus clear of the cathedral, gaining elevation, but terribly slowly—dipping and then rising again, clearly straining. They headed off at a creeping pace in the direction of the river while the octopus hung beneath, still as death. Reduced to the status of mere onlookers now, the three of us watched anxiously from our perch. Tubby's arm was bound up into a bandage and sling that Gilbert had cut from his own coat with his penknife. He was sweating, working to mask the pain of the wound. The old man's face was a mixture of emotions—wounds of another sort: a piece of his soul hung in yonder net, sold for a ball of whale excretion and at the expense of the monumental beast that had been as loyal as a dog. Gilbert's face changed, however, as I looked upon it, a wondering joy coming into his eyes. The octopus had began to haul itself upward with its several free tentacles, climbing the mooring ropes toward the nearest of the dirigibles, which was pulled lower in the sky as it took more and more of the weight.

God help them, I thought, swept up in utterly contradictory emotions. The dirigible had caught a right tartar in its net, and the men aboard her could have no idea of its deadly intelligence. We watched its inexorable ascent, the dirigibles swinging out over the river, their gondolas heaved downward in the stern, a great tentacle reaching upward, upward, groping at the whirring propeller, but not yet near enough to get a purchase on the gondola. In the next moments it would assuredly tear the dirigible to pieces.

And then at point midway between Blackfriars and Waterloo bridges, in that stretch of river known as King's Reach, they cut the ropes mooring the net. It plunged downward, the great tentacles pointing skyward in the moment before it fell into the river, casting up a vast plume of water as a farewell. The dirigibles swung around toward Greenwich, having been immensely successful, but only by a few lucky moments.

The octopus had disappeared out of the world, a dying god entangled in a net, perhaps poisoned by the fresh waters of the Thames mixed with the filth disgorged from London's sewers. Gilbert shook his head sadly and began to speak, to utter a eulogy, perhaps, but what he had in mind to say I would never know, for the first of the Fusiliers stepped out onto our balcony in that moment. He stooped to pick up Honeywell's fallen pistol, straightened again, and asked, "Which of you is Mr. Gilbert Frobisher?"

"Here, sir," Gilbert replied, looking lost and old, the weight of the long day crashing down upon him at last.

"You're arrested for public endangerment, general mayhem, trafficking in dangerous beasts, and the destruction of property belonging to the Crown. You lot also," he said, nodding at Tubby and me. "What's that, then?" he asked, nodding at the ball of ambergris.

"Nothing but a pasteboard pearl," Tubby lied.

"Relieve him of it," the man said to one of the soldiers, who did as he was told. —☙

The Ring of Stones

MY IDEA TO cast the blame at Lucius Honeywell's feet (dead men being famously unable to tell tales) fell on deaf ears. Although Honeywell had feet, there was nothing at all left of his face, which had been pulped. Lucius Honeywell had ceased to exist. To make matters more difficult, our arrival at the London Docks had been sensationalized by Gilbert's antics, and a host of people had seen the octopus emerge from the iron hold, the beast apparently mesmerized by Gilbert Frobisher, who had quite clearly climbed into the creature's arms and ridden his steed straight up the Victoria Embankment and into the sewer.

It was St. Ives who persuaded Alfred Russel Wallace to intercede on Gilbert's behalf, and the charges against the three of us were dismissed before the day was through, for the great man was fortuitously in London at the moment, and was still in favor with the Crown, having not yet insulted them with his socialist tirades. There were damages to pay, however, and the levying of an immense fine, and before the clock tolled midnight, Gilbert's ball of ambergris had disappeared into the Royal Treasury. Gilbert had lost his octopus, his ambergris, and his pocket-watch in one strange and lamentable afternoon.

The octopus had quite disappeared. The net was fished out of the Thames the next morning, containing a discarded beef cask and a dead sheep. There was a small article in the *Times* two days later regarding a cow that was plucked mysteriously from the deck of a barge in the Dover Strait. Some few days after that there appeared a report of a giant kraken haunting the waters of Eastbourne Harbor, where the *Nancy Dawson* once again rode at anchor, and an old sailor, far gone in liquor, claimed to have seen the monster abroad on the Downs. There was foggy weather on the East Sussex coast, however, and the descriptions of the alleged kraken were equally foggy.

GILBERT SUMMONED OUR little company to his Georgian mansion in Dicker a week after our return to London. This time there was no mystery about the summons. In his characteristic manner, Gilbert had landed solidly on his feet. He had sold the patent for his removable holds—'cargo boxes' as he now referred to them—to the Carnforth Ironworks, which had paid him a startling sum of money. Each of us was to receive a gold ingot for our part in the adventure of the octopus—each ingot weighing one hundred troy ounces. We made our way from London to Dicker by rail, Alice St. Ives and Dorothy coming along. We were in a festive mood, as you can well imagine, but Barlow, Gilbert's factotum, had the face of a worried man as he led us up to the third floor, where Gilbert sat looking out the high, bow window, watching his foggy yew alley through his birding glasses. He muttered something about being on the lookout for snowy owls, which he believed were nesting nearby. We expressed an interest in his owls. Perhaps he was telling the truth...

I returned the decorated speaking trumpet to him, and he took it with a sad nod of his head, peering wistfully for a time at the depiction of the rampant octopus.

He was fitting out the *Nancy Dawson* for another trip to the Caribbean, he told us at last. He meant to look in on Miss Bracken this time, and would be delighted if we were to come along as moral support, for he meant to ask her hand in marriage, if he found her alive and willing. All of us had lives to return to, however, and regretted that we couldn't accompany him. To my ear, 'looking in on Miss Bracken' was heavy with veiled, double meaning, and his gaze was repeatedly drawn to the window as he searched the misty night beyond.

It was some months later that Tubby brought us news of Gilbert's second voyage. The volcano on our uncharted island had fallen silent, and

Gilbert had moored once again within sight of the sea cave. Despite his aversion to being submerged in the diving bell, he had descended into the sunlit waters with Lazarus MacLean, and had left the speaking trumpet, heavily lacquered to keep out the salt sea, among the relics in the small, sad treasure trove within the ring of coral stones. —◌

The Here-and-Thereians

ALICE AND LANGDON St. Ives looked back toward Cannon Street Station as their hansom cab made its turn at the corner, rattling off in the direction of Ludgate Hill, bound for Smithfield. Alice had first come into Cannon Street Station the night she had met St. Ives, and she would forever have a romantic notion of the place. Its vast glass and iron roof disappeared behind buildings that were nearer-to, and a final train whistle diminished in the distance, drowned by street noise, the clatter and jangle of the cab, and horses' hooves clopping on the paving stones.

It was a festive sort of warm evening in late April, the streets full of people and the cabbie calling his horses by name as they threaded their way through traffic. St. Ives found that he was happy to be in London after four months at home in Aylesford, but that he was equally happy to have played the country squire for those four months. He had seen the first weeks of spring come into bloom in the Kentish countryside, and into his children as well, and the month of May, his favorite month of the year, was right around the corner, full of promise.

Alice, taking up a discussion interrupted by their arrival at the station, said, "…but you will admit that the more we learn about something the more we come to value it, given that it's a thing of value."

"Yes, indeed," St. Ives said. "We manufacture our enthusiasms, to be certain. I've developed a keen interest in your begonias, for instance, although three years ago I had very little interest at all. And I'm growing tolerably fond of Vicar Hampson's lichens, which I had always viewed as the outcasts of the plant family. But life is short, and we must pick and choose. The mind can only encompass so much. The opera is simply not one of my choices. The word 'caterwauling' comes to mind."

"I wonder what a caterwaul would look like—all toothy and hairy, perhaps, like a goblin or a bedraggled husband just waking up. Do you know that I mistook that word for years? I was disappointed to discover my error."

Happy to see that she was apparently letting him off his opera-house duties, he said, "Tubby and Gilbert will squire you to Covent Garden, one on either arm. You'll have a grand time while I fall asleep in my chair pretending to read."

St. Paul's loomed up before them on the right-hand side and then passed away in turn, and soon they rounded the corner onto Old Bailey, having traveled half the distance to the Half Toad Inn, where they would rendezvous with Tubby and his Uncle Gilbert. No doubt the two were already seated at one of the upstairs tables. St. Ives wondered what William Billson, the proprietor of the inn, had turning on the spit—a goose, perhaps, or a venison haunch. His stomach rumbled, his big guts devouring his little guts, as his father would have put it.

"What on earth is this, now?" Alice asked when they were held up at Newgate Street. She nodded in the direction of the Magpie and Stump, where a century ago people assembled to watch the public hangings at Newgate Prison or to pitch garbage and stones at people displayed in the pillory. Now a line of oak barrels reclining on india-rubber wheels was strung out along the curb in front of the pub. People sat within the barrels, fully contained except for their heads and arms, which were thrust through holes as if the passengers were captives in rolling stocks, the holes comfortably pillowed with padded leather. The barrels sported tiny ship's wheels, rain hoods, and raised storage boots attached to the backside. It was apparent that the barrelers were prepared to make a journey. They looked patently ridiculous, however, all of them wearing plum colored hats of varying shapes and sizes, yellow feathers in the hatbands. Many had mugs of beer in their hands, although several simply sat staring or sleeping.

St. Ives tried to puzzle it out—how they fit so neatly into their barrels—and then he spied the pairs of hinges here and there on the tops and sides and the several neat cuts that allowed the barrels to open up like a puzzle box. A man dressed in an apron and carrying a tray came out of the pub to collect mugs, and the train of barrels set out toward the river, roped together and hauled by two hefty boys in bright red vests and short pants, the jolliest of the barrelers breaking into song. One of the sleepers lost a hat, which cartwheeled away along the pavement on the breeze, and the second boy dropped the line and chased the hat down while the first red-vested boy labored on alone at a good clip, managing to ring a hand-bell at intervals.

St. Ives and Alice had a clear view of the eastern sky as the coach moved away up Giltspur Street. An approaching army of dark clouds had assembled in the east, low on the horizon—a storm blowing toward them on a freshening wind. St. Ives wondered idly whether it had dropped rain on Aylesford, watering the hops plants and the lawns.

They passed an open courtyard clustered with dozens of the wheeled barrels gathered in the shade of freestanding awnings, as if today were a barrelers' holiday. Not as jolly as the plum-hatted lot at the Magpie and Stump, most of this crowd was looking languidly at the road but apparently seeing nothing, reminiscent of chained-together prisoners contemplating their fate. Boys in red vests moved among them, apparently seeing to their needs.

"They're going to get a ducking in the storm if they don't find more useful shelter before nightfall," St. Ives said.

"Certainly they'll have gone home by then," Alice said. "They appear to have had a hard day. What a bizarre pastime, like gipsy caravans, but with keepers."

The coach soon turned onto Fingal Street, where the Half Toad Inn, an ancient, three-story building with quaint windows of colored, bull's-eye glass, sat at the edge of Lambert Court. The front half of a carved, wooden Surinam toad, cheerfully painted, looked out from above the taproom alcove where the street entrance stood. Two men came out through the door now, both of them laughing as they stood in the shadow of the toad, and in the moment before the door closed, St. Ives got a glimpse inside, where Lars Hopeful, the tap-boy, was just then passing by with two jugs of ale—the promise of things to come. It was a popular maxim that it was a better thing to travel than to arrive, but clearly there were notable exceptions, arriving at the Half Toad being primary among them. ⁓

The Tortoise in Winter

"Y OUR BARREL PEOPLE are what they call Here-and-
Thereians," William Billson told them after setting down two plates
of kickshaws: oyster-and-dill tartlets and deviled ham on toast. "The boys
in the red vests are just so—'Red Vests,' people say. Your lot at the Magpie
was the Purple Hats, West Smithfield faction. I don't know about the rest,
but they say there's nigh onto three dozen factions, some with a hundred
members and more by the day."

Henrietta Billson, who had married William close onto forty years ago
when he first bought the old inn, brought in a jug of ale and filled their
tankards, admonishing them to drink up and to eat the food while it was
fresh and hot, for doing otherwise was criminal. They were waiting for the
arrival of Tubby and Gilbert Frobisher, who were uncharacteristically late.

Alice, a great fan of oysters, swallowed a mouthful of tartlet and then
said, "So they're a society of some sort, these Here-and-Thereians?"

"Yes," Henrietta said, "and very much in the news—a phenomenon,
they call it, like the South Sea Bubble."

"We've given up reading anything but the *Maidstone Gazette*," Alice
said, "and it's tolerably free of news, which suits us these days."

"But surely you've heard of this man Diogenes?"

"*I've* heard of Diogenes," St. Ives put in while helping himself to deviled ham. "I remember the lesson well: Diogenes of Sinope, who lived in
Athens something over twenty centuries ago. He said cheeky things to
Alexander the Great and housed himself in a barrel, although some refer
to it as a tub and others a jar. He allegedly rolled it roundabout the city
in perpetual search of an honest man, whom he failed to discover. People

sought him out for philosophic advice. I'm happy to think that his star has risen again."

"I admit to never having heard of Diogenes of Sinope," Alice said.

"Nor have I," said Henrietta. "I meant the barrel-peddling man with the great walrus mustaches who sells headache powders in Bankside, at the foot of London Bridge. They say he's rich as your uncle Midas, although he has the face of a swindler."

"Headache powders?" St. Ives said. "I wonder if they'd have any effect on the pain in my sciatic nerve. It recently decided to betray me."

"Pains of all sorts," William put in. "The first envelope is gratis, they say, but customers come back looking for more once they've had a taste. We've seen them queued up down Borough High Street nigh onto eight o'clock at night, him set up under the electrical lights. A bruiser with a truncheon stood by to guard the strongbox."

"But the barrels is where the real money comes from," Henrietta said. "This man Diogenes is a sort of saint to them who takes the powders and buys his barrels."

"The man's no saint," Billson said, shaking his head. "Them that climbs into the barrels rarely climbs out again. More and more of them have taken to the river."

"To the river?" Alice asked. "Do you mean *afloat*?"

"Aye, ma'am, afloat."

"How do their barrels remain upright in the water?" St. Ives asked.

"Lead keels and copper bottoms. Some have outriggers, like the South Seas islanders. Some are rigged out with a mast and sail. A barrel is a dry sort of craft, and there's a jakes built in, what they call an 'evacuator' that…"

"None of that talk, Bill," Henrietta interrupted, giving her husband a hard look.

Tubby Frobisher entered at that moment, all eighteen stone of him, wearing a light flannel coat streaked with snuff that he had apparently tried to dust off. He had an out-of-sorts look on his face as he removed his disreputable Bollinger hat, smoothed the ratty peacock feather in the band, hung it on a peg, and slumped heavily into a chair. The Billsons avowed that they were happy to see him and then hurried out to put the halibut in the oven and finish the anchovy sauce.

"What's the good word, Tubby?" St. Ives asked him.

"No good word at all except that I'm damned happy to find you two here." He poured ale down his throat and banged down the tankard before saying, "We'll have to sup without Uncle Gilbert, and he won't be going along tonight to hear *Nabucco*."

"He's not ill, I hope," Alice said.

"No," Tubby said. "He's bought a barrel, a goddamned barrel. He's nothing less than Lord Mayor of the Primrose Hill Faction. He sent his man Barlow back home to Dicker and purchased a fabulously contrived kitchen barrel for Madame Leseur, his cook, to the tune of over four hundred pounds sterling. She spurned the barrel, refused to follow him, said that the English had finally gone mad, and has returned to Paris to live with her mother."

"That must have been a blow," Alice said. "Madame Leseur is the great cook of the world."

"She's correct about this barrel madness, and I speak literally," Tubby said. "I'm not the only one who thinks so."

"Lord *Mayor*, do you say?" St. Ives asked. "They're well organized, these factions?"

"Oh, yes. It's entirely necessary. I've been told that the term of office rarely extends past a few days. There's a decline in mental faculties. Pass me that plate of deviled ham if you will." He engulfed two of them before going on. "The newer members are enthusiasts, do you see, but that quickly passes and they begin to turn inward. Newer members rise up to take their places. They reach a point where there's no preventing them from taking to the river to be swept out with the tide. According to the *Times* they begin to conceive of themselves as eels, of all the bleeding nonsense."

"It's a swift decline, then?" St. Ives asked.

"An out-and-out tumble for some," Tubby said. "I mean to have a pow-wow with this human demon who calls himself Diogenes. He badly needs a thumping."

"Heaven help us," Alice said. "The three of us can surely talk Gilbert out of this madness without anyone being thumped. We'll pluck him out of his barrel and carry him away if we have to."

Tubby shook his head darkly. "I sought out the Primrose Hill crowd this afternoon in order to take Gilbert out by main force. There was a minister there, from what they call the Church of Diogenes. He was striding around the meadow gesticulating, filling their heads with rubbish, but they hung on his words like apes from a limb. A woman and several children arrived, looking for the children's father. The wife saw the man in his barrel in the midst of the crowd and they moved toward him directly, all of them sobbing aloud. The entire faction pedaled into motion, circling the barrels in order to protect their man, who apparently had no desire to leave. None whatsoever. His family might as well have been strangers. It was positively inhuman."

"Won't the police do something?" Alice asked. "This is insidious."

"No, ma'am. No law has been broken, and the current consensus is that people may do as they wish."

"And Gilbert wishes to live out his days in a barrel, then?" St. Ives asked.

"That he does, although what he wishes is nothing to me. I told him a flaming lie in order to placate him and the damned minister, so-called, who was the image of Beelzebub in a tailor-made suit. I was thinking of buying a barrel myself, I said to Uncle: the 'Jumbo,' identical to his own. He yammered on about accessories: a folding rain hood made of glass, a patent evacuator, a clean water reservoir with a purifier of charcoal and silver, a paddlewheel for river travel, an electric motor to run the whole business, including what they call a 'dry cell' battery to turn the wheels or paddles when a barreller is fagged out. There's no end to it: he's even had the Frobisher crest carved into the rear of the boot. I don't doubt that it cost him a fortune, although the barrel alone costs little. The common man can go to hell as easily as the rich man, do you see? It's the goddamned accessories that drive the price up. In any event, when I suggested that the two of us look into the Pennywhistle for lunch and a whet he turned me down flat. Can you imagine that?—A Frobisher having no interest in food and drink?"

"It's conceivable that he had already dined, I suppose," said Alice.

"On a sandwich yesterday evening. The powders are said to diminish appetite—some sort of bodily stasis, like a tortoise in winter. The Red Vests make sure they take their dose."

The halibut and anchovy sauce arrived, followed by roast pork, long beans, four types of mushrooms in gravy, and crushed potatoes swimming in butter and garlic—Gilbert Frobisher's sort of meal to be sure, now given up for life in a barrel and yesterday's sandwich. The conversation shifted to the opera, and St. Ives's mind drifted away, turning on the problem of the headache powders, what they might consist of—opiates? cocaine? chloral hydrate? He wondered about their medicinal effect and their curious connection to the barrel madness. Did they promote the desire for confinement, he wondered, or perhaps for an aquatic life? What had Tubby meant by the barrelers turning into *eels*? It was entirely likely that this self-styled Diogenes had synthesized an entirely new compound in a laboratory, like Mr. Stevenson's infamous Dr. Jekyll, whose "Strange Case" filled the bookstall at Cannon Street Station. A chemist might puzzle it out, although it would take time, and time was short.

"Good heavens!" Tubby said, bringing St. Ives out of his thoughtful stupor. "We must dress and be on our way. You're going to miss out, Professor. Lyle Worthnaught is to play the part of Nebuchadnezzar."

A not-very-clever reply entered his head, but he dismissed it. He was minutes away from abandoning Alice, and it was best to act the part of the gracious husband, especially because it had come into his mind to have an adventure of his own. It was an idea he had best keep to himself for the moment, lest Alice express her doubts about it.

Tubby swallowed the last of his wine and stood up, asking Lars Hopeful to fetch a cab in fifteen minute's time.

"I'm going out for a walk before the weather changes," St. Ives said, accompanying Alice to their room. "You can tell me about the operatic wonders I missed over breakfast in the morning. To my mind the Half Toad breakfast is reason enough to come into London." He said this last to placate her, and was happy when she agreed.

He fetched his umbrella and his coat, warned her that it would surely rain very hard within the next hour, bade her enjoy the opera, kissed her goodbye, and five minutes later climbed into a cab bound for London Bridge and Bankside, putting off his alleged walk until he had satisfied his curiosity about the infamous headache powders. ⌐°

Diogenes' Barrel

I T WAS EIGHT o'clock before St. Ives found his man. The storm was fast approaching, dark clouds moving across the moon and lightning in the cloudbank just to the east. A cold wind preceded the storm, the night looking to be a dirty one, and London Bridge was almost empty of foot traffic. The few remaining pedestrians hurried up or down Bankside or along Borough High Street, anxious to be home before they were drowned. St. Ives loved a storm, but he meant to conclude his business with Diogenes and find shelter before it broke.

Diogenes seemed to be of a like mind, for he was hurriedly closing things up in the glow of the lamp. His stall, into which he was squirreling away odds and ends, was a large, wheeled barrel that had bloomed into a complicated display case, hinging open in sections so that it stood some six-feet wide and tall. A long scroll that read "Diogenes' Palliatives and Wisdom" was still unfurled alongside, hanging from a long, sturdy pole lashed to the side of the barrel.

St. Ives had half expected that a man named Diogenes would have flowing hair and perhaps wear a toga, but the small man with mustaches grown down past his chin and a long, square beard looked like a professor from an out-of-the-way university, one who was profoundly unhappy with his students, perhaps with the world in general.

"I believe I'm addressing Diogenes?" St. Ives asked.

"Right you are," he said without looking up.

"Closing up shop, I see. Do you have time for one last customer? A friend of mine particularly recommended your headache powders."

"Half London will be recommending my headache powders before the month is past, including you, sir. We'll be quick about it if you don't mind. How many envelopes would you like? The first is free to anyone who asks. The second will cost you a shilling. Eight envelopes for one crown. That's a right bargain. Take my advice and buy sixteen. Save yourself a return trip, unless you develop an interest in a barrel-house. Half London will be recommending them, also. Let me offer you an illustrated brochure."

St. Ives took the multi-page pamphlet from him. He saw that there was a Holland Road address on the front above a sketch of the barrel shop. "I'm never averse to a bargain, or to a barrel, for that matter," he said as cheerfully as he could manage.

"Then we have something in common," Diogenes said, counting out sixteen little parchment envelopes that he slid into a larger parchment envelope, saying nothing by way of thanks to St. Ives as he took his coins. After glancing at the threatening sky he went back to reducing his barrel, closing drawers and banging home hinged compartments.

"How does one best consume a dose of the powder?" St. Ives asked.

Not looking up, Diogenes said, "I suggest stirring it into a tumbler of water, or of beer if you're inclined. Gin heightens the effect. Tea will do. An alternative would be to draw it up your nose through a common drinking straw cut off short or through a tightly rolled banknote. It goes to the head that way, straight into the enemy's camp. Consume two packets straightaway, and then single packets at the rate of four packets a day at even intervals. Another packet more or less won't hurt you."

"I was wondering also about the ingredients of the powders," St. Ives said as he tucked the lot of it away into his vest pocket, "the analgesic property, I mean to say. What makes it so effective?"

"Do I wear the face of a fool?" Diogenes asked him, looking past St. Ives's shoulder and giving his head a jerk just as the first drops of rain began to fall. "No doubt you wish to profit from another man's work."

"Not at all, sir. But I've got an interest in patent medicines and nostrums of all sorts. My curiosity is purely scientific, I assure you."

St. Ives was aware that someone was looming behind him now, and he stepped aside, thinking that it was perhaps a customer. The large, mule-faced man staring fiercely down at him, however, looked to be something else altogether. In a low voice the man said, "Move along, cully."

"Good day to both of you," St. Ives replied. He walked away down Borough High Street beneath his umbrella, still contemplating his rather desperate notion, one that would reveal the workings of the headache powders in short order. He looked back to see Diogenes climbing into a waiting coach and the horse-faced man wheeling the portable shop across London Bridge. ⟶

A Contemplation of Barrels

S T. IVES BENT in through the door of the George Inn just as the skies opened and the rain came roaring down, the cobbles in the courtyard disappearing beneath a mist of broken water. He was happy to see a fire in the hearth and equally happy to see an empty, lamp-lit snug with both a view of the fire and a window looking out at the street. He hung his damp coat on a peg, dug his note-book and pencil out of his vest pocket, bought a pint of porter at the bar, and settled into the snug, where he was unlikely to be disturbed on such an evening. He thought of Alice and looked at his pocket-watch, happy to see that she and Tubby would quite likely have arrived at Covent Garden before the storm broke.

After another moment of consideration, he removed the packets from his vest pocket, opened one of them, and sniffed the powder, which was a buff-colored substance, very finely ground. There was an unmistakably fishy smell to it, although not offensively so. He picked some up on his finger and tasted it—again the fishiness, and a tingling sensation on his tongue, the sensation and flavor rather more attractive than otherwise, which surprised him, given the odor. He patiently listed these things in his note-book along with questions and comments that came to him, pausing now and then to sip his porter and to watch the rain come down beyond the window.

The behavior of the Here-and-Thereians was baffling in six different ways, it seemed to him, as was the motivation of this self-made Diogenes, who was beginning to look like a behemoth of vice despite his diminutive size. Money would account for it, surely; money accounted for most of the world's ill-doing. He thought of Gilbert Frobisher now, who had so much money that he could buy and sell Diogenes a hundred times over. He owned a vast Georgian mansion in Dicker, complete with a six-acre pond with rowing boats. His giving up Madame Leseur, his longtime cook, was perhaps the strangest part of this entire affair, for no one on earth was fonder of food than Gilbert Frobisher.

"Another?" the bar man asked, looking in on him.

St. Ives looked up from his note-taking, slightly surprised that he had finished the porter. "Yes, thank you," he said, rearranging himself on his chair in order to take pressure off his sciatic nerve, although the effort brought him little relief. Gilbert was one of the few apparently happy men that St. Ives knew. He was rich, but there was nothing of the miser in him. He had an immense steam yacht moored in Eastbourne in which he traveled to tropical islands to escape the English winters, and he was perpetually busy the rest of the year compounding his fortune and trudging about the British Isles on the lookout for rare birds, nests, and eggs. In short, despite his age—well past sixty years—he was an active, cheerful man who would scarcely retire from a rich life in order to occupy a mobile barrel, or, God help him, to stand for Lord Mayor of a faction of barrelers who had abandoned their own lives and families.

It came into St. Ives's mind that it would be monstrously easy to infiltrate a faction of barrelers if he knew what motivated them. One must understand one's enemies, after all. His porter arrived, and he sat looking at it for a moment, at war within—hesitation doing battle with the bold stroke. Scientific curiosity sometimes demanded experimental zeal, it seemed to him, especially if the scientist was armored with a sound mind, clear intentions, and no troubling vices.

Having made his decision he carefully dumped the contents of two envelopes into his porter. The powder floated on top like a small island, and before it had a chance to settle, he said, "so be it," and he drank it off, emptying a third of the mug. Again he noted the distinctly fishy flavor, although it was somewhat disguised by the porter, and within a matter of moments he felt a general lightening of being, and, he realized happily, an almost total cessation of pain in his lower back and thigh. He got up out of his chair and strode back and forth. He could dance a jig if he chose to—there was nothing at all stopping him—and he cut a quick caper and spun on his heel. Well satisfied, he sat back down, raised his mug in an unspoken toast, laughed aloud, and with a feeling of great good health, drank off the rest of the porter.

Alice would surely frown at his…experimentation. *But*, he told himself, there was simply no other way to come to an understanding of their foe—if in fact they had a foe. His estimation of Diogenes, he realized, had risen considerably. The man's powders had metamorphosed the humble porter into something like the *elixir veritas* of Paracelsus.

He scribbled notes energetically: the novelty of the sensation, the clearing away of cobwebs in his mind, the feeling of contained, intelligent recklessness, and yet only a few minutes ago he had hesitated to consume the powder out of mere timidity. "Science," he wrote, "requires intrepid action," and he underlined the sentiment and added an exclamation point. He asked for a third pint of porter before noting that his reasoning powers were far more acute than they had been when he had walked in through the door of the George.

He was able to see now that Gilbert Frobisher was a man of considerable curiosity and enthusiasm who had simply made a virtue of these qualities. Certainly he had. There was much to be said for doing as one pleased if one was sure of oneself. St. Ives himself had never, he realized, been surer of himself than he was at this moment. The room roundabout him had a fine, rosy glow, as if it were alive with its own compounded history. Charles Dickens, a famous patron of the George Inn, had no doubt sat in this very seat, perhaps had written something brilliant while he drank *his* porter. What might he have written if he had access to the powders of Diogenes?

Emboldened by this notion, St. Ives drank deeply from his mug, squinting at the fire, which sprang apart into an enormous fan of colors like the tail of heaven's own peacock. The wood grain in the oak paneling was a collection of fabulous arabesques—shapes that threatened to leap out at him—and he could see, literally, it seemed to him, that the stones of the floor were dense with accreted time and with the elemental properties of the thousands of people who had trod upon them over the centuries.

He applied himself feverishly to his work, jotting down this whirligig of impressions, the words coming to him in an incessant rush. His mind had never been as sharp and vital as it was now, and his sentences were elegantly crafted, full of subtle wit, something near poetry.

He found that he was smiling broadly, very nearly a rictus, and he clamped his lips shut, startled by the phenomenon. In that moment the rain redoubled its wild fury, and he watched it fall in the gaslight out in the stormy London night, fascinated now by the very idea of water descending from the heavens and marveling that his hearing had grown acute enough for him not only to make out the sound of individual drops, but also the clear melody of their drumming. It came into his mind that he would swim back to the inn through the operatic rain, and he laughed aloud.

He called for another pint and a bowl of shelled walnuts, devouring the nuts one after another, caught up in the marvel of their shape. Each intricately contrived walnut half was exactly like its neighbors. How cleverly they fit together, enclosed snugly in their shells, safe from the weather, just as he was enclosed in his own safe snug, laughing at the roaring night. There was nothing foolish about Diogenes' barrels at all. Gilbert had seen that. They were a natural home, like the walnut shell or the shell of a snail. He contemplated on the bee in its hive and the tortoise in its domed chariot and the swallows and wasps in their mud nests. Nature was everywhere building barrels, to misquote the poet, and with great good sense.

He took out the brochure from the shop on Holland Road and scrutinized the various barrels and the countless contrivances that could be built into them. They were marvelous objects, these barrels—undeniable works of art and seaworthy into the bargain. His mind went back to the jolly, purple-hatted merrymakers outside the Magpie and Stump, and he was filled with a sense of longing that had no clear source or definition. "We know," he muttered, nodding his head. He was flooded with a sagacious joy and determination. He wondered exactly what it was he so fundamentally *knew*—but he could not put it into words. It was simply too vast, like trying to make sense of the sky.

He was distracted by his pocket-watch, which was lying on the table next to his empty mug, although he didn't remember having left it there. The perfectly round case of the watch attracted him—a barrel in its own right. It perfectly enclosed the workings—the intricately connected gears and springs that made up a living creature once they were put into motion. He saw in his mind's eye this circular creature of gears and springs stepping out of its case like a hermit crab from out of its shell and going off on a journey to find a more expansive abode. It would make an elegant illustration if an artist could capture its essence, and he was awash with the notion that he was quite close to grasping what the entire thing *meant*.

He opened the watch case and looked straight into Alice's face, a photograph of which was set into the inside of the cover.

He closed it hastily after noting that it was coming onto eleven o'clock; he had been running down mysteries for nearly three hours. He called for one more mug of porter, and when it came, he hurriedly opened another envelope of the powders, dusted the foam atop the porter, and then licked it away, savoring the flavor. If he could have five packets the first day, then he was still some way from overdoing it, and it had to be admitted that the effect of the powders brought about inarguable insight and clarity. His sciatic nerve had been silenced, and he meant to keep it that way.

He wondered at what time Diogenes set up his cart in the morning, for the urge was upon him to buy more of the envelopes of powder. He calculated the expense of a year's supply: 1,460 envelopes divided by eight per crown piece, and four crowns to the pound—something in the neighborhood of forty-five pounds for the lot with a few shillings leftover. He knew for a fact that Gilbert had paid twice that sum for a case of French wine—good wine, no doubt, but "good" under the circumstances was an arguable quality, since the wine deadened the intellect and…

"Are you quite all right, sir?" the bar man asked him, and St. Ives realized that he had been talking aloud, perhaps for some time now.

The man's temerity abruptly angered him, however, and he very nearly told him so. But on the instant the anger vanished, replaced by the benevolent thought that the poor brute was scarcely worth his ire. In fact the fellow was doing his best, no doubt. He considered offering him an envelope of the powders, but just as quickly decided against it. Until he had a safe supply of the envelopes, he would hold on tightly to the few he possessed.

"I've never been better," he said, and handed the man his umbrella, saying, "Keep it for your trouble." He took his coat from the peg, pocketed his pencil and note-book, and went out through the door into the courtyard, breathing in the delicious scent of the holy rain. He looked up at the sky and considered the clouds, none of them alike, and the fantastic shapes of the spaces between the clouds. Some sailed low in the sky and others higher, just as they damn well chose. What was a cloud, he asked himself as he walked along, but an ethereal barrel of rain afloat in the heavens?

It came to him that he should take out his note-book, find a sheltered place, and write this down, but now that he was moving, he was compelled to keep moving by an intense energy that raced through his veins and arteries. The bells of St. Magnus the Martyr were tolling the hour as he strode along Lower Thames Street past the bottom of Fish Street Hill, from which flowed a deep stream of water. He stood in the stream for a time, marveling at the water that filled his shoes.

Fish Street Hill!—the very name was laden with promise. "Hah!" he shouted, throwing up his arms and turning his face to the heavens. He angled up King William Street, the rain streaming down his face, past his open collar and into his shirt and off the tips of his fingers. Water rushed noisily through the rooftop gutters and poured from downspouts, contributing to the flood. He saw that the streets themselves were quite literally rivers—tributaries carrying the water that would fill the great London River and hence out to the sea, the Mother of all life on Earth....

He was immensely surprised to find himself looking up into the face of the massive toad that sat above the door of the Half Toad Inn. He had no recollection of time having passed or of having made any turnings since hearing the bells tolling midnight. —⟨

Water Dreams

H E AWAKENED SOME time later to find himself afloat on a broad river of great clarity. Far beneath the surface, water-weeds swayed in the current, and he could see transparent eels like ribbons of glass carried on the outward-moving tide toward the sea. The clear water was blood warm, the sky overhead blue as a robin's egg, and the silver sea lay in the far distance. It was no river he had ever known, and even in sleep—for he was aware that he was dreaming—he wondered if this river might be all rivers in one, the ideal of a river, perhaps sleep itself. He had the sensation of floating on his back and looking at the sky, although without moving his head he saw beneath the surface of the river: silver eels swimming toward their destiny in the sea, the shifting, translucent green of the waterweeds, the rippling sunlight.

—◌◌◌—

THE RIVER RETURNED to him carrying within it a blissful sense of ease and the awareness that he had been away for some indistinct length of time—asleep, he thought, asleep within the dream itself. He was borne out onto the vast, crystal sea, and soon was far from any visible shore, swept along on an ocean current—a river embedded in the sea—bound for a place of still-ness in a world of profound calm. He was filled with a longing for the place toward which he was bound, a shimmering, green world of unfathomable peace and clarity, of waterweeds and small, swimming creatures, and he swimming among them in the green-tinted sunlight. Something within him recognized this place—a place from his childhood, he thought, or a place from childhood's dream.

—◦◦◦—

He awoke shivering, a vicious ache in his head. The dream was still vivid in his mind—more real than the dark room around him. It was not dissipating or fading from memory, something for which he was profoundly happy, although he was full of regret that it was a thing of the past. He shut his eyes and attempted to compose himself, but his frightfully alert mind refused to be composed. He sat up, staring stupidly at the window and a grey dawn. Very quietly he arose from the settee on which he had slept and made his way to the dresser against the wall. With a shaking hand he dumped the contents of two packages of powders into the tumbler, filled it with water from the pitcher, and drank it off, standing still for a long moment to allow the powders to compose his fibers. —◦

Larkin the Just

ALICE CAME AWAKE in a rush, noting that she was alone in the room, her book lying open on the bed beside her. There was a beam of sunlight showing between the gap in the window curtains and not a hint of last night's storm. She sat for a moment, gathering her wits, recalling that she had intended to read until Langdon's return. She must have fallen asleep. She had left the lamp burning, but it had no doubt consumed its oil and gone out. Langdon apparently hadn't come in at all. He hadn't slept in the bed, not even atop the bedclothes. And yet his pillow was missing.

He *must* have come in. She saw now that the lamp oil was diminished, but not gone. Evidently someone—Langdon—had quietly extinguished the lamp, very late.

She climbed out of bed, seeing now that he had spent the night on the thinly upholstered settee, for his pillow lay upon it, as did a mound of plush cushions that he must have carried up from the benches in the taproom downstairs. What an odd business, she thought, although surely there was an explanation for it. It came to her that he might have caught a cold while walking in the rain and so spent the night on the settee in order to keep his distance from her. He must have burrowed into a heap of cushions for warmth, no doubt awakening early and going downstairs.

She poured a tumbler of water from the pitcher and started to drink from it. She recoiled, however, at the fishy odor that arose from the glass. There was a powdery residue floating atop the water. It hadn't been there last night. Suspicions came into her mind, but they were so

farfetched that she dismissed them, and after making herself present-
able as quickly as she could, she plucked up the cushions in order to
carry them down with her.

They were quite damp, she discovered, as was the meager upholstery
of the settee. Had he slept in his wet clothes? The corner of a well-worn
book, bound in morocco leather, was just visible under the front edge of
the bench—Langdon's note-book, she discovered when she dropped the
cushions and fetched it out. It was also wet. She looked for his coat on the
peg near the door, but there was no coat. She set the note-book on the table
next to the pitcher and basin, picked up the cushions again, and pushed out
through the door, hurrying down the stairs, where she replaced the cushions and went into the breakfast room.

There was no sign of Langdon, only Tubby Frobisher sitting with a
small girl, a child, with a shock of black hair pulled into pigtails. She was
dressed like an orphan in a play, the rips in her dress sewn up with whip
stitches using various colors of thread. The two of them were consuming
the contents of a rack of toast, a dish of jam, and a pot of coffee with evident greed. The girl, whose cheeks were blue with blackcurrant jam, did not
look up from her plate, but Tubby raised his knife, nodded to Alice, and
gestured at an empty chair. Then, apparently seeing the look on her face, he
asked, "What's amiss?"

"Have you seen Langdon this morning?" she asked, keeping the worry
out of her voice—an irrational worry, she assured herself. "He promised to
breakfast with us so that we could fill him with regret for missing the opera."

"Haven't seen him or heard from him. Perhaps he's gone out."

"Possibly," she said, and then went into the kitchen where both of the
Billsons were hard at work, William cooking sausages at the stove and
Henrietta emptying fruit and produce from baskets.

"Good morning to you," she said. "Have you seen my husband this
morning?"

"Aye," William said. "He went out just at dawn in a hellfire hurry."

"It was just when I was off to the market for produce," Henrietta put in.

"Did he say where he was bound?"

"Not a word of it, ma'am," Billson told her. "He didn't look back.
Seemed to be on a mission. He left a note, however, under the salt-cellar."
Billson found the message on a shelf and handed it to her—a damp piece of

paper torn from the morocco note-book. The writing was childish, barely legible. His hand had clearly been shaking. In one place his pencil had torn a hole in the paper. "Out for a time," it read.

"A time?" she muttered.

"Surely he had a good reason for going out," Henrietta said. "There's no one more sensible than the Professor. Sit down with Mr. Frobisher and Larkin and eat a bite. I'll bet a shiny new farthing that your man will turn up in due course."

Alice took a seat next to Tubby, who read the note and then reiterated what Henrietta had said about Langdon's being a sensible man. "Coffee will see you right," he said, filling her cup. "This is my great good friend Larkin the Just. We've just met this morning. William Billson introduced her to me as a rare plucked one, and I believe he told the truth. We're eating pre-breakfast toast and jam to stimulate the digestive fluids in preparation for breakfast itself."

"A sound idea," Alice said, forcibly pushing the worry from her mind. "Hello, Larkin the Just." She put out her hand and the girl shook it, perhaps a little skeptically. "How do you get along?"

"Prime, ma'am. Mayhem is my specialism, if that's your meaning by how I get *along*. You're quite beautiful. Are you royalty, then?"

"Royalty? No, but I met the Queen once. Surely you have nothing to do with mayhem?"

"Oh, yes, when we're paid to do it, or when we takes a fancy to it. We start it spinning, like a top, and then we're gone and leave it for others to put a stop to it."

"William Billson has known Larkin for a great long time," Tubby said. "He has the utmost faith in her loyalty, once she commits herself."

"Then so do I," Alice said, although it seemed to her that Larkin was more a wild animal than a civilized child. "How did you come to be called 'the Just'?"

"On account of I didn't gouge a man's eye when I could've." Her hand disappeared into the top of her shirt, and when it reappeared there was a hand's-length, cylindrical white object in it—bone, apparently—with a claw-shaped hook carved into the end of it. It hung around her neck on a strip of leather. "It's a gouger is what it is," Larkin told her. "It goes in at the side up along the bugger's nose, and then you give it a twist. It was give me by a sailor as knew my old dad, who carved it in Africa where he hunted it—the unicorn, I mean. It's a bit of its horn. I'm handy with it."

"*Unicorn* horn, is it?" Alice asked, staring at the girl for a moment, wondering whether she was being trifled with. Larkin couldn't have been above ten years old. "And where is your old dad today?" she asked.

"Dead of the pipe. We lived in Limehouse mostly, and he had a bed at Tai Ling's. I left when he copped it. They tried to take me to Mary Jeffries' to make a whore of me, but I run off. Don't remember my mum."

"I'm sorry to hear it," Alice said, and Larkin shrugged, as if she didn't much share Alice's sorrow. "Well, I'm glad you spared the…the man's eye. King Solomon would have approved. Certainly you have a fitting name."

The gouger had disappeared, and Larkin returned to her toast. Alice drank the strong coffee, thinking about Langdon again. At any moment he might walk in through the door, of course—this being a breakfast 'worth coming into London for.' It wouldn't be the first time he had chased away in pursuit of a suddenly appearing…caterwaul, leaving her a vague explanation. But there were bothersome elements in this, certainly—his sleeping in wet clothes, for instance, and being careful not to awaken her. Perhaps it had been mere gallantry, she told herself.

"Larkin and I mean to pluck Uncle Gilbert from his barrel today, if you're still willing to help, Alice," Tubby said, making room on the table for the plates of sausage, eggs, beans, bacon, and black pudding that were just then coming out of the kitchen. "He has a vastly high regard for you, you know. You have a way with him."

"Certainly I'll do what I can. How will we find him?"

"I was up and about early, and consulted with William Billson, who consulted with Larkin. Larkin has a crew of pirates, do you see, whom we've managed to employ as a private army. We've got a strict rule against gouging of any sort, you'll be happy to know. They scattered up and down as soon as we agreed upon a fee, and within half an hour two of them returned to report that there is to be a migration today at the base of London Bridge, near to where that quacksalver Diogenes does his business. The barrelers mean to launch at the turn of the tide. I'm assured that the Primrose Hill faction is involved."

"A *migration*?"

"Apparently they're taking to the water, God help them."

"It makes them into eels," Larkin said, "and they must go to sea."

"*What* makes them into eels?" Alice asked.

"The powders. Some goes quick, some slow. I know the Red Vests, and they told me. My mate Charley is one, and Jack Singer. It's what's in the powders, like I said. Glass eels dried out and ground up, along with what's called 'chemicals.' Old Diogenes lays the eels in the sun out Brompton way, by the cemetery. If it's hot out you can smell them to Putney. Charley told me, and he don't lie and I don't neither. They want to go home, the eels do. Their guts turn to mush afore they go, and they don't eat."

"And where is home?" Alice asked.

"Among the seaweeds," Larkin told her.

"The great Sargasso, or so it's reported," Tubby said.

Alice stared at him for a moment. "This Diogenes is an enterprising man."

"He's rich is what," Larkin said, "but Charley says his luck is out. Charley and Jack Singer mean to scarper before the rozzers take him."

"That would be the police," Tubby said to Alice, who nodded. "And that complicates our issue somewhat. If barrelling is outlawed, and the factions cut up rough, there'll be trouble for one and all. The Here-and-Thereians won't abandon their migration. We're a long chalk better off taking Uncle out of his barrel than out of Newgate Prison."

"I'm with you, then," Alice said. "How do we proceed?"

"I promised Larkin's crew two crowns apiece if they create what is commonly called a diversion—something short of mayhem, ideally. You and I will gouge Uncle out of the flotilla and spirit him away." —⌘

Holland Road

S T. IVES STOOD atop Blackfriars Bridge, looking down at the Thames, its murky water flowing very slowly as the indecisive tide debated the idea of turning upon itself and moving once again toward the sea. He put his hand into his coat for the tenth time in the last half hour, and was heartened by the feel of the bundled envelopes of powders, which had emptied half of his purse—1,500 packets all told, a veritable brick of them.

The rush of pleasure that coursed through him when he licked the powders from his fingertips troubled him somewhat. He thought of Alice and of the note he had left beneath the saltcellar. Surely she had found it by now and was...*content* to think that he was safe. The nagging sense of guilt hovered roundabout him like a spirit, however. Thoughts of his children came into his mind, and he pushed them firmly back into the shadows. He would contemplate family matters later, when he was steadier.

His breath caught in his throat, and his head abruptly began to shake as if he were palsied. He reached into his pocket, and his hand fumbled for an envelope. He poured it into his palm, sucking the dry powder back into his throat before carefully licking his hand clean and then swallowing a dram of Hollands gin from a pocket flask. He stood with his eyes closed for the moments that it took for his head to clear and his sanity to return to him. He recalled that yesterday—such a long time ago!—he had harbored ideas of opposition to Diogenes, and he now he considered the frail half-knowledge of hearsay, of the Billsons' warnings and Tubby's uninformed imprecations. Knowledge was mutable, he found, one plane leading to a higher plane. Or perhaps *plain* was the better word, for in some sense a man walked upon it throughout life, ever ascending, if he were lucky, to the great sea that held all secrets.

He removed the barrel brochure from his trouser pocket and gazed upon it with something like rapture. Surely it was within his powers to explain the nature of his…. The word 'compulsion' occurred to him, but that smacked of…. He rejected the word 'addiction' out of hand. And then in a moment of insight he saw that he and Alice might *share* a barrel, the two of them venturing out onto the great sea together. For a brief time he was satisfied with this, a very brief time, and then he saw that Alice would not comprehend the philosophy of the barrel, such as it was. Something like jealousy underlay this realization—not jealousy, surely, but the right of possession, perhaps—the right of property that was guaranteed to every subject…

To relieve his troubled mind he sampled another packet of the powders, just touching them to his tongue. Then seeing that he had dampened what was left on his palm—that he could scarcely dump them back into the envelope—he licked his hand clean, shook his head sharply, and drew in a deep breath of air. He had consumed two of last night's supply at Rodway's Coffee House across from Billingsgate Market early this morning, the smell of fish within the market and along the docks redolent in the air. Then he had gone into the market itself and had pondered the glass eels for close to an hour, living masses of them, hundreds of thousands of utterly transparent eels alive in vast basins illuminated by the sun, which had risen just high enough to shine through the glass roof. He had been struck with the notion of buying eels in wholesale quantities and releasing them into the river to set them free, but the money in his wallet was already bespoke, and when he heard eight bells ring out from a sloop in the Pool he had walked down to Borough High Street where the queue was already forming.

People were buying the envelopes in quantity, and Diogenes had taken his money without comment. This had seemed meaningful for a moment, but then he was indifferent to it; his mind was centered on the wonderful heap of envelopes that Diogenes had bound with string, and which were now safely in his pocket.

Pulling his eyes away from the river, he walked along Blackfriars Bridge to the Victoria Embankment and up a narrow lane above Puddle Dock, where he went into a gin shop. It was dim inside, with a long bar along one side beneath a decorated mirror. A woman with a mass of hair and a revealing bodice was busy dispensing glasses of gin to three men who went off to a table near the door and settled in as if they meant to stay. She smiled lasciviously at St. Ives when he ordered a glass, and then lost some of the smile when she got a better look at him.

"Been fishing, have you?" she asked, taking his shilling and wrinkling her nose. He affected not to hear her, and he turned away, finding his own table and sitting down so as to face the wall and conceal his actions. He carefully opened yet another packet of powder, dumped it into the gin, stirred it with his finger, sucked his finger clean, and drank down the gin. He sat for a time, letting it work its magic and remembering his elation last night when he'd had such marvelous powers of perception.

He looked at his skin in the gaslight. It appeared to be transparent, and he saw the complexity of bones and veins within his hand. He was a mere mechanism, it seemed, but a marvelous mechanism in a barrel made of skin, setting out on a journey of becoming. Becoming what? he wondered vaguely, and he stood up and went out into the road in order to discover the answer, for surely it lay in the sunlit morning and not in a gin shop. A tide of both elation and need had washed over him when he had consumed the glass of doctored gin, but a need for what? He would find the answer, no doubt, on Holland Road.

On Upper Thames Street he boarded an omnibus bound for Kensington High Street and Holland Park, and along the way he studied the barrels pictured in Diogenes' brochure. The accoutrements were little short of fabulous, and many of them necessary. He had a bare sixty pounds left in his wallet, and although the brochure did not reveal prices, it was clear that the sum would not do. He would cross that bridge, he told himself, when he came upon it.

For a time he closed his eyes and pictured the clear river of last night's dreams—portentous dreams, he saw now. His waking self could still see them within his mind, but as if through a telescope held wrong-end-to. He lost himself in the dream, however, and came out of it when he realized that the omnibus had reached Hyde Park. He climbed off at Church Street and went up past St. Mary Abbots, with its high spire aglow against a water-blue sky. He found Diogenes' shop on the Holland Street corner, and for a time he looked at the barrels in the window, each of them full of the promise of movement, of a happy return, of rebirth.

He smelled something musty and dank—his coat, he realized—and it seemed to him that he should rid himself of it before entering the shop, except that his brick of envelopes was safely stowed in one of its pockets. He made out his reflection in the window glass, seeing that his hair was awry and his collar gaping open. Turning away, he patted his hair into place as best he could with saliva, and he buttoned his collar and smoothed his coat. He squared his shoulders and went in through the door, a bell clanging from above, and he was greeted quite cordially by a thin man dressed in black like an undertaker's assistant, who said, "Good day to you, fellow traveler!"

"Thank you," St. Ives said. "I would like to purchase a barrel." He held out the open brochure. "This model. 'The Queen's Sloop.'"

The man recoiled, as if St. Ives's breath was rank, but then recovered and said, "An exceptionally useful vehicle, sir. Are you associated with a faction?"

"The Primrose Hill Faction," St. Ives lied, although perhaps soon it would not be a lie.

"A worthy organization. I've sold them many a barrel. The one you've chosen fetches an even three hundred pounds, sir, and it's warranted seaworthy and comes equipped with a tow-along, chambered cask stocked with dried beef, inspissated juice of lime, and ship's biscuit. For an added fee we can supply charts proofed against seawater with no fewer than ten layers of varnish. You've no doubt read the list of accoutrements listed in the brochure."

"Yes, of course," St. Ives said. "Three hundred pounds seems a nominal price." From his pocket he took three damp twenty-pound banknotes. "I'd be quite happy to pay these down and the rest with a draft on my bank."

The clerk stared at him for a long moment, looking past his spectacles and down his nose, which was wrinkled as if he had again detected an odor. St. Ives was aware of the fusty smell of his own clothing and also that his scalp and beard itched. He berated himself for not taking a few moments to shave this morning, although doing so would quite likely have awakened Alice, which…

He put the thought aside for the moment and attempted a smile, unsure whether he was being regarded with a look of mere assessment or active disdain.

"I'm afraid it's quite impossible," the clerk said. "My master Diogenes is happy to accept cash money in any form. Half a ton of farthing pieces in an ironbound chest would do, I assure you. But we have no use for cheques, bank drafts, promissory notes, or the annexation of firstborn children. If your funds are such that you can withdraw a sum from your bank, then I encourage you to do so. Good day to you."

With that the clerk turned away and began to polish the glass-topped counter with a rag. St. Ives had been dismissed. As he left the shop, a dissolute couple pushed in past him, and he heard the clerk shout, "Good day to you, fellow travelers!" as the door shut behind him. He watched from the shadowed entryway as they walked to the far side of the store, the clerk gesturing and nodding. Not three steps inside the door stood a barrel much like the one St. Ives had offered to buy. Whether it contained a cask of inspissated limejuice and ship's biscuit it was impossible to say, but he knew that it was quite possible that he could step inside, put his hands on the tongue of the barrel, and pull it through the door before the clerk was aware of it.

He felt the corners of his mouth turn up into a grin without him willing them to, and he pushed the door open, a vicious need having come upon him. The door-bell jangled and instantly gave him away. He saw the clerk whirl around and move quickly toward him, but already his hand was on the barrel, and he turned toward the door and pulled, nearly pitching forward when the barrel stood solidly in its place: the wheels were encumbered by chocks bolted to the floor. He abandoned it and leapt for the exit, pushing through it and fleeing along Kensington High Street, his coat flapping.

When he saw that he was not being pursued, he compelled himself to stop. He would surely be arrested otherwise. People were looking askance at him, moving out of his way. And in any event the vitality had quite gone out of his muscle and bone. He stepped into the first public house he passed, where he consumed two packets of powders in a tankard of ale, for he was thirsty as well as worn out.

Somewhat renewed by his dose, he made his way through Hyde Park, bound for Threadneedle Street where lay the Bank of England. It would be an easy thing to withdraw the necessary funds. Alice would quite understand, he told himself, when he explained it to her. He heard the sound of numerous hand-bells now, and a train of barrels rolled toward him down Serpentine Road, towed by no fewer than six Red Vests. "To the river!" the barrelers shouted, and as he stood aside to let them pass he felt a deep longing to be among them.

In that moment it dawned on him that it was May Day, a bank holiday, and that he was to be cheated of his barrel. He tried to recall how many packets of powder he had consumed since he awakened at dawn, but he had quite forgotten. His hand went into his coat, and he felt the brick of parchment envelopes, fingering the string that bound them as he trudged along in the general direction of Smithfield, his mind a cacophony of desire and despair. —

Tooley Street Stairs

ALICE KEPT A weather eye out for Langdon as she and Tubby crossed London Bridge on foot. His note still gnawed at her mind, both its brevity and its squalor being dead wrong. Larkin's strange comment about eels hovered in her mind, and she thought again of the fishy smell of the water in the glass. Her thoughts were half formed, however, and led her nowhere. She reminded herself that she had no reason to suppose that Langdon would be in the vicinity, but then it wasn't turning out to be a reasonable morning.

The bridge was lined with people watching the fun, and there was the usual complement of street urchins dashing to and fro, Larkin's pirate crew allegedly among them. It would be a famous opportunity to pick pockets and snatch purses, and she clutched her handbag tightly, wishing she had left it at the inn. She and Tubby perpetually dodged trains of barrelers jockeying for position to cross the bridge, and she could see that there was a crowd of them on the landing below the Tooley Stairs. Red Vests were helping to shift the barrels downstairs, or stood knee-deep in the river, at work binding barrels together into makeshift rafts, lines running through ringbolts fixed into the barrelheads so that the tide would take them down together. Others were stepping masts, outriggers, and sculling oars onto the more elaborate barrels.

Borough High Street was thick with barrelers, as was the causeway leading down behind Borough Market to the Thames. Barrels, both single and in train, stretched away along the south bank to Horselydown Lane and beyond. Several were mired up to the top of the wheels in Thames mud, having tried for the river and bogged down. A number were already afloat in the slack water, waiting for the tide to turn, and people on passing boats hollered ironical abuse at them, many leaning out with barge poles to shift the barrelers out of the way. There were hundreds of barrels, many hundreds, it seemed to Alice, the entire scene being outlandish in the extreme. There were constables in evidence also, no doubt standing by to read the Riot Act. Larkin the Just was somewhere in the crowds, waiting to give them a reason to do so, thereby earning Tubby's two crowns. Tubby, like his Uncle Gilbert, was as impetuous as he was generous.

The Primrose Hill faction, according to Tubby, wore green sennet hats, and Alice could see a number of them scattered in the general mob. Tubby pointed out two green-hatted clusters at the top of the stairs, waiting to come down, although whether Gilbert was among them was impossible to say, for the barrels hid their occupants below and the broad-brimmed hats hid their faces from above.

She spotted Larkin now, along with several of her small companions, the lot of them moving among the barrelers, searching for the barrel that sported the Frobisher crest—a rampant hedgehog with a flailing red devil in its teeth.

"They've got him, by God!" Tubby cried, pointing toward the landing. Alice looked in that direction and saw Gilbert clearly now. His raised paddlewheel spun at a good clip although he was still on dry land. The barrel hid the motions of his feet on the pedals as he tested the machinery. Like his compatriots, he was apparently anxious to be underway. Just as this thought passed through Alice's mind, however, Larkin snatched the hat from atop Gilbert's head and sailed it out over the river. She leapt upon his barrel and then hopped across half a dozen more, grabbing and flinging away hats with both hands as she capered along, her pigtails flying. Her crew—difficult to see how many—followed suit, and very quickly there were a storm of hats flying and children leaping and scrambling about, pushing barrels every which way and promoting a general outrage.

The watchers on the bridge and people in boats on the river cheered and hooted, but there was a panic among the barrelers, who knew they'd been besieged at the very moment that their migration was at hand. Many howled aloud, as if in physical pain. Tubby was moving toward the stairs now, using his bulk to bowl through the crowd and shouting, "Make a lane! Make a lane!" Alice followed in his wake as he cleared the way, increasing the general confusion as he heaved barrels to the left and right. Two stocky Red Vests confronted him, and he swept them aside as if they were made of paper.

Barrels were bouncing down the Tooley Stairs now and sailing out onto the water, where they splashed down and moved out into the stream, the migration carrying on apace, the tide flowing downriver at last. The way ahead cleared, and Alice saw Gilbert once again. Larkin straddled his barrel now, facing him and preventing him from unhinging himself from his prison, while four of her companions, a boy and three girls, all of them raggedy children, pushed and towed him into the mouth of an apparently empty alley upriver. His eyes were wild and his mouth worked and he swiveled his head this way and that as if searching for salvation.

Tubby and Alice pursued them, Alice seeing at that moment two policemen who were moving to follow suit, although they were hindered by the crowd, which was quieting down, the storm of flying hats having apparently ended.

"Take this!" Alice shouted at Tubby, and she pitched her handbag at him. "I'll follow to the Half Toad!" She turned then and ran toward the two policemen, who were still forty feet away. She dodged around a fallen barrel, its occupant trapped within it, and hollered, "Help! Help!" as loud as she could manage, putting a suitably distressed look on her face. "They've taken my purse!" she cried, pointing in the direction of Borough Market. "My jewels! They've taken my jewels!"

"Who has, madam?" one of the policemen asked, both of them happy to attend to her despite the wild antics of the people roundabout. They smiled at her encouragingly. "What did the blighter look like?" the other one asked.

"He's a small, stout man," she said, "with a terrible scar, his nose quite removed. Oatmeal tweeds. I…" She threw her hand across her forehead as if she were faint. "He'll escape if you don't hurry!" she sobbed out, and was happy to see their look of helpful determination as they raced away. At once she dashed back toward the alley, following its turns until she came out onto Bankside, which she followed to Southwark Bridge. Tubby and Larkin's gang had disappeared along with Uncle Gilbert's barrel.

She spent the following hour searching for the man Diogenes, always on the lookout for the two helpful policemen but managing to avoid them. Virtually everyone she asked knew of Diogenes and had various opinions about where he might have set up shop, but no one had seen him. She wandered up Bankside and Commercial Road to Waterloo Bridge and then back down again, finally turning toward Smithfield and the Half Toad. From the top of Southwark Bridge she could see that the river was dotted with barrels going down on the tide. Tooley Stairs were hidden from sight, but it was evident that although the migration had dwindled, it hadn't been entirely stopped.

The entire business abruptly struck her as funny—the mad barrelers, the flying hats, Gilbert towed backwards up the alley, the policemen racing off after her phantom thief. She began to laugh, and she covered her mouth with her hand, unable to silence the laughter. Frightened at her own wild energy, she forced herself to stop before the laughter turned to weeping, and she kept it in a firm grip as she walked up Queen Street through Cheapside.

As she approached the corner of St. Martin's Street, she heard the ringing of the barrel bells and barrelers chanting, "To the River!" over and over again like a mantra. A train of twenty or so barrels moved straight toward her, the occupants wearing yellow hats, the Red Vests running like thoroughbreds. When they drew up to the nearby corner, she saw among them a tall, leggy, hatless, disheveled man who rode along with his head nodding. She could not see his face at all, turned downward as it was, but it came into her mind that it was Langdon—the man's coat was very like Langdon's—and her heart leapt into her throat, a gasp escaping from her open mouth. The train of barrels rounded the corner sharply, and the sudden turn whipped the rear-most barrels hard sideways. The tether parted, and two barrels, suddenly loosed from the rest, overturned and caromed off a low wall adjacent to a haberdashery shop, the barrels flying to pieces, the occupants flung out. The rest of the train hauled away along Cheapside as if nothing had happened.

Seeing that a dozen people were surrounding the fallen barrelers, Alice stood on the pavement watching the train roll out of sight. It was patently impossible, she told herself, that Langdon was among them, reduced to such a condition. He had been himself yesterday evening—his intelligent, cheerful self. He could *not* have become someone else in such a short time. She repeated this thought firmly, resuming her trek toward Smithfield and berating herself for allowing her imagination to confound her. —☙

The Note-book

I GAVE UNCLE'S BARREL to Larkin," Tubby said in the tap-room of the Half Toad, "and she sold it for a mere sixty pounds to someone on the street, after which she converted the money to coins and distributed half of it among her piratical cohorts. She was keen to have the coins jingling in her pocket, as was the rest of the gang. They're all quite rich, but they'll be paupers by the end of the week. She's staked Uncle to a game of Old Maid."

"She had to sell the barrel cheap to be rid of it, I suppose," Alice said, gratefully accepting a glass of shrub from Hopeful. "I'm surprised she wasn't taken up by the police." She looked across at Gilbert, who sat at a table staring roundabout him like a man who had lost his wits, which of course he had, half of them anyway. Larkin sat opposite Gilbert, her back to Alice, dealing cards. There were stacks of crown pieces and shillings in front of both of them.

"They're playing for high sums," Alice said.

"I believe Larkin's money is safe at the moment, although Uncle is normally a wicked player. She was aware of your dodge with the police, by the way—knew just what you were up to. She quite approves of you."

"I'm flattered," Alice said, "and I quite approve of her, although the poor girl will be hanged if nothing is done to rescue her from her piratical life."

"Look at your cards, then," Larkin said loudly, perhaps thinking that Gilbert was partly deaf. When he failed to respond, she climbed to her knees on her chair and then reached across and looked at his cards, extracting pairs and discarding them into a pile. "You've got a good hand, Uncle. Wager five bob. Do you hear me?" Again he failed to respond, and she plucked up five of his shillings and put them into the middle of the table along with several coins that already sat there.

Alice walked across to watch the game. She smiled at Larkin and put a hand on Gilbert's arm. He sat morosely in his chair staring at his untouched tankard of ale, looking far past his age and pitifully unhappy. His clothes were disheveled and he had a high, fishy smell to him, having been encased in his barrel like salted cod.

"He won't attend," Larkin complained aloud. "It's the powders what does it. He wants his dose monstrous bad now that he can't have it."

"We've put the powders down the *loo*," Tubby said loudly. "It's no use pining away over it. Drink your beer like a good fellow and do as Larkin asks."

Gilbert turned his head and regarded Tubby as if he were a stranger, and Tubby looked sadly away.

"Mayhaps the powders have turned him into a frog," Larkin said quite seriously to Alice. "You might kiss him on the forehead, like the girl did to the frog in the well. It's in the fairy book. Do you want a sweet?"

"Yes, thank-you," Alice said, taking a piece of Larkin's molasses toffee from its packet and giving the parchment a twist. "I seem to remember that the girl in the fairy book cut the frog's head off into the bargain," Alice said. "I won't do that, but I will kiss him if you advise it. Do you read books, then?"

"Something like."

"Will you read to me sometime?"

"Will you kiss the frog?"

"Yes," Alice said, and she leaned over and kissed Gilbert on the forehead and then looked into his face. For a moment his eyes focused, and his lips moved as if he meant to speak. He blinked and looked around quizzically, but then seemed to disappear into his own mind again.

"Play a card, then, king frog," Larkin told him, waiting half a moment before reaching across once again in order to play it for him. Gilbert seemed to follow Larkin's fingers this time, and when she shifted backward into her chair, he leaned forward and plucked a piece of molasses toffee out of her bag. He began to put the entire wrapped sweet into his mouth, but Larkin snatched it away and informed him in a loud voice that he must unwrap it first, that he mustn't be the dog that ate dirty pudding. He sat with his mouth agape, waiting for her to put the toffee into it, after which he chomped down on it and sat staring as the brown molasses drooled out of the corners of his mouth.

"I believe he's coming 'round," Alice said to Larkin.

"He's a fat man is why. It's the narrow ones go down like sticks."

The phrase "narrow ones" reminded her instantly of Langdon, and she remembered the morocco note-book, which had been out of her mind since breakfast. She hurried to the stairs and ascended with a newly-revived feeling of dread. The book was where she had left it, still damp, and she took it to the window to open it, carefully turning the pages, the first of which were covered with sketches of plants and fish and animals along with brief annotations in Langdon's clear hand. There were dated barometer readings, rainfall totals, observations on the weather, on Johnson the elephant who lived in the barn, on the hops plants. There was a list of begonia species that had put out bloom spikes just last week—the color and size of the blooms, their curiously salty flavor, their lack of odor....

She came upon the page with yesterday's date, the time recorded as 8:18 p.m. Within thirty seconds' reading she knew what he had done. Her chest felt empty and her breath came in gasps. She sat down hard on the bed, remaining still for a moment with her eyes closed, trying to compose herself. She looked at the increasingly strange ramblings—pages and pages of scattered observations and wild statements. The handwriting grew in size and illegibility as the phrasing grew more and more eccentric and the exclamation points and under-linings more numerous. It was written evidence of a descent into madness that had apparently been well along by the time he consumed the second two packets of powders, evidently with great glee. The page was stained with what smelled like beer and fish, and the pages that followed were increasingly alien and incoherent.

She went back downstairs, taking the book with her. Larkin, she discovered, was speaking in low voices with Tubby, who arose when Alice walked in. The coins were gone from the card table, and Gilbert was asleep, snoring prodigiously with his head on the table.

"Larkin would have a word with you, Alice," Tubby said in a grim voice.

"And I need to have a word with you, Tubby. What is it, Larkin?"

"It's this, ma'am. Billy picked the man's pocket what we sold the barrel to. He can't help himself, can Billy, and it was dead simple because the man was an eel and stupid with the powders. I took the watch from Billy.

The thing is ma'am..." She held the watch up, the case open. "It's *you*. I just now saw it."

"Oh, *God*," Alice said, grasping the back of a chair to steady herself. She recognized the watch. She herself had purchased it and given it to Langdon as a birthday present two years ago. He had put a photograph of her in the lid. "Yes, it's a picture of me, Larkin. Thank heavens you brought it to me."

Tubby said, "It was Langdon, then, who bought the barrel for sixty pounds—a little over an hour ago. Did you suspect that he was taking the powders?"

"I feared it. My God, I *saw* him," she said, knowing now that it was true. "There was a train of barrels coming down along Cheapside, headed for the river. I couldn't believe it was he who was among them, but it was. It must have been."

"He's *bolting* down the river like the rest of them, ma'am," Larkin said, giving Alice the watch. "But we'll fetch him back if we hurry. Listen, Tubby. We'll have a boat at Pickle Herring Stairs. Do you know them?"

"Near London Bridge I believe, just..."

"Downriver. Dead across from the Tower. *Two* boats. I know where to borrow them. If he's already in the river, we'll have to follow him down. Hurry!" she said, and she dashed out the door, passing by the windows one after another at a run. —◦

On the River

OR THE SECOND time that day Alice found herself bound
for the Thames in a hansom cab. Not long past she had thought
the barreling amusing in its way, or at least some elements of it. Now she
thought of it as little less than satanic, and she had no patience for the
late afternoon traffic. Just past Cheapside, at Bank Junction, the cab was
at a dead stop. The sun was dropping down the sky, evening coming on.
She thought of what Larkin had said about following Langdon downriver,
and she envisioned doing such a thing in the darkness and of the river
funneling out into the sea at Gravesend, impossibly broad and with the
wide ocean beyond.

"I can't bear it," she said to Tubby, and then opened the door, climbed
down onto the street, hiked up her skirt, and set out at a run, dodging
around past Mansion House toward King William Street. She heard
Tubby holler something, and she looked back, happy to see that he was
following. People stared as she ran along, and she prayed that no one
would interfere with Tubby, perhaps thinking that his pursuit of her was
ill meant. She dodged in and out, catching her heel on a curb, stumbling
and nearly falling, taking to the road when the way was open and then
onto the pavement again when the traffic closed in. Tubby caught up with
her at Lower Thames Street, where they watched for a break in the crush
of coaches and wagons and people on horseback. The way was suddenly
open, and she took Tubby's arm, the two of them making a dash for it,
out onto London Bridge where they slowed down at last, the black smoke
from passing steamships rising roundabout them as they took a precious
moment to search the river for barrels.

Watermen plied their boats to and fro, dwarfed by the steamships and colliers, which were in turn dwarfed by the tall-masted ships moored in the Pool of London. Barrels bobbed along between the boats and ships, the migration moving forward in earnest, and it seemed little short of miraculous that the barrels weren't run down. She saw then that to the contrary there were empty barrels among them, some floating just beneath the surface, and she saw a man swimming tiredly, pawing the water like a dog, trying to reach one of the swamped barrels.

There were yellow bowler hats among the barrelers, and she pointed them out to Tubby, but of course she had no idea whether they were the same yellow hats as those she had seen in Cheapside. It was utterly impossible to tell whether Langdon was among them or already moving past Greenwich on the tide. Pickle Herring Stairs lay somewhere on the right bank opposite the tower, but there were too many impediments—ships and wharves and the swerve of the shore itself—to see them.

They moved on at a steady pace, glancing futilely at the river now and then, and soon arrived at the top of Borough High Street once more. It was evident that the migration was still in desperate progress. Many barrels had overturned, some occupants lying in a stupor, others crawling out and slogging down the bank, ankle deep in mud, or crawling toward the river on hands and knees. A profusion of police whistles were blowing along with a rising chorus of shouting and screaming.

The Metropolitan Police had obviously been ordered to put an end to the barrel madness—too late by half, Alice thought. The stairs and causeways were a lumber of overturned barrels. Some of the barrelers made away unhindered, but some resisted with a sort of tired violence, mad with desire to get into the river. The Red Vests were nowhere to be seen, having scarpered before things went bad, no doubt along with Larkin's friends Charley and Jack.

Alice held onto Tubby's arm as they angled across toward Duke Street in order to make their way downriver, but half way across Tubby stopped and shouted, "There's the scoundrel himself, absconding, by God!"

Not thirty feet distant stood the man Diogenes, frantically closing up his barrel in the shadow of a tree outside the corner pub. His sign was still open, hanging from the mast lashed to the barrel. A surprisingly large man with a long mulish face stood with crossed arms, blocking the view and evidently intent on defending his master. He peered past the edge of the building, then turned and said something to Diogenes, who slammed a hinged lid and bent over to release what was apparently the brake on a wheel.

Tubby reached beneath his coat and hauled out his heavy, blackthorn cudgel, which had been hidden, hanging by a cord. He slipped the cord over his wrist before hiding it behind his back. "I mean to put paid to their caper," he said hastily to Alice. "Across the way, take the first left turning and around to the right and straight on for Pickle Herring Street, and pray that Larkin is waiting. I'll be along directly."

"Nonsense," she said. "There's a likely looking police sergeant just over there, judging from his uniform. He'd be thrilled to collar Diogenes. I'll fetch him."

Before Tubby could protest she was off and running, covering the fifty yards with her hand waving. "The man Diogenes!" she shouted, pointing behind her. "He's there behind the corner of the pub, just at Duke Street. He's got a bully to defend him, so take care."

"Does he now?" the man said, blowing a long, double blast on his whistle as he started forward.

Alice saw two constables break away from the milling crowd in order to follow, neither of them, she was happy to see, being the constables who had been her champions this morning. She hurried after the lot of them at a distance, slowing and looking back as she passed the corner, determined now to make for the river instead of passing the ruckus on Duke Street.

Diogenes' barrel stood canted over frontward onto its right-hand axle, the spoke wheel hammered to pieces. The big man sat on the ground, holding his left forearm and looking furious. Diogenes hung from the mast that bore his sign, his coat yanked over his head and he struggling and hollering. Tubby was nowhere to be seen. He had been quick with his cudgel, but his necessary haste might have prevented him from committing a more dangerous crime.

At the river Alice stepped atop a narrow stone embankment that stood some six feet above the mud and moved along toward her destination, hurrying to catch up to Tubby, who had gone on to the stairs, no doubt. She trailed her right hand along a wall of old brick—the back of whatever buildings stood between Duke Street and the river. Just ahead, where the wall

ended, were the Tooley Stairs. She dropped down upon the landing, finding herself amid fallen barrels and a score of worn-out barrelers slumped
on the stairs, their migrations having ended at the edge of the river. Her
embankment began again beyond the landing, and she went on, making
her way to Pickle Herring Street where she nearly ran straight into Tubby.
They continued straight on, Tubby glancing over his shoulder, thinking
of constables, no doubt. There was no sign of pursuit, however, and Alice
gladly took his arm again, the way clear ahead. They waited for a dray to
pass in front of them at Battle Bridge Street, and then crossed Stoney Lane
unhindered, Pickle Herring Stairs lying not twenty yards ahead. Alice saw
Larkin and two of her crew heading toward the stairs in two boats. They
were near in to shore and in the shadow of a tall ship. Larkin's cohorts, a
boy and a girl, sat side-by-side in a down-at-heels scow, each pulling on an
oar. Larkin stood in the stern of a skiff, sculling her craft along at a rapid
clip with a single oar over the transom.

"Climb aboard!" Larkin shouted, when Tubby clapped onto the skiff's
mooring line. The two in the scow backed water and stood off ten feet.
"Miss Alice with me," Larkin ordered, "and Tubby into the scow!"

Alice did as she was told, sitting on a thwart facing forward, realizing
that they were already away, back into the shadow of the ship and heading
downriver. She looked behind to see Tubby climbing nimbly aboard the
scow as it bumped along the short landing, the bow heaving downward
with his weight so that it nearly took on water. It righted again and came
along in their wake, and soon they were into the sunlight once again, what
was left of the sunlight. The shadows on the river were long, now, and the
dome of St. Paul's would soon hide the sun.

"That's Bobby and Cooper in the scow," Larkin said to Alice. "The ones
who foisted your man's watch. He's got a sharp eye, has Bobby, and he don't
forget a man's face once he's picked his pocket."

Alice looked back, seeing that Tubby was rowing. Bobby and Cooper
were standing on the thwarts, Bobby looking through a short spyglass,
sweeping the river. They moved downstream, passing St. Catherine's Docks
on the left bank and a confusion of wharves and causeways on the right.
The barrels on the river were farther between now, fewer barrelers finding
their way into the river at all. Larkin sculled along at a surprising rate of
speed, passing the barrels that were merely borne upon on the tide. There

were far more men than women afloat, for some reason, but none of the men was Langdon. A ship blocked the sight of the opposite shore now, and Tubby crossed behind it, the scow disappearing as it went down the far side, then reappearing, the children still scanning the river. The minutes passed, the sun sank out of sight, and now there were no shadows at all, just a gathering dusk. Larkin moved toward the right bank again, where a dozen barrelers bobbed along in a loose cluster, none of them Langdon.

Once again they lost sight of the scow, and now they were swerving around the tight bend of the river into Limehouse Reach, with its maze of dockyards and wharves. Lighters moved from one to another, carrying tons of coal and goods from moored ships. The odd barrel drifted among them, but few and far between. Alice wondered with half a hope whether Langdon mightn't have got into the river at all. Perhaps he had struggled with the police and was sitting safely in a cell at Newgate Prison—the very thing that Tubby had feared. She prayed that it was so.

There was a piercing whistle now, and Larkin shouted, "Sharp's the word!" Alice saw that it was Cooper blowing the whistle, the boy Bobby pointing hard at a cluster of five barrels near the left bank, perhaps eighty yards away—four yellow hats—and even in the failing light Alice could see that Langdon floated hatless among them. She thanked God that Bobby had picked his pocket. Larkin brought the skiff around, shaving the stern of a lighter with four feet to spare and not condescending to reply when someone shouted a curse at her.

They approached at a good clip, the scow, the skiff, and the barrels drawing closer and closer together—close enough so that the barrelers perceived that they were about to be boarded. They shouted, endeavoring to grasp hands with their immediate neighbors. They gathered together like a school of fish that perceived a predator, their paddlewheels throwing bow waves as they surged forward. Tubby leaned hard on the oars in order to outdistance them and cut them off, and Larkin shouted, "Hold fast!" and drove straight into the mass, the barrels pushed apart, the bow of the skiff thumping into one of them, spinning it around.

"Langdon!" Alice shouted, reaching far out, waiting for a chance to grab the raised boot at the rear of the craft. Her husband's head jerked around, and he saw them now. The wild look on his face—the face of a madman, a stranger—made Alice hesitate, but then her own face hardened into a mask of determination. Langdon turned his ships' wheel hard a-port, driving away toward the left bank and into a current of swift moving water, Larkin following, sculling with wide, even strokes, reversing the blade with each turn.

Langdon was in the midst of the current now, outpacing them, his paddle wheel plowing along, throwing the water wide as they ran down through Limehouse Reach. His energy was clearly fading, however, the paddlewheel slowing and finally stopping. Alice reached down and plucked up the barrel's stern rope, which was trailing behind. "I've got him!" she cried.

But in that moment Langdon opened the hatches of the barrel, stood up, and attempted to leap out. The barrel rolled, and he was pitched facedownward into the water and sank beneath the surface. Alice had no leisure to remove her shoes, but she was thankful that she had worn trowsers beneath her petticoat. She hastily slipped out of her skirt and petticoat and rolled over the gunnel into the river, her eyes and mouth tight shut. She surfaced, got her bearings, and struck out after her husband, holding her head high.

Langdon was swimming desperately into the dark shadow between two moored ships now, his shoes and coat obviously dragging at him. Alice swam up alongside him, holding her head above the water and planting a hand under his right shoulder, scissoring her feet in order to propel herself upward and flinging him over onto his back with all her strength, then throwing her arm across his chest and bringing her hip up under the small of his back, stroking hard with her right hand and kicking her feet to keep them both afloat.

He arched suddenly as if he meant to fling himself into the air, and then splashed down, driving both of them beneath the water. She held on tenaciously, levering him over onto his back again, jamming her hip beneath him, and getting her head up, the dirty Thames water streaming from her hair.

"Easy," she gasped. "I have you now, my darling." He groaned softly, moving his lips as if trying to speak. Whether he understood her, she couldn't say, but he ceased to struggle. She heard a wooden clatter, and then heard both Tubby and Larkin shouting at her to hold on. An oar glanced off the side of her head, followed by a shouted apology. She flailed out with her free hand, banged her knuckles on the oar, and then got a grip on it, fearing that at any moment Langdon would cut another caper and break from her grasp. Tubby drew them in quickly, however, and with Bobby and Cooper pulling and Alice pushing, they heaved Langdon into the scow, where he lay on the flat bottom between the thwarts.

Alice grabbed onto the gunnel of the skiff, not daring to attempt to pull herself into it and risk overturning. As her breathing slowed it came fully into her mind that Langdon was safe, or at least alive. She thought of Larkin's admonition that she must "kiss the frog," and of Gilbert's very nearly awakening when she had done so. The thought was an element of hope that she held onto as tightly as she held onto the skiff. She did her best to be silent in her weeping and was happy that her tears would mingle with the Thames water still leaking from her hair. Larkin bent over to look down at her and said, "That's Drunkard's Dock right ahead, ma'am. Bobby and Cooper can fetch a barrow. We'll push your man up to Greenwich Road and find a hackney to fetch us back to the Half Toad." —⌀

Kissing the Frog

HUNDREDS OF BARRELS grounded on the Goodwin Sands, and an unknown number of barrelers drowned or lost at sea," Alice read. "They're still searching for bodies."

She laid the *Times* on the table and looked at St. Ives, who sat across from her, saying little. His hands shook uncontrollably from time to time, and he had elected to sit on them. The shaking was evidence of his head-first plunge into madness, and he was anxious to expunge as much of that evidence as he possibly could. With luck, he would be rid of the worst symptoms by tomorrow, and they could return to Aylesford. The guilt and shame, Alice knew, would weigh on his mind despite anything she could say to diminish them.

"The death toll would have been far worse if there had been heavy seas," Gilbert said. And then to St. Ives, in a perfectly cheerful voice, he said, "The tremors will pass away, Professor. I shook like a jelly when the poison was wearing off yesterday, but I'm steady now. It was a rapid decline, to be sure, but an equally rapid recovery. Are you still dreaming of the river?"

"Yes," St. Ives said. "I'm in the river every time I close my eyes."

"We share that, then. I'm rather happy about being there, however. There never was such calm, pellucid water in the waking world, such utter peace. I now understand the opium addict's regard for his pipe. Do you know that opium eaters employ people to awaken them from their dreams? They won't leave them otherwise, but would starve on their couches, the dream world being so very much superior to our own." Then, looking across to the table where Tubby and Larkin played a desperate game of Old Maid, he shouted, "Tubby's got a card in his sleeve, Larkin!"

"And who taught me that dodge when I was a mere boy?" Tubby asked, glowering at his uncle. "Do you remember drilling it into me? 'Shuffle me an ace,' you'd say, and then give me a sweet when I succeeded. You should have been taken up for ruining a child's innocence." He removed the half-hidden card from his sleeve and tossed it onto the pile of discards. To Larkin he said, "Watch your Uncle Gilbert *very* carefully when he deals cards, child."

Larkin scooped up the pot. "Fair is fair," she said, "and I'm not a child. You cheat, you lose your chink."

"Now see what you've done, Uncle. She's very nearly fleeced me. Loan me back ten bob, Larkin."

"I will, too, but you must pay me back fifteen."

"*Larcenous,*" Tubby said. "Are you quite persuaded to be her guardian, Uncle? You see how it goes with her."

"Doubly persuaded now that she's taken you down a peg."

"It's wonderful that you offered to be Larkin's guardian," Alice said to Gilbert in a low voice. "Are you quite sure you're up to the task—a girl, after all. Soon she'll be a woman, with all that entails, and a fierce one, too."

"My man Barlow and his wife have two girls of their own. Mrs. Barlow will rally round. And as for fierceness, why, the girl helped save the lot of us on account of it. I value her for it. I worry only that she'll find life in Dicker fairly mild. She knows something about birds, however, and there's famous birding on the South Downs."

Alice looked at St. Ives and discovered that he was gazing at her. "Is your memory returning?" she asked him.

"Yes, but in fragments. I recall consuming the first two packets of the powders at the George Inn, and again the following morning before I wrote that humiliating note and left if for Billson to find. My down-going course was so swift, however, that I very quickly became a mere sot, to my undying shame. Perhaps it's best that I don't recall it in detail." He picked up the morocco note-book from the table in front of him and looked into it. Immediately he shut it and set it back down.

"But I remember being in the Thames," he told her, "and you holding me. You said, 'I have you now.' I'd have drowned otherwise. I know that much."

Alice found that she was unable to speak, and so she took Larkin's advice and kissed him. —✧

Earthbound Things

The Aerial Spring

TWO MEN CROSSED the grounds of Bimbury Manor, the medieval ruin near Thurnham in Kent. The late spring morning, the nineteenth of June, was quiet, there being no one present save the two, one tall and one short, who followed an overgrown path toward a particularly wild section of woodland. It was a still day, the leaves and grasses a deep green. The heavy limbs of the Spanish chestnuts stretching above them had shaded the path for untold centuries, the trees having been planted by the lord of the manor in a distant age. The shorter of the two men, William Hampson, the Vicar of the Church of St. Mary the Virgin, carried a broad magnifying glass. He stopped for a moment to study a block of flint half hidden in a creeper-covered wall. Hampson was an amateur lichenologist, churchyard lichens being his specialty, although he was attracted to any lichen that grew upon old, cut stone, the older the better.

The other man was Professor Langdon St. Ives, a naturalist and adventurer who lived some five miles away in Aylesford with his wife Alice and his two children, Eddie and Cleo. St. Ives had walked the distance to Bimbury Manor early this morning when the sun was just up and the air was cool. He carried a haversack that he intended to fill with summer mushrooms. He had no compelling interest in lichens, but he and Hampson had recently become friends and the two enjoyed each other's company. Hampson had only yesterday sent to tell St. Ives of his accidental discovery of previously unknown standing stones in a meadow hidden deep within the woods beyond the old manor. If there were undisturbed lichens upon those stones the plants might conceivably be thousands of years old. Hampson had stumbled upon the meadow at evening and was unsure of his way home, and with night coming on he'd had no time to spare for it.

They followed the path downhill now, forded a stream, and went up another rise, climbing over a fallen tree and picking their way through a low, swampy area overgrown with fern, marsh orchids, and the asparagus-like shoots of club moss. No human footprints were to be seen on the damp trail save the three-days-old imprints of Hampson's boots coming down from the opposite way. There were the prints of badgers and deer, however, and they started a number of rabbits and surprised a large red fox that regarded the two men curiously for a time before turning and disappearing into the heavy foliage. The trail had quite disappeared by then, and they found their way only because Hampson, anxious to make his way back to his standing stones, had tied ribbons torn out of a blue handkerchief to conspicuous limbs.

"I'm very keen to ascend in your balloon, Professor," Hampson said as they trudged along. "I long to be aloft and that much closer to heaven, as foolish as it sounds when I say it out loud."

St. Ives had been up in the balloon a dozen times, tethered for the first several flights. Alice had no idea of his being blown out over the North Sea, however, especially with the Vicar riding along, and she recommended the tether, but Hampson was sensible of the danger, and rather enjoyed the prospect of an untethered ascent. "It doesn't sound silly at all," St. Ives told him. "There's something heavenly about a balloon ride, to be sure."

"I was offered the chance to ascend many years ago with Roger Kryzanek, the eccentric Polish balloonist, who was a friend of mine. Two days prior, however, I took a header down the sacristy stairs and broke my tibia, and I was cheated of the opportunity. It was months before I was steady on my pins. By that time Kryzanek had quite disappeared. He lived in Maidstone at the time, six children in all. That was twelve years back, almost to the day. Did you know Kryzanek?"

"Not first-hand," St. Ives said. "I've read about his exploits, however—those that were made public—especially of his strange disappearance above Sandwich. The Kryzanek mystery, as the *Times* called it, was very much in the news because of the report of a rain of periwinkles and nondescript pelagic crabs, bright orange, in a farmer's field on that same day."

"I recall the phenomenon," Hampson said, "or at least the rumor of it."

"Unfortunately, Alice recalls it quite well. She was a girl at the time, living near Plumstead."

"In what sense is the memory unfortunate?" Hampson asked, pushing aside the limb of a shrub and holding it for St. Ives.

"She believes, perhaps rightly, that I sometimes take too great an interest in scientific arcanum and that the habit lures me into dangerous waters. She herself is fond of mysteries only if they're safely imprisoned within the pages of a novel." He pointed now and said, "I believe I see one of your ribbons, away to the left there."

They clambered through the undergrowth toward the correct track, Hampson pointing out a stand of penny bun mushrooms to St. Ives. "Julia fries them with butter," Hampson said. "They're the prince of mushrooms, for my money."

"I'm with you there," St. Ives said as he set about gathering a goodly number of the largest.

When they set out again, Hampson said, "My brother-in-law Bates, the publican at the Queen's Rest in Wrotham Heath, witnessed Kryzanek's disappearance. He was one of the ground crew, you know—the chemist. Kryzanek preferred hydrogen gas to hot air, and Bates could brew up hydrogen gas by the tubful. He comprehends the art of it. As Dick Bates tells it, Kryzanek's balloon was drawn out of sight by a vortex of wind. He was heavily ballasted with sand, but not heavily enough, perhaps. One moment the balloon was visible, and the next it was not, as if it was yanked out of the sky with a shepherd's crook. Kryzanek was never seen again, poor fellow."

"A *vortex of wind*, do you say? What an unlikely notion. It's the sort of thing that Alice would be unhappy to hear."

"That was Bates's phrase, but it was repeated in the newspapers, which made it official. Your rain of periwinkles and crabs was written off as a hoax."

"Almost certainly it *was* a hoax," St. Ives said.

"Or a miracle," Hampson said, "which is an often overlooked possibility."

They found the ghost of a game trail and for half an hour made good time. Mushrooms of prodigious size grew everywhere, with enormous chicken-of-the-woods sending out fat gold rays from oak trees, and dense patches of chanterelles growing up through the deep mulch of the forest floor. St. Ives plucked up the chanterelles as he went along, putting them carefully into his haversack. The mushrooms were further evidence that the area was unexplored: they would certainly have been collected and eaten otherwise. Hampson's standing stones might indeed be previously undiscovered or, at the very least, long, long forgotten. The two men had agreed that they would remain so: there were too few wild places left in England.

"We're very near the meadow, if I'm not mistaken," Hampson said, pointing to yet another ribbon, and the two climbed a steep rise onto a hilltop at the bottom of which lay a grassy dell, perhaps an acre in size. The circle of weathered standing stones stood dead center—grey limestone richly colored by swathes of lichen. There was the sound of bees on the air and of an unseen fall of water, both of which increased the sense of loneliness.

The stones and the lichen, however, were suddenly of little interest to St. Ives, for he was distracted by something monumentally unlikely—a clamorous waterfall—a vertical, sunlit cylinder of water with no visible source, falling straight down out of the sky some twenty feet from the standing stones. It might have been an optical illusion, except that water was clearly splashing onto the meadow and running down to the edge of the woods in a wide rill and forming a small but apparently growing pool.

"I saw no such thing when I passed this way earlier," Hampson said, staring at the sight. "The meadow was dry. Now it looks for all the world as if someone has opened a tap in the heavens."

"There appears to be a vague disturbance of the air far above, perhaps at the source—the spring, as it were."

"I see a shadowy sort of fog, if that's what you mean, a stray storm cloud, perhaps, or the ghost of a cloud. You're the scientist, however. What do you make of it? I'm familiar with the notion of water pouring from a smitten stone, but not from a hole in the sky."

"Science does not account for either phenomenon," St. Ives said as the two set out downhill, passing among the standing stones. He put his hand into the falling water before tasting it. The water was surprisingly warm and was flavored with vegetation, as if leaves had steeped in it—yet another oddity: certainly not rainwater. He stepped back to avoid soaking his boots.

"Look there," Hampson said, pointing at the shallow brook that flowed away through the grass. A cylindrical fish, heavily scaled and about ten inches long, was pulling itself along with its pectoral fins, apparently going for a stroll. St. Ives retrieved the slippery creature and put it into his hat.

"Did this *fish* fall from the sky?" Hampson asked. "One would think such a thing to be patently impossible, Kryzanek's pelagic crabs and periwinkles notwithstanding."

"Indeed," said St. Ives, looking at the patently impossible fish. He had seen fossil examples of such a fish when he was a student at the University of Edinburgh and living examples from Africa and Australia that bore a family resemblance to it. "It appears to be a lungfish," he said, holding out his hat so that Hampson could get a good look at it. "Do you see the leg-like fins and the bony, independent scales—the way the scales do not overlap the way fish scales should?"

"I do, now that you point it out. And the creature seems to have an amphibious sort of fleshy tail on behind."

"So he does," St. Ives said. "He can walk as well as swim, and he hasn't been seen on earth—not this variety of lungfish anyway—for hard upon three hundred million years. If I'm correct, he's a living remnant of the Devonian era, although it quite possibly lived on for eons after most of the Devonian creatures had passed out of existence."

Hampson stared at St. Ives for a long moment, perhaps looking for signs that he meant to be humorous. "You've been reading Mr. Darwin, I see. In that argument, I'm firmly on the side of the angels, sir. I have no grudge against the opposition, but they may keep their apes."

"Mr. Darwin would have wept tears of joy to see this fellow," St. Ives said. "And you must admit that we're witnessing a wealth of unlikely natural phenomena here—this inexplicable waterfall as well as an extinct lungfish." He opened his haversack and laid the lungfish in among the penny buns and chanterelles, where it kicked for a moment and then lay still. He would be perfectly happy there until St. Ives could get him into one of the greenhouse aquariums. "You're *certain* that this fall of water was not here three days ago? The sun was low, after all, when you passed through. Perhaps there had simply been no reflection upon it."

"I've never been more certain of anything in my life. I would certainly have slogged straight through it. No, sir. Water has evidently recently issued from a hole in the sky, carrying with it an impossible fish. I'm happy to call it a miracle, which are few and far between in these grim latter days. What it portends, I cannot say. God moves in mysterious ways, according to Mr. Cowper's hymn."

"I meant to suggest only that the fall of water might cease as abruptly as it began."

"In that case give you joy, Professor. We have arrived on the day of days, apparently. I'll leave you to your lungfish and have a look at my lichens."

Hampson set out toward the standing stones, but immediately kicked something buried in the mud, just a corner of it exposed. He stooped, plucked it loose, and rinsed it in the waterfall—a ceramic beer bottle with a cork in it. Stamped into the stony clay were the words *T. Danes, Anchor Brewery, Aylesford.*

"What a disappointment," St. Ives said. "Someone has picnicked upon our far-flung meadow after all."

"I'm not certain I agree with you there," Hampson said. "The bottle was buried in a muddy pool that did not exist when I passed this way only three days ago. It hasn't rained since. Where are the footprints of the phantom picnicker? Why should we not assume that the bottle, too, has fallen from the sky, imbedding itself deeply from the force of its falling?"

"Perhaps it's the loaves and the fishes come again, although this time it's bottled beer and inedible lungfish."

"You mean to be waggish, but that's tolerably close to blasphemy."

"But a tolerably small feat for God, I'd suppose." St. Ives worried out the cork and tilted the bottle toward his nose to smell it. "No odor of beer at all," he said. He peered within now, a ray of sunlight shining into the dark interior and revealing what appeared to be a rolled slip of paper. He carefully withdrew it, trying not to tear the damp paper in the process—a sheet taken from a common pocket note-book on which were written several lines, although some of it was obliterated by damp:

'*...through the open door of the portal,*' it read. '*...China, but swept away... gas-bag quite destroyed, but fortune favored...The great god Fort quite possibly mad...My dear love to Pamela.*' Nothing else was legible, except for the name Kryzanek scrawled at the end of the missive.

St. Ives filled the now-empty beer bottle with falling water, replaced the cork, and laid it into the haversack with the lungfish. —◌

Open

I T WAS AN hour past closing in the library and the rotunda was
blessedly empty. Miss Julia Pickerel ran a lightly oiled cloth over the
marble plinths that held the tall candelabras, relishing the silence and the
beauty of the painted panels on the ceiling and walls and of the high, arched
windows that looked out over Bryant Park. The electric candles and globe
lights cast a rosy glow over the interior, it being dusk outside. She rarely had
a chance to be in the rotunda alone, and it seemed to her now that it was
very like being a duchess in a palace, although a duchess would be unlikely
to carry a tack-rag.

There was the sound of the creaking wheels, however, and she looked
up, annoyed at the disturbance. A short, stout man entered the great hall,
pushing a wheeled cart upon which sat two stuffed chairs, one atop the
other. He wore spectacles and heavy mustaches and had an amphibious
look about him. Miss Pickerel knew immediately who he was, although
why he was wheeling furniture through the rotunda was a mystery. She had
no desire to speak to the man and was anxious not to be recognized, and
so she turned away. She was an acquaintance of his wife Anna, a friend,
really, both she and Anna being members of the Parakeet Society. Some
weeks back Mr. Fort—Charles Fort by name, an eccentric of low Dutch
heritage—had squired Anna to one of the meetings, where he was evidently
bored and sat picking his teeth. He spent a great deal of time in the library,
although surely he ought to have gone away with the rest of the public when
the building closed and the doors were locked.

She heard his cart pass behind her, and after a few moments she looked
back, watching him as he rounded the corner at the far end of the hall and

disappeared through the high arch that led into the gallery. This struck her as another odd thing, for it was a comparatively small gallery with tapestry-hung walls. There was no exit from the room save returning through the arch. And the room was entirely without furniture. It had no need of chairs.

It went against her instincts to confront the man, who might be a dangerous lunatic. Evidently he had hidden himself in the library in order to avoid being ushered out when the library closed. Certainly he was up to no good. She stepped across into the shadow of a pillar and waited for his return. She heard shuffling and scraping noises, and then, in a voice fit for the deck of a ship rather than a library, Fort intoned the word *open,* as if it were a command. There was more shuffling, and a wooden bump, and then utter silence.

When she could stand it no longer, she sidled along the wall toward the edge of the arch in order to peer around the corner. The gallery was empty. Mr. Fort had quite disappeared, as had the chairs. The empty cart, however, sat abandoned in the middle of the room. There was no indication that anyone had entered the room at all, except for a small movement of the bottom corner of the great tapestry hanging on the east wall. It was her favorite, very old—a strange, rustic cottage on a cliff over the ocean, with a beam of sunlight shining on its arched front door.

She stepped inside the gallery and walked hesitantly toward the tapestry, which hung still now. She noted the absence of any breeze and considered the possibility that Fort might be hiding behind the tapestry, perhaps intending to leap out at her. She looked for the toes of his shoes in the narrow opening beneath the hem, but she saw nothing, and so she boldly pulled the edge of the tapestry away from the wall and looked behind it. There was no Fort, nothing but an innocent wall. She stared at the wooden wainscot, what she could see of it in the shadows. There was no door in it.

It came to her that there could not be a door; beyond the wall lay the City of New York. —⸕

Closer to Heaven

T HE FOLLOWING MORNING found St. Ives and the Vicar Hampson on the meadow once again along with sundry friends.

"Dead air, sir, at around three thousand feet," Hampson's brother-in-law Bates said. "Roundabout the height of your waterfall, I'd say. The dead air space is fifteen fathoms in height, give or take." He knelt before a windlass, its line tied to a small trial balloon that he had sent up to measure the speed of the wind. Bates was a large-framed man, his sleeves rolled against the warmth of the morning sun. His coat and hat lay on the meadow. The day was a twin of yesterday. "The anemometer says that the wind above it blows at two knots, and that below somewhat less."

"And it was something the same with Kryzanek—this space of dead air?"

"Just so, Professor. We sent up the trial balloon in just this way."

St. Ives nodded. To Hampson he said, "Do you find that this eccentricity reduces your desire to go aloft, Vicar? We could make a tethered ascent next weekend if the weather holds."

"Not at all, Professor. The world allows few adventures for a man of my age and station. And Roger Kryzanek was a friend of mine. These eccentricities, as you phrase it, have something to do with his disappearance, it seems to me. The coincidence is too great otherwise. If anything, my desire to go aloft has heightened." Hampson smiled up at the balloon that floated overhead—a cheerful red color, with the basket gondola dangling below. On the gas-bag itself was painted a black and gold carp, an authentic rendition of a fish that Alice had caught from a pond on their property. It had been painted just a week past by Theodosia Loftus, a talented gipsy girl who had become a particular friend of Alice's.

Hauling the balloon and its equipage into the time-forgotten dell had taken the better part of the night and the help of six men aside from St. Ives and Hampson. It had been rare good luck that a crew could be assembled on short notice. Dick Bates was fortunately free, as were his twin sons, both of them big men—several inches taller than St. Ives's six-feet, two-inches and weighing in the neighborhood of eighteen stone. Bill Kraken, from nearby Hereafter Farm, was tall and lanky but surprisingly strong and with infinite stamina. He and the brothers Bates had carried the silk-and-rubber gas-bag, rolled up and bound into a sausage. The fifth man was Hasbro, St. Ives's friend and factotum. He and St. Ives had toted the gondola, disassembled and lashed to a stout pole with many fathoms of line.

Young Finn Conrad, who occupied a cottage on the St. Ives estate, carried powdered sodium hydroxide and aluminium in a pack on his back. Bates functioned as chemist with Finn as his assistant. The two had been brewing hydrogen gas under the full moon since two in the morning, and the balloon was very nearly inflated. St. Ives could see that Finn deeply regretted not going along on the ascent, and Hasbro equally so. The balloon would hold more weight than that of St. Ives and the Vicar, but a heavier load would require more gas and more time spent on the ground and would make maneuvering slightly more difficult.

St. Ives had made light of the danger when he outlined his intentions to Alice last night. He would ascend, he said, only to have a look at the curious, cloud-like anomaly that seemed to be the source of the falling water. A breeze could push them off course, spoiling any effort to get reasonably close to their goal, in which case they would say quits and descend. There was no breeze to speak of this morning, however; it was a perfect day for a leisurely ascent. The gondola was stocked with a wickerwork hamper carrying St. Ives's quadruple-tube achromatic telescope and the usual stakes, line, and heavy mallet to facilitate an emergency mooring.

When everything was in train, St. Ives and Hampson climbed aboard the gondola, took the measure of things, and cast off. "Ten o'clock almost exactly," St. Ives said to Hampson. "I wouldn't have thought it possible."

The balloon rose vertically above the meadow, scarcely shifting on the breeze. The aerial spring, showing no signs of diminishing, thumped against the gas-bag, cascading down the envelope in sheets of water, some of it coming inboard and draining through the bottom of the basket. St. Ives and the Vicar stood clear of it along with the baggage.

The ascent was slow, but as long as they were rising at all, St. Ives had no desire to hasten it, since there was no recovering ballast once it was spilled. Very soon, however, the ground appeared to be a long way off, the dwarfed crew looking upward at them, shading their eyes against the morning sunlight. A small breeze shifted the balloon out of the fall of water, the grateful sun warming them, and St. Ives saw the coast in the distance—the city of Deal with the Goodwin Sands beyond and the ships at anchor in the Downs, the view startlingly clear through the telescope.

"Have a look through the glass, Vicar," St. Ives said, "but keep it inboard, if you would."

Hampson took the telescope and peered through it, apparently speechless for a time and taking in the view at all points of the compass—the literal compass that St. Ives pulled from his pocket. "There lies Canterbury Cathedral!" Hampson said. "And there in the distance, Professor—could it be that I'm looking into Essex?"

"Almost certainly you are," St. Ives told him.

"My brother Tom lives in Cambridge Town with his wife and daughters. I wonder if they can make us out, high aloft as we are." He waved heartily in that direction and laughed. "I'm positively giddy," he said. "There's Bimbury Manor, lying very neatly indeed among the trees, and Aylesford village, if I'm not mistaken. Can you make out your house and land?"

"I should think so," St. Ives said, taking the telescope from him. He quickly found the River Medway, and it was a simple thing to pick out his large meadow with its hops kiln, the barn and house, and the hops orchards roundabout, green and growing in the summer sun. And then he saw their resident Indian elephant, Dr. Johnson, being led out of the barn by Alice and the children. Old Mr. Binger the gardener was with them, as was Hodge the cat, although mouse-sized. St. Ives found that he was holding his breath, strangely moved by the sight of his tiny family going about family business without him, and at such a peculiar perspective. He was no great distance away, and yet it seemed as if he was on a different plane of existence entirely, and of course he was, he reminded himself, having left the Earth behind.

He willed Alice to look upward, but a shadowy grey twilight swallowed the balloon now and his family vanished. The balloon began to spin slowly—Bates's vortex, St. Ives thought, not much liking the idea. What could cause such a thing was a mystery—some sort of aerial Coriolis effect, no doubt—an effect that had swallowed Kryzanek and his balloon wholesale. They had entered the predictable dead air space now, and there was no breeze at all. Through the murk he could see what looked like a high wall of dark cloud ahead of him.

He consulted his compass and was surprised to see that the needle was spinning erratically, changing its mind and reversing half a spin, and then switching direction again, utterly confused. He fetched out his pocketwatch—fifteen minutes past ten o'clock. The cylinder of water began to thump atop the balloon again as they passed beneath, disturbing the quiet and swirling down the sides, falling straight toward the ground. The thumping abruptly ceased and the water washed straight through the side of the basket in a horizontal stream. Then the natural silence returned and the stream of water was gone. They had apparently passed through its apex and had risen above it.

Both men bent out over the void and saw through the grey dimness that the fall of water stood directly below them. St. Ives could make out the very place where it arched out of the darker shadow that they were fast approaching, the wavering wall of undulating twilight that grew blacker by the moment, very like a theatre curtain disturbed by actors passing behind it.

The balloon tilted now and dragged the gondola sideways into blind darkness, both men holding on tightly as the deck canted over. St. Ives thought of his final, infinitely lucky view of Alice, Eddie, and Cleo and his heart lurched. He considered the chance that he was leaving them behind for good and all, and attempted to put the thought out of his mind. He heard Hampson intoning a prayer—more useful than mere regret—but despite his efforts St. Ives could think only of his family, of having sold his rich bounty of happiness for a handful of idle curiosity. —೧

The Island

THE DARKNESS LASTED a long moment, followed once again by the narrow region of grey shadow. Then they came out into clear air again, although the sky was heavily overcast. The ground was visible below—very close below. It was not their world, however, neither the North Downs nor any landscape that St. Ives recognized. There were sheer cliffs in the near distance—black volcanic rock covered in verdant foliage—and a forest of giant trees stretching away from the base of the cliffs. A rocky coastline lay perhaps a mile away, although the air, which felt positively tropical to St. Ives, was so clear that it was difficult to gauge distance. He could see the spouts of whales rise from the calm sea beyond a horseshoe shaped bay.

He took in the view with a subdued astonishment, which was abruptly less subdued when he saw a rambling wooden house sitting above the bay on a rocky ledge. It seemed to be built right out of the cliff itself.

"I say, Professor," Hampson said. "What's this now?" He pointed toward the forest, from which four vast birds winged their way toward the balloon.

"Very large pelicans," St. Ives said without thinking. He was looking at his compass, relieved to see that it was once again behaving itself.

"Pelicans, forsooth," Hampson said. "Is it likely they'll eat us?"

St Ives gave the creatures a good look now and saw that they were not pelicans at all, but some species of pterosaur, with long sword-like beaks. He didn't believe in what was called mass hallucination, nor did he believe in living pterosaurs, although these certainly appeared to be alive—more stupefying evidence of…something. "If they're what I understand them to be," he said, "they're dedicated to fish and carrion—theoretically, of course."

"Then I pray that we do not have the look of theoretical carrion about us," the Vicar said, "and that the beasts are not inclined to spear our balloon simply for sport. We've found ourselves in a tolerably strange place, Professor. I'm not averse to finding our way out again."

St. Ives nodded, thinking of the unlikely lungfish, dwelling now in one of his greenhouse aquariums. That it had come from this very land was beyond doubt—a land that stood outside of time, in some sense, although his pocket-watch was ticking away as ever. He looked back at the cloudy darkness, at the curtain through which they had passed. It was some distance away now, an unsettling distance that was growing by the moment. On the meadow below a wide brook flowed along into that darkness, washing heaven knew what into the void. There were people moving along the shore of the brook, just visible in the twilight.

"Brace for a landing, Vicar," he said, drawing the gas-release lever downward to release a fraction of their invisible, precious hydrogen. "Be ready to dump ballast, but just a trifle if need be. I'll give you the word. Easy does it now." He closed off the valve, estimating that the balloon was descending at a reasonable rate of speed.

"Look below, Professor, there on the sward!" Hampson cried, his eye to the telescope, which he held in one hand.

St. Ives saw that a man was running down the slope of the meadow, evidently having dashed out from the edge of the forest. He waved his hands over his head, gesturing as if his life depended upon it. He was a stout man with a round, bald head, wearing spectacles and dressed in short trousers and gaiters.

"By *heaven*!" Hampson shouted. "*It's Roger Kryzanek!* No shadow of a doubt. His hair has vanished, and he's in a fair taking, bellowing like an elephant. And no wonder—he's been marooned for nigh onto twelve years. His hardships haven't clawed any of the flesh from his bones, I see." He laughed out loud, elated to see his old friend alive.

But his laughter ended when there appeared half a dozen savages, racing out of the trees and in hot pursuit of the Polish balloonist. They evidently gained on Kryzanek, who was pouring it on. The ground came up to meet the gondola, and a brisk cross-breeze pushed them along sideways when they touched down, the flat hull of the gondola bouncing and sailing like a stone on water. Kryzanek waited anxiously, looking back wild-eyed at the approaching men, two of whom carried spears. They were short men, hairy and dressed in ragged trousers hacked off at the knees and equally ragged shirts. Kryzanek grabbed the mooring line as it danced past and held onto it while capering along over the sward, coming on hand over hand along the rope. "Hampson! By God, Hampson!" Kryzanek shouted. "Haul me in, man!"

Hampson reached out and grabbed Kryzanek's forearm, trying hard to heave him aboard—an apparently impossible task—and St. Ives bent to help. It would be a close run thing, even though Kryzanek's weight put a stop to the gondola's capers. He levered himself over the side and tumbled in, but there was no rising again without dumping ballast, and now the savages were upon them—six men grappling the basket. They could dump ballast until doomsday and not rise an inch.

The six stood patiently, making no threatening gestures. Almost certainly they were not Paleolithic men, pictures of whom St. Ives had seen in a cave painting on the French coast. These had prodigious jawbones and were as much ape as human—a very ancient race, without a doubt. They were decorated with bits and pieces of cheap, pinchbeck baubles set lavishly with paste jewels. Each wore around his neck a primitively carved human head on a thin strip of leather. The heads was round and wore spectacles, like nursery rhyme illustrations of the man in the moon.

One of the savages was slightly taller than the others and wore red, ankle-length trousers, much faded and stained, and a pair of wire spectacles without lenses. He had a slightly superior air—the chief, St. Ives thought. The man pushed his spectacles up the bridge of his nose and inclined his head toward the ground, implying that the three in the gondola should climb out.

"Be damned to you," Kryzanek said to him between heaving breaths.

"I'll go over the side," St. Ives said. "We haven't a choice in the matter, it seems to me. Hand down the stakes and the mallet. We've got to moor her securely."

The chief stepped back to allow St. Ives passage, taking his arm in a gentlemanly way to steady him. Hampson passed along the sharpened wooden staves, and Kryzanek, shaking his head unhappily, hefted the mallet and looked hard at his so-far peaceful assailants.

"Best not to start a row that we cannot finish," St. Ives said to him, taking the mallet before Kryzanek crushed anyone's skull.

"I feared this," Kryzanek muttered. "He *knew*." The words conveyed no sensible meaning to St. Ives's mind. He set to work knocking in the stakes.

The four pterosaurs had swept around and were disappearing into the west now, where the sun was just breaking through the clouds. With luck, its warmth would heat the gas in the balloon and make it more buoyant— a good thing, certainly, if only they managed to take it up again with Kryzanek aboard. St. Ives nodded at his two companions to climb out, the gondola rising to waist height and riding easy, the mooring apparently secure. Without any more ado, the chief led the way into the trees, three of the unlikely savages ahead and three behind, conversing among themselves in a language that was mostly grunts, whistles, and gibbering.

The broad path led uphill, winding around toward the coastline and very shortly entering the forest, which soon became more jungle than forest, damp and vine-hung and smelling of decomposed vegetation. Enormous trees towered away overhead, and the air was full of birdcalls. Ferns grew out of the crotches of limbs, with blooming orchids and a wealth of smaller ferns rising out of the larger clumps—entire elevated gardens. Small monkeys moved high overhead, as did flights of butterflies with immense wings. St. Ives was thunderstruck by what he saw, but he pulled his mind away when Hampson's voice broke the spell, introducing Kryzanek to him.

"I've read of your exploits, sir," St. Ives said to him. "I very much hoped to meet you here."

"And I've heard of yours, Professor," Kryzanek answered.

"How so?" St. Ives asked, for it was a strange statement given that the man had been marooned for the past twelve years. His question was left to hang when an immense lizard appeared in a clearing forty feet away—a creature that might easily swallow a moderate pig—a monitor lizard, perhaps, but ten feet long if it was an inch. The reptile caused some excitement among the savages, one of whom hefted his spear and made as if to pursue it, although the chief whistled him back.

"It scarcely matters," Kryzanek said. "I shouldn't have raised the subject."

St. Ives's mind still dwelt on the giant reptile, and it was a moment before he made sense of Kryzanek's statement. There seemed to be no reason to pursue the subject of his own 'exploits,' however. For a time after that the three made familiar talk—friends mutually known, life in Maidstone and Aylesford, Kryzanek's family hearty and healthy.

"Twenty-six grandchildren in all," Hampson told him.

"God's rabbit!" Kryzanek cried. "*Twenty-six?*"

"You're a veritable patriarch."

"I live in horror of being a patriarch. But I can't say that I don't miss them—those of them that I know. I'll no doubt learn to miss those I don't know, for there's precious little chance we'll get off this damned island now. Did you find my message, then? I sent it down the river. I would have sent myself down the river, but you would have found a corpse instead of a bottle."

"We did find it," St. Ives said. "The bottle was half-buried in a puddle into which a miraculous stream of water fell from the sky—the very stream that flows across the meadow on which we landed."

"This fall of water was over Sandwich, then?"

"No, sir," said Hampson. "A meadow near Thurnham. I'm sorry to say there was no time to deliver your message to your wife Pamela."

"It was necessary that we get aloft without wasting an instant," St. Ives said. "I was worried, *am* worried, that the curtain, so to say, will simply vanish, as it must have done after you passed through it over Sandwich."

"You're in the right of it there, Professor," Kryzanek said. "And it will surely close when the current solstice tide has peaked."

"The *solstice* tide, do you say? I do not completely understand the term. What has it to do with the closing of the curtain?"

"You are no doubt well-versed on the subject of oceanic tides, Professor, but this is a tide of a different color—a cosmic tide, if you will, a sky tide. It's not scientific, perhaps—not in the canon, but it's inarguable."

"I'm inclined to argue with it," St. Ives said.

"A waste of breath, I assure you. I wore myself out contemplating it, but I finally accepted it and made myself at home, so that I could come to know this wild place. What I learned, to my dismay, is that the curtain, as you call it, will cease to exist when the tide passes full, marooning us utterly, and it doesn't care a groat for your doubt. We *must* be aboard your balloon when the tide is making. With luck we'll be drawn back through the portal. At the moment, however, we're prisoners of the great god Fort, whom I do not trust, not for an instant."

"*Fort?*" asked Hampson. "Strange name for a god. Do you mean a god in some abstract sense?"

"A living man. He's a humbug, is Fort—an American, who seems to relish my company, since the natives cannot be made to understand the nature of card games. They believe him to be a god, which he encourages by tricking them out in trash jewelry and supplying them with butterscotch. You'll meet him soon enough."

They walked into a well-swept clearing now. Overhead stood a multi-level cottage built in the heavy limbs of a banyan tree. A set of spiral stairs encircled the trunk. The several rooms, which were affixed to heavy aerial roots that had grown into the earth, were roofed with thatch, the uppermost section covered with what must be the gas-bag of Kryzanek's balloon, tattered and torn, although Kryzanek had made an effort to mend some of the tears. The walls of the cottage were made of sticks and wattle. There were lace curtains in the windows, moving in the very faint breeze that found its way through the trees.

"This is Scrimshaw, gentlemen—my home," Kryzanek said, gesturing at the edifice as they passed along the road. "Picturesque, ain't it? I've gazed upon the picture far too long, and when I saw your balloon descending at last the notion came to me that I might experience the joy of never ascending my stairway again."

On the floor of the clearing stood a wooden table with two crudely built benches and, strangely, an upholstered chair with a wooden deal table beside it. A half-eaten mangosteen and a leather-bound book lay upon the table, the book open, spine upward, no doubt to mark the place where Kryzanek had set it down when he'd sighted them. A broad patch of sky was visible through the tree's limbs.

"Surely you did not bring that chair along in your balloon?" Hampson said. "Nor books, I'd imagine, unless you meant to use them as ballast."

"Fort hauls these luxuries in through his private passage, Vicar, including what I needed to build this house—hardware, tools, even the window curtains. He's monumentally solicitous in that regard. He refers to his passageway as 'the second portal.'"

"Could he not haul *you* out through this portal?" asked St. Ives. "All of us, for that matter, if it comes to it."

"I almost dread answering that question," Kryzanek said. "You'll be inclined to argue with it, too. In a word, Fort comes from a future time. I've seen proof of it, and I have no desire to accompany him into a world even further from home and hearth than this one."

"From the *future*?" St. Ives said. "I very much look forward to meeting the man. Indeed I do."

"I pray it'll be a brief meeting. We're burning daylight, to use one of Fort's own phrases."

A tapir some four feet in height stared at them from deep shadows now, and a large upright creature moved along a heavy branch some distance beyond—an orang-outang or perhaps a gorilla. St. Ives realized that there must be a wealth of animal life on this…

"*Where are we?*" he asked Kryzanek. "Do you *know*? Has this man Fort told you?"

"Yes, he has," Kryzanek said, speaking to the back of St. Ives's head. "We're aboard a piece of our own earth that was blown into the sky in some ancient cataclysm—a floating island, if you will. It remains hidden behind what you referred to as the *curtain*, which is quite simply a mantle of invisibility, as the Welsh might say. This island floats unseen above the earth, stopping now and then when the tides are right. Currently we're over the North Downs, as you know. When the tide is in flood, Fort has the natives shovel odd heaps of debris into the stream, which carries the debris into the sky of our world—periwinkles and frogs and china plates, which fall to earth, astounding the citizenry."

"Why would a man do such a thing?" Hampson asked. "There can be no profit in it."

"Fort cares nothing for profit. He means to be jocose, I'm afraid."

"*Jocose?*" St. Ives asked. "I'm not certain I see the joke."

"Fort would tell you that the joke was on you, sir. He performs these strange feats largely to confound science, which wears blinders, if you will, denying everything that they cannot understand. Fort gives scientists things to deny and gives the local citizenry a thrill of astonishment."

At that point they rounded a bend in the road, seeing before them the cliff-side house that St. Ives had discerned from the air. Thick vines, heavy with purple blooms, snaked up the rough volcanic rock walls that formed the base of the wooden house. Mullioned windows looked out over the cove. The glassy but strangely ominous sea stretched away to the horizon, small islands visible in the distance. An enormous, toothy creature, perhaps a seagoing crocodile, peered up out of a bed of kelp for a moment and then sank beneath, and farther out to sea the black neck and head of what appeared to be a plesiosaur cut along through the oily swell.

What I wouldn't give for three hours time among the tidal pools with a net and a collecting bag, St. Ives thought. Such a chance would surely never come again. He would positively amaze the Royal Society. He would amaze the world! Perhaps the spring tide that Kryzanek feared wasn't absolutely imminent after all.…

An irritating voice in his mind warned him against foolhardy thoughts, and as they ascended a set of stone stairs, he wondered if in some sense it was Alice's voice—that in their years together she had become a sort of guardian angel. He should ask Hampson for his opinion on the subject.

They arrived at a verandah that sheltered a great, arched entry door, a door that swung inward now, although nobody stood in the doorway. The chief of the savages pounded the butt of his spear thrice on the planks, perhaps announcing their arrival to the god Fort, and then the six moved off and sat upon the verandah floor, immediately starting up a jabbering conversation.

"I'll lead you in," Kryzanek said, as they walked into the dim interior. "I warn you that Fort is some variety of devil—very persuasive. I mentioned that he comes and goes through what he refers to as a portal, where the date is some twenty years ahead of our own."

"You believe this to be true because you've accompanied him there," asked St. Ives, "or because he *told* you it was true?"

"I believe all of it to be true, Professor, although I haven't been to the future, so to say. I take his word for that. He has some curious proofs, however."

"What sort of proofs?"

"You'll discover them soon enough. The man is…unavoidable. He is obsessed with simple questions of time—questions simple to ask, I mean to say, but impossible to answer. He is concerned with the idea that alterations in the past will alter the future."

"I believe that they would," St. Ives said.

"Then you'd best think twice about lingering in this house. My own desire to flee motivated my great effort to be away in your balloon there on the meadow. The effort failed, but it proved nothing. You, sir, are his great experiment. He means to have his way with you because of who you are."

"This is all very cryptic," Hampson said.

"I'll make one thing about it clear, then. I mean to be away in the balloon with time to spare, and there is very little of that commodity left to us." With that he ushered St. Ives and Hampson toward the back of the house. ⟶

The Tell-tale Carp

THEY FOUND CHARLES Fort in his lamp-lit study, sitting in an upholstered chair identical to the chair in the clearing before Kryzanek's tree house. There were three other such chairs in the room. He was short but stoutly built, his hair cropped. His eyes, looking out through spectacles, held an amused look. "Gentlemen," he said, standing up and putting out his hand, "it's my great pleasure to see you at last. I've awaited your coming." He shook hands with St. Ives and Hampson, although Kryzanek declined the gesture. "Please, sit down," Fort said. "Drink a glass of this capital brandy." He fetched a decanter and a stack of tumblers from the bottom shelf of a table beside his chair.

"Do *not* drink it," Kryzanek said in a firm voice. "Not a drop. It's quite possibly a sleeping potion. We'll miss our tide while Fort goes about his business. This man is not to be trusted. His sense of humor is positively sub-lunar."

"Roger has an active imagination," Fort said, "and he's miffed that he owes me ten million in gambling debts."

"Ten million!" Hampson cried.

"Accumulated over twelve years of play."

"I suspect that he cheats," Kryzanek said, "but I can't make out how."

St. Ives listened with only half an ear. He found that he coveted the unlikely house, which was built of rough-cut planks of a dark, tropical wood. Here and there sunlight shone through chinks between the boards, glowing around vines that crept in with their showers of purple blooms creating a sort of indoor bower. There was an enviable view of the sea cove through a broad window, the wall of the room built at the edge of a sheer cliff. The plesiosaur, St. Ives noted, had disappeared, but from this height he could see that the water in the cove was crystal clear, with a kelp bed beyond in the open sea.

Books on natural history—many familiar to St. Ives and many not— were stacked on a nearby table built from the same rough planks as the wall, with more on open-shelved cases, although the majority of the shelves were taken up with large, lidded jars in which floated an array of fish and small mammals—shrews and octopi sitting side-by-side, coiled adders, a fetal shark, prehistoric ganoid fishes, skinks and toads, the head of a small ape—hundreds of jars all in all, Fort evidently being an avid naturalist.

"You're taken with my collection, Professor," Fort said to him.

"Very much so, yes. What is this long, tentacled creature in the conical shell?"

"A straight-chambered cephalopod. I found him trapped in a deep, tidal pool in my own cove. Fished him out with a net. Can you guess the era?"

"Devonian, I'd say."

"Right you are, although on this little paradise of ours many thousands of plants and animals avoided extinction. I wish only that I could have kept him alive. I'm not fond of killing things."

"Nor am I, although it's the lot in life of a naturalist."

"True enough. Did you see the ichthyosaur sporting in the cove when you were coming up the hill?"

St. Ives stared at him for a moment, thinking of the crocodile-like creature in the bay. He had identified the plesiosaur, but an ichthyosaur! "I believe I did," he said, "although I took it for some form of crocodile."

"Similar toothy snout, but it appears to be more fish than lizard. A link of some sort, perhaps, between the aquatic mammals and the fishes. Would you like to go exploring?"

"*He would not,*" Kryzanek said. "We've no time for it."

"Quite right," Hampson said, taking Kryzanek's side. St. Ives wondered whether Hampson had a Christian obligation to avoid looking too closely at the wonders roundabout them. They reeked of Darwinism. He wished that Kryzanek hadn't used the word "devil" to describe Fort.

"You're a lichen man, I believe," Fort said.

"I am," Hampson admitted, his face lighting up. Then it took on a suspicious cast. "How do you know?"

"I read of it in this very interesting periodical," Fort said, holding out his hand. In it was an issue of *The Graphic*, young Finn Conrad's favorite magazine. Hampson made no move to take it, so Fort handed it to St. Ives, who sat down now, caught up immediately in the mystery of the cover—an etching of a balloon ascent. There was a forest below the balloon, men in a clearing looking up, and above the balloon a sky with a shadowy cloud with a phantom wall visible within it—obviously the metaphoric curtain. A stream of water flowed out from within the cloud and fell away toward the Earth.

"What do you say to that, Professor?" Fort asked. "Racks your brain, doesn't it? Knocks you for a wallop?"

St. Ives had nothing to say to it. He studied the balloon. The gondola of the balloon was the image of his own, with two men, one tall and one short, standing within, the taller man holding a telescope. He realized with a shock of amazement that emblazoned upon the balloon was the painting of the tell-tale carp. There was nothing *similar* about the balloon in the illustration; it was in fact an illustration of his very balloon. His mind groped for an explanation, but there was none.

"Take a look at the date on the magazine, sir," Fort said, apparently enjoying this immensely.

"August, 1886," St. Ives read aloud.

"Over a year from now!" Hampson cried. "Surely this is a hoax."

"I can assure you it is *not* a hoax, Vicar," Kryzanek said in a flat voice. "Mr. Fort is not attempting to practice upon you. What the Professor holds is an actual copy of the magazine. Perhaps we should get on with this, Charles," he said tiredly. "The clock is ticking."

"You pay too much attention to the clock," Fort told him. "The clock is the first falsehood. No other instrument has caused humanity such pain and horror."

"I have half a mind to pitch you out the window, sir," Kryzanek said. "If we miss our tide, by God, my mind will wholly be made up. You're merely toying with us. Admit it to my friends here, and we'll be on our way."

"I'm having too much fun to admit any such thing, Roger. You always were a sort of schoolmarm." To St. Ives he said, "Have a look inside the front cover now, Professor."

Inside lay a small Manila paper pocket, glued in. A slip of heavy paper with a date printed on it was slid into the pocket. The day and month read

19 June—yesterday's date—but the year was 1906. St. Ives read it aloud for Hampson's benefit, and then to Fort he said, "This is proof of nothing, sir. Anyone with a wheel ribbon stamp could produce it. There's such a stamp in my own desk at home."

"But anyone did *not* produce it, sir. It was the work of a very pleasant librarian…"

"…*in* the New York Public Library," Kryzanek said, cutting him off. "For the love of God, Professor, I'll make it clear to you before my head bursts. You are looking at an *authentic* issue of *The Graphic*, borrowed by our grinning friend from a lending library in the city of New York, which he visits whenever he desires. In fact, New York City is his home. He travels back and forth, as I've told you twice now, through an unlikely door in that wall."

"Not quite true," Fort said. "I rarely travel whenever I choose. My visits generally take place during the hours that the library is open to the public. Now and then I make an exception."

"In a word, this magazine is impossible," St. Ives said. "I don't for a moment believe it."

"*Belief!*" Fort said. "Belief is the second bugbear, to my mind, very nearly as fiendish as the clock on the wall. If you disbelieve in what you hold in your hand, then perhaps you're dreaming."

"Perhaps I am. It's the simplest explanation for all of this."

"Capital!" Fort said. "If this is a dream then you're welcome to ride down the river in your gondola basket like Moses. That would be rare good fun in a dream. Not much fun if you weren't dreaming, perhaps, once gravity had its way with you. Are you the sort of Galileo willing to go to the wall in the name of what you suppose to be true?"

"Not for this truth, no, sir."

"Good man. Truth is a slippery eel at best."

"*Here's* the damned truth," Kryzanek said. "I'll put the case to you simply, Professor—the *facts* of the case. At this moment it is the year 1906 in the library accessed by this phenomenal door. The story illustrated upon the cover of that magazine has not yet been written. The author, one Jack Owlesby, is unaware that he will ever write such a story, let alone sell it to *The Graphic*. But he assuredly will, *if* in fact we depart this house immediately. If we do not, then he will know nothing at all of our sad story." He spread his hands and shrugged. "In short," he said, turning on Fort, his voice rising, "we have other *windbags* to attend to aside from the man who sits before us." He stood up out of his chair, giving Fort a look as if he meant his comment to sting, but Fort waved him down again.

"The Professor's curiosity is piqued, Roger. He has further questions. Rein in your impatience, man." Fort picked up a walking stick that leaned against the table and banged it on the floorboards. There was the sound of footsteps, and the Chief and his five men came silently in through the door, no doubt summoned by Fort's stick. Their looks were neither friendly nor hostile, although their very presence was ominous.

St. Ives realized that the carved wooden heads hanging around their necks was the image of Fort himself, which struck him as humorous for some reason. He hastily skimmed the magazine story, which told of the very adventure that he and Hampson were engaged in at present: the discovery of the standing stones, the aerial spring, the lungfish, the ascent. Even the story of Kryzanek's wild flight across the meadow was there, richly illustrated. He found another illustration of this very room, with a reasonable facsimile of Fort himself, sitting in his chair and looking at a pocket-watch.

"You know the author, I believe, Professor," Fort said.

"Quite well, yes, although not the illustrator, whose name I do not find here."

"You yourself will give this magazine to Mr. Owlesby, so that it can be published in this particular issue."

"Perhaps I will not," St. Ives said.

"But you *will*, for Jack Owlesby must write out your adventure and sell it to *The Graphic*, and I must discover it in my research years hence so as to prepare for your arrival. I've brought in two of these chairs, you see, thinking of your own comfort. Suffice it to say that if you did not give the magazine to Mr. Owlesby, none of us would be sitting here now."

"But if you keep us in this room yammering like a zoo ape we'll have been too long at the fair," Kryzanek said, "and then what? Do we turn to vapor?"

"Vapor? That seems unlikely," Fort said, working the fingers of both hands together like a spider on a mirror and staring wide-eyed at Kryzanek. "I'll make you a proposition," he said to St. Ives. "As an alternative to fleeing away in your balloon, you might consider making your own truth. Why not seize this opportunity to extend your stay on my little island? I saw the glint of desire in your eyes when you were looking at my jars. What if I told you there were wooly mammoths within two day's march? There are, you know—and even greater wonders. The opportunity will not come again if you leave now."

St. Ives found that he could scarcely speak when he considered the suggestion. He forced temptation back into the shadows and said, "But the island will move on. Two days might well turn into two months or two years."

"Or twelve years," Kryzanek said. "I suggest that we take the opportunity to return to Aylesford, Professor. *That* opportunity will not come again *unless* you leave now. It's time to slap the devil, Professor! Slap him down with your open palm!"

"Ignore the man," Fort said. "Roger sees devils under every bush. We're due to hover over China in several weeks. A month's vacation spent on this lost paradise, Professor, and then away you go in your balloon after a pleasant holiday in the Orient. I can show you wonders, sir."

Kryzanek stood up now, looking like thunder. "China! *Humbug!*" he cried. "There won't be a breath of hydrogen left in the balloon a month from now, as you well know. I've hovered over China fourteen times, and yet here I am on this accursed island while salvation is staked down on the meadow, opportunity leaking away." The six men by the door watched Kryzanek carefully.

Fort shrugged and removed his pocket-watch. He was fated to do so, St. Ives, realized, given the illustration in *The Graphic*. Fort held up his hand for silence, and then said mysteriously, "Sixty seconds to make up your mind, sir! Will you stay on, or will you walk away from adventure?" He smiled gleefully, counting down the seconds aloud, chuckling with laughter as if he saw a joke that no one else saw. He muttered out the descending numbers until he reached zero, shouting the word and pounding his hand down on the arm of his chair.

Nothing at all happened. Fort's joke had apparently fizzled like a penny squib. St. Ives looked about him, his mind working. The silence stretched, and then, strangely, a breeze smelling of books and furniture oil blew into the room as a section of the wall opened inward—the hidden door. There was the sound of voices from beyond the door, and then through it, impossibly, strode St. Ives himself, a pistol in his hand, followed by Alice. He trained the pistol on Fort. "Enough," he said. "Mr. Kryzanek will have his way now, Mr. Fort."

There followed an utter silence in the room. Hampson sat with his mouth agape. The six savages, apparently unhappy at the sight of the pistol, trod back toward the door through which they had entered, and then turned and fled in a body. Fort's smile was so broad that it disfigured his face.

St. Ives saw now that his future self—for that was the only explanation for what he was witnessing—was older, with a craggy face and grey in his hair—far too much grey. He looked tired, although not apparently unhappy. Alice was even more beautiful if anything than she was now. It came to him that there were two Alices at the moment, and he realized that the word "now" made little sense. Both of the newcomers were dressed in strange clothing—St. Ives in a plaid, double breasted suit with trousers that flared out and then in again at the ankles. Instead of a cravat he wore a small ribbon tie, more than moderately ridiculous. His hat was something like a homburg, but lower and with a garish band that matched his bow tie. Alice wore an evening gown with a peacock feather print and with pin-feathers from that same bird around the hem. She was hatless, with her hair curled atop her head.

"Alice St. Ives," Fort said, standing up and extending his hand. "My name is Charles Fort. I've been expecting you. Your husband and I have already met, as you can see. I'm charmed to make your acquaintance at last." To grey-haired St. Ives he said, "The pistol is not necessary, sir. I would never compel another man to do what he does not want to do. Life is full of hard choices, and I have merely endeavored to contrive an interesting example."

"Do put away the pistol dear," Alice said. "Mr. Fort shall not be shot." And then to the still-sitting St. Ives and not his alter ego, who was smiling as broadly as Fort, she said, "We're off to dine and then to the opera, dear. You bought the tickets as you promised. It's my birthday tomorrow, you know. You haven't forgotten?"

"Of course not," St. Ives lied. He had never had any taste for the opera—a lot of howling to his mind—and he regularly forgot Alice's birthday unless she invented a way to remind him, though she had never reminded him in this sort of outré fashion. *As he had promised?* Alice's presence in the room trumped the wooly mammoth, and in spades. "We'd best be away," St. Ives said hastily, nodding to his friends.

"*Away!*" Kryzanek said. "What an eminently sensible word under the circumstances. Charles, we take our leave. You'll never see your ten million, you know. Not a penny of it."

St. Ives stood up and nodded a goodbye to himself and to Alice, wondering whether it would be too farfetched if he were to kiss his wife. Hampson and Kryzanek were already out of their seats and heading toward the door, however, and the moment passed.

"You must play out your part, sir," Fort said to St. Ives. "*Take the magazine. The library won't miss it.*"

St. Ives did as he was told, although what he would do with the magazine he didn't know. As he went out through the door, he glanced longingly back at Alice, who waved at him and winked. Even then she and the elder St. Ives were turning toward the passage, the door still standing open, getting out while the getting was good. He would do the same, whether or not it was his destiny to do so.

The three companions made their way down the stone stairs unhindered and unfollowed. Kryzanek set out at a trot when they reached the path into the jungle, and St. Ives and the Vicar, were close on his heels. They passed Kryzanek's tree-house at a steady clip, Kryzanek not looking back, and when they arrived at the meadow it was clear that the sun, high in the sky now, had swelled the gas in the balloon, which was acting like a living creature, jigging in the breeze, straining to be away.

"In you two go," St. Ives shouted, giving Hampson the magazine. He dropped to his knees and laced his hands to give them a boost up, and then tied the mooring line around his waist for good measure before yanking out the stakes one by one and pitching them into the basket. He handed in the mallet, untied his life-line, and climbed aboard, the gondola settling lightly on the meadow with the added weight. Kryzanek was already dumping ballast, judiciously, thank heavens, and Hampson was once again intoning a prayer. The balloon rose, but the ground breeze swept them slowly toward the distant cliffs, Kryzanek cursing aloud and then apologizing to Hampson for the cursing.

"It'll come around," St. Ives said. "We *know* it will. Someone's got to deliver the story to Jack, after all."

"God between us and all harm," Kryzanek said, as if this were no time for optimism.

"No man is fated to do what he does," Hampson told them. "It's the great glory of being God's creation that we are able to change our minds, for better or ill."

"That, sir, is currently my deepest fear," Kryzanek said.

As if to further provoke Kryzanek, the balloon was still hauling them in a contrary direction, and despite St. Ives's foolish *we know we will*, he wondered unhappily whether he had just recently had his last glimpse of Alice—his second last glimpse in the past couple of hours, both glimpses from a distance that was very nearly fabulous. He looked down at the forest canopy, at the colorful birds flitting from tree to tree. A clearing opened below, and loitering at the edge of it were two of Fort's wooly mammoths, immensely shaggy creatures, each the size of a small cottage. St. Ives fetched out the telescope, thinking that it would take only a scant few minutes to descend for a closer look. As soon as the thought entered his mind, however, the balloon began to rise, and quickly.

The mammoths diminished beneath them as the balloon ascended into a piece of the sky in which the wind, blowing hard, was dead opposite to what it had been a moment ago. They were swept around toward the distant curtain like a ship caught in a tide-race. The curtain itself was agitated. Fissures opened and closed in it, flecked with pale streaks like angry whitewater on a rocky coast. The entire thing, it seemed to St. Ives, was disintegrating, and the fog that drifted in front of it was forebodingly thin.

Far below them the stream ran its course, and through the telescope St. Ives watched as Fort's men sent what appeared to be leaf-and-stick rafts downstream, heaped with a pale cargo of heaven knew what, playing out another of Fort's little joke upon the world. The balloon was still rising in an ear-blocking rush, making an incredible amount of leeway despite its speed. St. Ives wondered whether some force generated by the curtain was interfering with their forward travel—whether they would simply be dragged futilely up the sky, unable to cross through the curtain at all. There was nothing, St. Ives realized, that they could do to save themselves from such a fate, and he compelled himself to attend to the words of the psalm that Hampson uttered, his voice calm and clear.

And then in a wild, capricious caper the balloon was yanked suddenly downward, throwing the men into a heap on the deck of the gondola. They sorted themselves out as the balloon began spiraling madly, the horizon passing round and round before their eyes—the vortex of wind again, but with wild energy. Abruptly the spinning stopped, and the balloon sailed straight toward the curtain, the elongated gas-bag drawing away before them, towing the gondola away behind it now, the deck tilting precariously. St. Ives consulted his compass, which once again had lost its mind—a great relief.

The curtain appeared to be in a state of collapse. White, foam-like runnels cascaded downward within it, and here and there unnerving fragments of blue sky became visible through suddenly-forming windows. But *which sky*, St. Ives wondered as he held onto the railing of the gondola with a death grip. The rubberized silk of their balloon rippled and chattered, and the wind whistled in his ears as they were swept headlong into the darkness, the sky-tides pushing them toward the opposite shore, thank God. In the grip of the agitated curtain, the gondola bucked and creaked like a living creature. The three men held on, St. Ives uneasily watching the straining joints where the basket was lashed together with pitifully thin line.

And then they passed into glorious daylight, and the three clambered to their feet and set up a wild cheering. Below them lay the North Downs. The soft wind blew out of the east, carrying them toward home, and although they could not make out the meadow where their friends awaited their return, they could see Boxley Abbey no great distance below.

For a moment St. Ives allowed his mind to wander. He imagined regaling the Royal Society with an account of what had come to pass on this strange day—the invisible island, the prehistoric creatures, the lost race of men, Fort's house, the passage into the library, the as-yet-unwritten story that was in fact written by an unknown hand. It was a gaggle of lunatic conundrums to be sure, utterly ruinous to his reputation. The very notion of spinning out the tale was not to be countenanced.

He turned and looked back, seeing that the curtain had vanished from the sky. The world of the floating island had winked out of existence and would reside only in their memories evermore—or at least until he stepped into Fort's study twenty years hence. He patted his coat pocket, where lay the copy of *The Graphic*, his only keepsake. But then he remembered the lungfish and the beer bottle full of water from a lost world. Who knew what microscopic things—perhaps eggs or even larvae— swam within that bottle?

They set their sights on a broad sheep pasture, the sheep looking up at them as the gondola descended, settling on the grass not thirty feet distant from the Pilgrims Road and a bare three miles from Aylesford Village. ⟶

Earthbound Things

ALICE LAY THE copy of *The Graphic* on the bench in the glasshouse next to the aquarium that housed the apparently happy lungfish. She stared at St. Ives for a time without speaking. She wore the well-washed linen trousers and blouse that served as her work clothes, and there was a dusting of potting soil on her blouse. She'd been propagating begonias, reproducing them from rhizomes and leaves. The lush smell of the greenhouse—the plants and soil and aquaria—reminded St. Ives of the smell of the jungle through which he had tramped just yesterday—a jungle that he might have the fabrication of a dream if it weren't for the tangible truth of the magazine and the inarguable return of Roger Kryzanek.

He had seen the future, had seen his own and Alice's apparent happiness together, and he wondered now whether that happiness was assured or was simply one of an infinitude of possible futures—a future that might yet blink out of existence if he failed to give Jack the copy of the magazine that Alice had just been reading. It came to him that he had not had the presence of mind, there in Fort's study, to ask her about Eddie and Cleo, how they fared, what sort of people they had grown up to be. But he knew in the next moment that such questions must easily lead to poisonous answers, to the accumulation of regret for things that had not yet come to pass, or things that had. Still, he wondered what the answers would have been.

Alice pushed a wild strand of dark hair from her face with the back of her hand and picked up a porcelain doll's head from a large basket of such heads that sat next to the magazine, some of the heads cracked or broken, most of them whole. After looking at it for a moment, she said, "What you tell me makes no earthly sense. They clap people into Colney Hatch for asserting things far more mundane. If I didn't know you well, I'd send for the mad-doctor."

"*Earthly* sense? No, it makes not a bit of it. Fort has a regard for unearthly sense."

"What can this man Fort possibly gain by his eccentric behavior?"

"He has the theory that humankind must be awakened from their torpor now and then—that they dwell behind a veil, their time and their thoughts mortgaged to what they understand to be necessity. And so he causes it to rain limpets or frogs or porcelain heads in order to give people something startling to dwell on, and to watch the learned men of science deny the limpets and heads. He's either an artist or a madman, I can't make up my mind."

"Given how things fell out, I believe I rather like him."

"Tell me," St. Ives said. "If when I saw you come through that door, I had asked you about our future together, would you have told me?"

"No," Alice said. "Certainly not. I can conceive of nothing more ruinous to our happiness and the happiness of our family. Here's Cleo and Eddie, coming to feed the lungfish." She opened the door of the glasshouse and waved at the children, who dashed in out of breath. Cleo held a doll's head in each hand. Eddie opened his fist to show them a big earthworm.

"Can we try this fellow on old Kryzanek?" Eddie asked, boosting himself up onto the broad wooden workbench and kneeling so as to see down into the aquarium. "He's a fat worm. I've rinsed him clean." He dangled it over the water and then let it drop, the worm wiggling as it fell. The lungfish, newly named Kryzanek, darted forward and gobbled it down, then retreated to its hiding place. "I'll dig out more of them!" Eddie shouted, running out again.

"Poor worm," Cleo said. "Does Kryzanek want a doll's head, Father?"

"Not to eat, Cleo."

"I mean to play with, silly."

"Then, yes, almost certainly."

"Lift me up."

Alice lifted her, and Cleo dropped one of the heads into the tank. Bubbles rushed out of it as it sank, landing upright on the gravel so that it was peering out from behind a water plant. The lungfish swam over to have a look but was moderately indifferent, or so it seemed to St. Ives. Cleo plucked a fresh head out of the basket, and Alice set her on the ground again. She ran out shouting, "Eddie, come look!"

"I'm happy that Finn brought home a basket of these heads," Alice said, watching Cleo run across the meadow, "but no right-minded person would understand a rain of porcelain heads to be evidence of anything, even if they trekked out to your meadow to see the litter for themselves."

"Yes. None of this can be passed off as truth, although every word of is true. The three of us have agreed to keep silent. Think what would happen to Hampson's reputation as a sensible, Godly man if he were to say anything at all about our adventure. We would become the laughingstocks of the world."

"I cannot imagine what Mr. Kryzanek will say to his wife."

"He intends to say that his memory was shattered by a knock on the head. He's certain his wife will welcome him home without any sort of inquisition."

"Will you give the magazine to Jack?"

"I believe so," St. Ives said. "Jack will have no difficulty believing, but he might scruple at putting his name to story that he didn't write."

"But his name is already on it," Alice said. "Who *did* write it if not Jack?"

"There you have me," St. Ives said. "And here's something else. Happy birthday, dear heart. You can see that it's necessary, perhaps vitally necessary, that we take ship to New York City twenty years from now. That's my birthday present to you—a holiday in America and a night at the opera. What do you say to that?"

"I say that it's an odd thing to receive one's birthday present twenty years late."

"Then what would you like today? Anything you wish for is yours."

"I wish for you to pack a picnic basket. We'll gather up Cleo, Eddie, and Finn and spend the afternoon at the weir fishing. We'll eat deviled ham on toast and speak of sensible, earthbound things." —⁂